THEY HAVE HIDDEN AMONG US FOR CENTURIES

# ENDOSYM

## THE DARK FACE OF EVIL

By J. Henry Thomson

The events and adventures in this novel are fiction. The names, characters, places and incidents are either a product of the author's imagination or are used fictitiously and any similarity to persons, living or dead, business establishments, events or locales is entirely coincidental. The story and the glimpses of the lives and beliefs of the People of West Africa are based on the author's experiences. The secret Poro society exists, and the author has mixed fact and fiction into the story. The ancient statue is real, as is the leopard tooth. Their origins are fiction.


ISBN 10: 0985742607
ISBN 13: 9780985742607

# ACKNOWLEDGMENTS

It would take many pages to thank all the people who provided encouragement and support in the writing of this book.

Most of all, I wish to thank my editor Irene Hicks who provided not only corrections to my grammatical errors, but also her input to the story that made it come alive. Her energy, unflagging support and encouragement got me through the difficult periods. Without her constant efforts none of this would be possible.

I would also like to thank David McClellan and the other officers of the US Military Mission to Liberia who were part of the real adventure.

I cannot leave out the Indigenous Peoples of Liberia West Africa whose stories about ancient ruins, spirits of the bush and their shear joy of life was the corner stone of this novel and the one's to follow.

Finally and not least, for their caring interest, love, and constant encouragement, I thank my wife Linda, and son, Tim, who were there when it all begin.

ENDOSYM: *Two entities living in one humanoid body whose goal is to become the "Apex Predator" of the Planet.*

# 1

***It had been a twelve-hour flight to Monrovia, Liberia.***

"HANK, ARE YOU OK?"

"What?" he mumbled.

"I asked you if you were OK," she replied.

Hank rubbed his eyelids, stretched and looked toward the insistent voice.

"You were moaning in your sleep," she continued. "I thought you were having a nightmare or something."

A nightmare or something, he thought, one that he hadn't had for many years.

"Yeah, I guess I was in a pretty deep sleep," he answered softly.

"They said we'd be landing in less than two hours," she told him. "They're going to be serving breakfast in about thirty minutes."

The lights were still dim in the big Boeing jet. Most of the passengers still slept. He glanced at his watch. It was almost six o'clock in the morning. The sun would be just coming up when they landed at Roberts International.

"How about a cup of coffee?" he asked her.

"Sure," Lindsey answered.

Hank yawned, unbuckled his seatbelt, stretched, and made his way up the aisle to the serving cart.

Lindsey watched as he approached the flight attendant, a bleached blonde in her mid-forties. The two made small talk while the woman poured the coffee. Lindsey leaned back in her seat. She took a second look at the flight attendant. She imagined that the woman must have been stunning in her youth. Now, she had enough seniority to be what they called an "African queen," one of the lucky few who traveled the prized African circuit.

Hank thanked the woman and headed back toward his seat, holding one hot cup in each hand. Lindsey saw the flight attendant follow him with her eyes. She felt a touch of pride, as well as a tinge of jealousy. It wasn't the first time she'd seen another woman admire her husband.

No wonder. At forty-two Hank still had the physique of a man in his twenties. He stood six feet, three inches tall. He had broad shoulders and narrow hips. A few sprinkles of gray ran through his closely cropped hair. He hadn't changed much in the sixteen years they had been married.

"Here you are," Hank said as he carefully placed her cup on the corner of her tray table. He settled back into his seat beside her.

Lindsey leaned her head against his shoulder. She ran her fingers down his sleeve, over his wrist and clasped his hand firmly in hers.

Her coffee sat untouched while Lindsey closed her eyes. She didn't intend to fall asleep, but simply to pass the time until breakfast was served. Her thoughts drifted to their new duty station and this new twist in Hank's military career.

He had told her about the country's troubled history, its valuable national resources, and its superstitious, but friendly people. She recalled asking him if they would be in any danger. She was surprised that Hank had hesitated before answering her question. She had wondered if he hadn't told her the whole story. Sure, some of his knowledge was classified material, but it didn't hurt to ask. Hank had paused before reassuring her that everything would be OK as the Americans had strong political and economic ties to the emerging democracy.

Hank nudged her arm to warn her that the breakfast service was about to begin. Lindsey nodded and sat up straight. She resolved to keep a supportive and positive attitude.

An hour later, Lindsey peered out the window, scanning the horizon for her first glimpse of Africa. It won't be long now, she thought. Once on the ground, their ride would be waiting to take them to their new home.

Their adventure was about to begin.

On the ground, but not yet at the airport, Jim Parkinson wasn't so sure that the "ride" would get there on time. He took another look at his watch. Only one minute had passed since he had last checked it. Traffic barely moved. Flight 734 would be landing in about twenty minutes. He still had another ten miles to go.

"Why the hell did the Liberians build the airport so damn far from the capital?" he fumed. Just what he needed – being late to pick up the new defense attaché. Even worse luck, he thought, now the traffic had come to a dead stop.

"Drive over on the shoulder," Parkinson yelled to his driver. "Let's see if we can get by the back-up."

"Yes, sir," answered Songa.

This wasn't a bad job, working for the U.S. Embassy. Songa got along well with most of the Americans, but this Major Parkinson was his least favorite. Maybe it was because Parkinson was a black man. Songa felt that he looked down on his black African brothers.

Songa drove in typical Liberian fashion. He alternated between the brakes and the gas. He supplemented the foot movements with frequent honks and shouts. He wheeled the Chevy van to the shoulder and eased past the scene of an accident. A policeman raised his white-gloved hand in an attempt to stop the van. When he saw the diplomatic plates, he scowled and waved it on.

Parkinson looked through the shaded window at the twisted debris. Two taxicabs were now transformed into one obscene sculpture. No one had been seriously injured, yet that was an exception in this town. Thousands of taxis, wielded by aggressive drivers, tangled the traffic every day, injuring innocent passengers and pedestrians.

He remembered his first accident scene. Just days after he first arrived, he'd actually seen a pile-up in the making. A collision of four cars left five people dead. He recalled seeing the uncovered bodies spread out alongside the highway. He had never seen anything so brutal back home. Now when he or his wife, Maggie, went out during the day, they used the embassy drivers. He figured that gave them a slightly better chance of getting back home alive.

The van screeched to a stop in front of the main terminal. Parkinson flashed his diplomatic ID at the guard in customs and moved quickly into the area marked for the arrival of foreign passengers. He slipped the agent a five-dollar Liberian note, the typical bribe. Locals called it "a dash." This would speed up his passengers' progress through customs. He looked out the plate-glass window just in time to see the landing lights of the aircraft as it made its approach.

"I hope King is OK," Tim said to his mother.

"I'm sure he is, Tim," she answered. "The vet gave him that tranquilizer before we left. I'll bet he slept better than we did. Don't worry. You'll be seeing him in just a few minutes."

Tim never ceased to amaze her. He wasn't even fifteen years old, yet he was already more than six feet tall. He was in that awkward age – not a child, but not yet a man. It was hard to believe that in only a few short years, he'd be off to college and out on his own. She secretly hoped that their time in West Africa would bring special memories of their last time together as a family unit.

The plane touched down, jolting as its landing gear made contact with the runway. She leaned toward Hank and caught his eye.

"Ready for a new adventure?" he asked.

"You bet," she smiled. From her window, she watched the airport workers roll out the portable stairway. First off were the first class and business passengers. Finally, it was their turn. At the top of the stairway, Lindsey paused to take in her first impression of Liberia. The tropical heat and oppressive humidity hit her like the proverbial blast furnace. She clasped the hot metal railing and made her way carefully down the steps. Almost immediately, beads of perspiration broke out on her forehead. Strange odors – damp, decomposing vegetation, charcoal smoke, sweat and excrement – nearly overcame her. The combination of the heat, smells, twelve hours on the plane, and jet lag made her dizzy and nauseous.

Once inside the air-conditioned terminal, she regained her composure. She scanned the crowd, looking for Major Parkinson. They had communicated via letters and emails, but she had no idea what he looked like. His neat penmanship created an image of a bespectacled accountant.

"Lieutenant Colonel Martin?" said someone approaching Hank, "I'm Major Parkinson."

Lindsey turned to see an impressive black man in the uniform of an American officer. She flashed a quick smile, chastising herself for her first assumption.

"Mrs. Martin, I presume? Welcome to Liberia," he said, taking her hand.

"Call me Lindsey," she said as she motioned Tim forward. "This is our son, Tim."

"Pleased to meet you, sir," said Tim, shaking his hand.

"And all of you, please call me Jim. We don't always have to be formal. Here, we often use first names in everyday conversation."

They moved toward the baggage carousel.

"Once your luggage comes through, we can go. Since you're traveling on diplomatic passports, customs won't inspect your bags."

Right then the terminal echoed with the sound of a barking dog.

"Look, Mom! There's King!" shouted Tim. Two airport workers were pushing a cart with the German shepherd's kennel. The dog growled and barked at the two workers.

"Can we let him out?" Tim asked. "I have his leash."

"Why not?" Jim responded. He and Tim walked over to the crate. As soon as King saw Tim, he quieted down and wagged his tail. Jim helped open the door and fasten the leash. He stooped down and spoke quietly to the dog and got a good licking as a reward.

At the van, Songa wasn't too sure about the dog. King growled at the driver, baring his teeth. Jim reached down and held the dog's collar.

"Come here, boy," he said. "It's time you got acquainted with the Liberians."

A quick sniff at Songa's pant leg seemed to be enough of an introduction for King. His hackles down, he looked up at the man and turned to sniff the van's tire.

"Major Parkinson, oops, I mean Jim," Tim asked, "how come King likes you, but growls at Songa?"

"Well, I guess it's because I smell different," Jim replied.

"But you're both black," Tim said. Lindsey cringed at his comment, but the man didn't seem offended.

"Dogs are color blind. To them, all people look alike, but we smell different. Liberians eat different food than we do. As a result, their bodies emit a different odor. This is all new to King. It'll take him time to get used to his new home."

"Oh," said Tim, "I never thought of that."

It took them another twenty minutes to load the van. Time and King nestled in the back seat. Lindsey and Hank got in behind the driver. Jim sat in front to serve as the unofficial tour guide.

Tim stared out the window, taking in all he could of the passing scenery. At the outskirts of town, they came to a stop at a traffic light. Six young teenage girls stood beside the road. They wore short grass skirts and nothing else. A fine white powder covered their exposed skin. All were full breasted, their dark nipples jutting out from their smooth bodies.

"Holy smokes!" exclaimed Tim.

"Those girls are candidates for bush school," Jim explained. "They will go through secret rites that prepare them for their duties as women. Neither boys nor girls are considered adults until they go through bush school."

He told them that Liberia had two major language groups – the Kapel and the Kruman. The Kapel was the largest with a population of about one and a half million. The Kruman numbered about six hundred thousand. There were ten smaller ethnic groups that tended to speak either Kapel or Kruman.

The light finally turned green. Lindsey turned to glance at her son who continued to stare at the girls. He blushed and glanced down when he saw his mother looking at him.

"This will be quite an experience for a fifteen-year-old," she said with a smile.

People walked along the edge of the road, many balancing baskets on their heads. The people looked healthy, but abject poverty seemed to surround them. Houses were no more than a series of tin-roofed shacks clustered in random shantytowns. Although they saw some permanent buildings, all were in poor repair. Garbage and other refuse littered the streets. Thin, mongrel dogs pawed through the trash, looking for food scraps. Animal carcasses, likely traffic casualties, could be seen frequently along the road.

"Monrovia's population is around three hundred twenty-three thousand, but in the last few years a lot of people have left the interior and moved here. We figure that maybe one hundred thousand people live in the streets or in the shantytowns.

"The government is supposedly throwing up some low cost housing, but there's no way it can keep up with the growth. But this isn't what it all looks like. After the civil war, the US provided funds to rebuild the capital. The downtown area does have a nice business section with some decent shops. Embassy Row is well maintained. And, of course, there's Mamba Bluff, where you'll be living," Jim told them.

"Mamba Bluff?" Tim asked. "Does that mean there'll be snakes?"

Jim suppressed a laugh. "Oh, once in a while we see a snake, but they are usually busy getting away from the humans."

"Wow, this is really neat!" Tim said.

"Yeah, just great," Lindsey replied. But she was not so certain. Snakes weren't her idea of good company.

Jim's commentary continued as their car made its way through the city. For Tim, the drive had been filled with exciting sights and sounds. His first impression of Liberia would be indelibly etched in his memory.

"Mamba Bluff ahead," Jim said, as the van pulled in a wide, palm-lined drive. Now the housing was much different. They could see large, spacious homes. Some even had swimming pools.

"There are more than six hundred homes on Mamba Bluff, some worth millions. The embassy rents out several for its staff. Because there are only about forty residences on the embassy grounds, many of us live here. Most of the wealthy Liberians and other nationals live here, too. All six members of the attaché's staff are within a mile of each other. Your home is on Charles Street. The area is well patrolled by the national police. Rougings are pretty uncommon," he continued.

"What's a rouging?" asked Tim.

"A rouge is an old British term for a thief. Rouging is the same as a burglary," he replied.

About a mile later, they pulled up in front of a large yellow stucco house. A six-foot high concrete block wall surrounded the grounds. Broken glass bottles had been embedded along the top of the wall. They passed through a double entry iron gate and pulled up to the house.

"You've got five bedrooms," Jim said. "All together there are more than five thousand square feet of living space."

Eight black men stood at attention as the van came to a stop in front of the house.

"Your staff," Jim said, turning to Lindsey with a broad grin. "You have five guards, a houseboy, a yard boy and a cook. Let me introduce you. First, this is Everyday Walker, chief of the guards."

Everyday Walker moved one step forward and bowed at the waist. Barefoot and shirtless, he wore only khaki shorts. His bald spot was fringed with snow-white hair. His weapon was a rusty, single-shot twelve-gauge shotgun.

"Everyday Walker has been with this house for more than forty years," Jim explained. "He started when the Walkers built the house. They were an American family who worked at Firestone Rubber. These guards protect the house from rouges. They'll also serve as your staff when you entertain."

He introduced John Tarkoi, Zac Wleh, John Youbatie and Nelson Webe. Each was armed with a machete.

Hank shook his head. He wondered how secure they would be if their "armed" guards faced intruders with real weapons.

With a command from Everyday Walker, the men marched to a small guardhouse near the driveway.

The three other men came forward. Adam Sayeh, the houseboy; Charles Konabe, the yard boy; and finally, the only one with shoes, Abraham Karim, the white-uniformed cook.

At five feet ten inches, Lindsey towered over the Liberians. They must have been amazed to see such a tall white woman.

As they entered the house, they saw plush wall-to-wall carpeting. Expensive new furniture filled every room. Fine art hung on the walls. Someone had gone to great effort and expense to furnish the home.

"I hope the house is OK," Jim said with a smile. "The embassy got in a new shipment of furniture, and your place was re-done. My wife, Maggie, supervised the job."

"It's beautiful, really beautiful," Lindsey said.

"Look, Mom!" Tim called from a side door. "Look, what a great back yard!"

An expansive lawn sloped away from the house to the sturdy wall. Tim opened the patio doors. King dashed outside and bounded in his rediscovered freedom. A variety of flowers, shrubs and trees lined the edges of the property. One wooden gate, latched from the inside, opened to a steep hillside overlooking the Atlantic, just three hundred feet below the house.

"Folks, I know you've had a long flight and need some time to relax. Get settled in first, then we'd like you to come over to our house for dinner. Maggie's planned a little reception. You'll get a chance to meet everyone else. Until then, the refrigerator is full of food. Adam and Charles will bring in your luggage. Your household goods are due to come in tomorrow," Jim said. "I guess there's nothing else to say, except welcome to Liberia!"

After Jim left, the three stood silently in the living room in disbelief. They hadn't imagined such luxurious quarters. This whole adventure already seemed like it would be an amazing experience.

"Missy, would you and the master like some tea and cookies? Perhaps the young master would like a soft drink?" asked Abraham.

Lindsey had forgotten all about Abraham.

"Yes. That would be fine," she responded.

After the cook had left, she turned to Hank. "Honey, I don't need a cook."

"I guess you don't have a choice," he said. "They all come with the house."

"This is really going to be different," she said.

"You said you were ready for a new adventure," he smiled. "Well, this one comes with servants!"

# 2

***In Monrovia, the nation's capital, a dark blue Mercedes-Benz E500 rolled to a stop in front of the mansion gate.***

ARMED WITH AN UZI SUBMACHINE GUN, THE GUARD APPROACHED THE DRIVER'S window. He scanned the car's occupants and then nodded in the direction of the gate.

The heavy iron gate clicked and swung open. The Mercedes moved up the curved brick-lined drive and came to a halt by the wide stairs. Another five luxury sedans were parked several yards ahead. Arms folded in front of them; the uniformed drivers leaned against the sleek fenders. It wasn't uncommon to see such vehicles here for formal events. But this was different. It was almost midnight on a Wednesday.

A tall German driver got out. He walked around the Mercedes and opened the rear passenger door. The driver wore a white polo shirt and sharply creased black slacks. His shoulder holster held a large-caliber automatic pistol.

A thin dark-skinned man with white hair emerged from the back seat. He walked up the steps to the carved wood door. It swung open. Inside, he moved into the brightly lit entrance, turned right and walked down the hallway. His five-hundred-dollar Italian shoes tapped on the hardwood floor. He came up to a heavy wooden double door at the end of the hall. He twisted the brass knob, stepped in and closed the door behind him.

Floor-to-ceiling bookshelves lined the library walls. Thousands of leather-bound volumes were neatly tucked into the dark wood shelves. Thickly woven oriental carpets were artfully placed on the polished wood floors. A half dozen upholstered leather chairs were scattered around the room's perimeter. Thin, metallic floor lamps provided soft lighting. A massive inlaid mahogany table stood dead center in the room. Four high-backed chairs were on each long side. Larger chairs sat at each end.

Five men were already seated at the table. This new arrival moved to an empty seat. He did not speak, nor did he acknowledge the others' presence. The library door opened once again. A heavy black man – well more than three hundred pounds – walked in. Despite the bulk on the five feet-seven inch frame, he slid gracefully into the chair at the far end of the table.

This last man to arrive was Dr. George Nah Sarday, chancellor at the University of Liberia. The others all knew his story. He was once a lowly assistant professor of ancient African religions. Then twenty-five years ago he found the hidden valley and its mysterious secrets. Even though ten years junior to the others at the table, there was no question as to who was in charge. He looked first to his left, then to his right. He scanned his companions, nodding to each as their eyes met his.

On his left sat Steven Dowling, Liberia's President. Beside him was Thomas Karua, minister of finance. Next, was Steven Moya, Speaker of the House. Then, the next man was Julius Carpai, Minister of Defense. The last two were John Munah, president of Munah Industries, and Abdullah Ajami, owner and general manager of Liberia Rubber.

Of the seven, six were Kapel and had survived more than seventeen years of bloody civil war. Most had English first names; some had even assumed American surnames. After the 2003 peace accord, they assumed leadership roles in the new government. Only one was not a descendant of two black parents. The seventh man was the product of a marriage between a Kapel chief's daughter and an Arab merchant who had come to Liberia to make his fortune.

Originally, ten men had occupied the chairs around the table. Three seats were left empty as silent reminders of the lost brothers. Albert Carpai, Julius's brother, had died in the battle for Monrovia in 2003;

George Gabtu had succumbed to lung cancer; and a jealous husband had shot Albert Poste in 1998.

Here sat the seven most powerful men in Liberia. Their combined wealth surpassed that of the entire population of the rest of the nation.

The men bowed their heads and began to chant in unison in an ancient language. Few people alive today had ever heard these words, murmured in a tongue once whispered in the sacred land of Egypt before Moses had led his people to the Promised Land.

"My power and wealth come from you O Great One. Alone, I am weak. Together, we are all powerful. I will defend the brotherhood to death and reveal your secrets to no man," they chanted.

The ancient litany ended. Sarday broke the silence.

"Julius, do you want to tell us what happened in Singa yesterday?"

Carpai cleared his throat while choosing his words with care. "We sent a reinforced infantry company to Singa to collect the hut taxes. They were armed with the new M-16 rifles that came from the United States. Captain Mussafa Konah commanded the unit. Once they got to the town, a small boy handed the captain a note from Charles Morray. It ordered Konah to leave town before his men were killed.

"Konah, of course, refused. He deployed his platoons. Without warning, shots rang out. The People's Party militia had begun firing. It took only minutes. Konah was forced to surrender. Forty soldiers were killed. Another ten wounded.

"Morray confiscated all weapons, uniforms and gear and marched the survivors to the edge of town."

Carpai reached into his pocket and withdrew a folded piece of paper.

"Morray sent this letter to you, Steven," Carpai said.

"If your soldiers had captured Morray last year when we closed down People's Party headquarters, we wouldn't have this problem today," snarled Dowling.

But Carpai refused to be intimidated.

"Don't lecture me, you old fool," he said. "It was your idea to allow this opposition party. You said they would be no threat. It would look like democracy really was working in Liberia."

"Shut up, both of you," growled Sarday. "Give me that letter, Julius."
Carpai slid the crumpled paper down the table.
It read as follows:

> President Dowling, It is with deep regret that I write you this letter. You had the opportunity to give the people of Liberia the freedom of choice. You destroyed this chance when your soldiers tried to kill me. Mark my words; the time is coming when I will sit in your chair as the new head of state. The people will win!
>
> Charles B. Morray

Sarday's face darkened as he crushed the paper in his fist. His features taut, he whispered deliberately, "That goddamn bastard. He will never rule this country. I will drink his blood at the altar of sacrifice."

Sarday flung the wadded paper against the wall. Then he turned to Thomas Karua.

"Thomas, tell me of the negotiations with the Arab oil cartel."

"They are very interested in our proposal. They offer us $25 million U.S. if we can guarantee that no oil is pumped from the reserves beneath the Saint Paul River for the next five years."

"Will people wait that long now that they know we have so much?" Munah asked.

"Hell, they've already waited two hundred years to be rich. They can hold off another five," Moya responded.

"What about the U.S.? They're already pressuring us to start production this year."

Sarday seemed unconcerned. "That will be our job to handle the United States. Thomas, I want you to go back to the cartel. Take Abdullah with you. He can speak their tongue. Tell them that they have a deal, but it will cost them one hundred million dollars U.S. We want fifty million dollars now, and the rest in five years."

"They'll never agree to that much," said Karua.

"Of course they will. They have a stranglehold on the West. If we permit the U.S. to open our reserves, the price per barrel will plummet. They will lose billions. Mark my words, the cartel will agree to the deal."

Sarday pushed back his chair, stood, and left the room.

As soon as the door closed behind him, the remaining six leaned back in their seats. The tension had eased. Dowling turned to Moya.

"Are you coming over Saturday? My daughter Theresa and your son will be bringing the twins over to celebrate their third birthday. Jim Parkinson, Maggie and their boys are coming, too."

"I wouldn't miss their birthday for the world," responded Moya.

The six men filed out and headed for their waiting cars. Left alone at the mahogany table, Dowling twisted the cap on his fountain pen. His lips tightened. So far, he had managed to move hundreds of thousands of dollars into his European accounts. It would only be a matter of time until his hidden assets topped twenty million dollars. The future – far from this godforsaken country – would be all that he imagined. He caressed the smooth sides of the pen, tucked it into his vest pocket and tapped his chest with the tips of his fingers.

Sarday watched through the window in another room as the men climbed into their waiting limos. Except for Julius Carpai, the others were weak beings, but he needed them as he gained power. Soon the time will come when only the strongest would serve him.

# 3

*The Grand Pavilion in Monrovia, remodeled some six years earlier, was the site of many festive occasions enjoyed by the Liberian elite. The magnificent building could accommodate one thousand guests.*

LINDSEY, SEATED BESIDE HANK IN THE LIMOUSINE, CARESSED THE ENGRAVED invitation.

The President and Mrs. Steven Dowling
Request the pleasure of your company
At the One Hundred and Sixty-Fifth
INDEPENDENCE BALL
Thursday, July 26th
At the GRAND PAVILION, MONROVIA
Ashmum Street Entrance
Nine o'clock post meridian
Present at door
Dress: Formal

The doorman approached the vehicle. Lindsey looked at the officer seated beside her.

"I love your mess white uniform. You look so handsome," she said.

"That red evening dress isn't such a bad uniform either," Hank said. Lindsey's dark maroon silk dress was deeply cut, revealing more than a hint of cleavage. Two thin straps ran over her bare shoulders. Her lightly tanned skin, blue eyes and blond hair would cause many to stop and admire.

Arm in arm, the couple walked up the marble steps to the formal entrance. A Liberian captain snapped to attention, reached for the invitation and opened the door. Inside the grand foyer, they joined the reception line. The event had been touted as the highlight of the Monrovia social year. The guest list included high-ranking staff from embassy row, wealthy businessmen, and key government officials.

Fabric streamers in Liberian red, white and blue had been hung from the high ceiling. A soft breeze from the fans and air conditioning caused the bright material to sway gently, as if waving in celebration of the national holiday. The Monrovian symphony orchestra played a classical theme. Its musicians wore dark tuxedos and gold brocade vests.

The long linen-covered tables were laden with hors d'oeuvres – tiny shrimp, caviar, and crock truffles atop toasted bread. Fresh fruit, carved vegetables and petit fours were skillfully arranged around intricate ice sculptures. Tall crystal vases brimmed with hibiscus and black orchid. More tropical flowers and delicate ferns spilled from stone urns. Waiters, their trays heavy with crystal glasses glistening with French wines, wove in and out of the clustered guests.

The President himself – Steven Dowling – personally greeted the couples as they entered the main ballroom. As they waited their turn, Lindsey recognized some familiar faces. Jim Parkinson and Maggie stood at the front of the line.

Maggie, always one with good taste, had chosen a shimmering blue and silver gown that clung to her athletic form. Dowling kissed her warmly on each cheek, and then reached out to Jim, firmly gripping his hand. Lindsey marveled at the couple's presence. They were a study in deep, rich color. Jim's smooth dark skin, impressive height and toned physique paired well with Maggie's firm curves and lighter color. Maggie's friendship with Dowling's daughter had given Jim an open door to the executive mansion. Few attaches could match his connections.

The line inched forward. Soon it was their turn.

"Lieutenant Colonel and Mrs. Martin, I am so pleased you could attend our Independence Day Ball. I trust you feel welcome in our beautiful country?" Dowling asked.

"Oh, yes," answered Hank, "and we are especially enjoying your warm hospitality."

After obligatory small talk, Dowling's eyes moved to the next guest in line. Hank and Lindsey turned toward the ballroom.

"I'm amazed that he knows everyone's name," Lindsey said.

"The qualities of a true politician," Hank replied. "How about some wine?"

"Sure. White wine would be fine."

While Hank moved to the bar, Lindsey recognized Nancy Matthews. Her husband was Major Don Matthews, one of the two Air Force pilots assigned to the defense attaché's office. They flew the C-12 aircraft based at the airport. The Liberian office also served the ambassadors of four other small West African countries. The attaches made regular rounds, and the aircraft allowed them to travel without relying on commercial transportation. The twelve-passenger plane frequently had a few empty seats, which allowed family members to fly on a space-available basis.

Lindsey smiled when she saw Nancy. A short, plump brunette, Nancy never failed to make people feel comfortable around her. Not only was she a capable wife, she was also the mother of two children: Douglas, eleven, and little Chrissie, just six months old. The Matthews had nearly been rejected from the assignment because Nancy had been pregnant. But the paperwork had gone through. Nancy had flown to Germany to give birth to Chrissie. The child seemed to be thriving in Liberia.

"Hi, Lindsey," Nancy exclaimed, reaching out for Lindsey's hand, "will you be going to the soccer game at the international school tomorrow?"

"Wouldn't miss it!" answered Lindsey. "Tim's the goalie. He'd be broken hearted if we weren't there."

"Speaking of soccer, there's Joe Weah. God, is that guy good looking!" said Nancy.

Lieutenant Colonel Joseph Weah, commander of the Liberian Reconnaissance Battalion, stood a short distance from them. A blond secretary from the Swiss Embassy hung on his arm. Athletic and confident, the native Liberian sipped at his cocktail and visited with the French ambassador.

Weah was Liberia's only national sports hero. Sixteen years earlier, Weah had kicked the winning goal against the British in the Summer Olympics, claiming a bronze medal for his nation. He had later fought in the civil war and had been promoted to his present position in the new government. He was also the only Liberian officer to have been trained at the Special Forces Officers' Qualification course at Fort Bragg, North Carolina.

Unlike most Liberians, Weah stood nearly six feet tall. His grandfather, a Mandingo, had found a job as a metal worker and had settled in the village. Mandingos were a tall, mostly nomadic people, who could be found throughout West Africa, easily mixing with local tribes. Weah's grandmother was Kapel. Their son, Joe's father, had become a paramount chief. Considered by many to be Liberia's most eligible bachelor, Joe hadn't married. Few people, if any, would dislike Joe Weah. Even Tim had fallen under Joe's spell, as the affable Liberian had volunteered to coach the soccer team at Tim's school.

"Nancy, Lindsey!" Joe said, approaching them. "Are you ready for the big game?"

"Sure are," grinned Nancy. Joe's date, Ursula, was a tall blonde, about Lindsey's height. Her most significant attribute was an exceptionally well-formed bust. She reminded Lindsey of an overly made up call girl in a movie made in the forties.

"Your wine, my lady," said Hank, handing Lindsey her glass.

Social functions like this were no problem for Hank. Lindsey admired his ability to put others at ease. After sixteen years as an officer's wife, Lindsey had seen her share of receptions. Hank could play the chameleon with the best of them. He could please a boss or motivate a subordinate.

It was obvious that Hank truly liked Joe. It wasn't the same with some others. She had sensed his distaste for Julius Carpai, the minister of defense. When she questioned him about it, Hank was tight lipped. He said that it went back to his past assignment in Liberia before they were married. Maybe someday he'd tell her more. For now, that was enough. She didn't press the issue.

Shortly after midnight, people began to slip off to private parties or simply go home. The two moved to the foyer, pausing only briefly to say goodbye to those they passed.

Back home, King greeted them at the door, his tail thumping against the wall. Lindsey peeked in Tim's room. He slept soundly. The dog jumped up on the bed and curled up at the boy's feet.

"Good night, guys," she said, pulling the door closed.

Hank sat on the edge of their bed, still in uniform.

"I'm going to get ready for bed," said Lindsey, leaning over to kiss him softly on his neck. Minutes later she returned, totally naked. Hank looked up and grinned.

"You look even better without the red dress," he smiled.

"Let me help you out of that uniform, soldier," she said, running her fingers under the lapels of his jacket. Exercising restraint wasn't one of Hank's best qualities, but he forced himself to resist the impulse to shed his clothes quickly.

Instead, he waited as Lindsey methodically unbuttoned his shirt and reached inside to caress his chest. She pulled at his waistband and loosened his trousers. He fell back on the bed as she lifted herself over his hips.

Later, she reached over to turn off the lamp. "I'll always remember Liberian Independence Day," she yawned. "Good night, Hank. Sleep well."

"Don't worry. I always do," he answered.

Yet Hank didn't sleep well. Deep-seated dreams disrupted what should have been a perfect slumber.

In the valley again, the incessant drumbeat commanded his attention. Ceremonial fires illuminated the lush foliage. The compound took on an eerie, primordial glow. The statue stood on the altar. Its horns cast a shadow on the grass below. The eyes, like bottomless pits, drew him in. Once again, he felt the vertigo of free falling. His throat tightened and his limbs weighed heavy. He willed himself to hold onto his composure, yet the disorientation intensified. Now fear was his sole companion.

"It's just the goddamn dream!" he tried to shriek. "Come on! Come on! I've got to wake up!"

He struggled to find his control. This wasn't reality. Lindsey, his home, his bed – were reality. The scene began to fade. Now he was in charge. It couldn't overtake his will.

But his efforts were in vain. In a flash, he was back in the valley.

"Shit!" he thought. "All right, I know this is just a dream. Go ahead. You won't frighten me. Dreams are only dreams."

Yet tonight was different from past dreams. He sensed the cold grass on his bare feet. The heat from the fires warmed his exposed skin. How could it be? Here in the humid jungle, his breath condensed in the night air.

He was no longer on the hillside, but standing naked by the altar. Before, he was only a detached observer. Now, he was a participant. A stratified mist filled the night air. The statue was clearly visible, yet other dark figures remained partially hidden in the haze.

He tried to move, but his head would only turn part way. His legs seemed wooden and apart from his consciousness. When the mist began to fall away, he could clearly see the four men. Julius Carpai stood immediately before him. But it wasn't the earlier Carpai. Now it was the same man he'd seen at the reception – an older Carpai. Then there was Steve Moya, speaker of the House. He didn't recognize the third man. But Hank gasped when he recognized the fourth man. It was Steven Dowling, Liberia's President.

Carpai turned his eyes toward Hank before leaning toward Moya. Carpai pointed at Hank's groin and snickered. Hank instinctively tried to move his hands to cover himself, but his arms failed him. He blurted an explanation: It's cold. It shrinks when it's cold. Although the words formed in his head, they failed to come to his lips.

Now the drumbeat increased to one hundred beats per minute. A new figure emerged from the shadows. Naked and obese, it came to the foreground. Hank strained to make out its features. Soon it became clear – this was George Sarday, chancellor at the University of Liberia.

It all began to replay in his head. The thin form of the young Amahd once again lay across the stone altar. Unable to make his body move, Hank stared blankly into the statue's eyes. He felt himself falling under its spell. He remembered what had happened eighteen years ago.

A chant rose to accompany the drumbeat. Two men hooked their arms around Amahd's elbows and guided him toward the altar. The lanky boy was no match for the two grown men. They pushed and pulled until Amahd had been placed upon the stone altar. The boy looked up into the eyes of the idol. One man grasped the boy's head as the other held firmly to his waist. They stretched his thin form forward until his head hung over the altar's edge. The chanting continued in eerie harmony with the drums.

Now Sarday came forward and positioned himself to the right of the statue. In his right hand he was holding a long sword. The polished metal gleamed in the firelight. Sarday raised the blade high over his head. The drums reached a crescendo, and then came to an abrupt stop. The sword swiftly fell on Amah's slender neck.

It sliced cleanly through the spinal column. It cut through muscle and flesh, severing the head from the body. Falling forward, it seemed to drift toward the wooden bowl. Hank imagined the "thump" as it landed in the receptacle. Red mist sprayed from the headless corpse. The lungs released their last breath. The body contracted in massive shock. The arteries continued to spurt blood from the heart, which was still unaware of its useless effort.

At first, the bursts of blood shot more than three feet, spraying the statue. Then the pressure decreased, and the fluid slowed to dark ooze that dripped from the corpse and dribbled down the front of the altar.

"That's it," Hank ordered himself. "Time to wake up. I refuse to watch a repeat of ritual murder."

However, as much as he tried to will himself away from the scene, nothing changed. The brutal episode would be playing itself out once again.

Amahd's long, thin legs stretched out on the platform. The toes curled down and touched the stone edge. Hank could see a jagged scar encircling the boy's bony ankle. It looked strangely familiar. Where had he seen a scar like this before?

Then he remembered. It was just like the scar on Tim's ankle. Four years earlier, Tim had fallen from his bicycle. Now his fear took on a new intensity. This new victim was not Amahd. It was Tim.

A silent shriek again formed, but refused to come. Immobile, he felt the tears flow freely down his cheeks.

The chanting came to a stop. Each figure turned toward the altar. Only Sarday stood in place, his dark eyes focused directly on Hank. Then Sarday seemed to change before Hank's eyes. He appeared to be both a man and demon.

It was as though Sarday had become two beings in one body.

The thing that was called George Sarday gripped the sheath of the polished metal blade. Smiling, he raised the sword high over his head. The drums reached a crescendo. In slow motion, the sharp edge fell toward Tim's slender neck. Hank tried to scream once again. This time it was the cry of a desperate father about to watch the execution of his only son.

"Hank! Hank! Stop it! Stop it! What on earth's wrong?" Lindsey stood beside the bed, her face white with fear.

Hank sat upright. "Oh, my God ... Tim," he blurted. He rushed down the hallway and opened Tim's door.

King, alert, looked up, but Tim remained in a deep sleep.

Hank moved quietly to the boy's bed. Tim's left leg lay exposed. The thin, white scar circled his ankle. Hank reached out, touching the leg, sensing its warmth and vitality. He backed out of the room, softly released the doorknob, and moved silently into the bathroom.

He leaned unsteadily over the toilet. Beads of sweat had formed on his brow. Finally, he retched. Release of the vomit eased the spasms.

Lindsey cradled his spent body. "Hank, what's wrong?" she asked. "You've got to tell me what's going on." She helped him back to the side of the bed. He held his head in his hands.

"All right, I suppose it's about time I told you what happened," he said. It was right after he was wounded in Desert Storm, he explained. When his leg wound healed, he had been assigned to work with the Liberian army at Camp Jackson near the village of Naama.

They were a sorry lot. The officers held their positions because of political or social pull, not because of their qualifications. No one wanted to train. Colonel Julius Carpai was the biggest hurdle. An evil, ruthless commander, he stole from the payroll and bullied the villagers.

Hank's story went on for more than an hour. Lindsey sat amazed at his account of Amahd's ritual murder.

"My God, Hank!" she said. "Can't we do something? That Julius Carpai should be in jail for his actions. Certainly, he shouldn't be serving as minister of defense. "Isn't there anyone we could tell?"

"What could I say?" Hank asked. "I'm not sure any of it is real anymore."

Hank paused.

"There's more," he said, hesitating. "Sometimes I wonder if it's just a dream that occurred as a result of a malaria fever."

"Go on, dear," she said, "you might as well get it all out."

"I was discovered hiding on the hill. When they chopped off the boy's head, I think I yelled. Suddenly they were all looking up at the place where I was hiding.

"The guy with the sword reeled, pointed at me and shouted. Then the guards crouched and fired their rifles. Bullets ricocheted on nearby rocks.

"I turned and rushed downhill toward the trail. I ignored the stiffness in my left leg, still weak from the wound. Nothing mattered but escape. I sensed the presence of men in pursuit but resisted looking back. Wasted seconds could be deadly. My instincts told me that they were closing the gap.

"I took a sharp left off the main trail onto a less-traveled path. I increased my stride, ignoring the brush and vines that scraped against my uniform. Within minutes, the path widened. I allowed myself to slow, making careful steps through the darkness. It looked like I lost them but I kept moving, occasionally looking behind me. I saw nothing. I thought I had made my get-away.

"How wrong I was. Two steps later my flight came to an abrupt stop. Would you believe it? I ran headlong into that damn idol itself. But it was no longer just a small wooden statue; it had grown in size. It loomed over the path and blocked my way. The white eyes had turned red, the color of Amahd's blood. In its eyes, I could see the reflection of my own naked body stretched on the stone altar."

Hank stopped talking and sat on the bed staring at the wall. Then he continued.

"With no way to move forward, I cut to my right, thrashing through the brambles that tore at my flesh. Again, the brush opened up. This time I found myself at the mouth of a dark tunnel that sloped downward. I had no choice. I charged furiously ahead, dreamily aware of shouts and gunfire only seconds behind me. Although it was dark, my eyes adjusted to the scant light.

"I had entered a limestone cavern. I followed a worn trail deeper into the Earth. Then I realized that I wasn't alone. Warrior statues that looked like men with horns and tails stood as silent sentinels. I thought I was losing my mind. I ran faster and found myself in a subterranean grotto. In many ways, it resembled a Roman coliseum. At its center stood a granite temple. From behind its columns, I saw a reddish glow. As I got closer, there was the infernal statue sitting on a granite block. You know, like the statue of Lincoln in Washington, D.C.

"Everywhere I went, everywhere I looked, the statue followed. Although I struggled to fight its spell, it denied my escape.

"There was no way to move forward. My only choice was to turn and retrace my steps. In the shadows ahead, I saw something move. I couldn't see it clearly but I knew it was creature that the statue represented and it was waiting for me. Somehow, I knew that this hideous beast would drive me insane. I was sure that the statue in the temple was the lesser evil. I reeled and headed back down the path.

"Then I slipped and fell face first onto what I thought was the muddy floor. I pulled myself up on my knees and examined my slimy hands. I rubbed my fingers together and sniffed the substance.

"My God, I realized that it wasn't mud at all, but blood kept damp by the trickle of the cavern's own internal moisture. The floor of the tunnel was awash with the blood of thousands of sacrifices. I struggled to stand, but my legs gave way. The thing drew closer. I could smell its foul breath. It reeked of death and corruption. I struggled to my feet then slipped again falling forward as razor-sharp talons dug into my flesh."

"How did you ever escape?" she asked. Lindsey felt light-headed. She had been so close to losing Hank.

"That's the weird part. I don't really remember. I do remember this sixteen-year-old kid who had been assigned as my aide. His name was Charles Morray. He was supposed to keep up my uniform, polish my boots, and maintain the quarters. I didn't know how to deal with having a manservant at first, but that's the way they do things here. Morray led me to the valley. He left before the sacrifice.

"The next morning, they found me in my bunk. I was delirious and had a high fever. I remember being in and out of it for at least a week. The medic said it seemed like malaria. I took the pills and eventually got better," Hank said.

"What about this Morray? Did you ever ask him what he knew?"

"No. I never saw him after that. Someone told me that his company had been sent out to do border patrols. By the time they returned, our tour was up."

"Did you see Carpai after that night?"

"No. He had gone to Monrovia," Hank said.

"Do you think he knew you were a witness?"

"If he did, I'm sure I would have been killed," Hank answered. "Honestly, I don't really know what I saw. Maybe I temporally lost my mind. The dreams went away after a few years. They started coming back on our flight here."

Lindsey rubbed Hank's back, unsure of what to say next.

"What scares me is that tonight's dream was so different," he said.

"How was it different?" she asked.

When he told her that this time Tim had been the victim, Lindsey shivered. Somehow she had to help him get through this.

"Tonight's dream was most likely just a reaction to those old memories and being at the Independence Ball. All those men from your dream were there. You saw that Tim's just fine. Just try to get back to sleep. The reality is that you're here with me, and we'll get through this together."

In a matter of minutes, Hank slept soundly. His breaths came in even measures.

But now it was Lindsey who couldn't sleep. What was truth and what was fiction? Her husband wasn't a man who would confuse the two. Although she had done what she could to soothe his anguish, her concern had heightened. She began to recite the Lord's Prayer, an old habit from childhood. In the past, the words had helped her find stability when her world seemed out of control. Perhaps it would once again.

# 4

***In the conference room of the American Embassy, Douglas Baxter looked out the barred window at the blue expanse of the Atlantic Ocean.***

NO JUSTICE. NO JUSTICE AT ALL IN THIS WORLD, THOUGHT BAXTER. HE SAT IN the meeting, feigning attention. No use worrying about it. He had done his best. Now it was time to move on.

His hand moved in a tight circular motion as his pen drew tiny, black spirals on the yellow legal pad. For the last six months, Baxter had been the charge d'affaires ad interim. Basically, he had filled the role of the ambassador. At the end of the meeting, he would make the announcement. Then it would be over.

Baxter had regularly chaired the Monday meetings, relishing his role as acting ambassador. With thirty years of experience in the U.S. State Department, he had given his all to make himself indispensable. Certain the new President would nominate him as ambassador, Baxter had even ordered business cards. Then – just his luck – they had discovered the goddamned oil reserves. Liberia had become a political pawn. The new ambassador would be a political appointee.

Career diplomats weren't as useful. Most likely, the new ambassador lacked the knowledge and experience to run the country team, but that didn't seem to matter. Within the hour, he'd let the team know that the new appointee would arrive in two weeks. After the announcement, he'd offer his resignation. He looked around the table at what used to be his team. They would stay; he would be gone.

Lori Grant continued to babble on. She headed Liberia's Peace Corps. To her left sat Victor Ramirez, in charge of the office of the U.S. Agency for International Development. Next was Gordon Kennedy, the economics officer. His wife Jean served as the ambassador's secretary. The two had moved from post to post together. Beside him sat the medical officer, Dr. David King. He suppressed a yawn. He didn't hide the fact that meetings bored him. Neil Stone, chief of the U.S. Information Service, seemed to be taking notes.

Marsha Turner, a plump blonde in her mid-thirties, ran the consular office. She'd been with the embassy for six years. She was married to Wayne, a black American. Wayne didn't work, but spent his time buying African art. He made a profit by selling it, at a good mark-up, to others on the embassy staff.

The new defense attaché, Hank Martin, was next. Lieutenant Colonel Martin had only been in country for a few months, but Baxter liked what he saw.

The protocol officer, Bill Davis sat at Martin's left. A newcomer in the state department, Davis was smart. He'd move up through the ranks. Next to last was Bruce Ziegler. He caught Baxter's eye and flashed a grin. Ziegler served as first secretary. Like Baxter, Ziegler was a thirty-year man. He had joined the CIA right out of college.

The eye contact reminded Baxter that he had to find time to talk to him. Ziegler's wife, Donna, was the subject of some recent complaints. Ten years younger than her husband, the two had been married for only five years. Lately, comments had come in about Donna's habit of removing her bikini top while sunbathing at the embassy pool. Bare breasts were commonplace in Africa, but not for the foreigners. Donna had good reason to be proud of her large assets, but this wasn't the place to show them off. Even in her tennis whites, Donna could create quite a stir just walking through the recreation hall.

The last member of the team was Dan Hamilton, who served as political officer. Baxter didn't particularly care for Hamilton. The twenty-five-year state department veteran was still recuperating from his fourth divorce, but hadn't tired of women. He was on the hunt for any female who'd give him a second look. A true "Teflon man," Hamilton could always find a way out of a tough situation. Baxter wondered how he could have ever advanced as far as he had. Hamilton had a foul mouth that got even worse when he drank.

What difference did it make anyway? The new ambassador would have to deal with the team. It wasn't his problem anymore.

"Do you have any questions, Doug?" asked Grant, who was wrapping up her presentation.

"What?" Baxter stammered. "Oh, no. Thank you for your report."

It seemed like the meeting had finally come to an end. Several people began straightening their papers and reaching for their briefcases.

"Before we adjourn," Baxter said, "I have one more item. The President of the United States has selected our new ambassador to Liberia."

"Congratulations, Doug!" said Hamilton. Others smiled, pushed back their chairs and started to stand.

"Wait!" Baxter said, raising his arms, palms out. "I know many of you have expressed your support; however, the next ambassador will be a political appointee."

"Son-of-a-bitch!" growled Hamilton. "Who the fuck is he?"

"It isn't a he. It's Senator Victoria Ryan Johnson of Massachusetts."

"You've got to be shitting me. That's all we need. We've got to have a man with balls enough to keep a lid on things. The last thing we need is some female politician."

"That's enough, Dan," Baxter said. "We all have the choice to follow the President's orders or to go out looking for another job. No more comments like that at this table."

"Can you tell us a little about her?" asked Ziegler.

"Sure. She just finished her second term in the Senate. She's supposed to be quite popular with her constituents – she took seventy percent of the vote in her last election. She worked in the President's office when he was the governor of Massachusetts. As a senator, she helped stop that trouble in the Far East a few years ago. She's on the appropriations committee. Her husband worked hard to get the President elected. Both of them are supposed to be close friends of the President and his wife."

"So, just who is her husband?" Ziegler continued.

"None other than David M. Johnson, founder of NETTEL. He's supposed to be worth more than twenty billion dollars. The new ambassador will be here in two weeks. She's coming in her husband's corporate jet. He'll commute here, keeping his offices in Boston."

"Wow! A rich ambassador," commented Lori.

"Not only rich, but would you believe that she's been here before? She served as a Peace Corps volunteer here from 1990 to 1992."

Baxter continued to fill them in on what he knew about the new ambassador. But one member of the country team wasn't listening to the details. Hank Martin simply stared at the wall, lost in thought.

Victoria Ryan sure wasn't a senator back in 1992. Far from it.

Hank was commanding a Special Forces Mobile Training Team at Camp Jackson, near the village of Naama in Liberia. He'd been introduced to the Boston redhead who had come to teach school as a Peace Corps volunteer. They had spoken once or twice, but their relationship had been somewhat cool.

That all changed in a hurry.

One afternoon Hank jogged past Ismial Abram's store. The Lebanese merchant had married a local girl. The oldest of his three mulatto children, fifteen-year-old Amahd, helped run the store. His small generator pumped out the only power in the village. Anyone with spare change dropped by to take advantage of the cooler filled with chilled sodas.

Vicki was no exception. That afternoon she stood on the porch with her Coke in hand. She leaned against the railing, watching a child playing alongside the road. The four-year-old girl drew in the dirt, using twigs and rocks to make her designs. Vicki had agreed to keep an eye on the child while her mother went inside. She tucked a strand of her red hair behind her ear and smiled as the girl sang a song that Vicki had taught her older sister in school.

A movement to her left caught her attention. She recognized the American army officer from Camp Jackson jogging toward the town. He wore only brief swimming trunks and running shoes. His taut body glistened with sweat; his face reflected the concentration of an athlete. His only flaw was the scar tissue on his left thigh, the visible result of a bullet wound from Desert Storm.

Vicki had learned enough of the Kapel language to know what others said about this man. Since most Liberians were far shorter, this Hank Martin seemed like a giant. She'd seen the teenage girls snicker together behind upraised hands. They laughed, speculating on the size of his other body parts. Despite their interest, Vicki hadn't heard of any firsthand encounters. From what she knew, he hadn't slept with any local women.

The men had also commented on this American. They had noticed the scarring on his thigh. The ability to withstand pain was considered a virtue. It was a part of the initiation ceremony for both men and women. Whereas a disfiguring scar might repulse others, Hank's combat wound served as a badge of courage, winning respect and admiration from the locals.

Vicki's attention was split between the child and the man. She didn't see the little girl's brother come around the side of the hut across the road. Neither did she see the approaching money bus. These old twenty-passenger vehicles were the primary source of public transportation throughout West Africa. They hauled people, animals and cargo to the remote villages. Usually held together by spit and wire, they often broke down. They had their share of accidents. No wonder. Their drivers had come straight out of the bush. No training necessary. The only criteria for drivers seemed to be boundless courage and the willingness to drive at break-neck speeds.

At the same moment that the bus rounded the corner, the child spotted her brother. She squealed, jumped up and dashed into the road. Vicki screamed as the girl darted across the street. That only confused the child. She stopped, frozen in place. Inside the bus, the driver turned to his passenger – a bare bosomed young woman – who had asked how long it would take to get to the next village. He failed to see the child ahead, directly in his path.

Vicki reached out, her arms moving in slow motion, her legs wooden. The driver looked up, spotting the child. His foot slammed against the brakes. The wheels locked. The heavily loaded bus continued in its path directly at the girl. The driver forced the steering wheel to the right. A cloud of dust formed behind the vehicle as it skated on the loose gravel.

Hank saw the bus and the girl at the same moment. Anyone nuts enough to jog on Liberian roads had to be constantly on the watch. Without missing a stride, he rushed toward the child. He could see the girl – crying, but not moving. He could see the bus – the rusty bumper, bent grill and broken headlight.

He pushed himself to his limit, reaching the girl, scooping her up in his arms. He caught a glimpse of the hood of the bus rise above him. He dove to his right, throwing himself and the girl out of the path of the bus. He twisted, landing on his left shoulder and back as he slid on the rough gravel. Tiny pellets embedded themselves in his flesh. He heard a high-pitched scream in his right ear. Yet still the girl remained tightly enfolded in his arms. He choked on a brown cloud of dust as the bus roared past, its wheels missing his feet by inches.

Finally, the dust cleared. He looked up to find himself surrounded by people who had rushed up from all directions. Someone helped him to his feet. He still clutched the quivering child who wrapped her arms around his neck. Someone else handed him a torn t-shirt to help stem the trickles of blood spreading down his side.

Then the girl's mother reached out to reclaim her child. Beside her stood the Boston redhead sobbing with relief.

"It's all my fault," she cried. "I was supposed to watch her, but she ran out into the road!" She paused, looking at Hank. "Oh, my God, you're hurt!"

"I don't think I broke anything, but my shoulder is beginning to hurt like hell," Hank said.

"I have a first aid kit back at my place," Vicki said. "Let me see what I can do."

Just then, the crowd parted. The village chief appeared.

He reached out to shake hands with Hank in the West African fashion of popping fingers. Hands are clasped as in a normal handshake. As each individual pulls away, the middle fingers snap as they slide apart.

The custom goes back to the days when warriors snapped their fingers to prove there was no poison under their fingernails.

Everyone seemed to be talking at once. Many reached out to touch this man who had risked his own life for the child. Vicki moved forward, clutched Hank's elbow and led him through the crowd toward one of the mud brick huts that housed the Peace Corps volunteers.

The tin-roofed dwelling had two rooms, one in front and the other in back. The first room had three screened windows. Each window had shutters that could be closed at night. Curtains of thin fabric, faded and threadbare, bordered the screened openings. Under one window, a crudely constructed bookshelf held a couple of dozen dog-eared paperback books. Along one wall sat a worn rattan couch lined with green plastic cushions. Two matching chairs faced the couch, creating an informal sitting area. The kitchen area consisted of a small table with two folding metal chairs, a water filter, a kerosene refrigerator and a Coleman stove.

Hank's attention turned to the wall along the back. A thin wire had been strung loosely along the wall to display a half dozen old Poro masks. Underneath, a narrow table held a ceremonial drum with two crossed spears fastened to the wall above it.

"Sit here, near the window so there's better light," Vicki said, indicating the metal kitchen chair. She walked into the back room and returned with a first aid kit. She filled a pan with filtered water, immersed a clean terrycloth towel and knelt beside her patient.

"This is going to hurt a little," she warned. "I'm going to clean your wounds with soap and water and try to remove any rocks. If necessary, I'll stitch up the deep cuts. Then I'll treat the area with antiseptic and cover it with gauze."

For the next half hour, Vicki worked as efficiently as the team's medic. When she finished, she took a step backward to appraise her work.

"That should do it. Nothing was so bad as to require stitches. Come by in a few days, and I'll change the dressing."

"That's OK," Hank said. "The team medic can do that."

As he stood up, his arm upset the pan of bloody water. "Damn it!" he said. "This needs to be cleaned up before it draws ants."

Vicki grabbed some towels and began mopping up the spill. Hank slid to his knees in front of her, reaching out to help. By then, the late afternoon sunlight streamed in through the window at an angle, falling on Vicki's hair and shoulders. Her loose-fitting blue cotton dress hung open at the neck. Hank reached for another towel, but hesitated. He looked directly at her white breasts within an arm's length of his touch. He could see dark, red nipples and a slight blush of freckles.

His arousal was so immediate and intense that it shocked and embarrassed him. Foreigners became accustomed to seeing topless women in Liberia. Yet looking at Vicki exposed like this had caused an instantaneous response.

He looked up, only to find her staring at his swimming trunks. There was no hiding or explaining what he was thinking. Her cheeks reddened with her own embarrassment. That only served to increase the pressure of his erection. His thin shorts hid nothing. Vicki could see it, too. Still kneeling, she looked directly at his crotch.

She rose to her feet, her face still crimson. She cocked her head to the side. "Oh, what the hell," she said. "I'll probably hate myself in the morning."

She reached down to her hemline and pulled the dress over her head. She tossed it casually on the floor. Her fingers went to her black silk panties. Off they came. Now she stood, totally naked, facing Hank.

No matter how many women would pass his way, Hank would never forget the sight of the redheaded Victoria Ryan, standing in the sunlight on that hot West African afternoon.

"This way," she said, taking his hand and leading him to the back room.

Vicki's tour lasted another three months. The two shared her bed on a number of occasions, yet they never spoke of the future. There was no reason to hide their affair; after all, both were single. Yet the relationship had a kind of secrecy. Once they spent six days together in Cape Palmas, a resort in southern Liberia. Other times, if they passed on Naama's streets, they barely acknowledged each other.

When it came time for her to leave, they simply said goodbye. That would be their final farewell. No tears, no promises to write, and no plans to ever meet again.

"Does anyone know anything else about her?" asked Gordon Kennedy.

No one answered. Hank remained mum. No way he would raise his hand to report that the two had hit the sack a number of times when they were both stationed in Liberia. He couldn't help but wonder how the years had treated her. What would it be like working for Vicki? He'd soon find out.

"Just what we need, a goddamn woman who'll wet her pants the first time a shot is fired," growled Hamilton as they filed out of the conference room.

"Don't bet on it," Hank said.

"What did you say?"

"Nothing, Dan," Hank answered. "Nothing at all."

# 5

***At the Martin home, Lindsey had finally given up on Adam after five months of trying to train him how to dust the furniture. He'd never learn to pick up each object, dust, and then carefully set it back down. She'd just do the dusting herself. With Hank and Tim gone to soccer practice, she made the rounds in the bedrooms.***

SUBTLE CHANGES HAD TAKEN PLACE IN TIM'S ROOM. A BOTTLE OF AFTER-SHAVE sat on the dresser where a model car had once been displayed. The map of Disney World had come down. Taking its place was a poster featuring a scantily clad starlet.

Not long ago, Lindsey had made the mistake of poking her head in the half-open door to ask Tim if he wanted some ice cream. Wearing only his underwear, Tim blushed and hid behind the closet door. Since then, he had carefully locked the bedroom and bathroom doors behind him.

A full silhouette target affixed to the back of the bedroom door signaled another change. She had counted thirty-four nine-millimeter bullet holes in the heavy paper. His fascination with shooting caused her to pause. She wished she could rip the thing down and tear it to shreds. But that would violate the trust she shared with both her husband and her son.

It wasn't that long ago that she had seen him come home with the target in hand. Joe Weah had asked both Tim and Hank to visit the Reconnaissance Battalion camp to check out a new shipment of pistols. They had both fired on the qualification course. Hank couldn't stop talking about his son's natural ability. Tim had not only qualified, he had fired at the "expert" level with the pistol.

Lindsey had grown up around guns. She had shot skeet with her dad since she was nine. Her dad never missed deer season. Hank had taken Tim pheasant hunting many times. But hunting weapons were different from automatic pistols designed to kill other human beings. Now Tim had fired at the silhouette of a man on a paper target. Could he just as easily shoot a real man?

"Mom, we're back!" yelled Tim.

All three – Tim, Hank and Joe – stood at the bottom of the stairs, covered with sweat and dirt.

"You all had better clean up before dinner," Lindsey said. "Joe, I laid out towels in the guest bathroom."

"Do we have time to show you the new moves Joe taught at soccer practice?" pleaded Tim.

"Sure, it's going to be a while until dinner anyway," she said.

From a lawn chair on the patio, Lindsey watched the two men and her son, all shirtless, laughing and shouting as they kicked the soccer ball across the yard. King romped alongside them, pushing at the ball with his nose and barking enthusiastically. Both her men were tanned from the tropical sun. She hesitated. Indeed, they were both men. Tim now stood well over six feet tall. In so many ways, he had left his childhood behind.

Joe Weah was shorter than either Tim or Hank. Heavily muscled, Joe had a broad chest and a narrow waist. He had the classic washboard stomach of a weight lifter.

Abraham lowered the tray with the pitcher of iced tea and four tall glasses. Along with the beverage, he had arranged a platter of sliced cheese, crackers and fresh fruit.

"OK, gentlemen. Snack time," yelled Lindsey.

The three joined her on the patio, each grinning and damp with sweat. King plopped down near the table, hoping someone would throw a morsel his way.

"Joe, can I ask you a question?" asked Tim.

"Sure, Tim, what is it?"

"How did you get those scars on your back and chest?"

"Those are the teeth marks from the great crocodile spirit, *Nangma*," Joe said.

"Wow!" said Tim.

"Tell you what, sport. After dinner I will tell you how each Kapel man receives his scars when he escapes from *Nangma*."

Lindsey couldn't help but admire their friend Joe. He treated Tim as his equal. He seemed so comfortable around Americans. They were lucky to know him.

Abraham's dinner of roast lamb, sweet potatoes, mango and pineapple left them all full and relaxed. After her initial reluctance at having a Liberian cook, Lindsey had come to enjoy his service. Freed from meal preparation and after-dinner clean up, she had more time to visit. She, too, was looking forward to hearing Joe's account of the escape from the *Nangma*.

Joe leaned forward, tapped his fingertips together, and spoke in a low voice.

"I was born in the village of Zigda, high in the Liberian mountains. Even today, you cannot drive to my village. There are no roads, only trails. It is in a low valley, surrounded by high mountains covered with deep forest. People come from all around to go to Zigda. It is important, like your county seat. More than three hundred people dwell in my village.

"As a child, my life was no different from that of any other small boy. We worked, but we also played. I have fond memories of my life as a child. When Kapel boys and girls reach puberty, they go to bush school to learn how to become adults. The Poro spirits run the bush school. The Poro governs our lives. It is a secret society that guides and protects us from the evil spirits that live in the bush. Tim, do you know the old *Star Wars* movies?"

"Sure, Joe," he answered. "We have the whole series on DVD. They're neat."

"Remember how the Jedi knights could influence the Force? Remember, too, that there was a dark side to the Force?"

"Yeah, that's Darth Vader," Tim said.

"Well, the Kapel believe that a supreme force created the world. The missionaries must have been surprised to learn that the native people already believed in God. But it's a little different. We believe that God is far too busy to have time for the Kapel. Instead, good and evil spirits affect our lives. Even after a person dies, his spirit could continue to live in the bush and influence our lives. The Poro, just like the Jedi knights, fight the evil spirits. Sometimes, like Darth Vader, a member of the Poro can fall from favor and become involved with evil spirits."

Tim nodded. "I kind of know what you mean. Everyday Walker told me that members of the Liberian government sacrifice young boys to a demon that he calls the *endosym*. Every year, when the rainy season starts, this *endosym* comes to kill him. But Everyday says that his juju is too powerful, and he is protected."

"Tim," scolded Lindsey. "Everyday Walker is an old man. He is just telling you a fairy tale."

"That's not true, Mom. Everyday Walker is a powerful *zo*. You know, a witch doctor. When he was a young man, he brought up the demon from the dark depths of the earth. The *endosym* promised him fame and fortune if he would sacrifice people to him. When Everyday Walker refused, the *endosym* killed his family. But the *endosym* couldn't touch him because the spirit of the great leopard protects him."

Lindsey watched her son. He rambled on, as if reciting the old man's story from memory. She wondered if he was spending too much time with the old man. When they had first arrived in Liberia, she and Hank found themselves in a dilemma. They were required to attend an endless string of social functions. At fifteen, Tim was too young to attend, yet too old for a babysitter. Both had some anxiety about leaving him home alone so often.

They solved the problem by asking Everyday Walker, armed with his trusty shotgun, to share evening duties with Charles, the night guard. Hank had offered the older man a few extra dollars for his additional work, but Everyday Walker had refused, saying that it was his duty to watch out for the young man.

Often when they returned from a social event, they'd find the two playing checkers on the lighted front porch. In the weeks that followed, Tim spent even more time with the old man. He had picked up the Pidgin English of the working class and even knew a smattering of Kapel. She hadn't been concerned about their relationship until tonight. Now she wasn't too sure.

"Everyday Walker says that some of the big men in the government serve this *endosym*. He said that they kidnap young boys from the ghetto and sacrifice them to the *endosym*," Tim declared.

"Timothy Henry Martin," scolded Lindsey, "Everyday Walker is an old man. He is just telling you some superstitious mumbo-jumbo."

"No, he's not, Mom. I saw the leopard tooth he wears on a leather strap around his neck."

"Young man, Everyday Walker is a confused, old man. He is not, and has never been, a witch doctor. He's been a guard at this house for more than forty years."

She stopped. Hank, Joe and Tim all stared at her. She realized that she had been shouting. She took a breath and spoke in a more subdued tone.

"Honey, I'm sorry I shouted. Just understand that old men like to tell stories and have someone take the time to listen to them. There are no such things as *endosyms*."

No one spoke for several moments.

"Not necessarily," Joe said. "In Liberia, there have been men who tried to gain power by making human sacrifices to evil spirits. There are even stories about men who become one with a bush demon. They are called *endosyms*."

"Well, that's not the case now," said Lindsey. "Tim, there's no reason to take those stories for the truth."

Lindsey turned to Hank, expecting him to offer some support, but Hank's attention seemed elsewhere. He neither spoke nor looked her way. He remembered in his dream where George Sarday appeared to be both a man and a demon. Was Sarday an *endosym?*

"We kind of got off track," Joe said. "Back to my story. When we become teenagers, a masked Poro spirit called the *Ga Me* comes and takes us from our homes during the night. We go into the bush where we must live for six months. There, we learn the history of our people, how to hunt, how to build weapons and how to make magic potions. We boys become Kapel men and warriors. We learn many secrets that we share with no one, unless they are Poro, too.

"Tim, if you promise never to tell anyone, I will tell you some of the secrets of the Poro."

"I promise," nodded Tim. With a quick glance in her direction, Joe winked at Lindsey.

"OK, on the night the *Ga Me* came for me, my father whispered in my ear that my time had come. I was both happy and afraid – happy that at last I would be a Kapel warrior, but afraid of the unknown. That night I lay awake, waiting to be taken.

"At midnight, the drums begin to beat. I could hear them moving through the village. They stopped outside our door. My mother sobbed, but my father ignored her. He took my hand and led me to the door. I stepped into the darkness.

"Outside the *Ga Me* warned me not to speak. If I did, I would be punished. He led a line of boys out of the village, along the old bush trail, and into the mountains. Several hours later, we came to a raffia wall, blocking the entrance to the sacred Poro bush. Without a Poro escort, no one could enter. Those who tried would die.

"We came to a clearing. There were several small huts and one larger structure in the middle. We were told to remove our clothing. It was taken away. For the next six months, we would wear no clothing. When one of my friends complained, he was grabbed and pulled out of line. A masked figure came forward. Men held my friend while the masked figure whipped him with a leather strap. We all watched in fear as the strap cut into his back. Finally, the beating stopped and my friend was pushed back into our line. The *Ga Me* warned that any violation of the rules meant punishment. Repeated violations would result in death.

"The sun was just rising. We huddled together, frightened, tired, hungry and thirsty. Men came and told us to follow. We walked for hours, up the mountain and down the other side. Our feet throbbed;

every muscle ached. Some fell and were unable to get up. We lifted those who could not walk and carried them between us. We were told that all must finish, or none would finish. At sunset we staggered into a clearing. We were forced inside a large hut. We fell to the floor in exhaustion.

Joe looked at the Martins. All three were listening intently.

"In the morning, long before sunrise, we were awakened and led outside. We had been given no food or water for a full day. Our lips were cracked and swollen. We swayed as we attempted to stand upright. Before us, sat two iron pots. One had a steaming stew; the other filled with cool, clear water. Several boys ran to the water. They pushed and shoved to be the first to drink. Men came forward and held the boys by their elbows, pulling them tightly behind their backs. Again, they used the leather strap. We could only stand back and watch. This time the beatings were more severe. Finally, the limp and bloodied boys were dragged back to our line.

"The men left. We remained alone. We were uncertain what to do. Our stomachs hungered for food and water. Finally, after what seemed like hours, one boy stepped forward. He dipped a metal cup into the water pot. He hesitated, and then walked back to the line, offering the cup to one of the boys who had been beaten. A second boy moved forward to fill a cup. Then each, in turn, filled his own. We stood, cups in hand, together in our line. Slowly we lifted our cups to our dried lips. We drank. We drank together. Then we repeated our movements with the pot of stew.

"We learned the next lesson of the Poro – each man helps his brother. A brother is fed before a man feeds himself. The power of the Poro is in the whole, not the individual."

Joe sighed. To Lindsey, he seemed to have immersed himself in his story – almost as if he was reliving the frightening event. He paused and began anew without looking up for their approval to continue.

"The days became weeks. Our physical limits were tested each day. We learned to hunt, to make weapons and to kill with our bare hands. We learned to speak using only hand gestures. This language crossed tribal boundaries and dialects. One Poro may speak to another across a distance without moving his lips.

"When eight weeks had passed, our boyhood flesh had become firm. The soles of our feet were hardened, like rocks.

"One night a masked figure awakened us at midnight. It had the face of a young woman with light brown skin. We followed her into a deep valley. We approached a large compound surrounded by a tall fence. Stacks of burning wood illuminated the open areas, but we did not know what might be hiding in the dark shadows.

"We were told to line up. One by one, we were called forward. Each was made to lie on his back in the damp grass. One man grasped the boy's shoulders; another gripped the ankles.

"Drawing out a finely honed knife, the masked figure pulled at each boy's penis, stretching it to its full length. Deftly, the blade sliced through the foreskin. Some boys shrieked with pain; others fainted. When my turn approached, I vowed that I would silently endure the rite. I set my teeth firmly and held in my screams. When it was over, I returned to the line. Blood streamed down my legs, and I struggled to keep standing."

Tim winced at Joe's images of the sharp blade, the excruciating pain, and the bleeding wound. It all struck too close to home for the young man. But Joe continued. His stoic response to the rite seemed to have left him with an inner strength that would last throughout his life. Tim wondered if he could ever be as brave as his friend Joe.

"After all were circumcised, we were taken back to the hut. Some, arms supported by the shoulders of others, could barely walk – such was their agony. Yet inside the hut, it was less painful to stand upright than to sit. Men came in, washed us, and applied a healing salve to our wounds. Soon, our misery eased. We were fed a broth made from the flesh of our severed foreskins. By consuming the broth, we became one in the Poro spirit.

"We remained in the hut for ten days. Two suffered chills, then fever. They were taken away. We were told that the great crocodile spirit, *Nangma*, had eaten the boys. Their spirits would dwell in the Poro bush where they would live to serve *Nangma*.

"On the tenth day, we were taken outside. After the hut's darkness, the bright sunlight blinded us. Our eyes became accustomed to the light. We looked down at ourselves and at the others. We admired our new manhood. No longer children, our smooth members were proof that each had made the transition from boy to Kapel man.

"Now our lives in the bush school were transformed. We gained weight. We felt vital and alive. We were proud Kapel men, not mere children. Our teachers no longer hovered over us, watching for a violation of the rules. Now we obeyed because of our own will, not out of fear. We hunted together in teams. We ate what we killed.

"The day of our final test finally came. We would battle the great *Nangma*. We gathered together at dusk and filed into the bush. We reached the sacred home where the *Nangma* dwells. Each of us carried a spear and a knife. Men gave us cupfuls of a dark liquid. It would give us the power to fight the *Nangma*. They warned us that not all would survive the battle. Those who were lost would become its servants for eternity.

"I opened my throat and let the liquid flow freely into my body. I leaned back against a tree and waited my turn. I prayed that I would live to once again see my father and mother. I fell into a deep sleep. A short time later, I awoke. I was no longer in the compound, but on jungle trail. Even though it was deep into the night, I could see my way along the path. I walked forward, listening and choosing each step with care."

Joe stopped for a moment and took a deep breath. Tim wondered if this was the end of the story. It wasn't. Joe began again. Tim leaned forward with his elbows on his knees and his chin braced by his hands. He couldn't take his eyes away from Joe's lips. What more could Joe possibly have to say?

"Without warning, the largest leopard I had ever seen appeared before me. It growled, crouched and lunged toward me. I knelt, my spear pointed forward. The beast fell against my spear, its blade driving deep into its massive chest. The shaft snapped under its weight. It howled with pain and continued toward me. It threw me to the ground. Its razor sharp claws slashed my chest. I plunged my knife into its green eye, twisting the blade as it entered. It gave up its charge and fell lifeless to the ground before me. My arms and legs trembled, yet I rose to my feet. My broken spear lay embedded in its chest, and my knife protruded from its sightless eye.

"I ran ahead, down the trail. Within moments, I heard a low growl. I turned in time to see the beast rise again to its feet. It still lived! Pure hatred gleamed from its one remaining eye. I sensed its nearness, and I ran. I ran even faster, my lungs laboring as much from fear as from fatigue. Ahead, a large tree blocked my route. I panicked, crying for a way to escape. Then I saw an opening to my right. Heedless of the unknown, I left the trail and dashed into the bush.

"The forest opened up, and I found myself in a dark passageway. It sloped downward. I continued to run. I could hear the beast thrashing through the brush behind me. Despite the darkness, I could still make my way. Strange creatures lined the trail. Perhaps these were the giant winged guardians of the *Nangma*. I had penetrated the lair of the greatest of the Poro spirits.

"Panting, I continued my downward path. Ahead, I could see a reddish glow. I knew it was the *Nangma* itself. Behind, I smelled the humid breath of the wounded beast. But my fear of the beast paled to what loomed before me. No nightmare could compare. Even the leopard gave up its chase. Ahead, I trembled as I became aware of the presence of the great Poro spirit.

"I reversed direction and followed the leopard's hasty retreat. I felt the *Nangma* follow. Its odor stank of death and corruption. My foot struck a branch, and I lost my balance. Sharp fangs pierced my shoulder. At that moment, I was sure I would never return to my village as a warrior. My mother would hold tight to my clothing and weep at the loss of her son. My spirit was destined to serve *Nangma* for eternity.

"But I awoke. Once again I was inside the hut. I moved to one side. Spasms of pain ran up my spine. My arms and legs throbbed in rhythm to my heartbeat. In the distance, I heard the moaning of my brothers. I heard a man say that the *Nangma* had chewed us up and spit us out. Yet I would live. In two weeks, I would be welcomed into the Poro. A sense of well being came over me, and I fell into a deep slumber.

"It took fourteen days to heal the wounds from the bite of the *Nangma*. Finally, my brothers and I were released from the hut. Our teachers stood in the clearing. The *Ga Me* who had come for us so long ago pronounced that we were all brothers of the Poro. Once again were permitted to speak. Our voices croaked. We laughed and embraced one another. Out of the bush came our older brothers, our fathers and our uncles to join in our celebration. I saw my father move toward me. I reached out and enclosed his strength in my embrace. He encircled me, running his fingers through my hair and over the strength of my arms. To the beat of the drums, we marched back to the village.

"All our people lined the trail. They called out to us, using our old names, but we ignored their words. Now we had new Poro names, the names we would carry for the rest of our lives. My new name was Nah Weah. I would never again be known by my boyhood name. The child had been lost in the jaws of the *Nangma*, and a man had been born. We did not acknowledge our mothers; they wept at the loss of their children. As Poro warriors, women would serve us. We no longer would follow women's orders. We were now men."

Joe Weah's story ended. Hank, Lindsey and Tim sat without speaking. What could anyone say after hearing such a tale?

"But your name is Joe, not Nah," said Tim, breaking the silence.

"Joe is the name I have assumed for your world. People who want to succeed in the Western world do better if they take on an English name. But in my village, I am Nah Weah, not Joe Weah.

"You never spoke to your mother again?" wondered Tim.

Joe laughed at the comment, glancing at Lindsey. "Oh, no, I love my mother very much. After the ceremony, back in our hut, I hugged her and told her I loved her. However, to this day, on the streets of our village, my mother must be submissive."

Joe looked down at his watch.

"Look at the time! I didn't realize that it was so late. I have physical training tomorrow at six in the morning. Tim, you have school. I'd better call it a night."

At the door, Joe shook hands with Hank and Tim. He kissed Lindsey lightly on the cheek. After he was gone, Lindsey ran her hand along Hank's arm.

"Joe seems more like a brother than just a friend," she whispered. Hank put his arms around her and held her quietly.

"You know, I always thought it was tough to be a plebe in Beast Barracks at West Point. That was nothing compared to Joe Weah's ordeal in bush school.

# 6

***Sitting patiently in the outer office of the executive suite occupied by Liberia's President hadn't been easy.***

Only two minutes had passed since she had last checked the time. It had been more than an hour since Ambassador Ryan-Johnson had first entered the Presidential suite. Doug Baxter had warned her that it was customary to make the new ambassadors wait to present their credentials. One had cooled his heels and held his temper for more than three hours. Vicki hoped she wouldn't break that record.

She'd make the best of the wait time. She studied the opulent suite, marveling at the rich detail. They'd used native hardwoods in rich coffee and chocolate tones to panel the walls. She couldn't resist the temptation to slide her foot out of her high-heeled shoe, dipping her toes into the thick nap of the bronze-colored carpet.

Dowling's executive secretary had been noting her movements from his desk. A slightly built gentleman, he suppressed a self-satisfied smile as he watched her slip her foot back into the shoe. He shuffled through a pile of official-looking documents, but looked up when another, younger aide approached his desk. He glanced at the visitor, and then turned to the secretary.

"How stupid for the U.S. to send a female," he said in Kapel. "The role of women is to bear children and serve their men."

The secretary nodded and chuckled his agreement. Vicki stared ahead at an oil portrait of a former President. Neither man knew that this new ambassador understood their every word. During her tour in Liberia as a

Peace Corps volunteer, she had learned to speak Kapel. She had brushed up on her fluency by speaking to embassy employees. She had taken Baxter's advice, however, and hadn't shared her skills with government officials. He'd been right – this would give her significant advantage in dealing with the Liberians.

Ten weeks had passed since she'd first arrived in country. The question of oil exploration remained unresolved. Government officials had delayed issuing the permits that would give U.S. oil companies access to drill in the Saint Paul River Delta. Likely, today's meeting would be just another delay tactic.

The whole issue puzzled her. In so many ways, the influx of oil wealth could lead to a better life for the people. Government officials themselves would be among the first to benefit.

She had worked closely with her country team to find ways to break the deadlock. So far, she had been pleased with the professional and supportive group. Doug Baxter, deputy chief of mission, was truly a jewel. She had heard the rumors that Doug had expected to be appointed ambassador, yet he had stepped up and expertly facilitated the transition. She had asked him to continue to chair the meetings, while she acted as chairman of the board.

Lost in her reverie, the deep laughter of a dark man in an olive drab uniform broke her spell. Julius Carpai, the minister of defense, stood before the secretary. A second burst of laughter, a quick turn to the right, and Carpai passed through the door into the President's inner office. Seconds later, both Dowling and Carpai walked out together.

"Make sure she understands that we will not allow oil exploration to begin. As long as this terrorist threat exists here in Monrovia against Americans and third-country nationals, we cannot risk their lives," Carpai warned in Kapel.

"Don't worry, I can handle her," Dowling responded. Carpai left. Vicki remained impassive. Dowling approached her.

In slow, precise English, he said, "Madam Ambassador, please come in."

In his office, the President droned on about the country, the weather and the shortage of good help. Finally, he accepted the letter from the President of the United States, nominating her as ambassador.

"You realize, Ambassador Johnson," he said, abruptly ending the small talk, "we cannot authorize the search for oil. There is too much danger. Terrorists continue to stir up the radical elements. Of course, we want the prosperity and wealth this could bring our people, but we cannot risk innocent lives. As long as the rebel Charles Morray threatens the peace, there will be no exploration for oil."

"Mr. President," Vicki responded, "my people tell me that Monrovia and the delta have remained peaceful. The rebels are contained in Nimba and Grand Gedah counties.

"Of course, our excellent military force, under the expert leadership of Minister Carpai, has kept the insurgents at bay. Our concern is only for the safety of your company people."

"Mr. President, the U.S. would be happy to provide for the protection of our own people."

"Of course you would, but we in Liberia must take care of our own problems," he continued. "Oh, look at the time," Dowling interrupted himself. "I'm sorry, but I must leave now for the dedication of the new art building at the university."

He stood abruptly and escorted Vicki to the door.

Back in her limo, Vicki used her secure land-sat cell phone to call her secretary.

"Jean, contact Bruce Ziegler and Hank Martin. Tell them to meet me in my office in thirty minutes."

Something fishy was going on here. Carpai acted like he was the one in charge, not Dowling. They are clearly stalling. This deadlock had gone on too long.

"What's up, boss?" asked Ziegler, somewhat surprised by the hastily called meeting.

"I just got back from meeting with Dowling. He says the terrorist threat against Americans and third-country nationals is the reason for putting off oil exploration. I think they're deliberately stonewalling. What's your call, Bruce?"

"I think you're right about stonewalling. We know that Thomas Karua has met several times with members of the Middle Eastern oil cartel. At first, we thought they were just posturing for admittance to the cartel. Now we suspect that there might be a financial deal in the works. It would clearly be in the cartel's best interest to hold up or even stop oil exploration here. We also know that several late-night meetings have taken place at Dr. Sarday's residence.

"As for possible terrorist attacks," Ziegler continued, "that's just not Charles Morray's style. It's true that the People's Party has total control of the Nimba and Grand Gedah counties, but third-country nationals move freely there. Both the Liberian Mining Corporation and a French logging company move supplies and personnel in and out of the territory. Besides that, Monrovia has remained calm. We've had no hints of any terrorist activity here.

"Most Kruman are loyal to Morray, but we think only twenty percent of the Kapel are behind him. No Kapel leader has stepped forward to back the People's Party. Since the government here is ninety percent Kapel, Morray is better off staying in the Nimba and Grand Gedah. Some people suspect that the two counties might secede from Liberia and align themselves with Guinea," Ziegler concluded.

"Hank, what's your call on the military?" asked Vicki.

"Since the army's defeat in Singa, they've beefed up their forces along the Nimba border. There have been a few minor skirmishes, but neither side seems willing to prolong the battle or enter the other's area of control," Hank answered.

"Is there any way we could talk with this Charles Morray?"

"I recall a Private Charles Morray who worked with our mobile training team in Camp Jackson back in 1992. He'd be about the same age as this leader of the People's Party. But my understanding is that this Charles Morray graduated from the University of California," said Hank.

"I remember Morray," Vicki said quickly. "He was just a teenager."

Ziegler looked up, astonished.

"You guys were both stationed in the same town in Liberia in 1992?" he asked.

He thought he saw Vicki blush; Hank cleared his throat.

"I guess we may have run into each other once or twice," Vicki answered. But Ziegler wasn't convinced that was all there was to it. He'd been trained to catch people in lies, and this smacked of a whopper.

He looked first at Hank, then at Vicki. Each of them held deathly still, their eyes intently watching the others. Zeigler was certain that the two had more than just a casual friendship back in 1992. Vicki looked as if they'd just been caught banging on the couch. Hank's face flushed, and he stared at his clenched fists. Ziegler could read the telltale signs that they had something to hide.

Seeking safer territory, Ziegler changed the subject.

"I believe that he is one and the same. In 1992, Morray was still in the army and had been assigned to a security force to prevent the smuggling of coffee beans into Guinea. The soldiers were garrisoned at Morris Kerkula's coffee plantation. He took a liking to young Morray and had him permanently assigned to the plantation. Morray was educated at the local mission school.

"After his enlistment was up, Morray was hired as a plantation foreman. In 1998, Kerkula sent him to school in America. He returned in 2001, married Kerkula's oldest daughter and became the plantation's general manager. After that, Morray apparently found his own voice and began speaking out against the taxes on private farms. I guess you know the rest of the story."

"That sounds like the Morray I knew," Hank said. "Just before I returned to the states, Carpai sent a task force to curtail smuggling. Morray was in that task force."

Vicki remained quiet, lost in thought. Then she wondered out loud, "Is there any way that we could get Hank up-country to meet with Morray?"

"Morray's headquarters is in the town of Sanniquellie in Nimba County. However, I think we could arrange to fly him in. There's an airstrip at the Liberian Mining Company. He could use one of their vehicles.

The Kruman have allowed them complete access to the area," Ziegler said.

"Gentlemen," Vicki warned, "not one word of this leaves here. Don't discuss this with staff or family. If the Liberian government found out, the results could be disastrous.

"Hank," she continued, "I want you to assess Morray's intentions and determine if there really is potential for terrorism. It would be great if we could get him to keep a low profile until the oil companies get started. Who knows what the future holds? It looks like there is a good chance that Morray might be running this country some day.

"Now, what is our cover story to get Hank up there and keep the government from getting too suspicious?"

"That's easy," Ziegler said. "Hank has credentials in Upper Volta. Let's just say that Upper Volta's ambassador needs him up there for two weeks' TDY. He can fly up in the defense attaché's plane. They drop him off. One of my agents flies him into the mining company. After setting him up for a meeting with Morray, we get him back to Upper Volta and the DAO plane brings him back to Monrovia."

"What do you think, Hank?" Vicki asked.

"Sounds fine to me, but I'm not sure Morray will remember me."

Vicki shook her head.

"Hank, I guarantee that Morray will remember you. Let's do it. You can tell everyone that you'll be gone from ten to fourteen days. Be ready to go on Monday. Doug, get to work on the details. Both of you, I can't emphasize enough the importance of absolute secrecy."

# 7

***The recreation center on the U.S. embassy grounds in Monrovia was a favorite hangout for American diplomats and their families. It had large gym, an Olympic-size swimming pool and six tennis courts.***

AFTER WAYNE TURNER PLOPPED THE BARBELLS HEAVILY ON THE BLUE EXERCISE mat, he paused to study his reflection in the full-length mirror. Just this morning he had added a full forty-five minutes to his workout routine. He held in his breath and turned slightly to the right. Not bad for a thirty-eight-year-old, he thought. He hadn't noticed any difference in his build, nor had his weight changed since his college days.

Too bad he couldn't say the same for his wife.

Marsha had been one of the best looking co-eds on campus. But that was seventeen years and forty pounds ago. At least he had held up well. Although he took pride in his physique, not much else had gone his way. To put it bluntly, his life was nothing but a joke. No great career had ever materialized. No fame. No fortune. Now he was simply the unemployed spouse of Marsha Turner, an official in the state department.

It shouldn't have turned out this way, Wayne thought. Sixteen years ago, he had the world by the tail. Named an All-American at the university, he had been drafted by the Seattle Seahawks as a wide receiver. No wonder they wanted him. Swift and strong, he could magically seize the ball while surrounded by opponents. He could shuffle and sidestep his way out of many a jam. He posted the school record for single-handed touchdowns. No one had any doubt – especially Wayne himself – that he would make it big in the NFL.

On the way to success, he had won himself a trophy wife, the blond and curvaceous Marsha. Their love had grown, despite her father's disapproval. Marsha's dad had threatened to disown her. After all, how could his only daughter allow herself to be touched by a black man? Her father's face reddened, his pulse raced and his legs weakened at the very thought of that man's dark hands on Marsha's creamy white body.

Only the arrival of Toby, his light-brown grandson, had mellowed the older man. At least now he spoke civilly on the phone and had been able to endure an occasional three-day visit.

Wayne hadn't even stepped foot on a pro field, hadn't even sniffed the crisp fall air in a pro stadium, and hadn't even picked up his first paycheck. Nothing had gone right. At training camp, he grabbed a routine pass and rushed toward the end zone. Out of the corner of his eye, he glimpsed a defender reaching out to his left. He was tackled at the ten-yard line. The ball bounced out of his reach. He stretched, extending his arm in a futile attempt to recover it.

Fingers splayed in the green grass, three bones in his right hand fractured instantly when a defender's knee drove it into the soft soil. He remembered the ride in the ambulance, he remembered the surgeon shaking his head, and he remembered the dreams of his future as broken as the back of his hand.

Later, he coached at the local high school and taught tennis at the country club, but he remained the inadequate husband of the successful Marsha Turner.

After a tour in Washington, D.C., and postings in Europe, they had come here. At least in Liberia, he had found a hobby to occupy his time. He liked collecting and selling African art. At first, his interest had been stirred as a black man, tracing his roots through the art of West Africa. But the more he read and learned about the art of his ancestors, the more he grew to love the artwork itself. Besides that, there was money to be made in the dealing. His collection grew. He bought and sold African art and hoped to find the ultimate Poro mask.

Marsha didn't share his enthusiasm. She complained that more money went out than came in. Despite her objections, his obsession intensified. He looked for ways to pick up the extra cash it would take to buy more artwork.

Teaching tennis brought in a few dollars. After his workout, he headed for the courts. He patiently and tactfully monitored the moves of four middle-aged women, all embassy wives. It was still early, just a little past eight o'clock in the morning, but he felt unusually warm, especially as he raised his arm parallel to that of the dark-haired Donna Ziegler. His fingers clasped her wrist as he lifted her racquet. Although he controlled the serve, Donna managed the follow-through. His arm grazed her breast. Wayne mumbled an apology, but Donna just smiled slyly.

Two weeks earlier, Marsha and little Toby had left for the states to be with her father who had suffered a mild stroke. Wayne's presence wouldn't contribute to his recovery, so he stayed behind in Liberia.

He wasn't entirely sure, but since Marsha's departure, it seemed that Donna had been coming on to him. She often asked him to show her how to hold the racket. She stayed too close for too long. She had asked for private lessons and shown up in a tight t-shirt. Wayne watched as her full breasts bobbed freely, unconstrained by a bra. Just the day before, she had shown up unannounced at his house, offering a casserole for his dinner. She had commented on how lonely it must be to have his family so far away.

Even on the courts, she seemed to follow him with her eyes, like some men watch women and undress them in their imagination. But she was right. It had been rather lonely. After two weeks in an empty house, he had thought about Donna. He wondered what it would be like to see her buck-naked. A man like Wayne could only take so much teasing. Today he made up his mind that he would find out just how far she would go. Then, whatever happened, would happen. He leaned over to pick up his zippered racquet bag. His white polo shirt clung to his moist back.

Donna stood, arms folded, her racquet cradled against her breasts. Her nipples rose to stiff peaks as she studied the way Wayne's white tennis shorts stretched over his firm buttocks. She imagined the view from the front. She flexed her fingers then contracted them as if cupping his manhood. She swallowed and looked around to see if the other wives had noticed her obsession.

She wasn't sure what had come over her. Men often admired her body. Sometimes she'd pass a man, then turn around, checking to see if he was watching her. She wanted men to look, but she had never desired another man until she'd met Wayne. Liberia had been insufferably boring. It was nothing but meaningless social events and intolerable heat. And Bruce was always off on some trip. Maybe it was loneliness, maybe it was only the futility of life without purpose, or maybe it was this dark, muscular, smooth-talking male who stirred her desire.

The others had gone home to their daily routine. Donna found herself alone with Wayne.

"I have a new book on tennis at my house. You can borrow it if you'd like," Wayne said.

"Sure," she said. "I'd love to see it."

They walked the few blocks to Wayne's house. It was one of the large, two-story stucco homes that housed members of the diplomatic corps. He opened the wide front door for her. The large living room was decorated in dark green and blue. The air conditioning droned in its constant struggle to subdue the tropical heat. But Donna trembled. Was it the temperature, or simply being alone with this man?

Wayne pulled out an oversized red book and offered it to her. She held it gently, caressing its cover. But her attention was drawn to his collection of African art. She knew Wayne was an art collector, but she hadn't seen anything of this quality. Nothing she had seen in the local tourist shops compared to what Wayne had. She figured they could be museum pieces.

"These are exquisite," she said. "I didn't realize how extensive your collection was."

"I hope to acquire even more before our tour is up," he said.

Two dark statues caught her attention – one obviously male and the other female. Each stood about twelve inches high. The most vivid characteristic in each was its genitals. Below her protruding breasts, the female's vagina dominated one figure. On the other, the male's oversized, erect penis jutted outward and upward.

"What are those?" giggled Donna. "African porn figures?"

"Not quite," Wayne answered. "They are fertility dolls. The people believe that these dolls bring a successful union to a newly married couple. They are presented to a couple on their wedding night."

"But they are so disproportional."

"Not really. Africans take pride in one's sexual powers. Large breasts are considered a virtue, as is the large erect penis."

"I wonder if Vicki and Hank had fertility dolls like these watching over them while they made love," Donna said, more to herself than to Wayne.

"Who?" he asked.

"Ambassador Vicki and Hank Martin. Didn't you know that they were once lovers? Oh, not now, of course, but many years ago when they were both stationed here. Why, they were even friends with that Charles Morray, the leader of the People's Party."

She stared intently at the dolls; their exaggerated sex seemed to fascinate her.

"Vicki, Vicki, Queen Vicki! Now she'll send her knight, Sir Hank, into the jungle camp of Charles Morray. Will Sir Hank return? Will he win access to the oil reserves? Will she reward him for his efforts? Will the little dolls watch?"

She giggled nervously, stroking the male doll. Then she turned to face Wayne.

"How do I stack up?" she asked.

"From what I can see, pretty well," gulped Wayne. She carefully returned the doll to its place on the shelf. She crossed her arms in front of her, pulled at the hem of her t-shirt, and slowly lifted it over her head.

Wayne tried to speak, but no words came. She tucked her thumbs into the waistband of her shorts and pushed down both her shorts and panties in one movement. She stood, nude, before him.

"There," she said, staring directly into Wayne's eyes. "Now it's your turn."

Neither of them would have predicted Wayne's next move. He stood immobile. Then he felt dizzy and confused. He took two awkward steps backwards. He held his hands behind his back and braced himself against the wall. He watched as two nipples and a dark triangle came toward him. He turned his head to the side, averting his gaze from her nakedness.

To the right, Marsha's reading glasses and her unread mail lay on the end table by her easy chair. Toby's book bag hung from a hook in the hallway. He imagined Marsha's voice calling him from the kitchen. He thought of the bleep-bleep from Toby's video games.

"I... I... I... can't," Wayne stuttered.

Donna looked down, as if suddenly aware of her nudity. Her hands shuffled uncertainly between her breasts and the dark V-shape between her thighs.

"What have I done?" she wailed. She whirled and darted down the hallway. She slammed the bathroom door behind her. Wayne heard the click of the lock and Donna's muffled sobs.

Now it was Wayne's turn to tremble. What should he do now? What if she slashed her wrists, her red blood spattering the flowered wallpaper and staining Marsha's white terrycloth towels? Should he call for help? How could he ever explain the body of a diplomat's wife sprawled on his marble-tiled floor?

Then it was quiet. Too quiet. He held himself totally motionless, straining to hear some indication that Donna still lived. Nothing. No sound, nothing at all. He crept down the hall, each step taking him closer to the ghastly scene that would destroy his life.

At the door, he tapped lightly. No answer. Again he knocked, this time harder.

"Are you OK?" he stammered. Seconds passed. He thought he heard something move, but couldn't be sure.

"I'm OK," Donna whimpered. "Wayne?" she said so softly that he could barely hear.

"Yes?" he answered.

"Could you bring me my clothes?"

He dashed into the living room, scooped up her clothing and returned to the door. He rapped twice. The lock clicked, the knob turned and she reached out her hand.

Minutes later, the door opened. Donna walked directly past him to the front door. Wayne followed absently, playing the role of a gracious host. Her hand on the doorknob, she turned toward him, her eyes avoiding his.

"Wayne, I don't think I'll be taking tennis lessons anymore."

Then she was gone. Wayne closed the door. His heart rate returned to normal, but his mind still raced, replaying the image of the nude Donna before him.

"I need a drink," he said aloud.

At the liquor cabinet, he poured scotch into the heavy glass. He tried to lift it to his lips, but his hand trembled. He wrapped both hands around the glass and downed its contents in one gulp. He refilled it and emptied it again.

He had nearly lost everything he loved. What a fool he had been! Never again would he be so stupid, never again would he risk his marriage and his family.

He slumped into his chair, glass in hand. So what if Marsha had gotten fat? She was his wife; he loved her. He'd stick to the art collection. Someone else would have to be the ladies' man of Embassy Row.

Fifteen minutes and the two glasses of scotch cured his anxiety. His world had returned to normal. He had dodged the fatal bullet. Renewed and recharged, he wanted to get moving, to sense the freedom physical exercise would give him. It was just before noon. The mail would have come in at the embassy post office. Maybe Marsha had written; maybe Toby had sent a postcard.

Although it was only a few blocks away, the short walk, or maybe it was the hot sun, had left him feeling somewhat unsteady. He picked up the bundle of mail from the postal box, but he thought it would be a good idea to sit down for a moment or two before heading home.

He found a deserted bench near the pool. He looked through the magazines and advertisements. No letter. No postcard. Only Sotheby's had sent out its catalog. He thumbed through the thick pages, but stopped at a photo of a Poro mask from the Dan Tribe. Its members inhabited Liberia and the Ivory Coast.

"Only twelve thousand dollars?" he muttered. He would love to have a mask of that caliber. No way would Marsha agree to that much money. "Hell," he said aloud. "She bitches if I spend four hundred bucks."

From somewhere deep in his memory, he recalled a conversation at the Independence Day Ball with Julius Carpai, the minister of defense. He had chatted with him about his collection. Carpai bragged that he could find high quality masks for a reasonable price.

But Carpai had made it subtly clear that he would require something more than money in return. Wayne wasn't stupid. Carpai wanted information. Now who was stupid? The husband of a consular officer wasn't privy to any secret information. Wayne had to laugh. He wasn't even a very good gossip.

Once again he turned to the page with the mask. It seemed to be calling to him.

"Wouldn't it be something if I could provide Carpai with enough to at least let me see what kind of masks he's got?" Wayne wondered. Somewhere he had Carpai's business card. It must still be in the pants pocket of his tux.

But what could he possibly know that would snag Carpai? He searched his fuzzy memory, when it suddenly hit him. What was it that Donna had been babbling about? She had started chattering when she saw those figures. That was it – the male figure with its arousal and the female at the ready. They had gotten Donna talking. It had something to do with Hank and Vicki and some secret mission. He wasn't sure of the details, but he had the gist of it. There wouldn't be any harm in that. After all, it couldn't be anything special if Donna knew about it.

He walked back to his house and made a call to the defense attaché's office. "DAO. This line is not secure."

"Jim, this is Wayne Turner. May I speak to Lieutenant Colonel Martin?"

"Colonel Martin's not in today. May I help you?"

"No, I have a piece of African art I wanted to show him. Will he be in tomorrow?"

"No, I'm sorry. He'll be out of the office for two weeks."

"OK, thanks," Wayne said. He rested his hand on the phone for a moment, thinking about his next move. Maybe Donna had something after all. It was likely just enough to tweak Carpai's interest. He dug through the tux pockets until he found Carpai's card.

"Office of the minister of defense," said a receptionist.

"Yes, this is Wayne Turner from the American Embassy. May I speak to Minister Carpai?"

Within a matter of seconds, Carpai was on the line.

"Mr. Turner, this is Julius Carpai."

"Sir, we spoke recently."

"Yes, I remember."

"I understand you might have a Poro mask for sale," Wayne said.

"That is possible. We could meet to discuss the matter at the Victoria Pub on Mosman Street this evening. What do you say to seven o'clock?"

"Fine," said Wayne. "Just fine."

Carpai pressed his intercom.

"Tell Major Jalah that I want to take a look at the artwork we confiscated at last week's raid."

He couldn't help but grin. The consulate's husband had agreed to meet. Likely the guy would have no worthwhile information, but a clever man like Carpai wouldn't let an opportunity pass by unchecked.

"Who knows?" he said to himself. "I might just get lucky."

Some might think it odd to find an old English pub in the heart of West Africa. From the front facade to the smoke-filled interior, complete with high-back wooden booths, it could have been 1940s London. Expatriate Billy Thompson owned and operated the place. Only foreigners and wealthy Liberians frequented the pub. Wayne hoped that he wouldn't see anyone he knew. If he did, he would explain that he was thinking of buying a piece of art from Julius Carpai. After all, that was indirectly true.

A waitress, dressed like a serving wench, approached him.

"I'm meeting the minister of defense," Wayne said.

"This way, sir," she said, leading him to a shadowed booth in the rear. Carpai sat facing away from the entrance, a frothy mug of beer before him.

"Wayne, good to see you," smiled Carpai.

"Likewise, Julius," Wayne answered. He ordered a beer and slid in the seat across from Carpai.

"So, my friend, I understand you might be interested in purchasing a Poro mask."

"Yes, I might be interested," Wayne said.

Carpai reached down to the bench beside him and lifted up a cloth bag. He pulled out a Dan Poro mask complete with raffia headpiece. Intricately carved, its hand-rubbed surface glistened in the dim light. Wayne held it up to the table lamp. He turned it from side to side then placed it on its face. He looked for signs of wear and sweat stains on the inside. He was disappointed. Clearly, this was a new piece, likely made for the tourist trade.

"I'm sorry, Julius, but this is not what I had in mind."

Carpai acted surprised.

"I thought you wanted a good Poro mask."

"I do," Wayne said, "but not a new one."

"Wait," said Carpai. "I also have an old one. But since it is damaged, I wasn't planning to show it to you."

He reached in the bag again and pulled out a second mask. Again Wayne examined it under the table light. This one was old. Its seams had been mended, and it showed the unmistakable wear of actual use. This one was equal to or better than the one in Sotheby's catalog. This one was good – very good.

"It's not bad," Wayne said. "We might work out a deal."

Carpai passed his hand lightly over the carving.

"This piece is worth more than five thousand dollars. What kind of a deal are we talking?"

"I could give you perhaps three hundred dollars, plus some worthwhile information," Wayne offered tentatively.

Carpai laughed. He played the game well.

"I doubt if you have any information that worthwhile."

"What if I told you about the new ambassador and her former lover?" Wayne asked, measuring his response.

"Her lover... Lieutenant Colonel Martin." Carpai's expression changed. Had he taken the bait? Carpai could play hard to get.

"Wayne, I could care less what your ambassador and Colonel Martin did or are doing."

"They both know Charles Morray," Wayne interrupted.

"Half the country knows him. No deal," said Carpai, pushing himself back from the table. Beads of perspiration began to form on Wayne's forehead. Maybe if he elaborated a little, Carpai would give in.

"Wait a minute. There's more."

"What?"

"Martin is meeting secretly with Morray and his staff in Nimba County."

"So, what's so important about that?" Carpai asked.

"Don't you understand? The United States wants your oil. If your government is dragging its feet, perhaps Morray can deliver the oil faster.

"Don't forget that the United States backed Castro when he was just a rebel leader. The Cuban government fell. Then in Panama, when Noriega didn't do what the U.S. wanted, his country was invaded. He was taken prisoner and thrown in jail. Don't forget Bush and Iraq.

"You might want to guess again why Martin is meeting with Morray. He's working out a deal. It will be easy for Martin to get weapons and advisors to the People's Party. The U.S. has done it before. It can do it again," Wayne said with conviction.

Carpai didn't respond. It seemed to Wayne that several minutes passed. Finally, Carpai placed both hands on the mask and pushed it across the table.

"I want three hundred dollars for the mask."

Wayne pulled three one hundred dollar bills from his wallet. Carpai's long fingers reached out and grabbed the money. He stuffed it loosely in his pocket.

"We must do this again," Carpai said as he stood. He turned and walked out the rear exit.

Wayne began to reach out to the mask, but stopped. He backed his shoulders against the high bench seat and admired his prize. He grinned and wrapped his fingers around the chilly mug of dark ale.

The ultimate Dan mask sat in front of him, and it had cost him nothing but a few hundred dollars. He hadn't even given up any secret information. He only repeated the ravings of a confused woman. Carpai had bought it all – hook, line and sinker.

Yet he also vowed to never again provide any information to Julius Carpai. The comforting beer now gone, Wayne ran his fingers over the mask's deep eyeholes, its broad nostrils and its gaping mouth.

As he caressed the downward curve of the heavy lips, he pulled back his hand suddenly. Instead of a valuable prize, Wayne now felt a powerful spirit. The mouth formed a disapproving frown.

He felt a chill as he stared into the dark face of evil.

# 8

***Liberia's top officials sat in the President's executive office. Steven Dowling, at the head of the large mahogany table, cleared his throat, and then he spoke.***

"Our man in Upper Volta claims that Colonel Martin left the capital by bush plane this morning. He saw it head southwest in the general direction of Liberia. Julius, your information appears to be true."

George Sarday fumed.

"In the last six months, nothing has gone right. First, Julius's idiot nephew loses an entire company's worth of weapons and equipment to Morray. Then the oil cartel thumbs its nose at us. To date, we have less than twenty million dollars in our Swiss accounts. Those oil barons have the audacity to insinuate that we won't be able to stall the Americans from getting to our oil. Now, that woman ambassador dares to make a deal with Charles Morray!"

He added emphasis to his tirade by pounding his fist on the table while making eye contact with each man, one after the other.

"We will not tolerate this meddling by the United States. They will pay. And they will pay dearly. I want them to never, never forget."

Something seemed to be happening to Sarday. They all could feel it. It was as if they could almost hear his angry words in their minds. Steven Dowling shivered as he looked at Sarday. For just a split second, it looked like Sarday had horns sprouting out of his head. Then the moment passed.

"I have an idea," said Carpai cautiously.

"Go ahead, Julius. What is it?"

"Steven has told Ambassador Johnson that we could not allow exploration of the oil reserves because we feared a terrorist threat against the Americans. What if we stage a terrorist incident, and then blame Morray and the People's Party? Say, an assassination of one of the defense attaché's staff?"

"That's not enough," growled Sarday. "I want to really hurt them. Attachés die or disappear all the time. I want something that makes the front page of every newspaper in the U.S. I want this to be the top story on CNN."

Carpai's smile widened to a broad grin.

"What if we assassinated the entire defense attaché staff, including their families? They all live right here in Mamba Bluff," he said. His deep-set eyes shifted from side to side as if testing the others' reactions.

"We can't do that!" shouted Dowling. "That would be inhumane. No one kills women and children."

"That's the beauty of it," Carpai said. "If we convince the United States that Morray ordered such a hideous act, they will send in a military force to destroy his People's Party."

"What about Colonel Martin? If he's already in Morray's camp, he'll refute our claim."

"He won't if his family is dead. Americans are weak. He'll be too busy burying his dead to worry about deals with Morray."

"What are you talking about?" Dowling argued. "Are you all crazy? We can't do this."

"Shut up, Steven. You took the same oath that the rest of us took. The One we now serve demands this and even more," Sarday said. "Julius, do you have a plan?"

"I have four trusted men who can carry out the mission. They can eliminate the attaché's staff and their families."

"It is agreed. I want this to happen immediately – tomorrow night," said Sarday. He turned to Carpai. "Julius?"

"Yes, sir?"

"You will personally run this operation. I want no mistakes. In no way should this be linked to any of us."

"Maggie, this is Steven Dowling."

It took Maggie Parkinson a moment to register just who was calling. "Mr. President, what can I do for you?"

"Tomorrow night I have a special surprise for all of you. I want all of you to join us at our residence. I know that this is short notice, but we would be so disappointed if you and your whole family couldn't come."

"Sir, it's a school night. Maybe just Jim and I will come. We can find a babysitter for the boys."

"No, no, and no again. The whole Parkinson family is invited. You all must come. I won't take no for an answer," Dowling insisted.

Maggie hesitated. She transferred the phone from one hand to the other. She had never heard the President speak like this. He almost sounded frightened. She had become best friends with Dowling's daughter, Theresa. They had often been invited to informal gatherings, but the President had never contacted them directly.

"All right, sir," she said, unable to tell him no. "We'll be there, but we have to leave early."

"Great!" he said, sounding almost relieved. "We'll look forward to seeing you all. Say, around seven o'clock?"

"Sure enough," she said, still puzzled by his urgency.

Dowling stared at the phone he held in his right hand. He was sick to his stomach. He never dreamed it would go this far. He had accepted the sacrifices of victims to the demon as a necessary part of his commitment.

He had felt the power as each victim died, but this was different. Now he had gone against Sarday's directions, a step that could cost him his own life. But he just couldn't bring himself to allow the Parkinsons to become part of this. His daughter and Maggie Parkinson were like sisters, and the Parkinsons' two boys were so special to his family.

Hopefully, he would be able to get away with this without Carpai or Sarday finding what he had done. He placed the phone back on its cradle.

# 9

***The flight was headed for the iron-rich Nimba Mountains that stretched along Liberia's north-central border.***

HANK HAD SOME MISGIVINGS ABOUT THE FLIGHT RIGHT FROM THE START. When he first saw the plane, he had hesitated. The old, single-engine Cessna looked like it had been patched together with baling wire and duct tape. Yet Hank had a job to do. He had climbed aboard and settled into the passenger seat.

The pilot hadn't inspired confidence either. No-last-name Roy resembled a Kentucky hillbilly with an obvious aversion to bathing. He had sworn profusely as he forced the throttle in and out a half dozen times when the engine had sputtered. Fortunately, his charmed words had convinced the old bird to cooperate, and the flight had continued.

When they had neared the airfield, Roy had shouted, "Hang on, buddy! We're going in for a landing."

Straight-ahead Hank had watched the narrow dirt landing strip come into view in front of them. To the right, sat the mountain. Giant steam shovels tore up the earth, tearing open a red scar of iron ore. Monster-sized trucks hauled the ore to the crushers. From the crushers, conveyors carried it to waiting railroad cars. A locomotive pulling sixty ore cars crawled slowly from the loading site. It headed to the waiting ships at the Port of Buchanan.

Adjacent to the landing strip Hank had seen a village with several hundred brick homes. Clustered on a hill overlooking the entire site, the luxurious homes provided housing for the management staff.

The neighborhood included a large community pool. The Liberian Mining Company was a modern oasis in the middle of the jungles. It even generated its own power, which ran the entire operation and provided electricity to the homes.

Roy had leveled off the plane and begun the approach to the landing strip.

Then the engine had sputtered and stalled.

Cursing, Roy had yanked the throttle in and out again, but this time, the engine had stopped altogether.

"Shit, I think we are out of fuel."

"Shit," echoed Hank. "Now, what?"

"We put this baby on the ground, fast."

For the first time, Hank had become aware of the wind whistling by the windows. The ground had come up fast – way too fast for Hank's tastes.

"Hang on, here we go!" Roy had screamed loudly over the rush of the wind.

With a bone-jarring thud, the Cessna had hit the hard dirt strip, bounced into the air again then hit the runway again. They had been racing down the strip when the plane had begun to veer to the right. With no engine power, the plane's rudder couldn't respond. It had moved freely from right to left as it diagonally cut across the loose dirt. A pickup truck had appeared directly in front of them, growing closer by the second.

"Do something!" Hank had yelled.

"I can't," said Roy. "The rudder won't respond!"

Hank braced himself for the crash. At the last moment, the small plane had veered to the left, the right wing passing over the hood of the truck, missing the windshield by inches. Then, they had torn down the street between houses. Dogs, cats and kids had scattered in all directions. At the end of the street Hank had seen a large storage shed, and the plane had shot directly at it.

This time, there had been nowhere to go. There would be no escape.

Suddenly, the plane had started to slow. It had rolled to a stop six feet from the wall of the shed.

"I guess I should have used the brakes sooner," said Roy.

"Brakes!" roared Hank. "Are you telling me that this goddamn piece of junk has brakes?"

"Sorry, man."

Hank's legs trembled as he had stepped out of the plane, and he landed unsteadily on both feet.

Roy had turned to give his final instructions.

"Call on the radio frequency I gave you when you want me to pick you up," he yelled.

"Right," Hank had said as he headed down the street to the airfield. He forced himself to walk a straight line, yet his legs had still been shaking. If it were up to him, he hoped to never, ever, get in another plane piloted by Roy.

Hank spent the night on a narrow cot in a sparsely furnished room above the dining hall. When he woke up, his head was still spinning as he recovered from the wild flight from Upper Volta.

After getting dressed, Hank stopped by the company store and filled a wire basket with six cans of tuna, a can of Spam, and four partially dented cans of Campbell's vegetable beef soup. He grabbed a canteen and a packet of water purification tablets.

He had been granted the use of a surplus truck. He figured the four-wheel drive Ford should get him the thirty miles down the road to Sanniquellie, the county's capital. Likely he'd need the off-road capability. Flash floods often tore through the dirt roads, leaving deep ruts and uncovering large rocks. The government used to pay road crews to cut back the brush and to keep the roads passable. Since the People's Party had occupied Nimba and Grand Gedah counties, maintenance had ceased. After another rainy season, no one would be able to get through.

He passed through several villages along the way. They showed no visible impact of the occupation. Life went on as it had for centuries. Some hunters carried old shotguns, but he saw no other evidence of military weapons. Most ignored the white man driving a company truck.

He figured he was about ten miles outside of Sanniquellie when he noted a change. Young men stood in groups of four or five at about half-mile intervals. They didn't carry any weapons, but Hank picked out the figure of a man who stood on a high bank above the road. He held an M-16 assault rifle in his crossed arms. Hank's instincts told him that if a military threat showed up, the jungle would quickly be swarming with militia.

Bruce Ziegler had told Hank about an American missionary medical clinic in Sanniquellie. The Kruman had grown to love Frank and Karen Myers who had spent the last thirty years providing medical care to their people. Ziegler said that the Myers would help him locate Morray. He warned, however, that the Myers were not spies. Hank must do all he could to protect their neutral status.

Hank had to stop three times, asking for directions. He followed a winding road to the crest of a hill. Below him spread out five clay-walled buildings. Power lines linked them to a generator that sat inside a fenced compound. He could see a tin-roofed brick home atop a small knoll nearby. It looked like a mother hen, with a cluster of nearly thirty mud huts surrounding it. He could see small gardens and livestock pens. Dozens of people milled around; some could only hobble on simple, make-do crutches. Much more than just a clinic, the place had the feel of a thriving community.

Hank pulled up in front of what looked like the main building. Still early afternoon, it was already too hot. Odors of animal dung, cooking oil, and rotting vegetation mingled with the faint smell of antiseptic.

"May I help you, boss?" asked a black man wearing a white smock.

"I'd like to speak to Dr. Myers," Hank answered.

The man turned and went inside. Later, a tall white man dressed in blue surgery scrubs came out. He yanked at the fingers of his latex gloves, stretching the pliant material until the gloves snapped off his hands.

"May I help you?"

"Sir, I'm Hank Johnson from the mining company. I wonder if you can help me get in contact with Charles Moray?"

"What do you want with Morray?" he asked.

"We have concerns about the mine's security. Our managers want to work out a deal to make sure the mine is protected."

"Son, right now I'm dealing with two babies who are a little too anxious to get a head start in life. Why don't you plan on staying for dinner and spending the night? There's no place to stay in Sanniquellie. Besides that, what you're asking for won't happen today."

"I don't want to impose on you," Hank said.

"Nonsense. Since the shooting in Singa, Karen and I haven't seen a white face."

"At least let me pay for my keep."

"Your payment will be conversation," Myers said. "James, please show Mr. Johnson to the guest room."

"Right this way, boss," said the man in blue scrubs. White paint on baseball-size rocks marked the dirt pathway leading to the Myers' residence. Inside the small front room, Hank was surprised at how cool it seemed. The house had been situated on top of the hill. Screened windows on either side allowed the breeze to pass through, lowering the temperature, even on this sweltering afternoon.

James led Hank to a cozy room in back. A double bed took up most of the space. A worn quilt, sewn in squares of blue and white cotton, covered it. James opened the top drawer of the dresser and took out a thin terry towel and a block of homemade soap. He pointed to a door at the far end of the hallway. The shower was to the right of the privy.

After James left, Hank tossed his backpack on the bed. A shower sounded like a good idea.

He had expected to spend the evening dining on his can of Spam, but dinner with the Myers was a pleasant surprise. Local fruits and vegetables were served along with roasted goat. Frank opened a cool green bottle of smooth wine, and Hank relaxed, comfortable with this amiable couple that relished the opportunity to chat with their visitor. When they asked about his life, Hank found it difficult to stick to his story. He mingled fact with fiction until their curiosity had been satisfied.

"Tell me about yourselves," Hank said.

They had met in 1972 in Cam Ranh Bay in Vietnam. Frank had been an army doctor, and Karen had served as a nurse. Their courtship had been brief and their honeymoon was only a weekend at China Beach.

They spent sixteen-hour days in a field hospital. They moved from one mangled body to another, doing what they could to sustain broken lives. Inevitably, some would bear their wounds for the rest of their lives. Those were the lucky ones. Too many died; too many lives were lost.

"That's why we're here," said Karen calmly.

"How's that?" asked Hank.

She tried to explain the sorrow they both felt when they finally returned home. Not only had soldiers been victims of war, she said, but old people, women, children and tiny babies had also suffered from the violence. The couple's nightmares led them to seek comfort in the love of God. Each felt a calling to serve the helpless. They came to Africa.

Both their boys had been born in this very clinic, Karen said. She stood, walked to a nearby shelf and pulled out a photo album.

"This is Robert," she said. "He teaches third grade in downtown Detroit." She turned a page and pointed to another photo of Robert's three sons. She turned the page again. "And here is Peter. He's a missionary in Japan."

Both laughed, relating stories they'd been told of the grandchildren they loved, yet had seldom seen.

Hank leaned forward to see each photo and to hear each story. His cotton shorts had ridden up his leg, revealing his scarred thigh.

"Looks like you took a shot from a high-powered rifle," Frank said.

Hank explained that the injury had resulted in his medical retirement. He felt bad about his white lie. Lying to the Myers was like lying to one's parents.

The mantel clock struck ten o'clock. Frank yawned, and Karen nodded to her husband.

"Time to call it a day," said Frank.

Back in his room, Hank adjusted the mosquito netting and stretched out spread-eagle on the bed. The next day he'd meet up with Charles Morray. He wondered if Morray would remember him after all these years.

Before drifting off to sleep, his thoughts turned to his own family. At least they were safe and secure back in Monrovia.

# 10

*At Mamba Bluff, everything had gone flawlessly.*

An obedient and loyal agent of Julius Carpai, Major Oscar Jalah grinned inwardly as he rode in the stolen police cruiser. It pulled to a stop in front of the Matthews' house. It was just nine o'clock. Everything was right on schedule.

For the night's work, Jalah would take in fifty thousand dollars. Carpai had handed him a hundred grand. His share was half. Captain Mussafa Konah would get thirty thousand dollars. Lieutenants Alfred Drobia and Steven Menya would each net ten thousand dollars. He had already divided the cash, counting and stacking the money in neat piles, then stuffing the bills in manila envelopes.

The plan was perfect. Before midnight, the entire defense attaché staff and their families would be dead. What he had figured to be the most difficult part of the mission had gone without a hitch. The two national police patrol teams assigned to Mamba Bluff had been overtaken without a shot being fired. The four officers had been stripped, bound with plastic ties, gagged and locked in the water department's pump house. Likewise, it had been easy to remove the embassy guards. Since he and his men had been dressed in the stolen uniforms, the guards hadn't put up any fight. They, too, had been bound and gagged and left in the pump house.

Jalah took pride in his skillful acting. He and his three accomplices had talked boldly and openly about their leader, Charles Morray, and the People's Party. They had no argument with the Liberian nationals.

If they didn't resist, they wouldn't be harmed. He was confident the ruse had worked. Tomorrow everyone in Monrovia would be talking about Morray's brutal attack on the Americans.

They had divided the duties.

Jalah and Drobia would take out the Chambers, Davis, Matthews and Kelly families. The Edwards, Hanson and Parkinson homes were the responsibility of Konah and Menya. All four men would then meet outside the Martin house to kill Colonel Martin's wife and son. By midnight, they'd be out of Mamba Bluff.

Davis was first on the list. A bachelor, Davis lived alone. When he opened his door, Jalah shot him twice, point blank, in the chest. Carpai had provided the best of weapons – automatics with silencers. They fired with a soft spit, the noise easily muffled by the whir of the air conditioners.

Next stop was Matthews. After Jalah rang the doorbell, he waited. Soon a six-inch gap opened. A chain secured the door. Jalah heard the voice of a boy, about ten years old.

"Yes, what do you want?"

"I am Sergeant Kata with the national police. May I speak to one of your parents?"

"Mom," yelled the boy, "there's a policeman here who wants to talk to you."

Nancy Matthews came to the door and peered through the opening.

"Yes, officer, may I help you?"

"I'm so sorry to bother you at this hour, but we have a report of a rouging in the neighborhood. We noticed that you have no night watchman. We were concerned."

"Oh, my, I know he was out there earlier. I hope nothing happened to him."

"I'm sure everything is just fine," Jalah said. "By the way, may I use your phone to call my supervisor? Our car radio is not working."

"Of course, officer, please come right in."

Oscar Jalah could have laughed out loud. How gullible these Americans were! The woman slipped the hook out of its latch and opened the door. He and Drobia walked into the living room. He shot the woman and the boy while Drobia fired at the husband. Fewer than ten seconds had elapsed.

They turned to leave when Jalah heard a noise coming from the back of the house. Likely just a pet dog or cat.

"You stay here, Drobia. I'll check it out."

Jalah held the pistol rigidly before him and moved slowly down the hallway. He heard the sound again. It came from behind a closed door to his right. He carefully turned the doorknob. As the door opened, he scanned the room. He saw a crib in the corner. He walked in, approached the crib, and peered inside. Looking up at him was a baby, a small blond baby girl. She smiled. He laughed with relief.

He turned to leave, but remembered Carpai's orders – every man, woman, and child was to be killed. Without exception! He looked again at the child. She gurgled and smiled at him. Killing the others had been easy. This was different.

She reminded him of the young lamb. When he was a boy, his father had given him a knife. He had told Oscar to slit the creature's throat. It was to be the village sacrifice. That lamb, like this child, had shown no fear. It had no knowledge of what was to come. He knew the shame he would suffer if he didn't do as he was told. His father's hand help steady the knife as it made the swift cut. He had cried himself to sleep that night, still seeing the animal's eyes glaze over and lose their depth as blood gushed from the severed jugular.

He aimed the weapon directly at the child's chest. His hand shook. His eyes filled with tears. He couldn't do it.

"You must do it, you fool. That's what you're paid to do," he told himself.

He willed himself to pull the trigger. Again, a soft spit. The weapon jerked in his hand. The nine-millimeter round left the barrel of the pistol at eleven hundred feet per second. It struck little Chrissie Matthews in the chest. It tore through the soft, pink flesh and fragile bones, then passed through the coils and batting of the mattress and embedded itself in the hardwood floor.

Now there was no sound. Like the lamb, so long ago, the eyes became vacant and dull. Jalah wiped his nose on his shirtsleeve.

"When this is all over, I'm going to get goddamn drunk," he promised himself.

Back in the living room, he met up with Drobia. "Let's get out of here!" The two stepped out on the porch, closed the door firmly behind them and walked rapidly to the police car. Neither looked back.

Lindsey glanced at the clock on the dining room wall. It was only quarter past ten. She set the paperback book down. It hadn't been all that good. Maybe she'd start another. The house seemed so empty without Hank. He'd been gone for five days already. Since they had come to Liberia, she had been spoiled. He usually was home every night by dinnertime.

Tim and King had disappeared upstairs more than an hour earlier. He usually checked his Facebook page and played computer games before he went to bed. Tonight seemed unusually quiet. She reminded herself to talk to Everyday Walker about the night guard, Zac Wleh. Hank had found him asleep one night last week. Even tonight, when she had let King out about an hour ago, she couldn't find him.

Maybe a cup of tea would keep her company. She went to the kitchen, filled the teakettle, set it on the stove and turned the burner to high. Just as she had settled in to her chair to give the book one more chance, the doorbell rang. Perhaps it was Zac, she reasoned. Perhaps he was just late. He would beg her to keep his absence a secret from Everyday Walker.

Yet it wasn't Zac. Instead, two policemen stood on the porch. Every military wife dreads seeing men in uniform arrive while her husband was away. Without hesitation, she swung the door wide open.

"Yes?" she asked. "Is something wrong?"

"Are you the wife of Lieutenant Colonel Martin?"

Lindsey's knees grew weak. "Yes," she said quickly. "Has something happened to my husband?"

"No," one answered, "but we'd like to speak with you."

"Oh, thank God. Hank is OK," she whispered. Just then the tea-kettle whistled in the kitchen.

"One moment, please, my tea is boiling." She turned and rushed to the stove. She turned off the stove and slid the hot kettle to a cold burner. She turned to go back to the door but stopped in surprise to see that the men had followed her into the kitchen.

"Is your son here, Mrs. Martin?"

"My son?"

"Yes, where is your son?"

"Tim? Oh, yes, Tim," Lindsey hesitated. "Tim is staying at a friend's house tonight," she lied.

"That's too bad," said one of the policemen.

Lindsey felt her hand begin to tremble. Just then, a low growl came from the hallway. King had come downstairs, hackles raised. He growled again.

The other police officer reached for the black pistol on his belt. He pointed it at the dog.

"He won't hurt you," Lindsey said quickly. "Sit, King. Sit!" she ordered.

Just as the dog began to obey, she heard a soft spit. King yelped in agony. He whirled, biting at his hindquarters. Another soft spit. A red spray burst from behind the dog's right shoulder. He collapsed on the floor.

"You bastard!" Lindsey screamed. She rushed toward the policeman closest to her, swinging her arms. Her right fist connected with the man's nose. She felt the cartilage give way. He staggered backwards. The man with the pistol rushed forward waving the pistol before him. Lindsey ducked, but not fast enough. The heavy barrel struck her solidly across the right cheek. She stumbled backwards into the refrigerator. Her head slammed into the cool metal door. She felt a flash of pain; she saw stars, then only darkness. Her body slid to the floor.

Mussafa Konah ran the back of his hand gently across his face. Blood, too much blood. That damn woman! She had broken his nose. He pulled out his own pistol and aimed it directly at her head. He would kill the bitch and get this over with. He looked at her long, white legs and then a thought came to him. He wiped his hand over his bloodied face and lowered his weapon. It was bad enough that the boy wasn't home.

"Uncle Julius may want you dead, but first you will learn the power of a Kapel warrior!"

He reached down to the crumpled form, gripped the front of her light yellow sundress, and lifted the body off of the floor. The thin dress ripped at its seams, and the woman once again lay motionless. A second time, he stood over her. This time he tore at her bra and panties. He towered over the white woman, his feet planted firmly on either side of her long, pale legs. The sight of the pointed breasts and pink nipples instantly aroused him. He unbuckled his belt, unzipped his fly, and let his pants fall to his knees. He turned to Steven Menya.

"When I am done, you will have your turn. You can do anything you like, and then we kill her," he said.

Behind him, Menya smiled and ran his tongue over his lips.

In the valley again, Hank stood beside the altar. The smoke of ceremonial fires drifted through the darkness. He sniffed, aware of the odor of the man near him. All the same players were present, except for Julius Carpai. The massive George Sarday stood at attention near the statue, the executioner's sword rested in his crossed arms.

This time the demon-man was clearly visible. Sarday was an *endosym*.

Sarday turned toward the hut and barked a command. His words made no sense. Naked figures began to file out of the hut. Hank recognized each.

At the front of the line, walked Commander Earl Davis. Next came Master Sergeant John Edwards and his wife, Helga. Then came the Hanson family. Six-year-old Billy Hanson clung to his mother's hand. Next came all four members of the Kelly family. Next, followed the Chambers. Then, behind them, were the Matthews. Nancy cradled little Chrissie in her arms. Behind them, her husband, Don, and their son, Douglas. They all stopped before the altar. It was the entire attaché staff and their families. Only Jim Parkinson and his family weren't there. The group turned and faced the altar.

Another three emerged from the hut. Two were white, and the middle one was black.

"No!" screamed Hank.

Julius Carpai led them forward. On his right was Tim; on the left, Carpai gripped Lindsey's hand. The three approached the altar. Lindsey stumbled, struggling to move forward. Blood ran down her cheek, trickled over her shoulder and streaked across her breast. More blood coated the pale skin between her thighs. He saw dark patches of blood on Carpai's upper legs. Carpai turned and sneered at Hank.

Now Hank found his voice. He roared with anger, rushing forward to rip out Carpai's throat. Someone beside him held him back, yet Hank grasped the man's wrist and twisted. He heard a satisfying crack. The man howled and slumped to his knees.

A second set of arms wrapped around Hank's chest. Hank thrust his head back and slammed his skull into a man's face. The arms released their grip.

Hank raced toward Carpai, but again his forward movement was thwarted. He felt a bird-like creature grabbing at his back. Leather wings wrapped around his face, making it impossible to see. He yanked at the wings and hurled a large fruit bat to the ground. He pressed it into the earth with the heel of his bare foot.

Again he moved toward Carpai. The air filled with the sound of flapping wings. Hoards of fruit bats whirled around him. He flailed his arms, trying to fend off their attack. He caught one by its wings. Another clenched his back and nipped at his neck. Another bit deeply into the back of his hand, its razor teeth chewing at his flesh. He swung the body of a wounded bat, using it as a weapon against its brothers. Others clung to his legs, restricting his movement. He tripped and fell to the ground. The thick wings and black, furry bodies swarmed over him. He kicked and tried to roll away, yet they kept up their assault. He curled his limbs into himself and sobbed in surrender.

Lindsey stirred. Her eyelids fluttered, yet it was difficult to focus. She made out the hairy stubble on two black legs poised overhead. Between them, a penis jutted out, fully erect.

"No woman touches a Kapel warrior unless he wants her to," he screamed. "When we are through with you, you will know what it is like to be fucked by real men."

Lindsey rolled to her side in an attempt to slither out of reach. He kicked her in the back.

"No. No," she pleaded. Her whimpering caused Konah to roar with laughter. He knelt on the kitchen floor. The broken nose forgotten, he grabbed her legs, spreading them wide as he maneuvered her body toward the middle of the room. He leaned forward, his brutal manhood ready to bury itself inside the soft flesh. He opened his mouth to roar an oath of triumph.

Instead, a searing jolt of pain pierced his back. His broken body dropped to the floor, his arm fell across Lindsey's thigh. He rolled to his side, gasping for another gulp of air. It never came.

No sexual scene had ever engrossed Steven Menya, as did the sight of the white woman about to satisfy his partner's urgency. His own arousal had been so intense that he had failed to hear the sound of the shot.

Instead, he was surprised to see Konah writhing on the floor. A red pool formed near his mid-section. He whirled around to seek an explanation. A tall, pale boy, clad in white undershorts stood in the doorway. The boy pointed a pistol directly at him. He lifted his arm, ready to aim his own weapon at this adolescent who fancied himself a man. Before he could react, three nine-millimeter rounds pierced his chest, ripping the fabric of the stolen uniform, pushing through his flesh and burying hot metal in his failing body.

Tim let his hand drop to his side. The pistol fell harmlessly to the floor. He looked at his mother curled on the floor. Blood dribbled from a red smear on her cheek. In some ways, he was now a man, yet still a boy. His tears went unchecked.

"Mom! Oh, Mom!" he cried. His sobs came in short gasps. He reached for a small throw rug to cover her nakedness, but it slid to the side. He fell to his knees beside her limp body. He heard her speak.

"Tim," she whispered. "Tim, help me stand."

She reached up, grasping at the handles on the kitchen drawers. She managed to hold on only for a few seconds before slumping back to the floor. Tim hung his head. This was his strong mother, lying naked and weak before him.

"Tim," she said again. "Tim, you must help me get up. You have to help me get upstairs."

He got to his feet, moved behind her and reached under her arms. She stood uncertainly, waited, breathed deeply and took a tentative step. Together they got up the stairs and into her bathroom. She sat on the toilet seat and held her throbbing head in her hands.

"Tim, go to my closet. Get me some underclothes, jeans, a blouse and my hiking boots. Then get yourself dressed."

When Tim failed to move, she looked up. "Please, honey, hurry," she said.

She pulled herself up so that she could see her image in the mirror.

Her fingertips traced the gash, which measured at least two inches. It gaped open. She felt dizzy and her knees weakened. She set both palms firmly on the countertop until the nausea subsided. She opened the medicine cabinet and fumbled through the bottles and boxes until she felt the give of the brown plastic bottle of hydrogen peroxide. She twisted the cap and let its foaming liquid run freely over the cut. Again she felt faint.

"Mom," Tim said. "Mom!" He clutched her shirt, jeans and underclothes. He turned his head, respecting her nudity while stifling his embarrassment.

"Son, listen to me," she said with confidence. "Son, I want you to get the shotgun and shells, also a box of nine millimeter shells, and your dad's pistol belt and holster."

She paused, thinking of what else must be done.

"Get our backpacks and canteens," she said. She looked directly into Tim's eyes. He seemed distant, uncomprehending. "Tim," she said again, "do you understand?"

"Yes, Mom," he answered.

"All right," she said. "Go do it now."

"Mom, are you OK?"

Lindsey didn't answer right away. "Yes, but we don't have much time. You've got to hurry." Lindsey leaned on the counter, steadying herself. She daubed at the wound with a hand towel, soaking up the excess blood and peroxide. The bleeding had mostly stopped. She tore strips of adhesive tape and pressed them lightly over the gash. She had dressed wounds before, but never one so deep.

Another wave of nausea came over her. She paused to regain her equilibrium. She pulled down a bottle of aspirin, loosened the cap and let some fall into her hand. She gulped down five. Then she began the excruciating task of dressing herself.

Tim came back into the bathroom, his arms laden with equipment.

"Fill the canteens," Lindsey said weakly. She studied his face. He seemed more composed. A thin, clear trickle ran from his nostril to his lip, yet he set about doing as he had been told. When he returned, she handed him the pistol belt and holster.

"What should I do with this?" he asked.

"Put it on," she said. He had earned the right. He had saved both of their lives. She reached for the shotgun, loaded it with buckshot and chambered a round.

Tim steadied her as they moved cautiously down the stairs. Looking through the kitchen doorway, they saw one body on its side, the eyes dull and lifeless. The other twitched and moaned in delirium. Tim saw the stiff and still body of his dog.

"Oh, Mom! King's dead. We have to do something."

She squeezed her son's arm. "Tim, we can't help him now."

"But we can't leave him here."

"I know it's hard," Lindsey answered, "but right now we've got to get out of this house."

Tim nodded, and then let his head drop forward. Lindsey searched for words of comfort, but none came. Each one, mother and son, needed to mourn, but there was no time now.

Tim picked up his dad's pistol lying on the kitchen floor and put it in the holster. Then he pulled on his pack and handed the other pack to his mother. They went out the back door and headed to the gate overlooking the bluff. Lindsey used a small branch to lift the metal latch. Once through the gate, she removed the stick, and the latch clicked into place. If anyone checked, they'd think that no one had gone out this way because the gate was still locked from inside.

"What do we do now, Mom?" Tim asked.

"I want to see if anyone comes looking for those policemen. If no one comes within a half hour, we'll go for help."

They moved into the bushes, crouching low and taking turns peeking through a crack in the fence.

The job had gone quickly for Oscar Jalah and Alfred Drobia. Now it was time for the next move. Jalah pulled up behind the stolen cruiser in front of the stucco home at the end of the street. A curve in the road made it impossible to see this house from neighboring homes. He strained to look inside the police car. It looked like no one was in it.

"I told Konah that all four of us would take out the Martin family," he growled. Just like Konah to screw up. If it weren't for the fact that the imbecile was Carpai's nephew, he'd put a bullet in his thick head.

Jalah and Drobia paused at the front door. It stood ajar, open about six inches. He poked the barrel of the pistol into the gap and pushed it open wide enough for them to pass through. Inside, they paused to listen. Only the drone of the air conditioning could be heard. He noted one stairway leading to the upper floor; another went down to the lower part of the tri-level house.

He used his pistol to point at the stairs.

"You check upstairs. I take the lower level and the main floor," he whispered to Drobia. "Be careful."

Jalah moved downstairs, methodically checking the recreation room, the bar, and the laundry room. He peeked in the bathroom and into the wall-to-wall storage closets. Finding nothing, he came back upstairs into the living room and through the dining room. It was then that he spotted the body of a large dog in the kitchen doorway. He took a high step over the bloodied fur.

"Shit!" he said aloud. Lying with its back to the counter was the corpse of Steven Menya. Jalah saw three dark holes in Menya's chest. A pool of blood had spread out all around the body.

A second body – Mussafa Konah – sprawled on the kitchen floor, its trousers rumpled at the ankles. A small rivulet of blood had drained from a hole in the lower back.

Jalah's inspection was interrupted by a voice.

"What happened?" Jalah whirled around, leveling the gun in the direction of the words, his finger on the trigger.

"Jesus Christ, Drobia! I almost blew your head off. Don't ever come up behind me like that!" He shook his head to clear his thinking. "Did you find anything upstairs?"

"Only a lot of blood in the bathroom. Someone with no shoes had walked in it," Drobia answered. "See, over there by the refrigerator! More bloody footprints!"

Jalah knelt to examine the red blotches. Not Konah or Menya, he reasoned. Both still wore their shoes. Someone else had been bloodied. He placed his own shoe alongside one of the clearer prints. It was small and narrow, likely the footprint of a woman. A pile of clothing lay in the corner – sandals, a torn sundress, a bra and panties.

Konah's body lay in the middle of the kitchen floor. Jalah circled around the upturned buttocks. Konah's flaccid penis gave hint of his final act.

"The stupid idiot must have been raping the Martin woman," Jalah concluded. But still there were unanswered questions. Konah's gun sat on the table. Menya's fingers still curled around the trigger of his pistol. Someone else had gotten off three rounds before Menya could even pull the trigger.

"Oscar," Jalah jumped. "Oscar ...," someone said, barely audible. It was Konah – he still lived. Jalah moved closer to the wounded man in an attempt to understand his muffled words.

"What happened?" demanded Jalah.

"It hurts so bad," he cried. "I don't know. She said she was here alone."

"Where is she?"

"I don't know," Konah murmured. "When I came to, no one was here." He paused, taking a breath. "Please help me. It hurts so bad. I can't feel my legs."

"Mussafa, just take it easy. We'll get help," Jalah promised. He moved to the phone, reached in his pocket, pulled out a piece of paper with a phone number, dialed, and waited for an answer.

"Yes?"

"We have a problem," said Jalah.

"What is it?"

"I can't say over the phone."

"Where?"

"Last target."

"I'll be there in five minutes."

George Sarday watched as Julius Carpai hung up the phone.

"What's going on?" he asked.

"I don't know. I'll let you know when I get back."

"Be careful, Julius. Don't let anyone see you."

In a matter of minutes, Carpai parked his car a block away from the Martin house and threaded his way through the bushes. Jalah met him at the darkened front door and gave him a short account of what they'd found. Carpai walked to the dining room window and looked out into the back yard, brightly illuminated by the rogue lights.

"Have you checked out back?" asked Carpai.

"Not yet."

"Do it now."

As Drobia searched the yard, Carpai took another look at his unconscious nephew on the kitchen floor. Just as well, thought Carpai. He didn't want to talk with him.

He ran through the details once again. Too many questions and not enough answers. Where had the woman gone? How badly was she hurt?

"No one out there," said Drobia as he returned from the yard. "I opened the gate to the bluff, but no one was outside. The gate was still locked from the inside."

For a moment, no one spoke. Then Jalah broke the silence.

"What are we going to do now? Menya's dead. Massafa's hurt bad. I checked the bullet hole. He took it through the spine. He's likely paralyzed."

Carpai didn't answer. His thoughts ran to the stupidity of his nephew who had never done anything right. He had believed he had done his sister a favor in getting her son a commission, but now the idiot had put everything in jeopardy.

An idea came quickly. He turned to Drobia.

"Get kerosene from the storage room!" he ordered.

Everyone in Liberia had kerosene for lanterns. In the rainy season, power outages were frequent. Even homes with generators kept back-up kerosene lanterns.

"Give it to me," Carpai said when the man returned with a two-gallon can.

He went into the kitchen and began sprinkling the kerosene on Menya's body. He turned to Mussafa and doused his body. The movement brought the wounded man back to a state of semi-consciousness.

"Uncle Julius? What are you doing?" he managed to say weakly.

"Don't worry, Mussafa. Your pain will soon be gone."

"No, no," he moaned.

Carpai ignored the whimpering. He sprinkled the fuel in a wide swath, on the counters and over the furniture. He poured the last of it on the woman's dress then picked it up. He pulled his lighter from his pocket and ignited the fabric, tossing it in a pool of kerosene near Menya's feet. Flames erupted like a giant orange beast.

"Let's get the hell out of here!" yelled Carpai to the two men. From the porch he pointed at the two police cars and said, "Take the cars and get rid of them. Make sure you leave no fingerprints."

Jalah and Drobia dashed toward the vehicles. Carpai paused to close the front door behind him. He could hear the crackle of the flames and a roaring sound as the blaze began to consume the house. Then he stopped. Another sound caused him to hesitate. It was the pathetic wail of the dying man – his nephew – on the kitchen floor.

He bolted from the front steps and dashed to his car. He gripped the steering wheel. It was dark and quiet in the car, but soon everyone would know of the death and terror on Mamba Bluff.

Now he had to do what he could to find that Martin woman and her son. Even if they managed to escape, there would be no evidence to implicate The Seven. The People's Party was clearly to blame for the night's tragedy.

He still would have to face Sarday; that was bad enough. There was one bright spot – he'd no longer have to deal with his useless nephew.

# 11

*As they left the Presidential residence, the high beams from an oncoming car caused Jim Parkinson to squint. He whispered a mild oath at the thoughtless driver. Anything louder might wake up Maggie who had drifted off to sleep, her head tilted awkwardly forward. Both boys had curled up and gone to sleep before they had even pulled on the main road. Too late for a weeknight, Jim thought. The dashboard clock read half past eleven.*

He really hadn't wanted to socialize that night, but Maggie had called him at work yesterday with the news of the invitation. She had told him that the President himself had called. That had never happened before. The only guests would be Maggie's friend Theresa Moya, Dowling's daughter, and her family. Dowling had a copy of the latest Disney animated movie. It hadn't even been released in the United States. Jim figured the kids would like the surprise.

After the movie, Jim and Maggie had gotten up to leave, but Dowling insisted they stay for cake and ice cream. After that, he'd brought out a new video game. There was no way to stop the kids from trying it out. It would be past midnight when they finally got home. Jim yawned again. He was getting too old for these late night parties, even if it was just cake and ice cream.

Jim's thoughts were interrupted by the blare of a siren. In the rear view mirror he could see the flashing lights of another fire engine. He'd seen three since they'd left the mansion. It turned into Mamba Bluff.

He made out an orange glow to the west. Curious, he turned in the direction of what looked to be a large fire. He pulled to a stop at the road that turned toward the Martin residence. Police cars blocked the road.

"What's happening?" Maggie asked, suddenly alert.

"There's a fire up by the Martins' house. Hank's out of town. I'd like to check on Lindsey and Tim. You just stay here with the boys. I'll be right back," Jim said as he got out of the van.

A police officer held out his arm, blocking the way.

"Sorry, sir, but no one can pass beyond this point."

Jim reached for his wallet and pulled out his diplomatic identity card. The man pointed his flashlight at the photo, then at Jim, and handed it back. He nodded and Jim walked down the road.

Jim shook his head. It was always like this. He and Master Sergeant John Edwards, the only other black on the attaché's staff, had talked about how if you were a black American in Africa you had to spend half your time convincing police that you weren't a local. If he were white, he doubted that he would have been stopped at all.

As he neared the end of the road, he became concerned. The fire seemed too close to the Martin house. He increased his pace as he neared the corner. What he saw ahead caused him to stop in his tracks.

"Oh, my God!" he said aloud.

Flames leaped from the windows. Neighbors still in their nightclothes huddled in groups in the field across the street. He recognized Carl Dotson who worked for USAID.

"What happened?" Jim asked.

"Oh, hi, Jim," Dotson answered. "I really don't know. We heard sirens. When we came out, we saw the whole place on fire."

"Have you seen the Martins?"

Dotson shook his head. "No, Jim. Nobody has."

Jim moved through the crowd, asking the same question. Each time, he got the same answer. Maybe Lindsey and Tim had gone out of town. But, as far as Jim knew, only Colonel Martin had left. He could see their car still parked in the carport. He felt a sick feeling in his gut. No one could have survived that blaze.

Fire crews sprayed high arcs of water from five different trucks. They seemed to be getting it all under control. Jim turned and headed back to the car. He'd get his family safely home, and then get on the phone.

Once the boys were in their own beds, he dialed Don Matthews' number. He counted twenty rings, but still no one answered. He tried Arnie Chambers. Again, there was no answer. Then he tried Commander Davis, then the Kellys, then the Hansoms, and finally the Edwards. No one was answering the damn phones. Maybe the whole phone system was down.

He had better luck when he called Jerry Day, a CIA operative who worked for Bruce Ziegler. Jerry answered on the second ring.

"I'll be right over," said Jerry, after Jim had told him what he knew.

Jim brewed a pot of coffee. No sooner than it was ready, he heard Jerry's knock.

"Jesus, is that necessary?" Jim asked, noticing Jerry's nine-millimeter Beretta tucked in his waistband.

"You never know, Jim. You said that no one answered the phones. Let's go see if we can get Earl Davis up. He's just down the street."

It was now half past one in the morning. All the houses were dark, but the streets were well lit by the outside rogue lights. Jerry pushed the doorbell. No answer. He tried the doorknob. He felt the door begin to open. He drew his pistol and opened the door.

"Stand back, Jim," he cautioned as he moved into the entryway.

Jim followed close behind, almost running into Jerry as he came to an abrupt stop.

"Oh, no. Oh, my God," said Jerry. "We've got a big problem." The body of Earl Davis was sprawled on the floor. Three neat bullet holes dotted his chest.

Jerry got to his knees and picked up a shell. "Nine millimeter," he whispered. The two moved from room to room, but found nothing out of line. They pulled the front door closed behind them and walked back to Jim's house.

Maggie waited for them at the kitchen table, a half-full mug of coffee cradled between her hands.

"Jim, what happened?" she asked as soon as she saw her husband's face.

"Earl's dead. He's been shot," he said, lightly touching her shoulder.

"Jerry," he continued, "call your wife, Joan, and see if she'll come over."

While Jerry made the call, Jim headed to the closet and removed a metal storage chest. He carried it back to the kitchen and opened the two locks. He took out a 12-gauge riot gun and a nine-millimeter pistol.

When Joan arrived, she and Maggie embraced, both on the verge of tears. Maggie slumped in a chair, but then Jim's actions caught her attention.

"What are you doing?" Maggie asked.

Guns always had to be under lock and key. She knew that they would be too fascinating for her young boys. But now, Jim handed her the loaded pistol.

"I want you and Joan to stay in the house. Keep the doors locked and don't let anyone in. I don't know how bad this is, but I want to check out the rest of the attaché's staff before I call the ambassador. We'll take Jerry's car. If we're not back within an hour, you and Joan take the kids and get to the embassy."

"This can't be happening," Maggie whispered.

"Honey, I'm afraid it is," Jim said, reaching down to hold her in his arms. "We'll be back soon. I promise."

Maggie locked and bolted the door behind him, still holding the cool, dark weapon in her hand.

Neither Jim nor Jerry spoke as they drove to the first house. Jim held the 12-gauge riot gun in his lap. They pulled up in front of the Matthews' house. Although he hoped and prayed for the best, Jim had a sense that things wouldn't go well. He remembered this same feeling when he had made a next-of-kin notification to a family of an army pilot who had been killed in a helicopter crash.

He saw nothing out of place as they walked to the door. Doug's bike was propped up against the porch railing, ready for use in the morning.

He glanced at Nancy's gardens. She had loved the lush tropical flowers and greenery. Everything seemed peaceful – almost too peaceful.

Jim ignored the doorbell. He twisted the knob and the door began to give way.

"They must have let them in," said Jerry. He gave the door a gentle push, but something blocked it.

Jim looked down. Doug's outstretched fingertips caught on the bottom of the door. Carefully, Jim nudged the lifeless hand out of the way with the tip of his shoe. Doug had been shot five times, once in the face. Nancy's body was draped over her son's corpse. Perhaps she had tried to shield him with her own body. The boy had one bullet hole in the back of the head. Nancy's back was riddled with holes. Her sightless eyes stared at the body of her husband.

Jim felt of surge of vomit rise in his throat. His hand shook. He swallowed, suppressing his nausea. He pointed his weapon toward the back of the house and moved down the hallway. Jerry followed. They cautiously opened each door, one by one.

Jim would never forget the sight of little Chrissie Matthews, silent in her crib. It would haunt him for the rest of his life. Neither man spoke. Jerry pulled the door shut. Jim leaned back against the hallway wall.

"There was more than one guy in this," Jerry said, avoiding Jim's eyes. "This was a planned act."

Jim didn't answer. He knew he probably should say something, but no words came.

They moved on to the homes of the Kellys, the Chambers and the Hansons. One after another, they opened doors and found lifeless bodies. Finally, only the Edwards' house remained.

Jim's nausea had vanished. He felt no emotion. Each silent family had only served to harden his nerves. He felt detached, apart from reality. Just like in combat, he figured. Each death leaves the warrior less involved, more like an observer than a participant.

Perhaps there was a chance that Edwards had escaped the massacre. Edwards was the only other black man on the team. Maybe this hatred had been meant for whites alone. But Jim discovered he was wrong.

Master Sergeant John Edwards lay dead on the carpet in the middle of his living room floor. His wife, Helga, must have tried to make a run for it. Her body lay face down in the hallway.

They heard a noise in the dining room. Both turned, holding their weapons ready. Jim was aware of the pounding of his own heart. He raised his gun. No need. It was only Trooper, the family's terrier. The small dog held its tail between its legs and quivered.

"Come here, Trooper," Jim called. Trooper whimpered and took a tentative step toward him. "Come here. It's OK," Jim continued.

The dog yielded to Jim's coaxing and allowed him to run his fingers through its coarse fur.

"Come on, Jerry. There's nothing else for us here."

They drove back to Jim's house. Trooper snuggled in Jim's lap. Finally his shaking lessened. Maggie opened the door before Jerry had switched off the ignition. She rushed to Jim, embracing him and the dog.

"Where did you find Trooper?" she asked.

"At the Edwards. He's all that's left."

"What do you mean?"

"Maggie," Jim said, "they're all dead – every man, woman and child in the attaché office. Everyone – except us."

Maggie gasped. Now she began to shiver uncontrollably.

"Let's go inside. Let's get off the street," Jerry said. In the kitchen, Jim set the dog on the floor. Trooper shook with terror once again when the Parkinsons' cat hissed.

"Better get used to him, cat. He's your new roommate," Jim said. He led Maggie to a chair near Joan. He kissed her gently before going to the phone to call the Marine guard. He looked at the others and then issued an order.

"Pack up some things. We're going to make a run for the embassy." He got through right away. "Marine Guard. This line is not secure. Corporal Hawkins speaking."

"Corporal Hawkins, this is Major Parkinson. Wake up the Gunny. I need to speak with him immediately."

While he waited, many unanswered questions streamed through his thoughts. What could be going on? Were even more Americans lying dead in their homes on Mamba Bluff? Was the Liberian government being overthrown? Was the fire at the Martin house a part of the same attack? What happened to Lindsey and Tim? Why didn't they get Jerry and Joan? Where the hell were the embassy guards who were supposed to be watching the houses? What would happen to them? Could they make it out of Mamba Bluff alive?

"Gunny Sergeant Wilson here. How may I assist you, Major Parkinson?"

"Gunny, as the senior military officer in-country, I am ordering you to go to Threat Condition Echo."

"Echo, sir? That means that...."

"That's correct, sergeant."

"How bad, sir?"

"Sixteen. Two missing and presumed dead."

"Jesus, sir."

"Gunny, Jerry Day and I are going to try to make a run to the embassy. Activate the plan."

He hung up the phone. He turned and yelled down the hallway.

"Maggie, bring the cat cage. Both the dog and the cat go, too. It might be awhile before we come back."

He threw together a duffle bag, put on his battle dress uniform and combat boots. He kept the shotgun close by.

Wilson hung up the receiver. Never before had they gone to Threat Condition Echo. That meant that Americans had been killed by hostile action and the potential existed for a direct attack against the embassy staff.

"Wake up everyone!" he shouted at Hawkins. "I want full battle dress, Kevlar, and flak jackets. Have Corporals Smith and Jones open the arsenal and issue grenades. Set up the machine guns. This is Threat Condition Echo!"

"Is this an exercise, Gunny?"

"No, Hawkins. I think this is the real thing."

He leaned down and laced his combat boots. He picked up his M-16, loaded and on full auto. Outside the barracks, he stopped to listen. He heard no sound of weapons fire. Monrovia seemed to be asleep. But Parkinson had reported that sixteen people had died. Not an exercise, this was the real thing.

He broke into a run toward the ambassador's residence.

Vicki sat upright in bed at the sound of her doorbell. The clock on the nightstand read half past two.

Vicki wondered what was up at this time of night. Her instincts told her that whatever it was, it wasn't good. She reached for her robe and went to the front door. Gunny Sergeant Wilson stood at the door alongside her own guard.

"Wilson, what happened?" she asked.

"Ma'am, Major Parkinson just called. He said to go to Threat Condition Echo. He and Jerry Day are trying to reach the embassy."

"Echo?" she asked. "That means Americans have been killed."

"Yes, ma'am. The major said there are sixteen confirmed dead and another two possibly dead."

Vicki felt her knees weaken, and she leaned against the doorway.

"Ma'am, I have all eight Marines up. We're sealing off the embassy right now."

"Thank you, Gunny," she said. She closed the door and went to her phone. Only eight Marines, she thought, just eight Marines to defend the entire embassy.

Bruce Ziegler answered on the first ring.

"Bruce, this is Vicki. Call all members of the country team. Tell them to meet in the operations room in thirty minutes. Jim Parkinson has just asked us to go to Threat Condition Echo. He's trying to get here from Mamba Bluff."

She didn't wait for his response. She slammed down the phone. Her stomach churned. This nightmare was for real.

# 12

***They followed the riverbank away from Mamba Bluff.***

"WHAT TIME IS IT?"

"It's quarter past two. Mom, are you going to make it?"

"I've got to, Tim. Give me your arm. Help me up."

"God help me," she said to herself. She had slipped, that's all.

With Tim's help, she got back on her feet. She knew she should stop and catch her breath. Her head throbbed. She needed to hunch over, press her fingertips to her temples and just close her eyes. The nausea came in waves, weakening her knees and keeping her off balance. Slight concussion, perhaps.

They had been walking for more than an hour, heading east. If they climbed back up the edge, she figured they would be close to Tubman Boulevard.

After leaving the house, she had been looking through a crack in the fence when she saw Julius Carpai, Liberia's minister of defense, inside her living room. She had grabbed Tim's hand and the two slid down the bank towards the river.

This attack by the two policemen was no fluke. Carpai must have been behind it all, she reasoned. What did it mean? Was it somehow connected to Hank's involvement in the ritual murder so long ago?

She recalled his recent dream where Tim was to be sacrificed to that hideous statue. Was Hank's dream a glimpse into the future? They had asked for Tim. Maybe they weren't policemen at all. Maybe this whole night was only her personal nightmare. No way, she thought. She hurt too much for this to be a dream.

Tim had asked her where they were going. In truth, she didn't know. They were headed north along the riverbank. All she knew for certain was that they had to get away from Carpai.

At first, Lindsey had no trouble walking. In the last few minutes, she had tripped and fallen twice. She wasn't seeing clearly out of her right eye. Her depth perception was off. Each time when she got back up, she felt dizzy.

Even in the middle of the night, the humidity was oppressive. It must have been well over eighty degrees. When she wiped her hand across her wet hair, she felt a lump the size of a goose egg at the back of her head. She didn't remember hitting her head. Her side hurt. She remembered being kicked as the one policeman prepared to rape her. She didn't know how much longer she could continue. She needed to lie down and keep her world from spinning out of control.

"Let's see if we can make it to the top of the bluff," she said. "Tim, let's leave the backpacks and shotgun down here. You'll have to help me to the top and then go back to get our gear."

Tim slipped her arm over his shoulder, and the two started slowly working their way to the top. Several times she slipped, but Tim held on and steadied her. She was surprised at how strong he was. This wasn't just a boy, but a man beside her. His determination gave her the strength to take the last few steps to the top. He settled her down behind some brush, turned, and started back down the bank. She decided to close her eyes while he was gone.

She waited for the alarm to go off. It was a school day. She needed to fix Tim's breakfast. Hank was still in Upper Volta. He wouldn't be back until next week. This seemed like a crazy dream.

"Mom!"

Lindsey imagined she heard Tim calling her, but it was still too early to get up. She'd be up in few minutes. They still had time to sleep.

"Mom! Mom!" Now she opened her eyes again. She wasn't in her bed; she was lying in the weeds. This was no dream.

Tim helped her to her feet again. She was shaky. He reached around and held her waist to steady her. Her vision was worse. She was seeing double. She closed her right eye and tried again. They were in an open field above the river. She made out houses in the distance. She saw the streetlights lining Tubman Boulevard. Not far away she saw Sophie's Ice Cream Parlor. Now she knew where they were. They were less than a block from Charlie Marshall's house.

"We're going to Charlie's!" she said, turning to Tim.

Dr. Charles Jefferson Marshall was the veterinarian for the Monrovia Zoo. A British national, Charlie's father was the last colonial governor before Sierra Leone's independence. In his late fifties, Charlie was considered a bit of an eccentric. Never married, he lived alone. He raised snakes and sold their venom. The kids called him the snake man.

Since he was the only vet in Liberia, all of the embassy personnel took their pets to him. The Martins first met Charlie when Tim's class had visited the zoo. The three of them – Hank, Lindsey and Tim – had been treated to a behind-the-scenes tour of the zoo. The friendship had developed and Charlie had been a guest in their home on a number of occasions. They liked his sense of humor. Charlie could entertain them for hours with his stories of growing up in Africa.

Charlie's house was totally dark. He had no rouge lights. Perhaps he figured his reputation as the snake man would keep him safe. Ironically, he didn't have any snakes at his house. He kept them all at the zoo.

Tim banged his fist on the door. A light came on in the back of the house. Then, the porch light. Then the door swung open. There stood Charlie, all three hundred forty pounds of him. His red beard and sparkling blue eyes caused Lindsey to smile, despite her pain.

"Thank God you're home," she gasped.

Charlie sized up the two. Their clothes were covered with mud and grass stains. Both had scratches on their faces and arms. Lindsey's right eye was discolored. She had a bloodstained bandage on her cheek. The knees on her jeans were ripped and bloody.

"Come in!" Charlie said. "This sure doesn't look like a social visit."

Lindsey limped into the living room. "I've got to sit down," she said, sinking onto the sofa.

"Go get your mother a glass of water," Charlie said to Tim. "Find yourself something to drink, too."

Charlie lifted Lindsey's feet onto the couch and arranged pillows under her head. Tim returned with the water and a Coke.

"Is that a real gun on your hip?" Charlie asked.

"Yes, sir," said Tim.

"I guess you guys have some explaining to do."

Lindsey gave Charlie a brief account of what had happened.

"I see why you don't want to call the national police," he said. "What is it that you want to do?"

"In the morning, I'll call the attaché's staff and see if I can get someone to come pick us up. Hopefully, you'll let us stay here until morning."

"Of course, Lindsey," Charlie said. "But first, I need to have a better look at your face."

"But, Charlie, you're a vet, not a doctor," Tim interrupted.

"True. But all animals, humans included, are treated basically the same way. We use the same antibiotics. I can stitch up a wound as well as any people doctor. We need to clean and treat these injuries. It doesn't look as if there will be any doctors dropping by in the near future."

# 13

***At Marshall's simple home in Monrovia, Lindsey woke up, still hurting from their frightening escape from their home. She had to use her fingers to pry open her right eyelid. The left eye worked OK. She managed a blink. No longer was she seeing double. It was half past seven in the morning. She had slept for about three hours. Although she probably needed to sleep longer, she felt totally awake. Now they needed to get to the embassy. Not until then would she feel that they were safe.***

"THANK GOD FOR CHARLIE MARSHALL!" LINDSEY SAID OVER AND OVER AGAIN to herself.

He had cleaned up their scratches and stitched up the gash on her cheek. Charlie warned her that she'd need plastic surgery. Without it, she'd have a serious scar on that side of her face.

He had them all laughing when he told her she'd need a shot of antibiotics. First, he'd asked her what she weighed. He checked his book on primates and looked up the dosage for an adult chimpanzee. He told them that they wouldn't be able to sue him for malpractice because he didn't have a license to practice medicine anyway.

But now it was time to get moving. She sat up slowly and lifted her legs over the edge of the bed. Charlie and Tim had slept in the living room. Charlie had given her his own bed, a more comfortable place to sleep. When she stood, she felt a wave of nausea. It quickly passed. In the bathroom, she felt some pain as she peed. She noticed blood in her urine.

Likely her kidneys had been bruised when she had been kicked. She took off her blouse and began to wash up.

She knew now what a prizefighter must feel like after going fifteen rounds. The cheek looked better. Charlie had covered it with a flesh-colored Band-Aid. The area around it was swollen and discolored. Other parts of her body were dotted with bruises of varying shades of blue and purple.

She could smell someone cooking breakfast in the kitchen. Her stomach growled. She hadn't realized how hungry she was. She finished up and headed for the kitchen.

"Hi, Mom, are you hungry?" asked Tim.

"I sure am," she said, smiling at her son and giving him a quick hug.

"James is cooking up Spam, eggs and plantain," Tim said.

Both Charlie and Tim were sitting at the kitchen table nursing their cups of dark coffee.

James Doboy, a Liberian in a white lab coat, was manning the stove. Lindsey tried several times to reach Maggie Parkinson. Charlie's phone didn't seem to be working. She had given up and settled in beside the men to eat breakfast.

"I'll drive you to the embassy in the Land Rover as soon as you're done eating," Charlie said. "James, before we leave, I need you to go to the market and pick up six bunches of bananas. After I drop off Mrs. Martin and Tim at the embassy, I can take the bananas over to the zoo."

Charlie handed James some cash and the car keys.

"Hurry back," Charlie said. "We don't have all morning."

"We've found them."

"Where?"

"They're at Charlie Marshall's place. You know, the vet for the zoo."

Julius Carpai hung up the phone in Steven Dowling's office.

"One of the Reconnaissance Battalion's lieutenants was working the market on Tubman Boulevard when he overheard Marshall's assistant say that the Martins were at Charlie's place. That was brilliant having the soldiers search for the missing Americans. I told the battalion adjutant to keep the assistant there until we send someone to pick him up."

"So, what now, Julius?" asked Dowling. "The last thing we need is to spook them."

"Who do you plan to send?"

"Let's send Hans Kruger. Have him bring the woman and the boy to Sarday's place. We'll kill them there and dispose of the bodies. Also, remind him that we want no witnesses."

He'd been promised a bonus of fifty thousand dollars if it all went well, and he figured that there was no reason why it wouldn't.

Hans Kruger pulled the Mercedes onto Tubman Boulevard. Since he'd been hired as chief of security for the President, his Swiss bank account had grown to more than a million dollars. Today's bonus wouldn't be bad for one morning's work.

Kruger had been born in Andernok, Germany in 1965. Most people would have said he was from a normal, middle-class family, but from the beginning Kruger was different. A natural-born bully, he had always gotten in trouble for fighting. As a teenager, he loved being a part of the neo-Nazi movement. Sure, he hated Jews and ethnic minorities, but he had a general dislike for most people, regardless of their nationality. He loved the fear and intimidation the young skinheads could generate. He liked their look, too. His buzz-cut gave him a feeling of power. As if he would need it. At six feet four inches and two hundred forty pounds, he could overpower most anyone who crossed his path.

As soon as he could, he joined the German army. He had excelled in marksmanship and tactics, but his bully nature got him in trouble both on and off duty. When his enlistment was up, his superiors were glad to see him go. He took on a job as a bouncer and then saw an ad for the French Foreign Legion. He joined up, traveling to the world's hot spots. He specialized in martial arts and had become a principal instructor when his enlistment ended.

He was glad to leave the Legion. Even it had too many rules for Kruger. He became a mercenary, working for the highest bidder. His ruthless bent earned him lots of work as a highly paid killer.

Unfortunately, he had begun having knee trouble. The doctors told him to take it easy on his knees. At forty-one, he realized that he had only five or six more good years in the field. That's when he saw the ad for the job as chief of security for Liberia. His resume and his ability to learn foreign languages got him hired. Within months, he had mastered Kapel. The salary, however, was poor. He made only sixty thousand dollars a year.

But the bright side was that Liberia, like most African governments, had its hidden agendas. And then there was all that money under the table. Today's work was typical of the extra gigs. He was to pick up Lieutenant Colonel Martin's wife and son. He was to make sure there were no witnesses. He grinned. That meant he would be killing someone and making money doing it.

The open market lay ahead. He pulled to the curb when he spotted the lieutenant standing next to a man in a white lab coat. He spoke to both in Kapel. He needed to get them away from the crowded market.

"Lieutenant Mayon, you may ride with me to show the way to Dr. Marshall's house," Kruger said.

He didn't need directions; he just needed to separate the two men. He told Doboy to follow in the Land Rover.

Seated inside the smoked glass windows of the Mercedes, he reached over and struck the young officer in the temple, knocking him unconscious. Using both hands, he twisted the lieutenant's head. He heard a satisfying crack as the neck snapped.

He turned the key in the ignition and pulled away from the curb. The Land Rover followed closely behind. When they reached the turnoff to Marshall's house, Kruger pulled to the shoulder of the road. The Land Rover stopped behind him. Kruger got out, walked to the other car and opened the driver's door.

"Yes, boss?" asked Doboy.

"James, that's all I need."

With two lightning-fast blows – one to the left temple and a second to the throat – the man was dead. Kruger then returned to his car, pulled out the lieutenant's body, and dragged it to the ditch. Then he drove down the hill to Marshall's house.

Since the word had come of the attacks early this morning, the battalion operations center was a beehive of activity. Joe Weah had just walked over to the side table to refill his coffee cup when Major Thomas Sio tapped him on the arm.

"Good news, sir. Lieutenant Mayon called. He found the woman and the boy."

"Alive or dead?" Joe asked cautiously, fearing the worst.

"Alive. They're both alive," Sio said. "They're at Dr. Marshall's house."

"You mean the snake man who lives on Tubman Boulevard?"

"One and the same, sir."

"Have we picked them up yet?"

"No, sir. I informed the office of the minister of defense. They said they'd pick them up. He ordered us to stand down."

Joe looked down into his coffee cup, slowly stirring in his sugar. It took him a moment to respond.

"Good work, Tom," he said. "Tell the men I appreciate their efforts. Hey, I just remembered I have an errand to run. I should be back within an hour."

He set down his cup and walked out to his Hummer. The vehicle kicked up a cloud of dust as Joe hurried out the front gate. Joe figured that talking to Lindsey and Tim might shed some light on who was responsible for the murder of the Americans. More than that, he needed to see his friends, Lindsey and Tim. He had to know they were all right.

So far, this whole day had been unreal. Members of his battalion and the national police had searched every house on Mamba Bluff. It appeared that only families of the attaché's staff had been killed. Martin's house was nothing but burning embers. It was still too hot to search for the victims' remains in the rubble. Carpai ordered that the entire area be thoroughly searched before they confirmed that the Martins were indeed dead.

The area had been divided into sectors. Communicating by hand-held radios, Joe had kept a close watch on their progress. It was one of the lieutenants at the market who had phoned in the news that the two were at Dr. Marshall's house.

It would take Joe fewer than five minutes to get there.

Charlie got up to answer the doorbell.

"Yes?"

"Dr. Marshall, I am Hans Kruger. Minister Dowling has sent me to pick up Mrs. Martin and her son and conduct them safely to the American embassy."

Charlie recognized the President's chief of security. He had no reason to be suspicious.

"Come in, Mr. Kruger. I will tell them you are here."

Charlie walked into the kitchen, a broad smile spreading across his face.

"Good news, folks! They've come to escort you to the embassy."

"Oh, thank God," Lindsey said.

"Who did they send?"

"It's Hans Kruger, Minister Dowling's chief of security."

"Dowling?" asked Lindsey. "I thought you said someone from the embassy was here to pick us up."

"I'm sorry. The man said he was going to take you to the embassy."

"But, Charlie, how did he find out we are here? The phones don't work. Besides, I think the Liberian government is somehow involved in this whole ordeal."

A tall man with a German accent interrupted their conversation.

"You may be right, Mrs. Martin. That's why I plan to take you and your son directly to Dowling himself."

All three – Lindsey, Tim and Charlie – jumped. Behind them stood Hans Kruger with a .45-caliber automatic in his hand. Lindsey remembered they had left the shotgun and the pistol in the living room. Kruger was armed; they weren't.

Kruger fumbled in his pocket until he found two plastic wire ties. He handed them to Charlie.

"Dr. Marshall, tie their hands behind their backs."

"I certainly will not!" Charlie said.

"Fine. If you refuse, I'll shoot the boy in the knee. Then I'll shoot the woman."

To prove his point, Kruger aimed the pistol at Tim's right knee.

"All right, you bastard, I'll do it," Charlie said. He tied Tim's hands and then walked up behind Lindsey. "I'm sorry," he whispered.

"All right, folks, let's go meet the President," Kruger said.

"Sir, I can assure you that I will notify the British ambassador of this outrage!"

"I doubt that, doctor," Kruger said as he turned and fired two shots into Charlie's chest. The blast of the heavy weapon inside the small kitchen was deafening. Kruger calmly returned the pistol to his shoulder holster before grabbing Lindsey and Tim by their arms and leading them outside. In the last twelve hours, Lindsey and Tim had experienced enough stress to last a lifetime.

When Charlie Marshall had been shot dead right before their eyes, they lost all hope. The two followed meekly as Kruger led them to the Mercedes and locked them in the back seat.

The Hummer had just turned into the drive to Dr. Marshall's place when Joe saw Hans Kruger leading Lindsey and Tim to the car parked in front of the house. Joe pulled to a stop just as Kruger slammed the car's back door.

"Hey, Kruger, what's happening?" Joe asked as he climbed down from the Hummer.

"Not much, Joe, just doing some work for the President," Kruger said.

Kruger had recognized Weah when he pulled up. Since Joe was the commander of the elite Reconnaissance Battalion, somewhat of a national hero and a member of the inner circle, Kruger assumed that Carpai had sent him as a backup.

"I see you have the Martins," Joe said.

"No problem at all. It was a piece of cake."

"I'd like to speak with them for a moment," Joe said as he reached for the door handle.

"Sure. Sure, you can, Joe, but you'll have to wait until I get them back to Dowling."

"No," Joe insisted, "I want to talk to them now."

When Joe again reached for the door handle, Kruger grabbed his arm. Joe shoved him back.

"That does it!" yelled Kruger. He pulled the pistol from the holster. Joe spun, his foot flew up, and he struck the barrel of the gun with the toe of his boot. The gun flew out of Kruger's hand and skipped off the car's roof. Kruger didn't seem fazed by the move.

"Well, well. The colonel knows a little hand-to-hand combat. But I don't need a gun to take care of you," he snarled.

Kruger moved forward, his hands moving rapidly. His right and left fists alternated throwing crippling blows. Joe blocked the punches with his forearms and returned punch for punch. He struck Kruger a glancing blow to the cheek that caused him to stagger backwards.

"God damn it, you're making me mad, you kaffer!" Kruger swore, unafraid to use the rude, racial slur common in South Africa. "Now I am going to have to kill you!"

Kruger whirled, bringing his right foot up with a forceful kick. Joe turned in the nick of time, but the blow caught him on the shoulder, knocking him to the ground. Joe rolled away and jumped back on his feet. Kruger came forward again, lashing out savagely with his fists. Again, Joe blocked the punches.

Finally, Kruger landed a strong one to the side of Joe's head. Joe staggered backwards. Kruger moved in, following up with more hits. Joe felt himself losing ground. Kruger was by far the more skilled fighter.

"Having a problem, kaffer?" laughed Kruger.

Joe couldn't respond. He was losing the fight. Blood ran freely from his nose. His lip had been split. Kruger landed a vicious kick directly to Joe's chest. Joe found it difficult to catch his breath. He staggered and fell to the ground. He tried to get back on his feet, but he collapsed to the ground.

Kruger sensed his victory. He had killed many men in hand-to-hand combat. The last few seconds were the best. In two strides he stood directly in front of Joe who had managed to rise to a squatting position.

"Look at me, kaffer!"

Joe turned his eyes upward. He gasped for air. He had seen the blood running freely, staining the front of his uniform. He coughed up mucus and tried to speak, but no words came. Kruger placed a hand over each of Joe's ears. All it would take was a simple jerk of his arms. The neck would snap. It would be all over. Kruger smiled, savoring the moment.

Kruger's hesitation offered Joe one more chance. With the desperation of a dying man, Joe reared up. The top of his head struck Kruger in the chin. As Kruger's head snapped backwards, Joe reached up with his right hand. Palm open, it shot forward, connecting with Kruger's throat. It took every last ounce of strength in his body to crush Kruger's windpipe. Joe leaned forward in time to see Kruger fall to the ground, gasping for air. His body convulsed briefly. Then it didn't move at all. Joe knelt beside the man, checking for a pulse. Not finding any sign of life, Joe slowly rose to his feet.

He staggered toward the Mercedes. The back doors were locked. He opened the door on the driver's side. The back seat was closed off by a sliding partition. At first, he panicked. Then he saw the black button on the dashboard. He pushed it. He heard it click and the back door locks popped open.

"Oh, Joe! Please help us," cried Lindsey.

"Come on, Lindsey. Tim, let's get you out of here," Joe said.

The three of them made their way back into Charlie's house. Joe found a kitchen knife and cut the plastic ties. Lindsey located a bottle of antiseptic and cleaned the cuts on Joe's face. They gathered the guns and backpacks.

"Lindsey, I don't know what's going on, but we're in big trouble," Joe said. "From what you say, Minister Carpai, my boss, is responsible for trying to kill you both. He may be responsible for the deaths of the Americans. Now I've just killed the chief of security. It's likely that someone else will show up any minute. We have to get out of here – fast!"

"Where can we go? Where would we be safe?" Tim asked.

"We're going to Zigda," Joe answered quickly, heading out the door toward the Hummer.

Carpai paced back and forth. Where the hell was Kruger, anyway? He should have returned more than a half hour ago. His patience had run out.

"Major Jalah, come with me," he ordered. "We're going out there to find out exactly what's going on."

Not far from Marshall's front door, they spotted the body of Hans Kruger. It didn't take them long to find Lieutenant Sayon, James Doboy and Charlie Marshall – all dead. The two scoured the area, looking for clues as to what had happened. Then Carpai spotted the shiny dog tags partially covered by dirt.

"Weah," he said. "Of course, it all makes sense now. Weah was thick with the Americans. Somehow he got the best of Kruger. The Martin woman and the boy must be with him."

"What now?" asked Jalah.

"That's easy," Carpai said. He walked over to Kruger and fired a round into the body. He did the same to the bodies of the two Liberians.

"Why did you do that?" asked Jalah.

"It's simple. We claim that Colonel Weah is a member of Charles Morray's People's Party. He was involved in the assassinations. Just before we got here, I had a call from the fire inspectors. They found two bodies in the ashes of the Martin house. Unfortunately, they were burned beyond recognition," he smiled. "They came to the conclusion that they were the bodies of Mrs. Martin and her son. We accept that fact."

"But we know that the Martins are still alive," Jalah said.

"Right, but no one else does. We'll claim that the tip that they were at Dr. Marshall's house was only to lure us into an ambush. Weah killed Kruger, Mayon, Doboy and Marshall. We'll put a fifty thousand dollar reward out for Weah's capture – dead or alive. When we find Weah, we'll find the Martins.

"Now let's get the hell out of here!"

# 14

***Getting out of Monrovia hadn't been difficult. When the pavement ended, Joe explained that it would take three more hours of driving followed by a two-hour walk to get to Zigda, Liberia's most sacred village. Zigda had been kept relatively inaccessible to preserve its purity from outside influences.***

"But, Joe, why are you so sure that we'll be safe there?" asked Lindsey.

Joe explained that his father was the paramount chief. He'd be able to provide protection until they could contact the embassy. Despite Joe's confidence, Lindsey doubted that they could avoid Carpai's grasp, even in a remote village.

"Lindsey," Joe explained, "No government soldier would dare enter our sacred village without the chief's permission."

Miles of jungle passed by the Hummer's windows. Designed to handle the rough roads, the vehicle maintained a speed of fifty miles per hour. Exhaustion, warm sunlight and the constant rumble of the rough tires on gravel lulled Lindsey to sleep. Although she still had misgivings about Joe's plan, she gave herself over to his protection.

The Hummer's sudden braking interrupted her sleep.

"Shit!" said Joe.

"What's wrong?" she asked.

"A road block ahead."

At the top of a hill sat a military Hummer. Soldiers were searching the passengers of a money bus. Joe pulled off to the side of the road so he could assess the situation. Soon the passengers boarded the bus, and it continued down the road.

"Joe, what are we going to do?" asked Tim.

"We're going to make a run for it. This is a military Hummer, after all. Maybe they'll assume it's just another military vehicle. I'm going to see if I can sideswipe their vehicle and knock it into the ditch. Both of you, crouch down and brace yourselves."

Joe pressed the gas pedal to the floor, and the Hummer lurched forward.

Four soldiers stood alongside the road and watched as the Hummer approached. One soldier waved his arms overhead, indicating that the vehicle must stop. Yet Joe's speedometer climbed past fifty, then sixty, and then sixty-five. As he neared the roadblock, they were going almost seventy-five. When the guards realized that the driver was ignoring their orders, they dove for safety on the side of the road. Joe angled his vehicle toward the parked Hummer.

"Hang on!" he screamed. "We're going to hit!"

Lindsey braced herself and held her breath, anticipating a hard impact. She heard a loud bang and the crunch of metal as Joe sideswiped the vehicle. It flipped onto its top as their vehicle continued its wild rampage.

Joe looked in his mirrors. Behind them, a lone soldier stood in the middle of the road. He lifted his rifle and aimed at the cloud of dust in the distance. They were now hundreds of yards from the roadblock. It would be an impossible shot. Yet the soldier pulled the trigger, and the weapon bucked against his shoulder. Nothing happened. The Hummer disappeared from sight. The soldier shook his head, slung the rifle on his back, and walked toward the overturned Hummer.

Lindsey struggled to sit up as the vehicle swerved from one side of the road to the other. Joe brought it to a stop.

"Why are we stopping?" Lindsey asked, as she glanced down the road behind them.

Joe slumped over the steering wheel. "I've been hit," he whispered.

"Hit? How? I didn't hear a shot," Lindsey said. She leaned up to get a better look at Joe's back. Blood had soaked through his shirt, forming a dark spot on his right shoulder.

"Oh, God, Joe! We've got to get you to a doctor!"

"No. No, you can't do that," Joe said. "They know where we are. If they catch us, we're all dead. You have to help me get into the back seat. Tim will ride shotgun. Lindsey, you'll have to drive."

"Joe, I don't know how to drive this thing!"

"It's just like a car," he said patiently. "It has an automatic transmission. You'll do just fine. Now, help me into the back."

His breathing was labored. Lindsey knew she had no choice but to do as he said.

They eased Joe into the back. She urged him to let her tend to his wound, but he insisted that they had to keep going. The bleeding had abated. It had missed a major artery. Still, he couldn't raise his arm. He winced as he settled into the back.

Driving the Hummer took a little getting used to, but Lindsey found it was easier than she had thought. She forced herself to concentrate on the winding dirt road, denying her fears that Joe could die. She gripped the wheel and slammed down the accelerator. Who knew what the future held? For now, she had a job to do – drive this Hummer to safety.

Once out of the valley, the terrain became more rugged. Hills turned into low mountains. In the distance, she could see sharp peaks shrouded in low clouds. They passed through several small villages, slowing slightly. Soon the distance between the towns lengthened.

She pulled off at a Lebanese store. Tim went in and bought some canned food, boiled eggs and soft drinks. Tim's Pidgin English seemed to work. Lindsey couldn't believe how much at ease he was while talking to the Liberians. She could understand only half of what was being said. Tim had no trouble at all.

They stopped about a mile out of town. Both Lindsey and Tim were hungry, but Joe refused to eat. She insisted that he drink some water. Tim had filled the two canteens at a small stream. She was grateful that she had had the foresight to bring along the water purification tablets.

Joe permitted her to look at his wound when they stopped to eat. She got in the back alongside him. Behind them, she saw the hole in the canvas top where the soldier's wild shot had entered the Hummer. She gently eased Joe's arm out of his fatigue jacket and helped him out of his t-shirt, only to find a nasty hole about three-eighth-inch in diameter on his right shoulder about five inches below his shoulder blade. If it had entered his body just five inches to the left, it would have hit his spine.

Joe figured that most of the energy of the long shot had been spent before the bullet had hit. The wound still seeped blood, and the bullet was still lodged in his flesh. The wound continued to seep blood, and the area around it had begun to swell. Lindsey feared that if the bullet weren't removed soon, it could cause an infection. Again, she begged Joe to let her find medical help, but he shook his head and insisted that the bullet could be removed once they got to Zigda.

It was now almost five o'clock. About an hour and a half of daylight remained. Joe had told her they would come to a road that turned to the left. She had missed the turnoff and had to backtrack. No wonder she hadn't seen it. It wasn't a road, but a two-track trail into the jungle.

She slid the Hummer into low range, and it began a slow crawl up the trail.

# 15

*The charred remains of the Martin home on Mamba Bluff continued to smolder. Thin spires of smoke drifted upward from the hot pockets of debris. All through the morning, Everyday Walker had sat cross-legged, staring at the burning ruins of what had been his home and his responsibility for the last forty years. He watched the firemen spray streams of water, hack down walls, and finally remove three body bags – one containing the pet dog.*

THE FIRE MARKED HIS FAILURE. HE HAD LOST THE FAMILY AS WELL AS THE house he had guarded since it was built so long ago. His buttocks ached, his joints stiffened, and his useless hands lay palms up on his knees. It was too hot for an old man. Droplets of sweat formed on his balding head and rolled down the creases of his wrinkled skin. The burden of his eighty-five years weighed down on him. He shifted to his left, then to his right. The native people didn't linger in the tropical sun. Especially the old.

But Everyday Walker would not move until the spirit of the leopard revealed the whereabouts of Missy and Tim. Eyes closed, he began chanting in the ancient tongue of his ancestors. He recited the ritual phrases that had been etched in his memory many years ago. Lost in a semiconscious state, he rocked from side to side, murmuring. His right hand moved to the amulet hanging from a leather thong around his weathered neck. His fingertips caressed the charm, a smooth ivory tooth capped with a silver tip. It had been taken from a very large leopard.

He should have heeded his fears. Several months ago he had seen George Sarday in the market. Sarday had not aged in fifty years. That meant he was an *endosym*, a man and a demon in one body. Fortunately Sarday did not see him, but since that day he had felt the *endosym*'s power increasing. He should have warned the Martins, but who would heed the ravings of a simple old man?

If only he had been at his duties the night before. The power of the leopard might have prevented the fire. He had been remiss. He had spent the evening at the Goyam Bar, leaving Zac to guard the house. He had been drinking strong, dark beer with his long-time friends, fellow Liberians who had served the Americans at the old Firestone Plantation. One glass had led to another. Soon Everyday Walker's senses numbed, and he slid into blissful inebriation.

Somehow he had managed to walk back toward Mamba Bluff. He would spend the remaining night hours on the cot in the old guard house. But even as he reached the outskirts of Mamba Bluff, he knew the *endosym* had prevailed.

At first, he accepted what others had said – Missy and the boy had died. But later, as his consciousness cleared, he began to sense their life force. Only now, he struggled to learn where they had gone. Old men's minds usually took time to focus, but even more so when they are clouded with the aftermath of a night of drinking. He was aware that his own physical presence would soon be gone. Then his spirit would join those who watched from the bush. But now, his years had provided him with a better understanding of life's mysteries. He fell into deep thought, once again searching for answers to his questions.

He had not always been Everyday Walker. He was born Chea Geebe. He might have become the greatest *zo* in the chiefdom, had not the *endosym* robbed him of his birthright. His father and his grandfather had each been powerful *zoes*. Able to commune with the spirits, they were called upon to protect the village from the wicked beings that dwell in the sacred bush.

When he was only fifteen, he had killed a great leopard, the largest ever seen in his village. His father had been pleased. The leopard spirit had become his protector. One of its fangs still dangled from the cord around his neck.

His father had taught him how to communicate with the spirit world. When Chea himself had finally become a *zo*, his reward was a beautiful young virgin for his first wife. By the time he had reached thirty-five, he had two wives, two sons and three daughters. His power as well as his pride grew, but still he wanted more. What he wanted most was the power to destroy his enemies. He failed to heed his father's warnings and sought ways to invoke the evil spirits to work his will. His desire for more power began to consume his every waking moment.

He believed that his wishes had come true when the man who now calls himself George Nah Sarday passed through his village. Sarday carried a soft cloth bag. Chea's eyes became wide with curiosity as the man showed him yet another small bag, this one fashioned from black velvet. When he loosened its twisted ties, he brought out a bronze image of a man's face. It had horns protruding from the top of its head.

"This powerful spirit can grant a man great wealth and power," Sarday said, as his heavy-lidded eyes shifted from the small bronze face to Chea and back again. Unable to resist its magnetism, Chea handed Sarday twenty Liberian dollars. He pressed another twenty dollars into the fat hand. He demanded that he be taught the secret words that would release the spirit's power.

When Sarday had gone, Chea cupped the bronze head in his hands and slid it back into the velvet bag. He tied it to the thick cloth belt around his waist and went to his second wife's chicken coop behind her hut. He grabbed the largest black hen and stuffed it into a canvas bag. He checked to see that no one had seen him, and then he walked to the path that led deep into the bush.

Far into the jungle, he again looked around to assure himself that he was alone and unheard. He removed the small bronze image from the bag, placed it on the ground, cut off the chicken's head and dribbled blood over the face. As he recited the secret phrases, he saw that the area around the statue's head began to take on a reddish glow. Brightness soon encompassed his very being.

The clearing had disappeared. He now was within the walls of a large cavern. A stone temple stood inside the great room. A dark figure – not quite human – sat on a raised platform inside. It spoke in low, even tones. It claimed that it was an *endosym*. Chea was to go deep into the jungle valley until he reached the ruins of a sacred site. He must search until he found a worn, carved wooden statue. He would recognize it as the image of this strange being that roamed the bush. Chea's task was to reconstruct the sacred site, replacing the ruins with an altar worthy of the *endosym's* power.

When Chea returned to his village, he sought out ten men who agreed to help rebuild the site. With machetes and crude tools, the men slashed through the underbrush. Chea shouted in triumph when he discovered a weathered wooden statue. Termites had chewed into its surface. One leg had been broken off.

To repair it, Chea found a metal rod and pounded it into the body. He smoothed a flat board for a base. He positioned the statue so that it would stand upright. The men continued to toil. They cleared the area around the altar and encircled the site with a pole wall. They constructed a mud hut to the right of the altar. Soon the sacred site had regained most of its former glory.

On the next moonless night, Chea and his men gathered in the clearing. A young male goat, its legs bound tightly with rope, was placed on the altar. Its head dangled weakly at the edge of the stone platform. The men began to chant the ancient words that would invoke the *endosym*.

With a single blow of his cutlass, Chea severed the goat's head. Blood spurted from the neck, coating the statue. A reddish light illuminated the compound. The men fell to their knees in fear and awe as they felt the *endosym's* presence. It was pleased by the obedience, but admonished them. The only way to gain power and wealth was to make a human – not animal – sacrifice. After the light grew dim, the men gathered to consider the endosym's request. None wanted to bring a human being to the altar of sacrifice. Each vowed to leave the valley, never to return again.

But for Chea Geebe the *endosym* that called itself George Sarday refused to loosen its grip. The next day Sarday came to visit him. Despite his fear, Chea did not give in to its demands. Instead, he prayed that lives would be spared. Yet his prayers went unanswered. The next morning, he learned that a sickness had begun to spread throughout the village. His own father and mother had fallen into a fever. Three days later they died within hours of each other.

Chea stayed close to his wives and children, watching for any sign of illness, yet nothing could be done to save them from their fate. All fell ill. Even his brothers, sisters and their families succumbed to the illness. All died within the same week. The ten strong men who had helped rebuild the sacred site were among the last to die. When the sickness finally stopped, Chea Geebe was one of the few to survive.

The government claimed that the illness was one of the worst cholera epidemics ever to plague the country. But Chea knew it had been caused by the *endosym*. The answer lay between his fingertips – only the tooth of the leopard had protected him from death.

Nothing remained to hold him in the village of his birth. Alone, he moved into the city and eventually began working for an American and his family. George Walker was the general manager of Firestone Rubber Plantation. When he retired, the family decided to remain in Liberia. Chea stayed close to the Walker family, pledging never again to practice magic or to seek power and wealth.

When the Walkers built the house on Mamba Bluff, Chea took charge of the servants. Until the Walkers returned to America, Chea Geebe had never missed a day of work. He had become known as Everyday Walker. When the United States Embassy bought the Walker property, it was understood that Everyday Walker came with the purchase.

But now the house was nothing more than smoldering embers. It was sunset when his trance finally abated. The vision had come. Missy and the boy were on their way to a village in a green valley. All around the village were tall mountains. He recognized the place. He pulled himself to his feet, stretched his stiffened legs and set out on his journey.

# 16

***On the deeply rutted road to Zigda, Lindsey took one hand off the steering wheel and flexed her numb fingers. It had taken all her strength and concentration to maneuver the Hummer along the overgrown trail in the dense forest. Overhead, the tall trees formed a green tunnel, nearly cutting out the evening's remaining light. She patted her cheek, feeling for moisture along the gauze over her wound. Charlie had done a good job.***

SINCE THEY HAD TURNED OFF THE MAIN ROAD, THEY HADN'T SEEN A LIVING creature. Perhaps no one lived in this part of the forest, or they were hidden from sight.

She guided the vehicle around a corner. The road widened. The forest opened up. Ahead she could see that a narrow wooden bridge spanned a chasm. Only moments before, she had felt confident and powerful in her military vehicle. Now, she wasn't so sure. She came to a stop, braced her arms against the steering wheel and rested her head on her scratched forearms.

She opened the door and got out to assess the route. The river lay seventy feet below in the bottom of the cut. The bridge, likely a good one hundred fifty feet long, looked as if it hadn't been used in years. She tiptoed along the aging timbers, wondering if anyone had dared cross it on foot, let alone in a heavy vehicle.

Yet she had no recourse – they had to go forward. She returned to the Hummer and shifted it into four-wheel low. She eased it onto the first few feet of the bridge. She kept it in a slow crawl, frequently peering ahead, behind and to each side. Mid-span, she felt the left rear of the vehicle drop.

"Oh, shit!" Lindsey exclaimed.

Joe moaned. "What happened?"

"We're on a bridge over a river. I think the back wheel has gone through the deck."

"Give it gas," he said. "The Hummer is all-wheel drive. Each wheel can pull it along."

"OK, Joe," Lindsey said. Her upper legs quivered, and she could feel her underarms damp with perspiration. She pressed down on the accelerator, but nothing happened. She pushed it down even harder.

She could feel the Hummer begin to pull itself out of the hole. When the wheel freed itself, the back end gave a sudden leap. The movement startled her. Without thinking, she pressed her foot clear to the floor. The Hummer shot forward. She tried to correct her mistake by slamming her left foot on the brakes. Then she felt the bridge begin to shift beneath them. She heard the crack of timbers. The Hummer lurched to the left.

"Go! Go! Go!" Joe yelled.

She took her left foot off the brake and slammed her right foot again on the gas. The left side of the bridge creaked and dropped even lower. The Hummer began to slide toward the edge. Lindsey summoned all of her strength and forced the wheel to the right. The Hummer fishtailed. Yards ahead, she could see the end of the bridge, but it might as well have been miles away.

Her arms froze on the steering wheel. Whatever she did seemed wrong. Somewhere behind her and beside her, she could hear Joe and Tim screaming for her to turn to the right or to the left, to speed up or to slow down. She realized now that they were simply not going to make it. She could envision the Hummer twisting in a free fall to the river below. It would ricochet off the rock cliffs as it fell, spinning out of control until they crashed on the rocks.

Suddenly, she felt Tim's hand shaking her shoulder.

"Mom! Mom, stop!" he yelled. Not at the bottom of the gorge, they were two hundred feet down the road. Not bleeding and broken from their fall, they were inside the Hummer, safely riding on its solid, hard rubber tires. She pressed down on the brakes, and the vehicle rolled to a stop. She took a deep breath, opened the driver's door and walked back to the edge of the cliff. The entire left side of the bridge had caved away, leaving only one narrow timber spanning the crevasse.

"The valley of no return," she whispered.

It was now totally dark. Near the equator, the transition from daylight to dark is quick. She turned and walked back to the Hummer, to her son, and to her friend. She clicked on the headlights and put the vehicle in gear. Her heart rate returned to normal, and she forced herself to concentrate on the narrow road ahead. As the brush scraped the sides of the vehicle, she recalled hearing Hank complain that the wide Hummer, which had replaced the tried-and-true jeep, was too wide for the roads in third-world countries. Wide or not, she pushed forward, dodging trees and large rocks.

It couldn't be too much farther to Zigda, she calculated. Soon she saw a large clearing ahead. The high beams lit up a solid wall of jungle with trees more than one hundred feet tall. She turned the Hummer, shining the lights to the right and then to the left.

"Joe, what happened to the road?" she yelled.

Joe failed to answer. She got out, opened the back door and pressed her hand to Joe's forehead.

"Joe! Joe!" she said.

"What?" he answered groggily.

"You're burning up with fever. We've got to get to Zigda, but I can't find the road."

"No road," Joe whispered.

"What do you mean 'no road'?" she demanded.

"Don't you remember? From, here we must walk the ten miles along the bush trail."

"Joe, there's no way you can walk that far. I'll have to go for help."

"Lindsey, you can't go anywhere until daylight. No one walks in the bush at night."

"Joe, you'll die if we don't get help for that wound."

"No matter what happens, Lindsey, we must wait until morning. Then we can get help."

She held the canteen to his feverish lips. He managed to swallow some of the warm water.

"Please. Please, Joe, don't die on me!" she pleaded, kissing him lightly on the cheek.

"Don't worry. I'll make it," he whispered.

She climbed back into the driver's seat and brought her legs up to her chest.

"Mom, is Joe going to be OK?" asked Tim.

"I hope so, Tim. I hope so. He says we can't go on to Zigda until daylight. Try to get some sleep."

She stared out the windshield. A full moon covered the clearing with a silver glow. She could make out every blade of grass, every pebble, every detail in vivid profile. Tim had fallen asleep immediately, his head propped against canvas cover. Joe moaned, repositioned himself, and resumed his semi-conscious slumber.

She had to pee. The pressure was becoming unbearable. It was either wet her pants or get out of the vehicle and relieve herself. She couldn't hold it any longer.

"Damn it," she whispered as she lifted the door latch and stepped on the ground. She went only a few feet away, slid down her jeans, then her panties. She squatted, sighing with relief as the hot urine pooled beneath her. When she finished, she stood, but sensed that she was being watched. She pulled her clothes up and walked quickly back to the Hummer. The thin canvas would offer little protection. Even the shotgun and the pistol didn't ease her concern. She closed the door and looked ahead over the clearing.

To the right, she thought she saw movement. She waited, unsure of her first impression. A long, low form seemed to slink across the open area, moving toward them. It became clear that it was a leopard.

Its greenish-golden eyes looked directly at her. Its flared nostrils sniffed at the night air, its broad tongue visible as it panted softly.

Lindsey remembered the story Joe had told of his encounter with a leopard. She recalled the image of the spear dangling from the chest wound and Joe's knife firmly embedded in its eye.

The animal drew even closer. Only a few feet from the vehicle's front bumper, it stopped. Lindsey reached out until her fingers located the shotgun. She wrapped her hand around the cool metal. What good would it do? This was the largest leopard she had ever seen, far larger than those at the Liberian zoo.

Suddenly, its eyes locked with hers.

A second later the Hummer bounced. The leopard crouched, mid-hood, staring directly at her through the thick glass windshield. She stifled her scream, fearful that any noise or movement might cause the beast to rip open the canvas top with its powerful claws. It lowered its head, its eyes level with hers.

A sense of awe replaced her fear. She allowed herself to stare deep into its eyes. She fancied a wide grin forming on its thin black lips. It turned and looked into the window at Tim, who hadn't stirred.

As quickly as it had appeared, it leapt from the hood and sauntered back into the underbrush. For some reason, Lindsey was left with a sense of well-being. Her worries faded and her eyelids became heavy.

Finally, she dropped into a dreamless sleep. She had no idea if anyone even knew that she and Tim were still alive.

> CNN World News, First Watch – The President has vowed to take every step possible to bring those responsible for the murders of Americans in Liberia to justice, a White House spokesman said earlier today. Names of the victims of yesterday's alleged terrorist attack have still not been released.
>
> A team of FBI agents is expected to arrive in the nation's capital city of Monrovia later today to cooperate with the country's government on the investigation.

A second contingent, composed of medical examiners, will prepare the bodies for return to Delaware's Dover Air Force Base.

Officials say that eighteen Americans, one British national, one German national and two Liberians died in the attack. Reports say that children are among the victims.

The spokesman said that this is the single most serious terrorist attack since the September 11, 2001 attacks.

More information will follow as soon as it becomes available.

Lindsey rubbed her eyes as the bright sunlight streamed in the Hummer's windows. It was already seven o'clock. She unlatched the door and stepped out. She had expected to be stiff and sore from sleeping upright in the driver's seat. That, coupled with the beating she had received the night before last, should have resulted in more aches and pains. Instead, she actually felt refreshed.

She stepped out from the driver's side and opened the back door to check on Joe. He still was hot with fever. She shook him, but he didn't respond. She suspected that he might be slipping into a coma. Tim still slept soundly. Even her movements hadn't awakened him.

She heard a rustle in the grass behind her. She whirled to find two young boys, about eleven years old, smiling at her.

"Do you speak English?" she asked.

They didn't answer, but continued to smile.

"Please. We need help. We must get to Zigda."

"Zigda. Zigda," one said.

"Yes, Zigda!" she said more loudly. But it didn't do any good. They continued to grin, but not answer.

"Great. They don't understand English!" she said. Then she thought for a moment. What was Joe's tribal name?

"Nah, Nah," she said aloud. Then she pointed into the Hummer and the slumped body of her friend Joe. She pointed and said it again. "Nah, Nah. Nah Weah!"

Suddenly, it all seemed to register. The boys repeated the name, but then turned and ran into the jungle.

"Shit! Now what do we do?" Lindsey said. She turned to the passenger side of the car, opened the door and gently rocked her son. "Honey, wake up!"

Tim yawned and stretched.

"I'm hungry," he said before his eyes were even open. "Can we open one of those cans of beef stew?"

"Sure, Tim," she said. "One of us will have to walk to Zigda while the other one stays with Joe. I think he's slipped into a coma. We'll need help to carry him."

Tim opened the can and the two shared the cold stew. Tim made ready to leave. Tim would make the walk. If anyone there spoke English, Tim should be able to get help. Even if no one did, Tim knew enough Kapel to get his point across.

She reached over to help him put on his backpack.

"Mom!"

"Yes, Tim?" she responded.

"Mom, look!"

She turned. "Oh, my God," she said quietly.

Between twenty-five and thirty men emerged from the undergrowth. They wore only loincloths. Each carried a spear. This couldn't be happening, she thought. Even in Liberia, men no longer dressed like savages. Yet here they were, walking straight toward them. She considered firing the shotgun to frighten them off, but rejected the idea. There were simply too many of them. A hostile action might cause them to attack.

From their midst, a tall man with white hair came forward. Unlike the others, he didn't carry a weapon. His loincloth wasn't made of the common soft brown leather, but of rich leopard hide. He walked right past her and opened the back door of the Hummer.

"I need help to get him to Zigda," she blurted. "He is hurt bad. He is Joe Weah. I mean, Nah Weah. He is the son of a chief."

Lindsey spoke rapidly, forgetting that no one likely understood what she was saying.

The man turned to the others and said something in an unfamiliar language. Two men came forward and lifted Joe from the Hummer. Another two men brought forward a stretcher made of bamboo poles and a soft, brown fabric. Working together, the four gently placed Joe on the litter and moved off into the jungle.

"Wait! Wait a minute!" shouted Lindsey. "We have to come, too!" She started forward. Two of the men held her back and grabbed the shotgun from her hands.

"Mom!" Tim screamed. She struggled to get loose, but she was no match for their strength. Two others came forward and restrained Tim. One unbuckled the pistol from Tim's hip. Two of them searched the backpacks.

"What are you going to do to us?" Lindsey asked. "Please, we are friends of Nah Weah. Don't hurt us."

The two men took the ammunition from the backpacks. The weapons and the ammo were placed on the front seat of the vehicle. They thrust the backpacks into Tim's hands before heading off to join the others.

"Now what, Mom?"

"I think we were just told – no guns," Lindsey answered. "Come on. We'll follow them to Zigda."

They headed to where the men had disappeared into the jungle. She saw evidence of a bush trail.

"This way," she said to Tim. They had no other choice but to follow.

They went down the wide path that had been hacked out of the undergrowth. The men carrying Joe's stretcher had disappeared. Lindsey and Tim alternated running and walking for almost a half hour before they caught up with the warriors at the rear of the procession. The two men in the back turned and smiled as they saw them approach. Lindsey and Tim kept up, but stayed at a respectful distance.

As they fell into a steady pace behind them, Lindsey began to notice the beauty of the strange world they had entered. Tall, thick-leafed trees towered above. From their upper branches, she could hear the chirping of birds and the chattering of monkeys. On the stretches of trail where the sun filtered through the trees, multi-colored butterflies settled briefly on the broad leaves and then flitted away. In some areas, the jungle growth formed a green cathedral overhead.

Their trek took them over small streams, some spanned by rough-hewn log bridges. At one point, they crossed a raging river on a suspension bridge built entirely of tightly woven vines. It stretched more than one hundred feet across a ravine. It was held only by the knotted vines tied to tall trees on either side of the river. An engineering marvel, she thought, made without any modern tools.

Occasionally, the trail would lead to the crest of a hill. In the distance, she saw mountains carpeted in lush African green. Farther off, she made out higher peaks partially hidden in misty clouds.

About a half hour later, the group came to a stop. Lindsey and Tim cautiously approached the men who had settled Joe's stretcher near a stream running parallel to the trail. The tall man in the leopard loincloth knelt over Joe's motionless body. Lindsey thought she saw him insert something into Joe's mouth.

"Stop!" she screamed. "Don't hurt him!" She ran towards Joe. Two of the warriors stepped forward and held her by the arms.

"Please! He is hurt! Don't do that!" she pleaded, tears running freely down her cheeks.

The older man looked up and spoke sharply to the men. They released their grip. She ran forward and knelt beside her friend. She could see a white powder on his dry lips. The man turned Joe's head and poured a yellow liquid into Joe's open mouth. Joe swallowed, choked and then coughed. The man turned toward Lindsey. She saw a deep sadness in his eyes.

For the first time, she looked at his features. Something seemed familiar. Then she realized that she was looking into the face of Joe himself, but twenty-five years into the future. This must be Joe's father. She felt sudden relief – he was not trying to hurt Joe, he was trying to help. The old man nodded his head. She acknowledged his look with a nod of her own, then stood up and walked back to stand beside her son.

"He's Joe's father," Lindsey said solemnly.

"Did he tell you that, Mom?"

"No, but I know he is Joe's father."

Two men came forward, lifted the stretcher and resumed their journey. Lindsey moved ahead and walked beside the bearers, no longer lingering behind the others, she and Tim were now a part of the group.

Another hour passed. Lindsey thought she heard the beat of drums. At first it was only a faint rumble in the distance, but soon the sound became unmistakable. They crested a hill and in the valley below, she made out a pattern of dwellings and garden patches.

It was Zigda. Lindsey would never forget the first time she saw the sacred village.

It nestled on a stretch of low-lying land, bisected by a river. Above it were more rugged mountains, covered by dense forest. So many forested lands had been maimed by clear-cutting, but this was truly a virgin forest. The huts were roofed in natural thatch. Here no rusty, tin roofs marred the landscape. She saw well-tended farms, herds of healthy goats and orderly rows of crops. But the biggest surprise was yet to come.

As they rounded a bend in the trail, Lindsey stopped short. Ahead, lining both sides of the trail, stood the ebony-skinned villagers – every man, every woman and every child.

The procession continued down the trail with Joe's father in the lead. A murmur rose from the crowd as the two tall, white strangers passed through the gauntlet. For some reason, Lindsey felt no fear. She held her head high and smiled broadly.

A boy, perhaps five years old, reached out and touched her arm. She laughed and held out her hand. He grasped it, grinning and rubbing the light skin. Soon children surrounded her. Tim lifted the boy to his shoulders where he waved and laughed. More giggles and chatter accompanied the group as they entered the village.

The group stopped abruptly as Joe's father raised his right arm. The crowd quieted. Joe's stretcher was carried into one of the larger huts. A bent, wrinkled woman came forward. Joe's father spoke briefly to her, pointing at the two white strangers. She turned to Lindsey and stretched out her arms in greeting.

Lindsey took her hand, and the woman led her and Tim to a nearby hut. Inside, the woman lit a kerosene lantern. Its glow illuminated the worn face. Lindsey thought she saw tears in her eyes. Lindsey pointed to Tim.

"Tim," she said, pointing to her belly.

The old woman hesitated, as Lindsey repeated the gesture. Then the old woman nodded, pointed at her own mid-section and said, "Nah Weah."

Lindsey knew that this was Joe's mother.

The first day in Zigda was one of excitement, humor and sorrow. Joe's mother had left and returned with bowls of steaming rice, steeped in a meaty broth. She offered them a wooden tray covered with slices of banana and mango.

Tim picked around in the broth, searching for lumps of rice while avoiding the hot liquid and spicy bits of meat. He later learned that the dish was known as "country chop."

A bucket of cool, clear water stood nearby. Before ladling the water into the wooden cups, Lindsey dropped two iodine tablets into the bucket. Neither of them could deal with dysentery this far from civilization.

They felt satisfied after their meal. Tim wanted to explore the village. At first, she feared they might violate some taboo, but she was curious to find out what had become of Joe.

After the dark interior of the hut, they were blinded by the bright sunlight. They stood with their backs to the low doorway until they became accustomed to the light. They paused to take in the details of village life.

The town seemed to be laid out in a wide, circular pattern. A broad, common area formed the village center. Nearly one hundred huts of varying size fanned out from there. Tim took a few tentative steps forward. His foot collided with what he first thought was a dog or a pig. Recovering his balance, he heard the giggle and chatter of children who had scurried off to hide behind a pile of branches.

Bare-breasted women hovered over wooden mortars, grinding grain. Small charcoal fires burned in cooking kitchens behind the huts. Tim led the way; Lindsey followed closely behind.

The people smiled and nodded as they passed, murmuring unintelligible greetings. Tim smiled and answered in the Kapel greeting that he had learned from Everyday Walker. The tour ceased when Lindsey tapped Tim's arm. Joe's father approached them.

"Oh-oh," she said. "I think we're in trouble."

"Are you Lindsey?" he asked.

"You speak English!" Lindsey exclaimed.

"Of course, I speak English. I am the paramount chief. Three times a year, all paramount chiefs go to Monrovia to meet with the President," he said. Then he asked again, "Is your name Lindsey?"

"Yes, I'm Lindsey," she answered.

"My son speaks your name in his dream state. You must come with me."

"Come on, Tim," Lindsey said.

"No," he said. "He can stay with the young warriors." He pointed ahead at three young men about Tim's age. One was the warrior who had searched their backpacks.

"Tim's not a warrior. He is only a boy," said Lindsey.

"He's a warrior," responded the man. "I saw it in his eyes. He had killed his enemy."

Lindsey gasped. How could this man know of the violence they had experienced?

"All right," she agreed. Tim turned to the young men. He shook their hands using the traditional West African greeting of snapping fingers as they pulled their hands away. Tim didn't seem in the least bit anxious about staying behind. As a matter of fact, she realized, he seemed most willing to join the young men. They looked to him with respect.

She wondered if they sensed his courage at confronting and shooting her attackers.

"I am Togba Weah," said Joe's father. "You may call me Togba. Are you Nah Weah's woman?"

Lindsey blushed at his question.

"No, Joe is our friend."

She followed as Togba led her through the village. He explained that Zigda was an ancient village, isolated in the mountains. Here people lived as they had for centuries. No tin roofs were allowed. Guns were prohibited. No English was spoken, he told her with the same broad smile that reminded her of Joe.

"I will make an exception while you and the young warrior are our guests. Those who know English may speak to you in English. I have already told the warriors that they may speak to your son."

They stopped outside the large hut where Joe's stretcher had been carried. Inside, Lindsey's eyes adjusted to the low light. Joe lay on his side on a grass mat. A clean white cloth had been wound tightly over his shoulder. Togba reached out and placed a misshapen fragment of metal into her open hand.

"The bullet that hit my son," he whispered. "That is why no guns are allowed in Zigda."

Lindsey knelt beside Joe. She felt his forehead. He still burned with fever.

"Joe? Joe, it's Lindsey. Do you hear me?" she said, leaning close to his ear.

He didn't respond. His breathing seemed regular, but he remained unconscious.

"May I have some cool water? It will help bring down the fever if we can wipe his body with damp cloths."

For the next five hours, she stayed beside Joe. It was late afternoon when she stood to leave. She had taught several of the women how to swab the feverish body with damp cloths. She had pressed sips of water to his cracked lips and had been able to get him to swallow a small amount. She stretched, stared down at her friend, and prayed that he would wake from his deep sleep.

"Come with me," said a voice to her left. It was Salamatu, Joe's mother. She beckoned for Lindsey to follow. She led her to the edge of the village where a narrow trail led into the bush.

"A woman's place," she said. Long, deep trenches were cut into the earth. This is where the women straddled the ditches to relieve themselves. Without a second thought, Lindsey used the primitive facility.

Farther down the trail, they crossed a clearing and finally came to a crystal clear pool, constantly replenished by a waterfall coming from a high cliff above it. Smooth, white sand lined the pool's perimeter. About a dozen women, young and old, bathed in the pristine water. Boys and girls, none older than five or six, splashed in the water or played quietly on the sandy banks.

"Bath," said Salamatu.

"Yes, bath," nodded Lindsey. God, how she needed a bath!

Salamatu handed her a bar of soap. Lindsey took off her clothes and stacked them neatly on a large rock. She looked up to see that the others were all staring at her. They had never seen a white woman, let alone a naked one. Lindsey smiled politely and took a step toward the pool.

Two women approached and reached out to touch her. She stood still, assuming these women were simply fascinated by her pale skin. But when their fingertips caressed the dark bruises on her arms and legs, she knew they wondered what had happened. Her belly and breasts also carried the deep, purple reminders of her attack. Her eyes met theirs, and she could see their concern for her pain. They care, she thought, touched by their compassion. Lindsey stepped into the pool and allowed the cool water to soothe her. She floated on her back, gazing upward through the branches to the pure blue of the sky.

After bathing, she found that her dirty clothes had been taken. In their place, she saw a woman's tunic made of soft cotton. Salamatu helped her wind the dark purple fabric around her body, fastening it in a deep fold between her breasts. She told Lindsey that the white woman's clothes would be washed, mended and returned to her later. Until then, she must rest and allow herself to heal. Obediently, she followed the older woman up the trail and back to the village. One bare foot followed the other as she gave herself over to Salamatu's care.

Later, lying on a thick mat of dried grasses in Salamatu's neat hut, sleep came slowly. Although exhausted, Lindsey's mind couldn't rest. She was safe – at least for now – but where was Hank? Would their lives ever be the same again?

# 17

***At the Myers' clinic in north central Liberia, Hank began to wake up. He was confused. He wasn't sure where he was or why he was lying in a hospital bed.***

ALTHOUGH HIS EYES WERE CLOSED, HE WAS AWARE OF A BRIGHT LIGHT. He made a fist and used his knuckles to rub his eyelids. Still his eyes seemed glued shut. He used his fingers to spread the lids until his eyes adjusted to the sunlight pouring in through the screened window near his bedside. He curled his lips to moisten his dry mouth. Finally he became aware of his surroundings.

An inverted bottle hung from an IV pole. Plastic tubing ran from the bottle to his arm. He was lying in a hospital bed. But where?

He ran his free hand through his hair and looked from side to side. Where was he? Then he remembered that he had eaten dinner with Frank and Karen Myers in a village called Sanniquellie. He was on a mission to meet up with Charles Morray. It was all coming back to him. But how had he ever ended up in a hospital?

He heard the sound of approaching footsteps. A black man dressed in hospital whites poked his head around the corner.

"Miss Karen! Miss Karen! He is awake!" the man shouted down the hallway. A moment later, Karen Myers stood beside his bed.

"Well, so you decided to join us, Colonel Martin."

"Colonel Martin?" rasped Hank. "How did you find out?"

"We looked through your wallet and found your diplomatic identity card. But, don't worry, we haven't told anyone. But we are curious to know what's going on."

Hank turned his head and tried to suppress a cough.

"I'm sorry," Karen said. "Let me get you some water."

She poured him a glass of water from a white plastic pitcher on the bedside table. She held it to Hank's lips as he sipped the warm water.

"How long have I been here?" Hank asked.

"Let's see," she replied. "You destroyed our bedroom the night before last. I would say it's been close to forty hours."

"Forty hours? What happened?"

"Why don't we let Frank fill you in on the details. Right now we need to get some broth in you and get you up on your feet."

By evening, Hank was up walking. He was still somewhat wobbly, but Frank had asked if he'd come up to the house. He dressed and slowly walked up the pathway to the house on the hill.

"Come in, Lieutenant Colonel Martin," Frank said.

Hank felt uneasy; he hadn't liked lying to the Myers.

"I'm sorry I wasn't honest with you," he said.

"Let's just go into the living room and talk," Frank said.

Frank got Hank a soft drink and they both settled into the soft chairs. Small talk finished, Frank leaned forward and spoke directly to Hank.

"First of all, in all my experience with post-traumatic stress syndrome, I've never seen anyone still on active duty subject to such violent lapses. Just how long have you had these symptoms?"

"Whatever are you talking about?" Hank asked.

"Are you telling me that you aren't being treated for post-traumatic wartime stress?"

"No, sir, I've never had a problem," Hank said.

"Well, something is certainly wrong. Two nights ago you went completely berserk. We woke up before midnight to the sound of breaking glass. It took five of us to hold you down before we could get a sedative in you. One orderly had his arm broken. Another got a bloody nose. After that, you were unconscious for a day and a half."

"No way," Hank said. "I can't believe I would have done that. Nothing like that has ever happened before."

"Have you had headaches?"

"No, no headaches."

"How about dreams or nightmares?"

Hank looked at the doctor. How could he know?

"Nightmares, yes," Hank said slowly.

"Tell me about them," Frank said.

"You'll think I'm going crazy," Hank said, shaking his head.

"To tell the truth, right now you are crazy. You could really hurt someone – including yourself. Look, I'm your doctor now, whether you like it or not. What we say here will not leave this room, but you'd be better off telling me what's happening."

Hank hesitated. This kind of thing was foreign to him.

"All right," he said. "I'll tell you the story, but I have to warn you that what I'm about to tell you could cost you your life if the wrong people found out about it."

Hank started at the beginning. He told Frank about how he had met Charles Morray in 1992. He told about witnessing the ritual murder in the sacred bush. He explained that he had been fine until the dream came back to him on the flight to Liberia. He described how the dream later changed to where his son, Tim, had become the victim.

He told Frank what had changed in the dreams. Now he recognized other members of the government. The original ones had aged through time. Then he related the horror of his recent dream – the presence of the attaché staff and their families. Then he told him about Carpai and Lindsey and Tim. By now, he was shaking and tears ran down his face. Frank reached over and put his hand on Hank's shoulder.

"Am I really crazy?" Hank asked.

"God, son, I wish it were that simple, but I don't think you are," Frank said. "I've lived in Liberia for thirty-five years. Things are different here. I believe that an evil force has touched your life."

"Impossible," said Hank.

"No, not impossible," Frank answered. "Karen and I have spent our lives spreading the gospel of Jesus Christ. We truly believe that Jesus is our savior, but you recall that Satan tempted Christ. In the book of Matthew, chapter eight, verse fourteen, Jesus drove out the evil spirits from men who were demon-possessed."

Hank relaxed as Frank continued to soothe his fears.

"Karen and I were so naive when we came here to Sanniquellie. We tried to convince the people that evil spirits didn't really exist. Their powerful *zoes* couldn't heal them nor change their lives. That approach didn't work. Few people came to the clinic. Those who came wearing country medicine in pouches around their necks were treated, but I would try to destroy their folk medicine. Yet we were unable to reach the people.

"Finally I took my concerns to God. I felt I needed to work out a compromise with their healers. I praised those who came with country medicine. I even referred an occasional patient to a *zo*.

"One day an old man came to the clinic wanting to know more about Jesus. I had learned enough of the language to understand him. We met regularly. Weeks later I learned that he was one of the most powerful *zoes* in Nimba County. Over the years, he and I have learned from each other."

"OK, I'll buy that, but tell me how these evil spirits can affect me," Hank said.

"About ten years ago," Frank said quietly, "someone dropped off an old tribal mask. I hung it right here in the living room. Each morning the mask would be lying on the floor. I decided to get up in the middle of the night to see what was happening. The mask was already on the floor. I picked it up. As soon as I did, the room became cold – so cold that I could see the condensation of my own breath. When I touched the wooden face, I felt I was no longer in my own home, but in a strange and terrifying place. My soul was being pulled from my very body. I didn't know what to do but to recite the Lord's Prayer. I repeated it over and over. Before long, I was back in this room. In the morning, I burned the mask."

"Are you saying that what I am experiencing may be based in reality?"

"Yes," said Frank. "At least part of what you have seen is real."

"That means something might have happened to my wife and son," Hank said, anxious for their safety. "I have to get back to Monrovia immediately."

"Yes, son, I'd say you do, but first you need to speak with Charles Morray."

"I don't have time to wait for him," Hank said, already getting to his feet.

"You don't need to wait long," Frank said. "Morray will be here in five minutes."

"Five minutes? How did you ever arrange that?"

"Well, son, now I have to be honest with you. You see, I've known Charles Morray for years. You might be surprised to learn that Karen and I are godparents to his children."

In five minutes, just like Frank had promised, they heard a knock at the door. Three men, two dressed in para-military uniforms and carrying Uzis, came into the room. The third wore a tie-dyed shirt, slacks and open sandals. Frank hugged him as a father would hug his son.

"Colonel Martin, may I introduce Charles Morray," said Frank. "I believe you two have met before."

"It's been a long time," said Hank, reaching out to shake hands. Morray was of medium build with closely cropped hair. His features reflected the proud heritage of members of the Kruman tribe. He had changed over the years. Hank would never have recognized this man as the young Private Morray from Camp Jackson.

"About seventeen years, to be exact," said Morray.

But Morray, like Hank, didn't have time for reminiscing.

"I do wish we could chat about our past adventures," Morray said in impeccable English, "but, unfortunately, we do not have that luxury. Dr. Frank has told me that you are here in an official capacity."

"Yes," Hank said, "we are hoping that you can work with us to stabilize the situation between the People's Party and the Liberian government."

"I'm afraid that's impossible, Colonel Martin," said Morray. "Dr. Frank, didn't you tell him?"

"No, Charles, I thought you should be here for that."

"What the hell is going on?" demanded Hank.

Morray asked if they could all sit down.

"Two days ago in Monrovia, terrorists attacked American families in Mamba Bluff," he began. Hank felt his stomach tighten. He held his breath as he listened to Morray talk.

"No names have been released, but the government radio says that at least eighteen people were killed. We've heard on CNN radio that your President will stop at nothing to bring the terrorists to justice. In Liberia, martial law has been declared. President Dowling claims he has evidence that it was members of the People's Party who were responsible. They say that Lieutenant Colonel Joe Weah is involved and that he is personally responsible for the deaths of several people."

"Joe Weah?" Hank asked. "Impossible!"

"The government is offering a reward of fifty thousand dollars for his capture and arrest."

"I have to get back to Monrovia – now!" Hank said, getting to his feet.

"General Martin, please listen," Morray insisted. "You need to know that I would never have ordered an attack on the Americans. No matter what the government is saying, my people are not involved."

"I believe you," Hank said. "Is there any way you can get me safe passage out of the territory?"

"Yes, but you'll not be able to get into Monrovia until daylight. The government has imposed a dusk-to-dawn curfew."

Hank had no choice but to wait.

Once again Hank sat in the Liberian Mining Company truck. He was on the outskirts of Monrovia, waiting for sunrise. He had parked next to a power pole. On it was stapled a poster with Joe Weah's picture and details of the reward for his capture.

The waiting gave him time to think – too much time. Lindsey and Tim might be dead. After all, he had seen them as prisoners in his nightmare. All this business about evil spirits was too bizarre. His job had taught him to deal with reality, not the supernatural. His encounter with that evil seventeen years earlier had never quite left him, but he had struggled to bury the incident deep in his subconscious.

Reality, to a soldier like Hank, was a full-metal jacketed bullet fired at twenty-six hundred feet per second. Now this concept that reality consisted of two sides – the spiritual as well as the material – made life much more complicated. Could it be true that he could see into the future? Were his dreams predictions of what had already happened or what would soon happen? If a man like Frank believed that some sort of demon had existed since the beginning of time, perhaps it was true.

Rays of sunlight finally broke over the top of the hill. Hank turned on the ignition and pulled out onto the road. As he entered the city, he saw groups of soldiers posted at several intersections. Even so, he saw shopkeepers set up their goods and people begin to fill the streets. It looked like business as usual for Monrovia.

Even the tree-lined streets of Mamba Bluff had a sense of serenity. The yellow crime scene tape across the gate at the Chambers' house was his first clue that all wasn't right. He accelerated, turning in the direction of his own home.

Before he had left Sanniquellie, Frank asked that they take a moment for prayer. At first, Hank felt awkward standing there holding hands with Frank and Charles Morray. They bowed their heads as Frank's soft words offered comfort.

But surprisingly, Hank had felt a sense of peace. His tension lifted. Now, so near their home, he prayed again. He prayed that he would find his wife and son safe at home.

"Oh, God, no!" he said aloud when he rounded the corner to his own address. There was simply nothing left. Blackened timbers were piled haphazardly. Nothing recognizable remained. At his gate, he saw the same yellow tape, running across the drive. He lowered his head against the steering wheel, then slowly turned the truck around and headed toward the embassy.

Liberian soldiers guarded every gate along Embassy Row. Two armored personnel carriers and a tank sat at the main entrance to the U.S. embassy. He pulled up to the inspection point and pulled out his diplomatic identity card. A soldier waved him ahead. When he reached the gate, a Marine came to the truck door and saluted.

"Colonel Martin, everyone has been looking for you," he said.

"I've been out of town," Hank answered.

"Sir?"

"Yes?" Hank.

"I'm really sorry about your family."

So this was it, Hank thought. He nodded, "Thank you, private."

He drove slowly up to the main building. His limbs felt weak. He opened the door and his boots touched the pavement. Each step was slow, as if he were wading in hip-high water. He concentrated on controlling his breathing. He warned himself not to hyperventilate.

In the front office, the ambassador's secretary saw him come in the door.

"Hank? Thank God, you're OK!" she said, pushing the intercom button on her desk. "Ambassador Johnson, Hank Martin just came in."

Hank walked around the secretary's desk and went straight to Vicki's door. She stood at her desk, her eyes ringed with dark circles.

"Oh, Hank, where have you been?" she asked.

"They're dead, aren't they?" he asked. Vicki hesitated, looking first down at the pile of papers on the desk, then straight at Hank.

"Yes, Hank," she answered. "We found the bodies the day before yesterday. They found all three – the bodies of Lindsey, Tim and the dog. They were burned beyond recognition."

She moved around her desk and reached out to Hank. "I'm so sorry, so very sorry," she said, taking him in her arms.

It was Vicki who cried like a small child.

Tears streamed silently down Hank's cheeks. His world had just come to an end.

# 18

***Soldiers had been seen on the trail to Zigda. Lindsey had heard the drums, but it had meant nothing to her. Then Tim had run up to her, telling her that his new friends had translated the drum message. She dropped the cloth that she had been using to cool Joe's body and ran to find Togba. She found him sitting on a low stool in the main square.***

"TOGBA, SOLDIERS ARE COMING. WE MUST HIDE YOUR SON!"

His dark eyes looked steadily into hers.

"They cannot enter Zigda," he said.

"You don't understand," Lindsey pleaded. "They have guns. You only have spears."

Togba laughed at her words.

"We have more than spears. The *Nangma* has sealed the village. No one may enter or leave Zigda. Anyone who tries will die."

"That is the spirit of the crocodile?" asked Lindsey.

"So you know of the Poro spirits?" Togba asked.

"I've heard of them."

"Then you should know the great power of the Poro. No man can enter Zigda."

The chief's confidence did little to ease Lindsey's fears. She realized that he didn't intend to defend the town. She turned to find Tim. They would have to find a place to hide.

Major Oscar Jalah strolled confidently along the bush trail. Minister Carpai would surely offer a fine reward when he killed Weah and brought back the woman and the boy. It had only been logical that Weah would try to hide out in his village. Jalah and forty soldiers marched forward to finish the job.

They had crossed the damaged bridge and found Weah's Hummer parked nearby in a clearing. A pool of dried blood on the back seat indicated that one of the three had been hurt. The stupid fools had even left their guns and ammo in the vehicle. This would be easy, not unlike tracking a wounded animal.

Several men had been sent ahead to scout the trail. One of them returned, out of breath.

"What is it?" Jalah asked.

"Bad juju, major. The Poro have blocked the road."

"What do you mean? Could it be bush school business?"

"No. No, it is the sign of the great *Nangma*. We cannot pass."

"Let me see for myself," growled Jalah.

He walked ahead with the men until they reached a raffia wall that blocked the trail. In front of the wall, they saw a human skull stuck on a stick. Beyond the wall, they could see the body of a goat, impaled on a stick. It appeared the animal had been alive when its body had been pierced. It sat in a pool of its own blood. Jalah swore. He would not be stopped from completing his task.

"Captain, they are just trying to scare us," he reassured the man. "Raffia and a dead goat cannot stop the Armed Forces of Liberia. Look, I will show you."

Jalah walked past the skull, parted the raffia curtain and came to a stop by the fly-covered goat.

"See," he boasted. "There is nothing to fear."

He laughed, and his soldiers laughed along with him. Jalah grinned; he had won them over.

Just as he turned to continue down the trail, the sky darkened. A mist began to encircle his feet. He could feel the coldness in the air. His breath condensed in front of his face.

No longer could he see the trail. Instead, he saw strange, bright-eyed creatures lining a pathway that led to the entrance of a dark tunnel. He heard his own screams as he turned to run.

Back in the warmth of the sunlight, his soldiers held him until the screams subsided.

"Sir, what happened?" asked the captain. Jalah couldn't speak. He gasped for breath. Ashamed, he looked down to see his own urine running down his leg.

"We cannot enter," he said firmly. "We must go back and report our findings to Minister Carpai. Until Weah and the Martins leave Zigda, there is nothing we can do."

Everyday Walker gained a new respect for the ravages of time as he left the city. He remembered how he had once been able to walk twenty miles in a single day and not be tired. He could have gone the one hundred eighty miles in nine days at his steady pace. If he had pushed himself, he could do it in six. Now, even with two rides on the money bus, he had gone only one hundred seventy miles.

It had been four hours since he had gotten off the last money bus. The sun seemed hotter than he ever remembered. It beat down unmercifully on his stooped body. One step followed the other, slow and steady.

Ahead he saw five army trucks alongside the road. Two soldiers leaned against the front fender of the lead vehicle. They ignored the old man when he passed.

When he came to the broken bridge over the river, he knew why the trucks had not crossed. The planks had collapsed, making the bridge only safe for foot traffic. The old man picked his way cautiously over the rotting timbers. He wondered where the other soldiers had gone.

Soon he came to the Hummer, abandoned in the middle of the road. Another fifty feet ahead, he saw where the road ended and the trail began. He paused by the vehicle, his attention focused on the windshield.

The night before, while he had been dream walking, he had crouched on the hood of this very vehicle. He had seen Missy and the boy. She had looked deeply into his eyes. He watched her fears fade away. She was no longer afraid of this creature. She was certain that a dream spirit had possessed it. It would not harm her nor her son.

Deep into the forest, he found it easier to walk along the cooler trail. He increased his pace. When he heard voices, he slipped quietly into the underbrush. A few minutes later, a large group of soldiers passed by his hiding spot. Their nervous chatter told him that they were afraid. After they were gone, Everyday Walker stepped back onto the trail. Nearly a half hour later, he realized why the soldiers were frightened. He had reached the raffia barrier. The soldiers had met the great *Nangma*.

He drew close to the human skull. He opened his knapsack and placed several items in neat piles. Then he took off his clothes. He fastened a leopard hide loincloth around his waist. He drank the dark liquid from a small brown bottle, grimacing as the foul elixir ran down his throat. He would need to take in the antidote for the poison before he continued his journey. He folded his clothes and put them in his sack. Besides the loincloth, his only other garment was a leopard tooth necklace that dangled from a cord against his bony chest.

He parted the raffia and passed by the goat's body. Now Everyday Walker had once again become Chea Geebe, the great *zo* who had once triumphed over the *endosym*. It would not be long until he once again would do battle.

The trail on this side of the barrier looked no different from the trail before it. Suddenly, he felt a prick in his thigh. He reached down and pulled out a dart that had been lodged in his flesh.

Although the Poro believed that the spirit of the *Nangma* would keep out anyone who dared enter the sacred bush, there was a back-up plan. Men hid in the bush armed with blowguns and poison darts. Their victims would die a painful death. But Everyday Walker was unconcerned.

The antidote would protect him. He kept on walking.

The next challenge would be even greater. He would have to call on the spirit of the leopard for protection. Ahead, lay the next ambush where warriors waited with spears. He sat down in the middle of the trail and began to chant in the ancient tongue. A few minutes later, he stood, stretched and moved on down the trail.

Gola Kulua alerted the others. An intruder approached. They crouched down, ready to attack. Gola couldn't understand why the stranger continued to advance. Usually the poison worked sooner. He wasn't concerned; the spears would stop the man.

An old man came around the corner. A stupid, old man, thought Gola. He would die for violating the warning. He watched him come along the trail. He had crystal-white hair and a bald spot on top of his head. The man wore only a loincloth. He carried no weapon. Gola felt a fleeting sadness that this man who had lived so many years would soon die. He raised his spear in readiness.

The man had vanished. In his place a large leopard lumbered down the trail. It looked directly at Gola and issued a warning snarl. Gola saw such malevolence that his legs weakened. He trembled, yet the leopard casually walked past his hiding place.

He peeked out again once the beast had passed, but saw only the thin backside of the old man disappear around a bend in the trail.

"What did you see?" Gola said to a man near him.

"A great leopard," he answered. The others had all seen the same thing. Gola turned to the drummer.

"Send the word that a powerful *zo* is coming to Zigda!"

The drumbeat sounded the message. On a distant hill, another drummer relayed the warning. A powerful *zo* was on his way.

Lindsey saw the jubilation of the people when they learned that the soldiers had turned back. She hadn't believed that superstition alone would keep them safe.

As the drumbeat increased, her heart began racing again. Perhaps they hadn't retreated after all. She paused to listen. Togba entered the hut where she had been bathing Joe.

"Are the soldiers coming?" she asked.

"No," Togba said with a smile. "The drums say that a powerful *zo* is coming to Zigda. He will help our *zoes* drive out the spirit that keeps Nah Weah in his deep sleep."

Lindsey nodded, still unconvinced. The day had gotten even stranger.

Not long afterward, the people gathered along the trail, awaiting the arrival of the great *zo*. Lindsey and Tim stood to the rear of the crowd near the top of the hill.

"Mom, what do you think this *zo* will look like?" wondered Tim.

"I have no idea, Tim. The *zo*es who have tended Joe are just a bunch of old men."

The crowd fell into a hush as Togba raised his arm. Even the goats and the chickens quieted. Lindsey could see the brush move near the top of the hill. Everyone fell to his or her knees.

"I guess we'd better kneel too," Lindsey said.

"This is just like they do for the Queen of England," Tim whispered.

But moments later, Tim was once again on his feet.

"Look, Mom!" he shouted. "It's Everyday Walker!"

Tim began to break through the crowd. Lindsey reached out to stop him, but she moved too late. Tim was already running up the trail. She feared for his life. Instinctively, she moved forward. She saw the figure rush toward him.

"Oh, please, God, don't let my son die!" she prayed.

The two met in the middle of the road. They wrapped their arms around each other. Lindsey stifled a scream when she saw the white hair around the man's bald spot. It was Everyday Walker! Impossible, she thought. She looked around her. She was the only one besides Togba standing in the kneeling crowd.

"The young warrior knows the *zo*?" asked Togba Weah.

"Yes," answered Lindsey. "They are good friends."

"Then you and the young warrior must be present tonight when the Great *zo* drives the bad spirit from my son. Tonight the great *Nangma* will cleanse the village of evil spirits and the *zo* will release the spirit that holds Nah Weah in the sleep world," he said.

As they walked back into the village, many averted their eyes as they passed Tim and Chea Geebe. They gave them wide berth as befitting such important beings.

Later, Tim sat cross-legged outside the hut, wolfing down his large wooden bowlful of country chop. In the three days they'd been in the village, he'd gone from picking through the strange contents to relishing each spoonful.

"How resilient teenagers are," thought Lindsey.

Tim had adapted quickly to village life. He had picked up even more words in Kapel. He told her that he had been asked to go on a hunt the next day with the young warriors. He explained that as long has they were visitors in the village, he had an obligation to help feed its people. He had seemed so happy about going that she hadn't told him not to go.

"Mom, Everyday Walker.... I mean, Chea Geebe, will wake Joe up. Soon he will be well enough for us to get help and find Dad," he said confidently.

"Honey, let's not get our hopes up too high. He is an old man."

She wanted to prepare Tim for possible failure. After all, Joe's condition hadn't changed. He still was deep in a coma. Everything she knew told her that Joe needed to be in a hospital, not on the floor of a jungle hut being tended to by a former embassy guard in his eighties who barely spoke English. A magic wand couldn't make Joe well again.

"Chea said that he knew we were in Zigda," Tim told her. "He said that he saw us in a dream while he sat in our yard. He said that our house had been burned to the ground."

"Yes, Tim," she said, indulging him. How easy it was for a teenager to accept such an unbelievable story.

"He said that last night he paid us a visit in the body of a leopard," Tim continued.

Lindsey couldn't believe what Tim was saying.

"Say that again," she said.

"Chea said that he has the power to take over the body of an animal. He can see through that animal's eyes. He said he entered the body of a great leopard. He found us in the Hummer. He told me that he sat on the hood of the Hummer and looked in the window. You were awake, but I was asleep. He said he smiled at you. Was that true, Mom?" Tim asked.

Lindsey could do no more than stare at her son. She hadn't told anyone about the leopard. There was no way that Everyday Walker could know about the leopard unless the story was true.

"I guess maybe I did see something last night, but I don't remember. I was too sleepy," she sighed.

She didn't want to encourage Tim, but her evaluation of the old man had changed. Maybe there was something to this *zo* thing after all.

She would know soon. It was already dusk. Togba had told her that someone would come for them before the devil danced. All others must remain inside their huts until morning.

"Bak, Bak," they heard someone say. Tim rose at the greeting and went to the entrance.

"Mom, it's time to go," he said. It was totally dark on the moonless night, yet she could still see the silhouettes of the nearby huts. They were deep in the mountains, a hundred miles from electric lights. She had never seen the stars so bright. She craned her neck to see the Milky Way, a silver band stretching across the sky. A man tapped her arm, indicating that they must follow him to the hut where Joe had been taken.

Inside, a single kerosene lantern hung from a center post. In the corner, Lindsey saw only Joe's mother and two sisters. He led Lindsey and Tim over to them and pointed to the ground, indicating that they must sit. He said something to Tim in Kapel.

"What did he say?" asked Lindsey.

"He said that no one must leave the spot where they now sit until the drums stop beating. Anyone who dares move will die. Once the drums begin, no one may speak or it will anger the spirits. It is also forbidden to look at the great *Nangma*. Anyone who does will die a horrible death."

"God, was he serious?" asked Lindsey.

"Yes, Mom, very serious. We'd better not talk anymore," he warned.

Joe lay totally naked before them. Lindsey felt no embarrassment. For the past three days she had spent most of her waking hours caring for him. Now he was lying there alone. Even in the low glow from the lantern, she could see that he had lost muscle and weight. His body was being consumed from within by infection. If he weren't treated soon, he would surely die.

It seemed impossible that three days had passed so quickly. The two of them were trapped. They couldn't leave. There was no communication into or out of Zigda. Just a short time ago she had been an army wife – planning meals, attending meetings, and arranging for the next soccer game. Then she was running for her life and immersed in a totally alien culture. She bowed her head.

"God, I know I don't talk to you like I should, but tonight I ask that you heal Joe Weah. He is a good man who doesn't deserve to die. Watch over Tim and Hank and grant me the strength to be there for each of them. Amen," she prayed.

When she looked up, she noticed that the door of the hut had been left open. She thought for a moment about getting up to close the gaping hole, but then she remembered the admonition not to move.

The three other women looked terrified, but Tim smiled with confidence. It must be difficult for him to sit still for so long, she thought. She closed her eyes, listening to the chirp of crickets and the steady croak of frogs.

Suddenly, there was no noise at all. It seemed to her as if someone had come in and turned off a radio. The only sound she heard was her own breathing. The open door continued to concern her. It was unusual to leave it wide open. Again, she heard her own heartbeat. Then she realized it was not her heart at all, but the distant beat of drums. It became louder. It was then coupled with shrieks and cries of something not quite human. She shivered, although she wasn't cold. The sound of drums and cries continued. Time moved slowly, much more slowly than before. First, the sounds came from one side, and then shifted to the other. Soon she became accustomed to them, and her mind began to wander.

Her musing came to an abrupt end as the drums became louder. A high decibel scream came from the darkness outside the doorway. She imagined a man in costume at the door. A drummer would be beside him. But she remembered the warning not to look. Instead, she shifted her gaze to Joe's family. The women had stretched face down on the hut's dirt floor. She glanced at Tim. She lifted her finger and pointed at her eyes, closed them and then bowed her head as if in prayer. She peeked at Tim. He nodded and closed his eyes tightly.

"Let this be over with soon," she prayed.

She shivered again, but this time from the cold. It felt like she was sitting in a freezer. The abrupt chill caused her to gasp. She opened her eyes a crack. A cold mist had settled near the ground around them. She sensed a presence in the hut. It seemed to move and flow to every corner. It covered her body. It felt wet and cool. It felt dead. She wanted to scream or run away. Then, just as suddenly as it had come, it withdrew.

The hut became warm once again. She lifted the lid of one eye only. She saw three old men standing beside Joe. Their naked bodies were covered with a white dust. It was a scene from the beginning of time, she thought. They knelt beside Joe and began to chant. One painted a white stripe from Joe's forehead, down his chest, over his stomach and to his groin. A second man removed a necklace – a leather cord with what looked like a large tooth. He set the tooth on Joe's forehead.

A green glow started to spread from the tooth across Joe's face. It continued until it had basked the entire body in the green light. Lindsey couldn't believe what happened next. Joe's body began to fade away until it vanished entirely. The mat and the green glow remained, but Joe had disappeared. Then, just as suddenly, Joe was again on the mat and the green light had vanished.

Lindsey stared at the men. No longer did she peek from half-open eyes. Now she stared straight ahead with her eyes wide open. When the old man reached for the tooth, he looked directly at her. She held her breath. She had violated a taboo. She feared for her life. She looked directly at the man. Then he winked at her.

It was Everyday Walker.

Without uttering a word, the three men left the hut. Lindsey didn't move. A cricket chirped. Then she heard another. The frogs began to croak again. Someone coughed then coughed again.

"Water. Water," she heard someone say. It took her a moment to realize that she had heard Joe speak.

"Oh, my God!" she exclaimed. "He's awake! Quick, bring some water!"

She couldn't control her own tears. She knelt beside Joe, amazed at his recovery.

"Thank you, God! Thank you for bringing us Everyday Walker!"

# 19

***Back on U.S. soil, a small crowd had gathered at Dover Air Force Base.***

CNN World News, First Watch – The President's limo has just pulled up to the aircraft. The President and the First Lady will accompany the caskets as they are taken to the hangar where the families are waiting. Lieutenant Colonel William H. Martin has just shaken hands with the President. Colonel Martin accompanied the bodies of the slain Americans. Sadly, those bodies include Colonel Martin's own wife and son. Martin escaped the attack because he was on assignment in Upper Volta.

In so many ways, this is truly an American tragedy, so reminiscent of the September 11 attacks. In this incident, a number of children also died, including an infant only six months old. Sources say that even the children were shot execution-style.

The entire nation is saddened and outraged at this vicious attack.

Now we can see the tail ramp of the C-17 being lowered. The contingent of pallbearers, made up of members from all branches of the military, will carry the caskets inside the hangar for a private memorial service. The Air Force band is in place.

"This is Zac Wingdale reporting live."

Afterwards, Hank tried to remember what happened at the service. He could recall walking alongside the President from the plane into the hangar. The President and his wife had moved from family to family, expressing their condolences. He shook hands, embraced them, stopped to listen, and relayed the sympathies from a grateful nation.

Finally, the two had reached Hank's family. Suddenly his parents seemed older, more fragile. Likewise, Lindsey's father and mother, Virgil and Susan, who had once been so strong and vital, seemed also to have aged. They all huddled together, each consumed by a private sorrow, yet united in their love and concern.

After the service, the families were quartered in guest lodging. The military had generously extended every courtesy possible to the mourners. As soon as the mortuary staff completed its examination, each set of remains would be dispersed to different hometowns throughout the nation. Lindsey and Tim would be buried next to Lindsey's grandparents at Riverside Cemetery in Spokane, Washington.

Maybe it was pure fatigue. Maybe it was the fact that Hank no longer had to shoulder his sorrow alone, but for the first time in days, Hank slept solidly through the night. When he awoke, American sunlight streamed through his window. He felt somehow at peace. Although he was more rested, he felt strangely vexed. He had dreamed of his wife and son. They had still been in Africa. Green mountains, a waterfall, and neatly tilled fields surrounded a cluster of huts. Even more bizarre, he dreamed of Everyday Walker's white hair, broad grin and twinkling eyes.

He got up and took a long, hot shower. He had just pulled on his pants and was buttoning his shirt when he heard a soft rapping at his hotel door.

"Dad!" Hank said when he opened the door. "Come on in."

Hank had been surprised to see his father standing alone outside his door. He stepped inside and laid his arm on Hank's shoulder.

"Hank," he said haltingly, "your mom and Lindsey's folks wondered if you'd like to visit the chapel with us."

Hank hung his head. This was yet another hurdle.

"Sure, Dad," he said.

The days had run together. He realized that it must be Sunday already. Hank's dad stared at the toes of his shoes.

"Hank," he said.

"Yes, Dad."

"Son, I've never been very good at expressing my feelings. I don't know why. But, I just love you so much I thought it didn't need to be said." He took a deep breath before continuing. "I just always wanted the best for you. Lindsey... and Tim... They were so special," he sobbed. "Hank, I just want you to know how much I hurt and cry for your loss."

The dam that had held back the tears finally broke. Hank and his father held each other close, each man openly consumed by wrenching sobs.

"Dad, I loved them so very much. I don't know what I will do. Sometimes I just want to die. Oh, God, why did this ever have to happen?"

Neither answered the question. There was no answer. They pulled themselves together. Hank's dad wiped away his tears with his weathered knuckle.

"Come on, Hank. We've got to get ready for church. We will need all our strength."

"I know," said Hank.

"Dad?"

"Yes, son."

"I love you, Dad," Hank said.

Since the bodies had been brought in, the staff had worked straight through the night to complete the examinations and prepare the bodies for burial. Seals were broken on the aluminum caskets. Each neoprene body bag had been opened, and the remains placed on the stainless steel tables.

To most people, the naked, often mutilated, dismembered, burned or partially decomposed bodies of the dead would result in nightmares. But for Dr. Alex Robinson it was just the opposite. He had become a forensic pathologist because it offered him the chance to practice a form of medicine far less traumatic than dealing with the problems of the living.

These bodies, the subject of headline news, hadn't been difficult to autopsy. Robinson had spent days of laborious work following the September 11, 2001 terror attack. In those cases, he had seen many sets of remains that were crushed or burned beyond recognition. Recovery crews had collected bits and pieces of human flesh. The staff had to determine the identity of each piece. After weeks of work, they ended up with a pile of flesh that couldn't be identified. Those remains had been cremated. A small portion of the ashes had been placed in bags to be buried with each incomplete, but partially identified, body.

As for this shipment from Africa, only two human bodies were yet to be examined. The first sixteen had been victims of bullet wounds. The morticians would have no problem preparing those cadavers.

The three burned corpses were another story. They had each been placed on the stainless steel tables. A lab assistant had opened the bag that contained what was left of the dog. Robinson's primary assistant, Dr. Roger Voss, began to make notes on his clipboard. He noted the body weight and condition before he began his dissection. A nine-millimeter bullet had been embedded in the dog's hip. Another round had passed through both lungs. He made his notations, set aside his paperwork and moved to Robinson's side.

Robinson hadn't yet decided where to begin on the two sets of human remains. Each had been more severely burned than even the dog, although the report indicated that all three bodies had been recovered from what had been the kitchen. He wasn't even sure which one was the male and which was the female. Fortunately, he had medical and dental records on each. Both had undergone thorough physical exams less than six months earlier. Both were taller than average. The female had been five feet ten inches tall; the male, six feet one inch.

Measurement alone would take some time. The feet had been destroyed. The bodies had curled inward as the muscles and fat were scorched from the outside. The best identification would come from the teeth, which remained intact inside the blackened skulls.

"Roger, how about you take that one. I'll take the other," Robinson decided. "Let's find out who's the boy and who's the girl."

Robinson reached for his scalpel. He cut the backs of the legs and pried them apart to determine the gender. Even in an intense fire, the genitals were often spared from total destruction.

Only moments later, Robinson stepped back and called to his assistant. "I've got the male here."

"Wait a minute," Voss answered. "Mine's a male, too."

"Impossible! We're supposed to have one of each," Robinson said. "Well, let's take them apart and see what we can learn about these folks."

The two worked side by side for the next two hours to complete the autopsy. Back at his desk, Robinson tamped the pages of the report on his desk before stapling them together. He thumbed through the data again.

Both were male. No doubt about that. Bone measurements indicated heights between five feet six inches and five feet eight inches. Joints indicated no recent growth. Obviously, both were adults. Both sets of teeth indicated no modern dental work. They'd found evidence of kerosene on the bodies, which intensified the damage to the flesh. One had died of multiple gunshots to the chest. The other had a single wound to the spine, likely not serious enough to have been fatal. Robinson concluded that this victim might have been burned alive. He placed his reports in manila folders and turned to Voss.

"Roger, see if you can find out if Lieutenant Colonel Martin is still on base. I need to talk to him," said Robinson.

Hank dreaded the intense emotion he knew he'd have to face at the church. Once again he would be vulnerable, his composure put to the test. He saw many of the same faces that had been at the memorial service. Families of other victims also sought solace through their faith. The army chaplain's words brought a sense of calm. It made Hank recall that moment of prayer with Frank Myers and Charles Morray back in Africa. Finally, he felt some hope for the future. Strange, he thought, how experiencing the depths of despair could lead to a sense of renewal.

Afterwards, the family walked down the concrete sidewalk to the rental car. Hank jingled the car keys in his pants pocket, getting ready to unlock the car.

"Lieutenant Colonel Martin?" someone said. A trim, middle-aged officer approached.

"Yes? May I help you, sir?" Hank answered.

"Let me introduce myself," the officer said. "I'm Dr. Alex Robinson. I know this is an awkward time, but I'd like to speak with you in private as soon as possible."

"Sure," Hank said, excusing himself from the family. He walked with Robinson to the blue Air Force sedan parked in the same lot. After the two got in the vehicle, Robinson reached into the back for a black briefcase. He took out two file folders and handed them to Hank.

"Colonel, these are the copies of the autopsies we did on your wife and son."

Hank looked at the man and hesitated. Why would he give him something so hurtful as the medical reports? He was about to refuse, but something in the man's demeanor caused him to pause. He opened the first folder and scanned the dark print. He opened the second and read it quickly.

"Is this some kind of a sick joke, Colonel?" Hank asked, suppressing his rising anger.

"Not at all," Robinson answered. "That's what we found."

"But I don't understand," Hank persisted.

"This says that we have the bodies of two adult males. The DNA tests won't be back for another two weeks, but I'm betting that these cadavers aren't Caucasian."

"Good God!" Hank gasped. "Then who the hell are they?"

"Colonel Martin, there's no way I can tell you that," Robinson said. "All I know is that the bodies recovered from the fire in your house are definitely not those of your wife and son. I have no idea where they really are. We only know that they are missing."

Hank had heard the man's words, but he froze in place, unable to react. He covered his eyes with his hands before running his fingers back through his hair. He shook his head in disbelief. What could he say?

He reached for the door handle and stepped out of the car. Robinson got out, too, and the two men stood silently behind the car. Robinson waited to see how Hank would respond.

"Thank you for the information, sir," Hank said, calmly reaching out to shake Robinson's hand.

"You're welcome," Robinson said. "I hope you find your wife and son."

"I will find them," Hank vowed, "or die trying."

Later, Hank broke the news to Lindsey's parents.

"Do you really think they could still be alive?" asked Lindsey's mother as the family waited for breakfast to be served.

"We don't want to stir up false hope," said Hank's father. "What are you going to do?"

"I need to get back to Liberia," Hank said. "I'll be on the Wednesday night flight out of JFK. Meanwhile, we'll postpone any funeral service. We'll tell everyone we're waiting for the DNA identification. I'm already on emergency leave. I'll stay on leave while I search for Lindsey and Tim. Right now, I have three days to go over the intelligence files and get together some things I'll need in Africa."

Hank reached out for his coffee mug, but then pulled back his hand. He looked around at the other people who loved Lindsey and Tim.

"Hope," he said aloud. "At least we have hope."

# 20

*John's Bar on Fayetteville, North Carolina's Hay Street catered to the military crowd. Over the bar hung a bigger-than-life size photo of John Wayne in his colonel's uniform from the movie* The Green Berets. *The walls were lined with photos of actual Green Berets. The place looked like a quasi-museum of the Vietnam era. War relics included a bullet-riddled Viet Cong flag.*

IT WAS STILL EARLY, JUST PUSHING FIVE O'CLOCK. HANK AND HIS FATHER HAD been on the road for almost five hours. The older man had seen his share of bars, but his career in the Corps of Engineers hadn't really prepared him for this one.

Two gnarled men, likely in their late fifties, leaned against the bar. They continued their small talk, not even bothering to look up when the two Martins came up behind them.

The bartender was a real piece of work. The burly guy stood at least six and a half feet tall. His polished head towered far above most of his customers. He'd lost his eyelashes, which made his eyes appear too small for his wide face. His upper arms, thicker than most men's legs, bulged out of the sleeves of his taut t-shirt. His gut hung out over the top of his belt. Hank's dad was impressed – clearly, no one would mess with this one tough dude.

"Green Berets are pussies. Rangers lead the way!" Hank's dad had heard someone shout. The brazen talk made him freeze in place. His own son had issued the threatening words.

The two men at the bar turned around slowly. The massive barkeeper growled, "Who the fuck do you think you are?" He whipped around the corner of the bar. His ham-sized fists doubled up in readiness.

"Son, what are you doing?"

Hank grinned broadly, ignored his father, and moved directly toward the frowning hulk.

"Hank! Stop! Let's get out of here!"

They were too late. The bartender had grabbed Hank, lifting him off the floor as if he were a child.

"Lieutenant Colonel Martin," the bartender chuckled, "you son of a bitch! You're the only man with the balls to say that kind of shit in this place!" He reached out and held Hank in a vice-like grip. Then his voice softened. "God, sir, I was so sorry to hear about what happened to your family."

"Tiny, that's why I'm here. Everything is not what it seems," Hank explained. Then he remembered that he hadn't come in alone. He turned to his father.

"Oh, gee, I'm sorry, Dad," Hank said. "Let me introduce you to Command Sergeant Major Retired Wilber G. Sprague."

Hank's father had frozen in place. Things were moving much too swiftly. The big man reached out to shake his hand.

"Sir, it's a pleasure to meet you. Just call me Tiny."

"Dad, Tiny was my senior non-commissioned officer when I commanded my first 'A' Team."

"Larry, take over here," Tiny said to a man at the end of the bar. "These two men and I have some talking to do. By the way, bring us three beers."

Tiny led them to a dark booth in the rear. "OK, sir, fess up. What's happening?"

For the next two hours, Hank told the two of them everything that had happened since he had witnessed the ritual murder in Liberia in 1992. He told them of his recurring dreams and about how he met Charles Morray and Frank Myers in Sanniquellie. He also talked about what he had discovered when he went through the files at the Defense Intelligence Agency.

"I know that what I have just told you might sound completely crazy, but I have a gut feeling that everything I saw in those dreams has at least a thread of truth. I know for a fact that Julius Carpai is a part of this whole thing. The reports that President Dowling's chief of security has been killed lead me to believe that some kind of government plot exists at the highest level. Then there's this story that Joe Weah was involved with the terrorist attack. I just don't buy it. Finally, after meeting with Charles Morray last week, I have to believe him when he says that he and the People's Party are not involved."

Tiny frowned, folded his thick arms over his wide belly and looked Hank directly in the eye.

"Sir, if it had been anyone but you that just told that story, I would be checking to see what he'd been smoking. But I was at Mott Lake when Joe Weah came through the 'Q' course. You're right about Weah. We have had only a handful of foreign nationals who successfully complete the Special Forces Qualification. Weah not only succeeded as a student, but he was also a team player. I'd say he's definitely pro-American."

Now it was Hank's dad who needed to speak.

"Son, what you have told us may well be true, but you have absolutely no proof. I doubt if your ambassador, or the President himself, is going to cancel relations with Liberia because you think its leadership is evil. Hell, even if you had a videotape of Carpai and Dowling pulling the trigger, I don't think our government would jeopardize those oil reserves just to bring them to justice. I know this may sound cruel, but with the economy in the mess it is, I think you'll be on your own on this one."

"I know, Dad. If Lindsey and Tim are alive, I'll have to get them to the embassy by myself. I can't believe that the Liberian government would let them live. Obviously, if they were involved in the killing of the two men at our house, then they know too much," said Hank, twisting his empty beer glass in his hands.

"According to the intelligence reports I read yesterday, they haven't captured Joe Weah. Rumors have it that he's in a village called Zigda.

Apparently, the Poro, the secret society of West Africa, has sealed off the area. Even the Liberian government will not violate the closure. Troops have been stationed on the road leading to the village. I guess they're waiting for the Poro to lift the blockade. The Liberians claim that there was a false report of Lindsey and Tim being at Charles Marshall's house. They say that Joe Weah was responsible for all the murders there – Marshall, Kruger, Marshall's houseboy and one of Weah's own lieutenants. I believe that there is a connection between what is going on in Zigda and the so-called terrorist attack. If Lindsey and Tim are alive, I think I will find them in Zigda. That's where I'm going," Hank concluded.

"You know, sir, you can't take a task force and invade the nation of Liberia."

"I don't have to, Tiny. Liberia already has the task force. I plan to appeal to Charles Morray for help. That's where you come in. I still have my diplomatic passport and an open visa for re-entry into Liberia. I just extended my bereavement leave to thirty days. Now, I need the tools of your trade – nothing that sophisticated, just the basic tools."

"Sir, not a problem. But according to my stomach, it's time for some good Chinese cuisine. Come on, the guys can close the bar."

They followed Tiny's red pickup along Yadkin Road and into one of the older housing developments. A short woman of Chinese descent met them at the door of the brick, ranch-style home. She stood no more than four-and-a-half feet tall.

"Hon, I brought home some visitors," Tiny told her.

"Hank!" she squealed. Hank bent down to kiss her on the cheek.

"Mai Lee, this is my dad, Bill Martin."

"Please, please come in. Tiny called to say he was bringing home guests, but I had no idea it was you, Hank." Her expression turned quickly from joy to seriousness. "I dreamed of Lindsey and Tim," she said, looking directly at Hank. "They were in a village deep in the jungle. There was a black magician with them."

"What did you say?" Hank asked. Mai Lee repeated her story.

Hank's face turned grim as he stared at his clenched fists.

"Hank, what's wrong?" asked his father.

"Dad, I never told this to you and Tiny, but I had a similar dream on Saturday night."

Mai Lee broke out in a laugh and leaned against her husband.

"Hank, after being married to this man for almost forty-two years, he still does not believe that some people can see into the spirit world. I know that both Lindsey and Tim are alive," she said. "Now, all of you come in. I have a surprise for you. Our youngest daughter will be joining us for dinner."

Standing in the hallway was one of the most stunning women Bill Martin had ever seen. Ann Sprague wore a Nomex flight suit with captain's bars. Unlike her mother, Ann was close to six feet tall. She was slender with raven black hair, ivory skin and green eyes.

"Oh, Hank," she cried, throwing her arms around Hank's neck. "I was so sorry to hear what happened, but Mom keeps insisting that Lindsey and Tim aren't dead after all."

"She may very well be right," Hank said. "We've just discovered that the bodies found in our house were likely Liberian men."

He abruptly stepped back and held Ann at an arm's length.

"My God, you're an aviator!"

"Yes, sir. I fly with the 82nd Airborne Division. I'm also airborne and air assault qualified."

"Last time I saw you, you were still in college. Are you married?"

"No, I haven't found anyone who could compare to you or Daddy!"

It didn't take Mai Lee long to have their dinner ready. Small white porcelain bowls arrived, one after the other. The finely chopped vegetables, delicate pink shrimp and steaming rice amazed Bill Martin. Although he'd eaten Chinese food many times, he'd never before sampled such a unique combination of flavor and texture.

As they ate, Tiny and Hank talked about old times. Story after story was followed by hoots of laughter. Occasionally, one or the other would pause to rub a fist under an eye, wiping away a tear. Hank's dad was fascinated by their stories. He had never before seen his son quite like this. Sure, he'd attended promotions and change-of-command ceremonies, but as a professional engineer, Bill had considered the Special Forces somewhat less competent and less professional. Now he realized that was far from true.

Before long their appetites were satisfied and their laughter nearly spent. Tiny stood, rubbed his belly and looked at each in turn.

"Gentlemen, would you join me downstairs?"

Then he looked again toward his daughter.

"Captain, would you care to accompany us?" Ann glanced at her mother.

"Go ahead, dear. All you soldiers can visit Tiny's 'I-love-me' room. I'll clean up after dinner."

"Thanks, Mom," Ann smiled, giving her mother a quick hug.

Tiny's basement had been transformed into a museum of memorabilia, yet it – like Tiny himself – seemed solid and comfortable. A big screen television was built into one wall. Deep brown leather chairs, one extra large, faced the screen. Tall stools were lined up in front of a highly polished bar. A deep sink and a well-stocked refrigerator completed the mini-kitchen.

The walls, paneled in mahogany veneer, provided the backdrop for photographs, trophies, plaques and certificates. A lighted display cabinet showcased the smaller items. Bill leaned down to read some of the inscriptions. He recognized the Distinguished Service Cross, the nation's second highest award for valor.

He saw a photo of Hank, Tiny and the rest of the Special Forces "A" Team on the wall.

In another photo, Tiny was in dress blues, saluting a newly commissioned second lieutenant, his own daughter Ann. Bill grinned. He knew the significance of the silver dollar stuck to the corner of the photo frame. The coin was the traditional gift given by a new second lieutenant to the first non-commissioned officer who saluted. Ann had honored her father, giving him her silver dollar.

Bill's tour of the mementos was halted by the clank of glasses on the bar. Four brandy snifters stood at the ready in rigid formation. Tiny poured half an inch of golden liquid in each – one for Hank, one for Ann, and one for Bill. His thick hand wrapped around his own as he held up his glass.

"To Lindsey and Tim," he said.

"To Lindsey and Tim," the others said in unison. All four raised their glasses and swallowed in one gulp. Without speaking, they set the empty glasses on the bar.

"All right, Colonel Martin, let's see if we can get you some tools."

Tiny picked up what appeared to be the TV's remote control. He pointed it at the wall and pushed a series of buttons. Bill heard the faint whirr of a motor. The paneled walls slid open. Behind them was a thick steel door. Tiny again pointed the remote. This time he fingered a second series of buttons. The heavy door swung inward, revealing a well-lit room.

"Right this way, folks," Tiny said.

The vault was about the same size as the den itself. Bill shook his head in disbelief as he took in the array of weapons, stacks of boxed ammo and cases of plastic explosives – enough weaponry to arm an entire infantry battalion. He figured that there were close to one hundred tiger-stripe camo uniforms and one hundred boxes of jungle boots stashed along the back wall.

"Have anything particular in mind?" Tiny asked.

"I need a nine-millimeter with a silencer, a back-up nine millimeter, two knives, a set of jungle boots, a tiger suit, camouflage sticks and ammo. And," he added, "at least one box of your special ammo."

"Any plastic or blasting caps?"

"No," said Hank. "I'll be carrying the stuff in my suitcase on the plane. It will have a diplomatic seal on it, so it won't be opened, but I can't afford to have an explosives dog find my goodies at Kennedy."

Tiny moved to a rack loaded with pistols.

"This will work for your main gun. It's a nine-millimeter with a built-in laser sight. As you lightly place your finger on the trigger, it activates the laser."

Tiny pointed the weapon toward the far wall. A light touch made a small red dot appear on the wall. He squeezed the trigger, and they heard a click as the hammer fell on the empty chamber.

"It's sighted to within one half inch at one hundred fifty feet. Whatever the red dot marks is ground zero for the bullet that follows.

The gun is threaded for the new aluminum alloy silencer, much lighter than the old-fashioned ones. Only drawback is that they are good for only about three hundred rounds."

"That won't be a problem," Hank said.

"That's OK. I'll throw in an extra silencer in case you get carried away. Oh, by the way, the gun carries a 20-round magazine."

Tiny tossed Hank a ten-shot Glock, small enough to hold in the palm of the hand. With the Glock came an ankle holster. After Tiny had gathered together everything that Hank had requested, he set two boxes of nine-millimeter rounds on the table.

"The ones with the red tips are the specials," Tiny said.

"What are the specials?" asked Bill.

"Dad, Tiny makes them himself. He takes a standard hollow point one hundred fifty-grain bullet, drills out the tip, fills it with liquid mercury, and then melts lead over the top. They don't pass through the body; they fragment. Therefore, they won't wound a bystander. However, it tears apart the body it hits. The bullet literally explodes. Even a slight wound quickly becomes fatal. The liquid mercury contaminates the massive wound. They are designed for one purpose – to kill."

"My God, this stuff isn't legal. Aren't you afraid you would go to jail if anyone found out about this arsenal?" asked Bill.

Tiny laughed.

"No problem, sir. I have an arms dealer's license. More important, my customers guarantee there is no problem."

"What customers?"

"Langley and Delta Force. All of these weapons are sterile. They can't be traced back to me or to the United States."

Bill shook his head.

"Tiny, this has been quite a night. I feel that at least my son will be equipped to handle any situation. Thank you for your friendship and support."

"My pleasure, sir. Your son is the finest officer and soldier I have ever known. I would give my life for him," Tiny said.

# 21

*In Zigda Lindsey made her way down the now-familiar path to the women's bathing pool. She had been up earlier than most. Perhaps she could bathe alone. She preferred solitude and privacy to the noisy chatter and curious stares when the women came together.*

THE DAY BEFORE, TIM HAD PICKED OUT THE DRIED THREADS OF THE STITCHES from her cheek. It had taken unusual restraint to keep her fingernails from scratching the irritating itch. At the last moment, she had thrown a small make-up mirror into her backpack. Without it, she wouldn't have been able to examine the healing wound. It looked like she would have a permanent scar. Charlie, the vet turned emergency room doctor, had done a fine job of pulling the gash together. His tiny stitches reminded her of the neat handiwork on her grandmother's quilts. Once the redness around the wound faded, she would be able to use make-up to hide all but the slight dimpling where the stitches had pulled on the skin. Perhaps even those would fade with time. As the days passed, she was healing. Even the deep bruises were fading. She prayed that time would also mend her broken family.

When she reached the pool, she saw only one old woman seated along its sandy edge. Lindsey smiled and greeted her in Kapel. The woman nodded, fastened her cotton skirt firmly under her thin, hanging breasts and mumbled a phrase that Lindsey recognized as an expression of leave-taking.

Now the pool was hers alone. She undressed, neatly stacking her shirt and pants on the bank. She tiptoed into the cool water, and then plunged headlong into its depths. She turned and floated on her back.

Deep green, leafy branches provided partial shade, yet still caused her to squint in the morning sunlight. She was once again amazed by the brilliance of the blue sky. She rolled over and reached for a small bar of soap in a stone dish on the bank.

Lindsey realized that it wasn't the best shampoo, but it was better than nothing.

She rubbed the soap through her hair and rinsed it before lathering her body. Once again, she dove into the pool, savoring the brief sense of freedom and renewal. Beads of water hung on her lithe body as she climbed out of the water and settled onto a straw mat on the shore. She pulled a thin plastic comb through the tangles in her hair. She stretched out on her stomach, allowing her body to dry in the morning sun.

The warm sunlight, even here in this remote African village, was the same sunlight she knew from back home.

"Home," she sighed.

Five days had passed since Joe's miracle recovery. Lindsey had watched as his eyes opened, and he scanned the crowded hut. Like a child abruptly awakened from an afternoon nap, Joe had blinked his eyes and asked for a drink of water.

Just the next day, he had gotten to his feet and taken his first short walk outside the hut. Within a mere forty-eight hours, Joe seemed his former self – strong, friendly and at ease with himself. On his third day, he felt strong enough to go along with Tim and three of the young warriors on a hunt. Proud and boisterous, the hunters had returned with two carcasses tied by their hoofed feet to two long poles. Joe still felt tenderness on his shoulder, but his arm and hand were nearly back to normal.

The successful hunt couldn't have come at a better time. A feast had been planned to celebrate the planting of the season's rice. Women rose early to begin roasting the butchered goats and forest antelope over the open pit fires.

By noon, the beat of drums announced the arrival of lesser Poro spirits. Masked, costumed figures paraded into the village, trailed by clusters of small boys. These weren't the invisible spirits, but actual physical beings. People lined the wide pathways to watch their entrance. People laughed and poked at them with blunt sticks.

This was only the first of many events. Elsewhere in the village, people gathered to dance. Others formed impromptu bands, beating out the rhythmic melodies common to West Africa. As dusk arrived, a large crowd came into the open central square. Small fires had been lit around the edge to provide light for the night's activities.

Lindsey had been led to an honored location and was seated next to Joe. She searched the crowd, looking for Tim. He had spent yet another day with his young friends. Lindsey assumed they had not yet returned. Joe leaned close to her ear in order to be heard over the din of celebration.

He explained that the festivities helped unify people for the communal workday. Early the next morning, everyone would take part in clearing the land to prepare new rice fields. In this part of the world, rice grew in open fields. Timed to coincide with the beginning of the rainy season, the young plants thrived in the soggy earth. No need for rice paddies here. The fertile new ground and heavy rains provided the ideal growing conditions.

Suddenly, the drums began to beat more loudly. People began cheering.

"What's happening?" Lindsey asked.

"The young warriors will compete in hand-to-hand combat," Joe answered.

"Combat?"

"Well, I guess you could say it's more like wrestling," Joe said. "In bush school, the boys are taught ways to take down the enemy. Once he's on the ground, it's easier to kill your enemy with a spear or a knife. In this contest, two men stand on a ten-foot square mat. The first man to throw the other off the mat or to throw him to the ground is the winner. The top five winners earn the right to dance with the young virgins. Forty of the best warriors will compete to reach the top five."

"Do they all pick wives?"

"No, I never did, and for five years in a row before I left Zigda, I was always one of the top five."

"Joe," Lindsey asked, "why haven't you ever married?"

"I've never found the right woman," Joe said. "Look! The forty are coming forward to stand before the chief."

The crowd parted and a line of young men emerged. All were barefoot and wore only leather loincloths. Their bodies were coated with shiny oil. Lindsey counted as they moved into the open.

"Joe, I only see thirty-nine. Where is the fortieth?"

"He's coming," Joe whispered.

When the last man came forward, Lindsey heard cheers from the crowd, but she raised her hand to her forehead in despair.

"Oh, my God! Joe, I can't let this happen!"

The last warrior was none other than Tim. Clad only in the leather loincloth, his long, lean body reflected the red glow of the firelight.

"Relax, Lindsey. No one gets hurt in these matches. It's just a friendly competition."

"But, Joe, you don't understand. Tim's just a boy," Lindsey protested.

"Boys of only twelve compete in bush school. Tim's almost fifteen," Joe said.

"All right, so he's fifteen, but you said that only warriors participate. Tim's no warrior. He had no tribal scars. Those are men out there. Tim could get hurt."

"Lindsey, the worst that could happen is that he will end up on his butt in the dirt," Joe said. "You may not think of him as a warrior, but our people do. Tim faced a greater challenge than most when he saved you. When he got here, he embraced the greatest *zo* in the country. Few people even dare look directly at a *zo*. He has everyone's support. Sit back and relax. He'll be joining us soon, and he'll be none the worse for wear."

What could she do now? Lindsey had to rely on the confident words of their friend.

Soon the competition began. Joe was right – this was similar to the judo matches she had seen when Tim took lessons two years earlier. He had worked his way up to a green belt, but then decided to take karate instead. He pursued that for a while until he took up something else. The only consistent sport for him was soccer.

The chief called out the names of the combatants. In the fourth match, he chose a man in his late twenties. The heavily muscled man stepped forward. He bowed to the chief. When the name of his opponent was announced, Lindsey shuddered.

"Tim," the chief said.

The white-skinned American boy stepped boldly forward. He planted his feet firmly on the mat and bowed to the chief. He did not glance once at his mother.

"This isn't fair, Joe," Lindsey said. "Your father just picked the biggest man in the group. He must be ten years older and a good seventy pounds heavier."

If Joe had intended to respond, he didn't get the chance. The chief signaled for the match to begin.

For Tim's opponent, Junga Sayeth, this would be no adolescent game. For seven seasons, Junga had danced with the virgins. A fight with this tall, pale boy was beneath his dignity. No matter what people had said about Tim's power, the story of how he had killed two soldiers could not be true. The match would end quickly. The boy would regret that he dared think himself equal to a man. This boy had not earned the right to stand with true warriors.

Junga made the first move. He lunged forward, intent on kicking the weakling off the mat. Tim saw him coming and stepped quickly to the right. His opponent missed and barely recovered his balance. He let out a low animal growl and grabbed at Tim's wrist. The move had always worked before, but the white boy twisted his wrist inward, breaking the hold.

Angered, Junga grasped both of Tim's shoulders. His large hands dug into Tim's flesh. Because he was focusing on his grip, he failed to heed Tim's footwork. Tim swept his right foot against Junga's left ankle. Again, Junga struggled to keep his balance. He released his hold.

Without a pause, Junga resumed his stance and moved forward once again. Now he held Tim's forearms. Tim countered by clasping his opponent's arms. Locked together, the heavier Junga pushed Tim backward. He had him now. One more thrust and Tim would be in the dirt.

The next moment should have been his victory, yet he felt his head spin, and Junga flew through the air, landing heavily on his back at the feet of the onlookers. He had been thrown off the edge of the mat. He lifted his upper body and got up on his elbows. He was breathing hard from the sudden impact. He looked up into the night sky and then into the smiling face of this pale upstart.

Junga let out a fearsome shriek, charged forward and grabbed Tim by the throat. Now he would strangle the last breath from this outsider. But Tim countered the chokehold by bringing his clasped fists straight up between Junga's hands. Tim took a step backward and assumed a defensive karate stance. Both stood ready, awaiting the other's offensive.

"Stop!" yelled the chief. "Stop!" Then he repeated his order in Kapel, adding, "The white warrior has won. You have lost. Do not bring embarrassment on our people."

Junga turned and walked out of the square.

"I can't believe it!" Lindsey said. "Tim used a judo throw to win the match. Hank always claimed that Tim had a natural ability in the martial arts, but I would never have believed that he could win against an adult." Lindsey spoke rapidly, caught up in the thrill of Tim's success.

The physical combat resumed. Tim confronted two other warriors and easily won both matches. To Lindsey's amazement, Tim had become one of the five finalists. Cheers and shouts filled the night air as the young men stood proudly before the chief. Lindsey wrapped her arms around Joe, hugging him tightly.

"What happens now, Joe?"

"Just watch," he said. The drumbeat intensified. The crowd parted and twenty young women surrounded the proud, but trembling, warriors. Their firm bodies moved to the rhythm of the drums. Short grass skirts were wrapped around their waists. Their dark breasts in a variety of shapes and sizes bobbed to the rhythm of the drumbeat. They lifted their knees, some directly in front of the perspiring young men.

Lindsey gasped as she realized that the short skirts were their only covering. Their bold leaps raised their skirts, revealing the dark area between their legs. Some reversed direction and leaned forward, offering their smooth dark buttocks to the gaze of the spellbound young warriors.

Tim shuffled his feet, his eyes cast downward. The dancers tightened their circle, moving to within an arm's length of the warriors. One warrior reached out, his fingertips only inches from a pointed nipple. Following his lead, other arms stretched out, some grazing a shoulder or a leg. The girls pulled away, and then once again moved in closer.

Lindsey shifted in her seat, her hip nestled warm and comfortable next to her friend Joe. Her tenuous composure began to disappear when she saw Tim's arm reach out to caress the sleek upper arm of a well-formed virgin.

"Joe, what's this all about?" she whispered.

He moved nearer so she could hear, his arm pressing against her. "The warriors see the most eligible young women in the village. Once the rice is harvested, they have first opportunity to offer a bride's price to the girl's father. That's why the men try so hard to win, both for honor and for their choice of the women. I guess you could say the strongest males select the finest women."

"Great," Lindsay said. "My fifteen-year-old son may be finding a wife!"

But there was nothing Lindsey could do but continue to watch the tantalizing performance. She sighed in relief when she heard the drums begin to fade. She watched as the young women vanished into the crowd, leaving the warriors looking tired and spent.

Two men came forward. One held a leather pouch filled with liquid. The other passed out five cups fashioned from black gourds.

"Now what's going on?" Lindsey asked.

"The five get the first of the palm wine," Joe said.

"Palm wine? Tim doesn't drink wine!"

"In Zigda, he can, and he is," Joe, answered. Trickles of the milky white beverage ran down Tim's bare chest. He followed with still another cup, until people came forward to escort the staggering boys to the sleeping hut where the five would spend the night. Relieved that her son would drift into an exhausted sleep, Lindsey sighed. What a night! Tim had certainly received a lesson in African life.

By now the fires had died down. Only glowing coals remained where flames had once blazed so intensely. People moved randomly to their huts. Lindsey chose her steps carefully in the darkness. Only dim lantern light illuminated the inside of her hut where she would be sleeping alone tonight.

She kicked off her shoes, unbuttoned her shirt, took off her bra, and slipped out of her pants and underwear. Naked, she ran her hands over her breasts and brought them to rest on her hips. Although no longer a young virgin, the night's fervor had left her strangely unsettled. Sleep wouldn't come easily.

The quiet, after all the night's pandemonium, should have calmed her. Instead, she stood still, almost as if she expected someone. For a moment, she thought she heard a slight movement outside her door. She turned. Behind her, stood Joe. Startled, she blurted out his name.

"Joe! Joe, what are you doing here?"

He didn't answer. She made no move to cover her nakedness. Instead, the two remained immobile, as if waiting or wanting the other to do or say something. Confused, Lindsey tried to sort out her emotions. Hank had been her only lover for more than sixteen years, yet she wanted Joe to see her like this.

The pulse of the drumbeat and the primitive pull of the sensual dance had captivated each of them. Neither spoke. Lindsey looked into his eyes. She thought she detected sadness.

Suddenly, Joe turned and bolted out the door into the dark. Their moment was over.

# 22

*Morning in Zigda was a quiet time – especially quiet on the morning after the celebration.*

LINDSEY AWOKE LATER THAN USUAL. SHE HADN'T SLEPT WELL AT ALL. FINALLY, in the early morning she had fallen into an exhausted sleep. About noon, she saw Joe coming toward her hut. As he approached, she thought he seemed more distant, more reserved. Their easy friendship had been tainted by unspoken emotion. Lindsey regretted the change. In so many ways, their lives had intertwined. Things would never be quite the same again.

"Lindsey," he said, not waiting for her response. "Let Tim know that we'll be leaving Zigda this afternoon."

"Leaving?" she asked, shocked by his directness.

"Yes, we have to get to Nimba County. If we can reach Charles Morray, he may be able to get us across the border. Hank has no way of knowing where you are. He probably thinks you're both dead."

"Yes," Lindsey said, lowering her eyes. "Yes, I am anxious to reach him. He had been out of the country on assignment. By now, he might very well think we've been harmed. No one really knows where we are." She hesitated for a moment, biting her lower lip. "But, Joe, I thought no one was supposed to leave Zigda."

"The chief will lift the Poro roadblock after we're safely on our way," Joe answered.

"But how can he do that unless he's the...." Joe stopped her, resting his finger on his pursed lips.

"Yes, Lindsey, my father is the *Nangma*, the greatest of the Poro spirits."

By late afternoon, they were ready to leave. She knew Tim wasn't a bit happy about their departure. He had adapted to village life and still wanted to learn more. He had made friends and won their praise and affection. Even Lindsey felt a touch of sadness. The land was beautiful, and the people were warm and accepting. Although military life had taken her to many strange lands, she had never before been so at ease in a new community.

Five warriors were assigned to accompany them. They would avoid the main trail. Instead, they would skirt the mountain and join up with a secondary route leading from another village. Joe said it would take a good eight hours. They would reach Zorzor by midnight.

It seemed like every man, woman and child had come to say goodbye. One after another, they filed by, shaking hands or offering a quick embrace.

Finally, the great *zo*, Chea Geebe, who they had first known as Everyday Walker, stood before them, a wide grin spreading across his weathered face. He wrapped his thin arms around Tim, slapping him heartily on the back. The two hugged, and then popped fingers. When he got to Lindsey, he stopped.

"Missy, the power of the leopard will protect you on your journey," he said. His gnarled fingers lifted the leopard tooth necklace from around his neck.

"No," Lindsey said, "that is your powerful juju. Without it, you will have no protection."

"You must take it, Missy. The *endosym* still hunts for your spirits. It will not rest. Besides, the great leopard had two fangs."

He reached into a small pouch attached to a leather cord around his waist and held up a second fang of the great leopard. Lindsey bent her head forward. Chea hung the necklace with the leopard tooth charm around her neck.

"You dear man," she said, kissing him lightly on the cheek.

People clapped and cheered, celebrating their friendship. Chea rested his palms on her shoulders and looked directly at her.

"No white person has ever done that. You and the boy treat me like family. Chea has no family. Your spirits and my spirit will be family. The leopard spirit will be with you always."

Lindsey thought she heard a catch in his voice and imagined she saw a tear in his eye. She watched as the fine and faithful man turned and walked away.

The last man to come forward was Joe's father. He shook his son's hand, then Tim's hand. Lindsey knew that women were considered lower-class citizens. In public, a man never touched a woman. To her surprise, the paramount chief and great Poro spirit of the *Nangma* reached out and held Lindsey's hand in his own.

"You have saved my son's life, and you and your son will always be welcome as members of our village."

The two snapped fingers. Then Lindsey, Tim, Joe and the five warriors started up the winding trail into the mountains.

By seven o'clock, it was dark. Their pace slowed, but Lindsey was surprised at how easy it was to move along the jungle path. Joe told them to take small steps to avoid tripping. Two of the warriors took the point. Unlike a silent combat patrol, the warriors talked continuously. Joe explained that at night in the jungle, noise would help, not hurt. It wasn't a good idea to surprise a leopard or other wild beast. Also, snakes would scatter, sensing the vibration of stomping feet.

Tim did his part, chattering with Sabo Weah, Joe's cousin. Sabo was three or four years older than Tim. He had attended a mission school and spoke excellent English. The boys had become good friends. Three others were older men. Although Lindsey didn't know their names, she recognized their familiar faces. The fifth was Junga Sayeh, the warrior that Tim had bested in the first match. She wondered why he had been selected. Perhaps he would learn that to lose in a game did not reduce his importance in the tribe.

They had made better time than they expected, arriving in Zorzor an hour early. They stayed hidden just outside the village while one of the warriors went to the hut of the village chief. Zorzor was one of the dozen or so villages that fell under Joe's father's authority as paramount chief. They would be among friends.

A short time later, the man returned with two others and led the group to a solitary hut at the edge of the village. They would stay quietly inside until an hour before sunrise.

Arrangements had been made for a produce truck to pick them up the next day and take them to Sanniquellie. The three would be hidden in the back to avoid detection in case government soldiers stopped them.

"We have about five hours. We might as well get some sleep," Joe said.

"Mom, can I sleep outside with Sabo? Tomorrow morning the warriors will go back to Zigda."

"All right, Tim, but don't wander too far from the hut." She watched as they disappeared in the darkness.

The ringing of the bedside phone brought him out of a deep sleep.

"Carpai here."

"Sir, this is Oscar. We have located Weah and the Martins."

"Where?"

"In Zorzor. We got a call from the telephone exchange in Zorzor a little after midnight. Someone used the number on the reward poster."

Carpai couldn't help but smile. Finally, something was going right.

Just the day before, Dowling had been in an absolute panic. They had gotten word that Lieutenant Colonel Martin had returned to the embassy. Then CNN reported that the bodies found in the fire might not be Martin's wife and son. They had planned to eliminate the woman and her son along with Weah. Now that Martin was back in the country, Carpai had a better idea.

"Oscar, I want you to alert the Air Corps chief of staff. Have three choppers prepared for immediate departure to Zorzor. Also get Dr. Eduardo

Torres out of bed. He will go along. I want the woman and the boy brought back sedated. Kill Weah, but bring back his body."

"Yes, sir," Oscar answered. "I will have the troops on the ground in Zorzor in less than two hours."

Unable to sleep, Joe pressed the light button on his Casio watch. It was just half past three. He struck a match and lit the kerosene lantern, keeping its flame low. Lindsey rested on her side, breathing softly. Two of the warriors curled on mats on the floor. The other three and Tim stayed outside to keep watch. Joe had intended to wake everyone in one hour.

No use lying here awake, he thought. He got up, quietly opened the door and stepped outside. A moonless sky made the stars shine brightly. He could see no lights in the town. The village was quiet and dark. He heard the barking of dogs farther down the road. He walked behind the hut to a grove of palms, unzipped his fly and emptied his bladder.

A few yards to the right he noticed one of the warriors reclining against a tree. Might as well get everyone started, Joe thought. He finished, zipped and walked over to the silent man. He shook him gently, careful not to startle him. No response. He shook him again, this time more forcefully. The man's body slid sideways and remained still. In the darkness, Joe strained to see the man's features. He fumbled his way to the man's chest and moved his fingers upward, trying to detect a pulse. He slid his hand to the neck and immediately pulled it away. He had felt a deep gash, the throat slit from ear to ear.

Joe crouched close to the ground. His heart began to pound wildly as adrenalin surged through his body. He knew he had to act quickly. He turned toward the hut. From behind a grove of palms, he thought he saw movement. He hid behind a tree and peeked out. Dark figures had encircled the hut. He heard a splintering of wood as a uniformed man slammed his heavy boot into the thin door.

Bursts of automatic weapons fire rang out from inside the hut. He heard Lindsey's screams. Two dark figures came out, dragging Lindsey as she struggled against them. One man seemed to be in charge. He barked out orders. Joe thought he heard the approach of even more soldiers. He watched as three soldiers tied Lindsey's hands behind her back and forced her to the ground. Likely these three would hold her hostage as the others searched the area.

If Joe was going to do something, he had to do it immediately. He moved through the palms, working his way to the back of the hut. He felt around in the dirt until his hand located a fist-size rock. He picked it up and scraped it against the rough siding. He paused for a few seconds, and then resumed scraping.

"What's that noise?" asked one of the soldiers.

"How should I know?" asked another.

"Check it out!" Joe heard the man coming around the back. The man turned the corner, pausing in his attempt to see in the darkness. Joe watched, as the man seemed to give up. He hadn't found anything unusual. Just as he was about to turn, a hand with the strength of a steel vise covered his mouth. The last sound the soldier heard was the snap of his own broken neck.

Joe dragged the crumpled body a few yards away. He pulled off the soldier's fatigue cap and jacket. He pulled the cap down tightly on his head and slipped his arms into the jacket.

"Did you find anything?" someone asked from the front of the hut.

"Nothing," Joe answered.

So far, so good. Joe had been taught how to operate in the dark. The trick was to transform oneself into something other than a human shape and remain still. Joe had stretched flat on the ground against the back wall of the hut. The first soldier had almost stepped on him as he came around the hut. He never looked down to check the ground in front of him. His carelessness had cost him his life.

Joe picked up the man's rifle and moved to the front of the hut. One soldier sat cross-legged on the ground beside Lindsey. The other stood in the shadow. It took Joe three long strides to reach the standing soldier. He brought the rifle up in a vertical butt stroke and struck him soundly in the jaw. The soldier on the ground had no time to react. Joe turned and drove his boot square into the side of his head. The force of the kick pushed him backward against the wall. With the sharp steel of his knife, Joe ended both of the soldiers' lives.

Joe wiped his bloody knife on his victim's jacket, and then cut the ties that bound Lindsey's hands. He reached down and helped her to her feet. She turned her head away from the dead soldiers. Sickened by the smell of blood, she struggled to contain her nausea.

"Oh, Joe, what's happening?"

"Soldiers are all over the village. Somehow they found out that we're here."

"Tim. Where's Tim? We've got to find Tim!" she cried.

"Not right now. First, we have to get out of here and find a place to hide. I counted at least thirty soldiers. There may be even more."

Tim and Sabo had made their way through the darkness to the bank of a stream about three hundred yards from the hut. They had spread out their mats, intending to sleep. This was likely to be the friends' final night together.

Sabo had been the first to extend his hand in friendship when Tim had arrived in Zigda. Even though Sabo was seventeen – two years older than Tim – they had hit it off immediately. It seemed as if they had always been friends.

Sabo was Togba Weah's nephew. He had come to live with his uncle's family after his father had died from fever more than five years earlier. Since Togba's sons had already grown and left the village, Sabo became more like a younger son than a nephew. Determined to help Sabo succeed in life, Togba had sent him to the mission school in Gabanga. Sabo had spent half of each of the previous four years there. He learned to read, write and speak English fluently.

Instead of sleeping, the two had spent the night talking. Time had slipped by. Both had yawned, ready at last for some rest. Tim had no idea what time it was, but he figured that dawn couldn't be too far away as the stars had already begun to lose their brightness. He had just leaned back on his elbows, ready to curl up in sleep when he heard the blast of automatic weapons fire.

"What was that?" whispered Sabo, suddenly alert.

"It sounded like gunfire," Tim said. "Let's find out what's going on."

They rolled up their mats and started up the trail. They crept silently toward the hut, fearing what might await them. Near the doorway, they saw the corpses of two soldiers. Tim spotted an M-16 rifle lying on the ground. He picked it up, flicked off the safety and peeked through the shattered door. Inside, the dim light from the lantern revealed two bodies sprawled on the dirt floor.

"What do you think happened?" asked Sabo.

"It looks like the soldiers came for us. Mom and Joe aren't here. Either they were captured, or they got away. We need to find them."

Back outside the hut, Tim scanned the ground until he found the second soldier's weapon.

"Here, Sabo, you need a rifle, too."

"I don't know how to use it."

"It's easy. All you do is turn this little lever here. It's called a safety. Then just point the barrel toward your target and pull the trigger."

The two moved down the road, staying in the shadows. They could make out sounds coming from some of the huts. People were beginning to awaken. A group of four or five men stood next to the Lebanese store. The boys picked their way carefully along the street, pausing every few yards to check for danger.

In Zorzor, like in many of the smaller towns along the main road, transmission lines brought electricity to the village, but to save money, the power was shut off from eleven at night to four o'clock in the morning. Tim and Sabo paused near a light pole. They lifted their rifles, ready to resume their search when the streetlights came on.

The sudden change from darkness to brightness startled each of them. Sabo's finger had rested lightly on the trigger of the M-16. He flinched, and his finger curled around the trigger. The rifle went off on full automatic.

"Run!" yelled Tim. The burst of fire further confused Sabo. He remained frozen in place. Soldiers now appeared from out of nowhere. They rushed toward the boys while wildly firing their own weapons. Tim could have turned and run, escaping into a dark side street. Instead, he tackled his friend, lying on top of him to protect him from the hail of bullets. In a matter of seconds, soldiers had crossed the street and fallen upon the two boys, wrenching the rifles from their hands. They were jerked to their feet, their hands bound behind their backs, and they were marched up the road and out of town.

Joe and Lindsey had taken shelter in the ruins of a burned-out hut. Part of the roof had collapsed, but they had found a small open space in the rubble. They heard the bursts of gunfire just as the streetlights had come on.

Joe peered through a crack in the blackened boards. He could see armed soldiers swarming through the village. His estimate of thirty men had been far too low. It wouldn't be long until they were found. Even though he still had the M-16 from one of the soldiers, they were boxed in with nowhere to go. When discovered, Joe had already decided to give up. He knew he would most likely be shot. But, for some reason, it seemed the soldiers wanted to take Lindsey and Tim alive. Perhaps his death would give the two of them a chance, no matter how slim.

He heard the crunch of boots in the gravel before he saw the soldiers coming. He turned to see the silhouettes of two men framed in the dark timbers of the doorway. Two others stood behind them. The four picked their way through the burned boards. The beams of their flashlights flitted from side to side.

Joe knew they would be seen as soon as the soldiers moved forward. Motionless, he tried to slow his breathing. He looked to his right where Lindsey crouched beside him. He lifted his hand in an attempt to steady himself. It was all over. He turned to her.

In the dim morning light, he could barely make out her features. He gasped in amazement as he watched a greenish glow spread from her face to her chest and then encompass her entire body. He shook his head and raised his hands in surrender, waiting for the inevitable impact of bullets that would tear his life from him. So this was what it was like to be seconds away from death. He waited, but nothing happened.

Then he heard the soldiers talking.

"There is something in here," one said.

"Yes," another answered. "It is large. It is an animal – a huge leopard!"

"Shoot it!"

"No, don't shoot. It is too big. It wants us to leave. We must leave now!"

All four soldiers turned and crept slowly away from the hut. Joe still stood motionless, his hands high over his head. His arms shook and his breaths came in short gasps. He lowered his hands slowly and dropped to his knees behind the pile of charred boards.

Lindsey still seemed to glow. He reached out and touched her cheek. The glow vanished as quickly as it had appeared.

"Joe, will the soldiers look for us here?"

"What?" Joe asked in disbelief.

"I asked if the soldiers would look for us here."

"Lindsey, didn't you just see some of them come into the hut?"

"What? I closed my eyes for only a moment. It was so strange. I imagined I saw Everyday Walker standing in a clearing. Next to him sat a huge leopard. Wasn't that strange?"

"Yes, it certainly is," Joe, replied.

"Lindsey," he continued, "I think we'll be safe here. The soldiers have moved on."

A half dozen armed soldiers escorted Tim and Sabo from the village. They walked for nearly a half hour then stopped in a clearing. The brush had been burned to prepare the land for the rice planting. Three large helicopters, each capable of carrying thirty combat soldiers, had landed in the field. When Sabo tried to speak to Tim, he'd been pushed to the ground and told not to speak. The one white man among the soldiers had come forward and offered them each a drink from a canteen. Tim thought he spoke with a Spanish accent. About an hour later, nearly seventy soldiers marched into the clearing.

"What's going on?" whispered Sabo.

"Shut up, boy!" ordered one of the soldiers. He slapped Sabo across the side of his head with an open hand.

Tim watched as the soldiers approached. He saw that a Liberian army major led the group. Next to him, chatting like an old friend was Junga Sayeh.

What a bastard, Tim thought. Sayeh must have been the one to betray them.

The two sauntered up to them. Standing tall over the seated prisoners, Sayeh looked down at Tim.

"You may have danced with the virgins, but that was your last dance," he snarled before turning to Oscar Jalah. "The other boy is the nephew of the paramount chief. He lives in Togba Weah's hut."

Jalah raised his eyebrows in keen interest. Originally, he had planned to kill the native boy and hold only the Martin boy as prisoner. But perhaps taking this other boy would ease Carpai's anger when he learned that Weah and the woman had again eluded them. He turned to an officer behind him.

"Put them on the chopper with Dr. Torres. Load up the soldiers. We will be flying back to Camp Jackson."

Two soldiers stepped forward. They prodded the boys with the barrels of their rifles, bullying them to their feet and pushing them in the direction of the waiting chopper.

"I will get part of the reward, won't I?" asked Sayeh.

"Of course you will," smiled Jalah. He pulled out his pistol and shot Sayeh point blank twice in the chest. Blood gurgled from his throat as he fell to the ground. Jalah holstered his pistol and headed for the helicopter. As they lifted off, he looked back down at the village of Zorzor.

"Damn, missed them," he grimaced.

But now he had a plan. He would tell Carpai that the boy and the chief's nephew had been alone. Weah and the woman must have gone ahead. He wasn't about to let Carpai know that Weah had bested him.

Lindsey was unable to control her trembling.

"Oh, Joe, what are we going to do? They have Tim and Sabo!"

The two had stayed hidden in the hut until it was full daylight. The routine sound of people going about their morning activity told them that the soldiers had left. They scrambled into the forest and up a trail to the top of a hill overlooking the rice fields. They could see the soldiers lead the boys to the helicopter. They had heard the pistol shots and seen Jalah step over Sayeh's body. Joe reached out and cradled Lindsey's hands in his own.

"Lindsey, the boys are alive. The man who just killed Sayeh is a major who works for Minister Carpai. For whatever, reason, they want you and Tim alive. As long as the boys are alive, there is hope," he said. "As for us, we have got to get to Charles Morray. Come on now, that produce truck is waiting to take us to Nimba County."

Dr. Eduardo Torres ground the butt of his Cuban cigar into the dirt. He sat on a bench in front of the headquarters building at Camp Jackson. He looked at his gold watch. It was now half past eight in the morning. He needed to be back in Monrovia by ten o'clock. It was a good two-hour flight. God, how he hated flying in helicopters! At Camp Jackson, Major Jalah had told him to sedate the two boys. Their limp bodies had been placed in the back of a truck.

He couldn't figure out why Carpai had wanted both of the boys. It was also strange that one of the two was white. Over the years, he had sedated a number of young boys for Carpai. But that had been different. Those poor bastards had all been homeless street urchins. He never bothered to ask what Carpai wanted with the young men. He didn't want to know. He suspected that the boys would never be seen alive again. Most likely, these two would also disappear without a trace.

Too bad, he thought. The white kid had shown some guts. When he had prepared the hypodermic needles for the injections, two soldiers easily restrained the native boy as he slipped the point of the needle into his arm. The white boy was a different story. He fought, even though his hands were bound behind his back.

He had jumped to his feet and had landed a fierce kick to one soldier's crotch. Another man had tackled him from behind. He managed to throw that soldier over his shoulder and take off running. It took another four men to finally wrestle him to the ground. As they held him securely,

Torres rammed the needle into the boy's hip, right through his jeans. At least now, they were both out. The sedative would keep them both under control for at least the next five hours.

What a disaster his life had become! Dr. Torres could remember so clearly how proud he had been when Fidel Castro himself had handed him his diploma. He had been top in his graduating class from the University Medical School in Havana. He was destined to be one of the greatest doctors of the revolution.

Unfortunately, he had one flaw – he had become addicted to his own prescriptions. An embarrassment to his own government, he had been stationed in Angola to support Cuba's troops. When Cuba backed out of Angola, Torres elected to stay. While some might call him a defector from the communist regime, Cuba was glad to be rid of him.

A Cuban medical degree couldn't guarantee him a position in a reputable hospital, but it was good enough for Liberia. He worked at Monrovia's Medical Center. Ten years earlier Julius Carpai had learned of Torres' drug addiction during an investigation into missing hospital supplies. After his arrest, Torres had expected to be sent to Beliyela, the nation's penitentiary. The stories he had heard of the conditions there made Devil's Island, the notorious French penal colony, look like a day at the country club.

He had resigned himself to his terrible fate when one day he had a personal visit from Julius Carpai. He'd been offered freedom, a second chance in the hospital, and a significant increase in pay. In return, Torres would provide discreet medical services for the minister of defense, no questions asked.

He looked down at his watch once more, only to be interrupted by Jalah who walked toward him with a cell phone in hand.

"Time to go?" Torres asked.

"Carpai wants to talk to you first," Jalah said, tossing him the phone. He caught it in mid-air.

"Yes, sir," Torres said. He paused, listening to Carpai. "No, sir. I could never do that. I am sorry. That is not possible."

Jalah stood nearby, listening to Torres' side of the conversation.

"The minister wants to speak to you now," Torres said, handing the phone back to Jalah who held the phone to his ear, nodded and then snapped it closed.

"What did Carpai tell you?"

"He said to shoot you if you didn't do what he asked."

"You've got to be kidding," Torres gasped.

Jalah pulled his nine-millimeter and pointed it directly between Torres' eyes.

"Not kidding at all – not in the least," said Jalah, moving his other hand up to steady the one with the gun. Torres had been there when Jalah had shot that informer back in Zorzor. He had no choice.

"Have someone bring me my medical bag," he said.

# 23

***Produce trucks lined up at the Zorzor loading dock.***

It was now nearing the hottest part of the day. Joe and Lindsey sat in the shadow of the shed that housed the fruit and vegetables. The day's events had wrung their energy and sapped their spirit. Tim and Sabo had been captured. Their warrior-guards had been slaughtered. They had witnessed Sayeh's betrayal and brutal murder. They had talked about Sayeh and had agreed not to disclose his cowardice. The people in the village would have enough to deal with when they learned what had happened.

They had hoped something good would come of it all. Joe said that he was certain it would unite the people in anger toward the Liberian government. He thought it was unlikely anyone else would turn him in for the reward money.

Two wood crates had been placed toward the front of the truck's bed. The crates were big enough to conceal one person in each. Workers laid stocks of green bananas around them, hiding the crates. The two would only have to endure the hiding place for a matter of minutes. More than that would be disastrous for them in the stifling heat.

There would be one driver and two laborers. Lindsey climbed into the cab and huddled between Joe and the driver. The workers perched in back with the bananas. They started off down the road. Two hours later, the driver pulled off onto a small side road. The men moved the bananas, opening up a passage that led to the empty crates. One man pulled on the wooden lids and Joe and Lindsey each crawled into their cramped cells. The lids replaced, the bananas were once again stacked on top. The workers got into the front seat. The driver shifted into reverse, backed out onto the main road and continued on the way to Sanniquellie.

Minutes later, Lindsey felt the truck slow down as it approached what she thought was a military roadblock. She heard the sound of heavy boots on gravel and the click of a metal weapon.

"Where are you headed?" a voice said.

"To Sanniquellie. To exchange bananas for coffee beans," the driver answered.

Lindsey held her breath. Rivulets of perspiration poured down her face. She heard the grinding sound of the clutch as the heavily loaded truck lurched forward. Joe had assured her that the search would be more thorough when the truck returned. It would be inspected for weapons and illegal passengers. The government was more interested in what came out of the territory than what came in.

They remained hidden for took another ten minutes. The driver pulled to a halt on a side road. The workers jumped out and removed the bananas. They pried open the wooden lids. The men reached under Lindsey's arms, lifted her wilted body and leaned her against the vehicle. She sipped at a canteen. Even warm water offered some comfort. Finally she was tucked back in the cab between the driver and Joe. She rested her head against Joe's shoulder. The heat of the day combined with the rumble of the engine made it impossible to stay awake. She drifted into a deep sleep.

An hour later, Joe shook her awake. He helped her out of the truck, and they said goodbye to the men who had helped them escape.

"What now?" Lindsey asked.

"We have to find a member of the militia who will tell us how to contact Charles Morray. Let's go over to that bar across the street."

As they crossed the street, Lindsey felt dozens of pairs of dark eyes watching her. Clearly, a tall white woman in the company of a Kapel man in Sanniquellie was not an everyday occurrence. In the bar, a radio played loud calypso music. The two settled in at a small, wooden table away from the window.

"What would you like to drink?" Joe asked when the bartender approached them.

"I'd love a Coke," Lindsey answered.

Speaking in Kruman, Joe ordered a Coke for her and a beer for himself. They sat in silence until the drinks came. Once served, the two slowly sipped their beverages without speaking. Finally, the back door creaked open and a young man, about twenty-five years old, came to their table and spoke to Joe in Kapel.

"Liberian army spies are not welcome in Sanniquellie."

"What makes you think I am an army spy?"

"Are you saying that you are not in the army?"

"Yes, I am in the army," Joe answered.

The man reached in his back pocket and withdrew a piece of paper. He laid it on the table.

"I believe this is you, Lieutenant Colonel Weah."

Joe looked at the poster. "It's a good likeness, but I was much younger in that picture."

"It says here that you are worth fifty thousand dollars."

"I am honored," Joe said.

"Who is the white woman?"

"She is the wife of Lieutenant Colonel Martin. He is a friend of Charles Morray."

"And what do you and the white woman want?"

"We want to see Charles Morray."

A slight smile crept over the young man's lips.

"You need to visit the clinic. Go out of town and follow the road down into the valley."

Without saying goodbye, the man turned and left.

"What was that all about?" Lindsey asked.

"We were just told to go to the medical clinic."

"Why?"

"I believe that is how we will find Charles Morray. Are you ready to go now?" Lindsey nodded. "This way," Joe said, leading the way out to the street.

Karen Myers rested her reading glasses atop her head. She had completed her notes on the patient's medical form. She stood and looked out the screened window. A tall, blond woman walked beside a well-built Kapel man. The two had just crested the hill.

"Daniel, go get Dr. Frank," she said to a young man in a blue cotton shirt. He turned quickly and ran into the clinic. Moments later, Frank Myers stood beside his wife.

"What is it, Karen?"

"Look who's coming down the trail," she answered. "We don't see anything like that very often. I wonder who they are."

"We'll know shortly," Frank said.

As the two drew closer, Frank squinted, and then slapped his hand on the table.

"I'll be damned. It's Mrs. Martin, and, unless I'm mistaken, the infamous Lieutenant Colonel Joseph Weah."

"Are you sure?" asked Karen.

"Yes, I'm sure."

Frank felt a shiver run down his spine. He remembered Hank's story of the dream where he had seen his wife naked with a gash along her cheek. This woman approaching them had a distinct red scar on her face. He had listened to the reports on CNN that had substantiated the fact that Martin's dream had been at least partially true. The people he had described in his dreams had indeed been killed. The first reports indicated that Martin's wife and son had died, too. Now Martin's wife was walking directly up to the admissions table, unless he was seeing a ghost.

"Mrs. Martin, Colonel Weah, I am Dr. Frank Myers, and this is my wife, Karen. Welcome to our clinic."

"How do you know who we are?" Lindsey asked, unable to hide her astonishment.

"It's a long story," Frank answered. "Why don't the two of you come up to the house?"

# 24

*Hank pulled out of Monrovia onto Tubman Boulevard on his way to the up-country highway. It was now about half past one in the afternoon. He had hoped to be on the road by noon. Talk about Murphy's Law working overtime. His plan had been simple. He figured the old Liberian mining company truck that he had driven down from Sanniquellie would just as easily get him back up-country to Zigda.*

THE FIRST THING IN THE MORNING, HE HAD WALKED INTO THE EMBASSY MOTOR pool. He asked where the truck had been parked. The mechanic on duty pointed to the far corner where they kept the junkers. Although it had been brought in less than two weeks earlier, the truck had been cannibalized. No tires. No wheels. No battery.

Fortunately, Jim Parkinson had come to his aid. Jim had signed off the requisitions on the DAO budget for tires and a battery. A search through three junkyards netted four wheels. Only Jim knew he was back in Liberia. If Vicky knew, she would try to stop him.

He was on the road out of Monrovia within hours. He glanced in the rearview mirror. Two military Hummers had followed him from Embassy Row. He pulled over to the shoulder. Just in case he needed a weapon, he reached down and pulled the Glock from his ankle holster. He placed it between his legs and rested his right hand in his lap.

The first Hummer came to a stop in front of him. The second Hummer pulled up behind. Soldiers got out and stationed themselves around the truck. Seven held Uzis. Each weapon was pointed directly at Hank.

Remaining calm, Hank questioned their tactics. Why they had chosen this location to confront him? After all, if they were planning to kill him, they could have done it anywhere.

A Liberian army major, wearing mirrored sunglasses, walked up to the driver's door. Despite the glasses, Hank recognized Major Oscar Jalah. He knew that he worked directly for Julius Carpai.

"Major Jalah, what brings you out on a nice day like this?"

"Colonel Martin, welcome back to Liberia. Please accept this small token of our appreciation."

Jalah handed Hank a small cardboard box. He saluted, turned and snapped his fingers. The soldiers returned to the Hummers. Both vehicles wheeled around and headed back towards the city.

Hank stared at the box. He figured it wasn't a bomb. After all, Jalah didn't need to blow him up. All he had to do was to simply shoot him.

Hank carefully opened it. Inside, he saw a single sheet of folded paper. He picked it up. Under it was a small object wrapped in aluminum foil. He unfolded the paper and read its typed message.

"Lieutenant Colonel Martin, you are a fool to come back to Liberia. We know everything you do. We are watching every move you make. You should have stayed in bed with your lady ambassador instead of trying to make a deal with your old friend, Charles Morray. Your stupidity resulted in the deaths of your friends. But you don't seem to get the message. Now you must go to Charles Morray and kill him. If you have not killed him within two days, your son will die a long and horrible death."

The note was unsigned.

Again, Hank wondered what they were planning. They had certainly chosen a strange way to deal with him.

He picked up the foil-wrapped object. Inside was something enclosed in plastic wrap. He could see through the clear wrapping.

"Oh, God, no!" Hank gasped, letting the object fall back into the box. He slammed the truck into gear, took a wide U-turn, and almost collided with an approaching taxi. He wove in and out of traffic until he reached the front gate of the American embassy. The Marine guard saluted and waved him through.

He drove directly to the medical clinic, ran up the steps and burst into the front office.

"Where's David King?" he demanded.

"Sir, he's with a patient. Would you please have a seat?"

Hank came around the desk and took long strides down the hallway until he reached an exam room. He threw open the door only to find King with his stethoscope in hand. Cindy Brooks, an embassy secretary, perched on the end of the exam table.

"Sorry, Cindy, this can't wait," Hank blurted out.

"Jesus, Hank, what are you doing?" asked the doctor. Hank didn't bother to answer his question.

"Doc, you need to tell me if this matches anyone in the embassy fingerprint file. Also let me know how old you think it is. As soon as you know, bring the information directly to Vicki's office."

"What is it?"

"A severed finger."

"Hank Martin, is this some kind of sick joke?" Cindy snapped, grasping the exam gown and holding it tightly against her breasts.

Hank ignored the woman. As suddenly as he appeared, he was gone.

He sprinted across the parking lot until he reached the ambassador's office.

"My God, Hank, what are you doing back in Monrovia?" the secretary asked.

"It's a long story, Jean. Is Ambassador Johnson in now?"

"Yes. She's with Jim Parkinson and Bruce Ziegler. She asked not to be disturbed."

"Just the people I need to see," Hank said, walking directly to Vicki's door. Jean could only watch as he passed her desk and opened the office door without knocking.

The three – Vicki, Jim and Bruce – all sat around the coffee table. All of them looked up at once. "Hank, where did you come from? What are you doing here?" Vicki asked.

"I'm sorry, Vicki. I didn't tell you that I flew in yesterday. I wanted to keep you out of this. But things have changed."

"Hank, what on earth are you talking about?"

Before he could answer, Vicki's secretary stood beside him.

"I'm sorry, Ambassador Johnson, he just barged in."

"It's OK, Jean. Pull the door closed behind you," Vicki said.

When the door closed, Vicki looked directly at Hank.

"All right, Hank. You need to start talking."

But Hank didn't talk. Instead, he handed her the unsigned note. After she read it, she passed it along to the others.

"When did you get this?"

"About forty-five minutes ago. Oscar Jalah, Carpai's assistant, handed it to me on the up-country road."

"Any witnesses?"

"Only the seven soldiers who were pointing their Uzis at me."

"Hank, this just doesn't make sense. How can you expect us to believe that Carpai is holding your son hostage and that he wants you to kill Charles Morray?" Vicki asked, shaking her head. "That's impossible."

Someone knocked rapidly on the office door.

"Now what?" Vicki said. "Come in!"

Her secretary peeked around the edge of the door. "I'm sorry to interrupt, but Dr. King is out here. He said that Colonel Martin had asked him to come here."

"What is this anyway, the Mad Hatter's Tea Party?" she asked. "All right, tell him to come in."

Vicki tapped her pen against her left palm and glared at Hank.

"Hank, I know you've been through hell with the loss of your family. I assure you that I sympathize with your grief, but I don't like to play games."

Dr. King slid through the partially open door and stood silently, looking at the ambassador.

"All right, David. Why did Colonel Martin want you to come to my office?"

"He didn't tell you?" the doctor asked.

Now she had a chance to take a good look at the doctor. His face was pale and his hand shook. He spoke slowly, deliberating on each word.

"The fingerprint shows that the severed finger was from the fifth digit on Tim Martin's left hand. The finger was surgically removed at the second joint. Exposed bone indicates that enough tissue remained to sew up the end of the finger. At least the bone had not been sawn in half. Amputation where the bone is cut has a significant potential for infection and possible death. Based on the elasticity of the tissue and the complete lack of decay, I would estimate that this occurred sometime earlier this morning."

Vicki stared at the floor. She took a long, deep breath and exhaled slowly. Hank sank in a hard-backed chair and buried his face in his hands.

"Thank you, doctor. Please close the door when you leave."

Hank dropped his hands to his lap. Vicki looked at him, expecting to see abject sorrow. Instead, she saw pure hatred. She shivered, about to offer words of comfort, when Hank began speaking.

"I need to tell you what happened. It's going to take some time."

"Take as much time as you need," Vicki said.

"It started in 1992 when you and I were living in Naama...." Hank described what he had seen at the ritual murder and about Carpai's involvement. He told of his recurring dreams. Then he told them of the dream where Tim had been the victim. He talked about the people he had seen in the ceremony. He told them of the terrible episode in Sanniquellie and how that dream included the members of the attaché's staff and their families. He told them how Jim Parkinson's family had been missing from the dream.

He went on to explain how he had found out that Lindsey and Tim hadn't died in the fire. Finally, he related his belief that the two were still alive.

His story went on for nearly an hour. When he stopped, neither one spoke. Finally, Vicki broke the silence.

"But you have no actual proof that the Liberian government is involved. My God, the implications of that are enormous. You imply that so many of the nation's top officials are a part of this. Sarday, Moya, Karua,

Dowling and Carpai. And you say there are even two others. You're saying that they're devil worshippers. You're saying that they have a part in the murder of these American families. Do you realize that the President would have all of us locked up in an insane asylum if this ever got out?"

Jim Parkinson raised his hand to interrupt. "I believe him, Vicki," he said.

"Why, Jim?"

"When I was just a kid, a tornado hit our town. It touched down less than two blocks from our house. Twelve people were killed. We were just lucky. The house didn't lose a shingle. For months, we helped other people get their lives together after they had lost everything. We actually felt guilty that the tornado hadn't hit our home.

"After the terrorists hit Mamba Bluff, we found ourselves the only survivors. Maggie and I felt that same kind of guilt. We didn't even want to talk about it out of fear that something horrible might still happen to us.

"In Colonel Martin's dream at Sanniquellie, he said that my family was the only one missing. He said that Dowling was a part of this group.

"Well, the night of the attack, it made no sense that Dowling would invite us over to see that movie. I had tried to close my mind to that night's events, but now that I think back, Dowling acted strangely all evening. He seemed nervous. We tried to leave several times, but he insisted – no, demanded – that we stay longer. We felt we had no choice but to stay.

"As you know, Maggie and Theresa Moya are good friends. Theresa is Dowling's only daughter. That friendship got us invited to a number of functions through Dowling. But we had never before been invited to his house on such short notice. I think that he knew what was going to happen that night. For his daughter's sake, he figured if we weren't home, we wouldn't be harmed."

When Parkinson's story came to an end, Vicki stood and walked to the window. A few moments later, she turned and faced the men.

"That's still only circumstantial evidence, and weak evidence at that," she said. "But there are some things that we can do.

"Bruce, I want you and Jim to send reports back to your agencies to let them know that we have some intelligence that indicates that Morray may not be responsible for the murders. Also, let them know that there are possible links to the Liberian government. Don't mention any names."

She paused, taking a deep breath.

"Also, we need to send to Washington Dr. King's report and the finger. It has to be preserved and sent back as evidence that Tim Martin is still alive as of today."

"Well, I can do a hell of a lot more than that," Hank growled, getting to his feet. "I'm going to Charles Morray."

"Hank!" Vicki said. "You're not going to kill Charles Morray. That wouldn't help, and they wouldn't release your son. You know the state department policy on hostages. We don't negotiate."

"Vicki, I never said that I was going to kill Charles Morray, and I couldn't give a rat's ass what the state department policy is. I knew from the start that there was no official way out of this. I knew I was going to be out there on my own."

"You're not going anywhere. I am your boss, and I am ordering you to stay put."

"Madame Ambassador, you had better discuss that with your new defense attaché. As of Monday I was reassigned to Washington, D.C. You are no longer my boss."

"As the ambassador of the United States, I'll have you arrested if you try to leave the compound."

"You can try, lady, but it will take more than a couple of teenage Marines to stop me. Besides that, someone is likely to get hurt."

Hank slammed the door as he stormed out of the room. The others sat stunned and speechless.

"Are you going to have him arrested?" Jim whispered.

"Jim, I could never do that," she said. "Gentlemen, would you all please leave now? I have some serious thinking to do."

After they had left, Vicki rushed for her private restroom. She reached the toilet in time to empty the contents of her churning stomach. Sinking to her knees, she sobbed aloud. In public, she had to maintain the strong image of being in charge. Here, locked in her bathroom, she cried for Tim's agony and Hank's suffering. Perhaps even more was yet to come. They might still find out that Lindsey had already been killed.

Vicki wondered how she would have handled the situation if it had been her husband's finger wrapped in aluminum foil and delivered in a cardboard box. What would she do in response to the threat? If only David were here to offer comfort and advice.

She got to her feet and pressed her open hands firmly against her middle. At the sink, she rinsed out her mouth and daubed the tears from her eyes. Now she knew what it was really like to be the ambassador – all alone, at the top, and in charge.

Rather than returning to his office, Bruce walked through the embassy grounds until he came to a bench near the recreation hall. Tall palms offered some shade. He needed some time alone, time to think things over. He replayed the facts in his mind. The note had said something about how Hank should stay in bed with the lady ambassador. It referred to some deal with Charles Morray.

He was puzzled by something else he'd heard. The fact that Vicki and Hank had known each other in 1992 wasn't common knowledge. He had guessed at their intimate relationship during the meeting right before Hank left to meet with Morray. Whoever wrote the note claimed to know about the meeting. Only Vicki, Hank, and he had been there when they came up with the plan. Who else could possibly know?

Then it came to him – there was only one other. He stood and headed to his quarters.

"Hi, Hon!" said Donna as she saw her husband come in the back door.

"Donna, I need to ask you a question," he said, leaning against a kitchen counter.

"Sure, what is it?"

"Just before the terrorist attack, do you remember when I told you about my suspicion that Hank Martin and Ambassador Johnson had a thing going when she was a Peace Corps volunteer here? I think I also mentioned that Hank was planning to meet with Charles Morray."

"I guess so. Why?"

"Did you tell anyone?"

"No, no, of course not. You know I'd never do that."

Bruce had spent five years in CIA interrogation. He had been trained to observe eye contact, physical reaction, and voice modulation. He could pick out a liar ninety-nine percent of the time. He moved toward her and grabbed her by the shoulders.

"You're lying! Who did you tell?"

"Bruce, you're hurting me! Stop it! I didn't tell anyone. I swear I didn't tell anyone!" He dug his fingers deeper into her upper arms.

"You're lying! You're lying!" he screamed. "Seventeen people are dead. One was a six-month-old baby girl! She's dead because someone found out. I will have to live with that. You will have to live with that. Now, who did you tell?"

Donna shook with fear as her tears streamed down her cheeks. She knew that Bruce had worked in black operations. He was capable of doing horrible things to people. She'd never seen him like this before. His eyes showed the intensity of his anger.

"It was Wayne Turner!" she gasped. "I might have said something to Wayne. We didn't do anything, Bruce. We just talked. Please, please... you're breaking my arms. Please stop! You're hurting me!"

He released his grasp. She slid to the floor, sobbing uncontrollably. She looked up in time to see the door slam.

Wayne Turner was shocked to see Bruce Ziegler standing at his door.

"Bruce? What can I do for you?"

Bruce pushed his way inside.

"Who did you talk to?" he demanded.

"What are you talking about? Are you nuts or something?"

Then Wayne remembered the morning after tennis when Bruce's wife had come to his home. Had Donna told him what happened?

His first impulse was to try to explain his way out of it. Then he took a second look at the angry man before him. Bruce was only about five feet ten inches tall and weighed around one hundred fifty pounds.

Wayne figured he could pick him up with one arm tied behind his back.

He pondered his options. What did he have to worry about? Who the hell does he think he is?

"Look, man," Wayne said firmly. "I don't know what your problem is, but you can get your skinny butt out of my house right now!"

Bruce Ziegler didn't seem to hear.

"Who did you tell?" he asked again. "You're going to tell me, and I'm not going to leave until I find out!"

Wayne's options narrowed. He concluded that he'd push the puny little fart out the door. He'd report Ziegler's forced entry to the ambassador.

Without another word, Wayne reached out and wrapped his large hand around Bruce's right wrist. It wasn't much different than grabbing a little boy's arm. He could snap it in a second.

Bruce stared at his wrist as if he had suddenly discovered that someone was holding it. Now Wayne spoke.

"That does it! I'm going to hurt you, little man. I have no idea what Donna can see in a little white shrimp like you. What she needs is a real man," he said still holding Bruce's wrist.

In a split second, Bruce's left hand had shot forward. He dug his fingers into the pressure point between Wayne's neck and collarbone. Wayne's knees buckled under him as an agonizing pain shot through his body. He dropped to the floor. Bruce's fingers wrapped around his wrists and dug into the soft flesh. A second, more severe bolt of pain shot up his arms.

"Who did you talk to?" Bruce demanded.

Wayne sobbed. He struggled in a fruitless effort to get away. "I don't know what you want!"

"Who did you tell about Hank Martin planning to meet with Charles Morray?"

Through the pain, Wayne began to focus on what Bruce was asking.

"I, I told Julius Carpai."

Bruce released his hold and fell back into a chair.

"Do you know what you did?"

Wayne pulled himself up and made his way to another chair across the room. He rubbed his wrists, trying to get feeling back into his aching arms.

"I didn't do anything wrong. It was just gossip I told him," Wayne explained.

"Wayne, you murdered seventeen Americans. You ruined hundreds of lives. It was because of you that those families were brutally executed. You're going to have to live with the faces of those poor people in your dreams for the rest of your life."

Bruce got up and walked out the door, never once looking back into the face of the startled Wayne Turner.

Wayne remained in his chair, trying to regain his composure.

He shook his head as he thought through what had just happened. What he had told Carpai wasn't anything secret. As a matter of fact, he had even made up some of it. He had led Carpai to believe that Hank was somehow working with Morray to get military aid to the People's Party.

He recalled Carpai's reaction. He had given him the valuable Poro mask. Wayne got up, but still trembled. The mask hung on the opposite wall. Its dark wood and intricate carving continued to enchant him, and then he remembered Carpai's reaction to what he'd told him.

"My God!" he said aloud. "Bruce was right after all. How could I be so stupid?"

Wayne had convinced Liberia's minister of defense that the United States was going to dump the nation's established government for the People's Party. Carpai was ruthless enough to commit murder so he could send a message to the U.S. He was cunning enough to blame it all on Charles Morray.

Wayne had sold out his country for an old wooden mask. He screamed out in his frustration, took the mask from the wall and hurled it across the room. It splintered to pieces. He slumped back in the chair and buried his face in his hands.

Vicki logged off. It was part of their daily ritual to chat online. She couldn't tell David what had been happening, but it was comforting to have a little contact, even though it was only electronic.

She heard a knock at her door. She checked the time – ten o'clock – too late for visitors. Perhaps it was Hank. Maybe he'd come to his senses and decided not to go out on his own to get to Charles Morray. Instead of Hank, Bruce Ziegler stood in the doorway.

"Bruce?" she asked, astonished at his disheveled appearance. "Bruce... God, you look horrible!" she blurted.

"Look, Vicki, sorry to bother you at this time of night, but what I have to say can't wait."

Vicki thought she caught a whiff of alcohol.

"You're not drunk, are you, Bruce?"

"No," he answered. "It would be a hell of a lot easier if I were. May I come in for a few minutes?"

"Sure," she said, leading him into the living room. "Let me fix you a cup of coffee. Looks like you need it."

A few minutes later, Vicki carried in two mugs of coffee. When she handed Bruce his cup, she saw that he used both hands to hold it. Whatever he had in mind, thought Vicki, it can't be good.

He handed her a sealed letter.

"What's this?" she asked.

"My resignation. It's effective as of today's date. Donna and I will be on a Swiss Air flight tomorrow morning. My career is over. Maybe my marriage is as well. Only time will tell."

"I don't understand," Vicki said. Bruce leaned back and began his story. He admitted his violation of security when he told Donna about Hank's trip. He told Vicki how he had even speculated about Hank's relationship with her in 1992.

He paused, cradling the mug.

Vicki only listened, not visibly reacting to the story. Then he told her about how Donna had told Wayne Turner the story. Turner had passed the information on to Julius Carpai.

Vicki set her cup on the coffee table and folded her hands in her lap. She had always regarded Bruce as one of her finest staff members. She had valued his expertise and professionalism. She longed to tell him that he was forgiven. She also wanted to scream at him, blasting his stupid indiscretion. His weakness had destroyed too many lives. Even more lives might yet be at risk. He had also jeopardized her role as ambassador.

Finally, she just nodded, creasing the fold of the letter tightly between her fingers. The next morning, he'd be gone. Jerry Day would replace him as first secretary. After Bruce had left, she returned to the computer. She quickly composed a brief statement on her computer, ordering Wayne Turner out of the country. She would ask the FBI to investigate possible charges of espionage. She printed the memo, switched off the computer and began to get ready for bed.

No more tears. Tomorrow she'd get a handle on the situation.

# 25

***Tim and Sabo were running side-by-side down the bush trail toward Zigda.***

THEY WERE SURROUNDED BY AN INDIGO BLUE, THE SUN SAT STRAIGHT overhead. Tim and Sabo had pulled so far ahead of the other warriors that they would easily win the final phase of the competition – the race to the finish. Before they started, they had vowed to each other to clench hands as they crossed the finish line together. It would be a tie. Both would be honored as the greatest African warriors in this contest with other young men from every village in the area.

The final turn lay just ahead. They could see the village of Zigda in the valley below. All downhill now, they lengthened their stride. Both let out a scream of victory when they finally saw the taut line of yellow plastic, which marked the finish. Sabo laughed out loud as the two pushed themselves even harder. Just a little faster, Tim thought, and they could almost fly.

Ahead, just beyond the finish line, he would see people he knew in the waiting crowd. Mom and Dad, Joe Weah, all of his friends from school, and even the attaché families waved them on toward the finish. Nancy Matthews held up little Chrissie so she could see the oncoming runners. Chrissie giggled out loud, as babies often do.

Togba himself lifted a big black and white checkered flag. Now less than one hundred yards remained. Side by side, the two broke through the plastic tape at the same time. Tim lifted his arms above his head in a victory salute. Sabo beside him, Tim bent over to catch his breath.

First, it was complete silence. Then only darkness. Tim focused on his own breathing. A thick fog made it impossible to see clearly. Sabo stood beside him. He gripped Tim's left hand so tightly that it hurt. Sabo's hand seemed so cold. He imagined it was a frozen package of meat, not a part of Sabo's anatomy. He tried to form the words to tell Sabo not to squeeze so hard, but words wouldn't come. He turned his head to look at his friend, but Sabo had disappeared.

Instead a midget, less than three feet tall, had taken Sabo's place. Its naked body was covered in a thin gray powder. Two pointed horns sprouted from the top of its oversized head. Tim gasped and tried to make his body move, but he was frozen in place. The creature's horse-like face glared up at him as it bared its long yellow teeth. The red-veined eyeballs stared at him. Tim forced himself to look into the white orbs. They had no pupils. He opened his mouth and his lips formed a scream, but no noise came out. He willed himself to pull away, but his weakness left him helpless.

The creature laughed. "Your soul will be mine!" it said in a childish whine. It reached out its curved talons and guided Tim's hand toward its mouth. As if it were snapping a pretzel, it bit off the end of Tim's little finger. A bolt of pain shot up his arm. Never before had he been in such agony. He heard his own shriek, coming from deep in his throat and from the depths of his lungs. His tormenter only grinned more broadly, its black-forked tongue lapping Tim's blood from its white lips. It opened its mouth, revealing red liquid and tissue from inside the dark cavity. It reached out and lifted the next finger, salivating as it readied itself for a second bite.

It was just like the nature show on television. Wild dogs attacked a wildebeest. It struggled, rolling, kicking, as the dogs ate it alive. Tim had asked if it felt any pain. His mother had told him that it hadn't. It would have gone into shock, desensitizing it from the sharp teeth that ripped its failing body.

"Mom, you're wrong!" he screamed. "It hurts bad when you're being eaten alive."

But his mother didn't answer.

"Oh, God, oh, please," he cried. "Please, someone help me!"

The creature's sharp teeth were just inches from Tim's next finger. Instead of biting, it stopped, then looked behind Tim and screamed.

"Kill him!"

The fog parted. Tim could now see the face and form of Junga Sayeh who held a pointed spear above him. Tim tried to shake his head. Junga was dead. He was sure he was dead. He had seen the dark holes where the soldier's bullet had gone deep into Junga's chest. Yet this Junga raised his muscled arm, preparing to follow the creature's demands.

Just then, a massive animal emerged from the shadows behind him. With one sweep of its powerful paw, a leopard knocked the spear from Junga's hand. It raked its razor-sharp claws across its victim's chest, exposing his bright red ribs. The animal lunged at the body, driving it to the ground. Its teeth sank into Junga's throat, nearly severing the head from the body.

With a violent roar, the leopard turned toward the dwarf-creature whose face reflected its fear. It dropped Tim's hand and scuttled away on its stubby, bowed legs.

It didn't go quietly. Tim heard its final scream fade into the fog.

"You haven't won yet, Chea Geebe. I will have the boy's soul!" Tim's chest heaved with uncontrollable sobbing. He held his mutilated left hand in his remaining good hand. He braced himself for the animal's inevitable attack. He closed his eyes, yet experienced an unusual calm.

Instead of claws, he felt the rough tongue of the huge cat, gently licking his bloodied hand. He gritted his teeth and awaited the pain. Rather than the crunch of the animal's jaws on his mutilated flesh, he heard a throaty purr. He looked down and saw the cat washing away the blood. It reminded Tim of his dog, King, and his friendly lick. The pain had subsided to only a dull throb.

His attention shifted from the leopard to what he thought was the sound of a voice, although he wasn't aware of another presence.

"Tim, the *endosym* has taken only a small portion of your soul. You must continue to fight. The spirit of the leopard will help you, but you must ultimately win the battle by yourself. Here in the den of the *endosym*, do not eat or drink. If you fail to heed this warning, your soul will be lost."

The voice faded. The leopard stood, stretched and vanished in the mist.

"Wait! Wait, don't leave me alone!" Tim called out. The earth beneath him began to shake, and he felt pulled to another level of consciousness.

In the semi-darkness, Tim looked up to see a ray of light pouring in through a small barred window. He blinked and tried to focus on a dark form that stood over him. He sighed with relief when he recognized the face of his friend Sabo. He began to pull himself up to a sitting position, but fell back, screaming with pain.

"My hand," he moaned. His left hand was swaddled in gauze. "What happened? Where are we?" Tim asked.

"They must have drugged us," Sabo answered. "When I woke up, we were in this cell."

Tim saw that they were in rough concrete block room. It measured about ten feet on each side. On one wall about five feet from the floor, a ten-inch hole let in a beam of sunlight. The opposite wall had a heavy wooden door with a small, barred window.

"What happened to my hand?" Tim asked.

"I don't know," Sabo said. "All I remember is a white man sticking a needle in my arm."

"We must be in some sort of army camp," Tim said. His left hand continued to throb. He began removing the bandage.

"Why are you doing that?" Sabo asked.

"I have to know. I had a horrible dream." He pulled back the gauze until he could see the swollen tissue. "Jesus, it really happened!" he said.

The little finger on his left hand was gone. He held his hand up to the light to get a better look. Everything about it looked clean. He slowly re-wrapped the gauze. Strangely, he wasn't all that upset. The loss of his finger had now become a part of who he was. He had no choice but to live with it.

"Tim, where do you think we are?" Sabo asked.

"I don't know, but I think we're in big trouble."

Tim eased himself to his feet. He held his left hand near his chest, elevating it to minimize the throbbing. It hurt, but he could handle the pain. He peered through the bars on the door window. From what he could see, the cell was a part of a large circular hut. Several other rooms lined the far wall. Those doors had no windows. A large opening on the far side led to a grassy area. That opening provided the only interior light.

Tim heard movement. He hurried back to the mat where Sabo sat. The lock clicked, and the door swung open. A man in the fatigues of a Liberian soldier stood in the doorway. Speaking Kapel, he ordered the boys to remain seated. He carried a nine-millimeter pistol and pointed it in their direction. He backed out, picked up a bucket and set it inside the door. He placed two bowls of steaming rice and chop on the floor.

"Enjoy yourselves," he said. The door closed, the lock clicked, and he was gone.

Neither boy moved nor spoke. Finally Sabo stood up and walked to the bucket. It was filled to the brim with clear, cool water. He dipped his cupped hands into the water and lifted them to his lips. Tim's right hand reached out and pushed Sabo's hands from his mouth, spilling the water on the dirt floor.

"What did you do that for?" asked Sabo. "I'm thirsty."

"Don't eat or drink anything. I was warned in a dream that if we ate or drank anything in this place, we would lose our souls. I think the water and food could be poisoned or drugged."

"It looks OK to me, Tim."

"We can find out real easy," Tim said. "Let's pour the water on the floor and dump out some of the food. Then we'll lie down. When someone comes in, we'll pretend that we're asleep."

Only a matter of minutes passed before they heard people approaching. They curled up on the floor.

"Hey, boys, wake up! Wake up, boys! Come on, we're letting you go home to your families."

"Are they out?"

"Yes. The magic powder works every time. They will be out until morning. When they awake, the powder will make them so thirsty that they'll want to drink more water."

"Are you going to pick up the bucket and food bowls?"

"Not now. I'll get them in the morning. Let's go eat."

After he was sure the men were gone, Tim whispered to Sabo.

"What did they say?"

"You were right. The food and water are drugged. One of the men said that he would come back in the morning to get the food bowls and bucket. That may be our only chance to get out. Maybe we can overpower him," said Sabo.

# 26

***Hank had just passed into Nimba County. His hands tightly gripped the steering wheel. He'd been on the road for more than five hours. In less than an hour, he would be in Sanniquellie.***

NO ONE STOPPED HIM AT THE EMBASSY. HE REGRETTED HIS BLOWUP IN VICKI'S office. He'd been angry about Tim's abduction. He had been frustrated with the lack of U.S. support. He bristled when he thought of the Liberian officials who were behind all this death and grief. It looked like they would walk free.

He had passed the government buildings in downtown Monrovia. It had taken all of his willpower not to burst into the office and blast Julius Carpai between the eyes. But he knew he wouldn't get away with it, and Tim would still die. At least there was a chance for success if he could make it to Sanniquellie.

Tim's mutilation tore at his heart, and he still didn't know the fate of his wife. The pragmatic, professional soldier tried to bury the hurt. What surfaced was a special operations expert, capable of killing an enemy with surgical precision.

One of Hank's greatest talents was the ability to "worst case" any scenario. Planning for the worst, at least in his mind, usually resulted in a greater level of success. The worst case here was that Tim would die a gruesome, painful death. Sadly, the best case he could come up with was that Tim's death would come quickly. He knew that these bastards would never willingly release his son. Seventeen years earlier, he had witnessed their total disregard for human life.

Hank scoffed when he thought of that letter telling him to kill Charles Morray. Carpai was a fool if he thought that Hank would do what he asked just to save his son. The letter and the severed finger hadn't brought Hank to his knees. On the contrary, it had pushed Hank over the edge. He was beyond the fear of losing his job, obeying the law or turning the other cheek. These men would die for their crimes, and Hank was determined to be the instrument of their deaths.

He slowed the truck as he came into the village of Sanniquellie. He passed the market and the small shops and followed the winding road to Frank's clinic. It was almost six o'clock. He pulled up near the house, climbed the steps and knocked on the door. Frank opened it.

"Colonel Martin, what a pleasant surprise. Please come in. We were just sitting down to dinner."

"Sir, I hate to bother you, but it is imperative that I get in touch with Charles Morray."

"That's no problem, but let's have our dinner first. We'll all think better on a full stomach." Hank would have preferred to continue on his mission, but something in Frank's demeanor told him to respect the man's wishes. Frank led him around the corner and into the dining room. Five people – two men and three women – were already seated at the table.

Joe Weah and Charles Morray stood. Charles' wife and Karen Meyers and....

"Oh, God!" Hank cried. "Lindsey!"

She jumped to her feet and called out his name. Her chair fell backward, crashing to the floor as she rushed into her husband's arms.

"Hank! Oh, Hank!" she sobbed, burying her face in his embrace.

Hank hugged her tightly. It was really her – warm, vital and alive. He ran his hands through her hair and down her back. Then held her out at arms' length to reassure himself that it was really Lindsey. His finger traced the red scar on her cheek.

"I love you," he whispered in her ear.

"Hank, they have Tim," she said.

"I know," he replied.

"Folks," interrupted Frank, "I know you need to talk. But, as a doctor, it is imperative that we all eat first. Food in the stomach helps the brain function!"

They sat, joined hands and bowed their heads. "Our Father in heaven, we would ask that you be in our presence this evening. We do not know why such evil exists, but we do know that through your son, Jesus Christ, we can prevail against all evil. Help these people to do what they must do. Give them comfort, and bless this food to the nourishment of our bodies. We ask these things in the name of your son. Amen."

Hank squeezed Lindsey's hand. His anger hadn't been forgotten, but now he felt a renewed sense of composure and hope.

Frank had been right about the food. It helped bring the world into perspective. When they finished their meal, they sat down in the living room.

"Start at the beginning," Hank said to Lindsey. "What happened the night you escaped?"

Lindsey told of the terrible night. She told them of how Tim had shot Carpai's men. She told them of how she had seen Carpai himself in the house just before they escaped.

Joe explained about how he had found the two of them at Charlie Marshall's house. He described how Major Jalah had captured Tim and Sabo.

When Lindsey and Joe had told their story, Hank realized that the time had come to tell them what had happened since he'd first witnessed the ritual killing so long ago. He told of the horrible dreams that haunted him. Finally, he talked about the letter that threatened Tim's life if Hank failed to kill Charles Morray. He deliberately did not mention the amputation of Tim's finger.

"Would you kill me to save your son?" asked Charles.

"No," answered Hank. "No matter what I do, they intend to kill Tim. There's only one thing for sure here – I will kill Julius Carpai."

"Colonel, they won't have a chance to murder your son if we can rescue him first," Charles said.

"But I have no idea where he is."

"Yes, you do. There is a place near the Saint Paul River where no Liberian dares go. It is a place of great evil where men see strange visions."

"My God!" Hank exclaimed. "Are you telling me that the place where I saw that ritual killing still exists?"

"The evil has grown even more powerful. You know how powerful it was on that night so long ago."

"I remember you tried to convince me to leave, but I wouldn't go. I stayed to watch the ceremony. It was all so strange. I felt as though I had entered another world."

"Colonel, when I found you, you were out of your mind. I had to hide you from the men who searched for us. After they had gone, I took you back to Camp Jackson, but you didn't know who I was. It seemed as if you had been drugged. If we try to rescue your son, it will have to be only you and me. No other Liberian would dare enter the sacred bush."

"You can make that three," Joe said. "I'll go with you."

"It is very dangerous. We might fail," Charles said.

Lindsey, who had been listening intently to their talk, interrupted them.

"Perhaps this will help," she said. She lifted a leather cord from around her neck. Its charm looked like the tooth of a leopard. The tooth was capped in silver.

"Everyday Walker gave this to me when we left Zigda," she said. She went on to tell about how they had found out that he was a great *zo*. He was really Chea Geebe. She could tell by Hank's expression that he was skeptical.

"Hank, I swear that I saw it glow with a green light when it was placed on Joe's chest. Minutes later, Joe came out of the coma. He gave it to me because he said it would offer us protection from what he called the endosym. Please, Hank, wear it!"

"All right," Hank said. "But I think a nine-millimeter pistol is all the magic I'll need."

Hours later, the men completed their plans for Tim's rescue. They put on military fatigues. Hank's tiger suit was what they call a sterile outfit. It couldn't be traced back to the United States. He smeared his face, hands and arms with camouflage makeup.

Lindsey knew this side of her husband had existed, but she had never seen it up close. She shuddered. How could this evil transform the man she loved into a fearsome soldier?

"You're sure that we won't run into a roadblock between here and the valley?" Hank asked.

"The soldiers only man the up-country roadblocks during daylight hours," Charles explained. "There are too many spirits in the bush. Besides that, the officers are too lazy to stay with the soldiers. We've found that we've been able to move freely at night. However, if we are successful in rescuing your son and Joe's cousin, we'll have to hide out during daylight. It may take several days to get back here to Sanniquellie."

"We'll use your mining truck," Joe offered. "These trucks are so common that it will draw little attention. Our greatest concern will be Camp Jackson. They have two hundred soldiers there. Carpai can call them up quickly."

Lindsey stood in the kitchen doorway. Hank saw her watching in silence. He got up, walked to her and enfolded her in his arms.

"We'll be leaving in about five minutes," he said, holding her close. "Don't worry. I'll find our son and bring him back."

"You be careful, Hank. I don't want to lose you," she said, kissing him gently on the cheek.

Hank turned to Joe and Charles.

"Let's go, guys."

"Hold it, gentlemen," said Frank. "You're not going anywhere without a little help from above. Frank led the group in prayer. Then he embraced each man. When he got to Hank, he had something more to say.

"Remember what I said about saying the Lord's Prayer. I believe you are facing something supernatural. If you again feel the presence of something in that valley, say the prayer over and over," he cautioned. "Be careful, son. Don't worry about Lindsey. Karen and I will take care of her until you return."

Lindsey lingered at the door until the truck's taillights disappeared over the crest of the hill. Karen came up behind her and rested her hand on her shoulder.

"Come on back into the house, dear. You're going to need some sleep. Tomorrow you can help out at the clinic."

Lindsey looked again down the road where she'd last seen Hank. Reluctantly, she turned and went back into the house.

Charles drove. Hank and Joe squeezed in beside him. Two of Charles' men rode in back. Nearly three hours later, the old mining truck pulled to a stop alongside the road.

"Take the truck into Gbarnga," he told the men. "Stay there until tomorrow night. It's now about one o'clock. Be back here tomorrow night at the same time. Wait here two hours. If we're not back by then, go back to Gbarnga and return the following night. If we don't show up then, you might as well assume that we've been captured or killed."

The truck disappeared into the darkness, and the three of them crossed the bridge over the Saint Paul River and turned left down a rough road that headed west. About ten minutes later, Charles led them off the road and onto the bush trail. When Hank had last made the trek some eighteen years ago, it had been in daylight. Nothing looked familiar now.

Charles hiked quickly along the trail. Hank and Joe followed close behind. Their only light came from a half moon that filtered through the jungle foliage. Hank and Joe had learned their patrolling techniques at Fort Bragg, North Carolina. Charles' only training was as a private in the Liberian army. Yet, like his African brothers, he had learned to hunt and stalk animals in bush school.

All three were armed with M-16s. Each carried extra twenty-round magazines. In their rucksacks, each of them had five fragmentation grenades and a three-day supply of food. Hank also carried four one-pound blocks of C-4 plastic explosive, ten non-electric blasting caps, detonation cord, fuse and fuse lighters, and two white phosphorous grenades. He had strapped his nine-millimeter pistol with an aluminum silencer to his waist.

When Charles raised his hand, they stopped.

"We're almost at the entrance to the sacred bush. Once we pass the barrier, we must be particularly careful. There are guards in huts on the hill overlooking the valley. At night, none of them will be on the trail, but they've set up booby traps that shoot poison darts. One nick would be fatal."

He reached into the undergrowth and cut down a thin stalk of bamboo. He stripped off its leaves until he had an eight-foot-long pole. He cut another two poles and gave one each to Hank and Joe.

"Colonel, hold the pole out in front of you. Let the tip touch the ground. They've used monofilament-fishing line to make trip wires. They're really hard to see. When the pole hits the line, it will trigger the darts. Since the pole is out in front, the darts will miss you."

"I understand," Hank said, "but you need to call me Hank. We're all equal here. We'll live or die together."

"All right, it's Hank then," Charles grinned.

"Are we ready to go?"

"Lead the way!" Hank said.

As they continued down the trail, Hank thought how fortunate he was to be with these two men who were willing to risk their lives to save two teenage boys. They had the courage to cross the line and openly oppose their government and its leaders. These men themselves were leaders. He had seen Joe work with the soldiers and officers of the Reconnaissance Battalion. Charles led the People's Party. He had tens of thousands of followers. He had joined so many other brave men who, throughout history, had dared take on an unjust government. When this was all over, Hank thought, he vowed to do whatever he could to help Charles and the People's Party overcome the evil that had consumed their country.

They rounded a bend and came face to face with the raffia barrier. Joe held back the raffia as Charles and Hank stepped through.

"There should be no problem now until we reach the next warning," Charles said.

Hank made a conscious effort to control his anxiety. He remembered what it felt like to take his first parachute jump in airborne school. His head throbbed and his throat was dry. He willed himself to keep calm. He worked to bury the images of terror from so long ago. He was so consumed in his own thoughts that he almost bumped into Joe.

Charles had come to an abrupt halt. A thin line of white powder stretched across the trail. He saw decaying human skulls dangling menacingly from a post. This served as the final warning.

"Why didn't we go through the jungle like we did the last time?" Hank asked.

"Because, in the dark, we could lose our way. It's already half past four in the morning. We must hide out in the jungle above the valley before it's fully light. We'll keep to the trail. But, remember," Charles warned, "walk in my footsteps. I'll lead the way and look for booby traps."

He took out plastic garbage bags from his rucksack.

"Put these on over your boots. It will keep the powder off your feet. When we get to the other side of the barrier, we'll stop. We'll take off the plastic from one boot, step out of the powder, then lift the other foot and remove that bag."

Joe went first, then Hank. Charles followed. He backed across the boundary, lightly brushing away their tracks behind them. When they got to the other side, they removed the plastic bags and turned to survey the path. There was no indication that anyone had crossed the barrier. Charles folded the plastic bags and tucked them into his rucksack.

The concentration necessary to cross the barrier had taken Hank's mind off his frightening memories. He felt more confident as he followed Charles, who held his bamboo pole out front and carefully checked for trip wires. Charles suddenly stopped, knelt and pointed to the ground ahead of him. He flicked on a small pocket flashlight. They could see a fine monofilament line running about four inches above the ground.

He used his pole to poke at the line. A poison dart flew through the air and lodged in a tree on the other side of the trail.

They'd gone less than a hundred feet when Charles stopped again. Another line crossed the trail, but this one was four feet above ground. Within the next half hour, they found and tripped three more booby traps.

Hank continued to be impressed with Charles' skill. He imagined that he would have been an excellent point man in a combat situation. His natural instincts could save an entire squad. Finally, Charles announced that they could continue at a normal pace.

Hank felt even more at ease. He was pleased that he had been able to conquer his fear. But his confidence was premature.

He thought he caught a glimpse of something near the edge of the trail. He stopped and looked again. He saw nothing unusual, but still he felt unsettled. Likely an animal, he told himself. His newfound calm evaporated. Beads of sweat formed on his brow. Swallowing became difficult.

Ahead something scooted across the trail. He'd only seen its movement, yet it was enough to fill him with terror. It was a dull gray, like the statue, but it seemed to be a living thing. He gasped, struggling to take in sufficient air.

He saw no sign of Charles or Joe. He was alone, deserted, abandoned. The empty trail stretched before him in the faint moonlight. He whirled around, checking behind him. Impossible, he thought. Only seconds before, he'd been following Joe's back only ten feet ahead of him.

Now he felt cold. He shivered, partly due to fear, partly due to a sudden drop in temperature. His fatigues, which were soaked in sweat, drew the chill deep into his body. While his teeth chattered, he struggled to catch his breath. He wanted to step forward, but his legs couldn't obey. Even his hands felt heavy. He froze in place, gasping.

The brush ahead of him rustled. A dark figure moved toward him through the semi-darkness. When he'd first looked through his binoculars to see that horned statue in 1992, he could not imagine how anyone could have created such a macabre creature. Now he knew.

The inspiration for the statue stood before him. It was the living duplicate of the image that had haunted his dreams. The light gray body stood no more than three feet in height. Overhanging brows, like those of a Neanderthal, shaded the blank eyeballs. Two horns protruded from the hairless scalp. It proudly thrust out its male genitalia.

He heard it speak; its childlike voice evoked pure evil.

"I almost had you the last time you visited my home. You are a fool to dare enter this place. The boy is mine. I will drink his blood and eat his soul."

"No!" Hank gasped.

"What can you do to stop me, you foolish mortal? After your son, your wife will be mine. I will ravish her body then drink her blood. You will be forced to watch as I consume those you love."

Hank sank to his knees. Frank's words came back to him. The Lord's Prayer, he had said. He had told him to recite the Lord's Prayer. Hank coughed and began slowly.

"Our... our..." he sputtered. He couldn't continue. He tried once again. "Our Father who art in heaven..." Finally, the familiar prayer rolled from his lips. Breathing became less labored. He said it again. This time it came out even stronger and without hesitation. The rhythm of the words soothed his anxiety.

All the while, the creature stood by, watching. But Hank was able to stare at the vile form without flinching, without retreating.

Annoyed by the litany, the demon emitted a high-pitched scream and covered its eyes with its talons. As quickly as the creature had appeared, it vanished. Only a funnel of gray dust whirled where it once stood.

Hank covered his face with his hands to avoid the noxious reminder of the creature's presence. When he opened his eyes, he saw Joe and Charles directly before him.

"Hank, are you OK?" Joe asked, resting his hand on Hank's shoulder.

"I think so," Hank said, struggling to stand.

"What happened to your fatigue jacket?" Charles asked. "It's glowing green."

Hank ran his palms over his chest, reached inside and pulled out the leopard tooth necklace. The tooth itself was the source of the green light.

"It's like I'm holding a firefly in my hand," he said. He could see the green light reflected on his companions' faces.

"I've never seen anything like this in my life," he continued.

"Lindsey was right," Charles said. "Chea Geebe has given you a very powerful amulet."

Hank looked down at the tooth in his open hand. It no longer glowed.

"That, and Frank's prayers didn't hurt either," Hank said.

He grinned at the two men and reached down to pick up his gear. Then three moved down the trail and into the sacred valley.

# 27

*In the cell together, Tim and Sabo waited for dawn. The first rays of sunlight filtered through the tiny window. Tim lightly shook Sabo's shoulder to wake him.*

"It's getting light," he whispered. "We must be ready."

They had moved the water bucket close to the two sleeping mats. Their plan was simple. When the guard came in to pick up the food bowls and water bucket, they would jump him and try to escape.

Tim's hand had hurt so badly that he had been unable to sleep. He thought about his mother and Joe Weah. He didn't know where they were or even if they were still alive. His thoughts also ran to his father. He didn't know if his dad had any idea of what had happened to them. At one point, he was on the verge of tears.

He wanted his mom and dad. He thought of his dog, King. Poor King. They had killed him. The ache in his heart and the ache of his hand were almost unbearable. It was too much for a fifteen-year-old boy.

He clenched his teeth. He moved from sadness to anger. What right did these people have to hurt others? He wished he were bigger and stronger. He visualized himself as a movie action hero. He would surmount all odds by destroying the bad guys and rescuing his mother.

Despite the jumble of thoughts that filled his head and prevented sleep, he kept coming back to one thing – he and Sabo must escape this horrible place.

Then the lock clicked.

"This is it," Sabo whispered. Both boys pretended to be fast asleep. They heard the guard approach and bend over to pick up the bucket.

"Now!" yelled Tim.

Both boys jumped on the guard. It might have been much easier except that this guard was particularly large for a Liberian. He weighed well over two hundred pounds. He shook his shoulders, and the boys dropped to the floor. He laughed and pulled out his pistol.

"So the magic powder wore off," he said. "On your feet, both of you!"

They struggled to stand. Tim still stooped in agony. When he'd fallen, he had landed on his left hand. The pain shot through his arm and up to his shoulder.

"All right, both of you, up against the wall!"

Tim finally was able to stand upright. His anger began to consume him. This wasn't the way he had imagined it would happen.

"Come on, boys. Move!" the guard ordered.

"No!" responded Tim. He brought his right foot up in a karate kick. He dislodged the pistol from the guard's hand.

It flew across the room and landed on the floor. Tim head-butted the man in the stomach while Sabo leapt on his back. The guard crashed to the floor and both boys fell on top of him. He shoved out his hand, and Tim was pushed back against the wall. The impact left him dazed. His ears rang. He sat immobile, trying to focus.

When his vision cleared, he saw the guard astride Sabo, the huge hands tightening around his friend's neck. Tim tried to get up, but he screamed in agony. He had tried to push himself up with the injured hand. He fell back hard on his rear, causing yet another jolt to his body. He rolled to his side.

His arm lay stretched out on the dirt floor. Only inches away from the fingers of his right hand, he saw the guard's pistol. He reached out and clasped its cool metal. He chambered a round and pointed it at the guard's head.

"Stop it! Let him go!" screamed Tim.

The guard ignored him. He continued to choke the life from Sabo. It would only be a matter of seconds before Sabo would be lost.

Tim squeezed the trigger. The pistol recoiled in his hand. The guard gave out an angry growl, holding his right arm with his left. He got to his feet and came toward Tim.

Tim fired again. This time he hit the man directly in his broad chest. The guard looked down at himself, screamed and charged forward. Tim fired twice more at point blank range. The man's momentum carried him right toward Tim. His body slumped forward and landed on top of Tim.

Tim crawled out from under the dead man. He pulled himself up and staggered to his friend's side.

"Come on, Sabo. Get up! The other guards will be here any minute. We've got to get out of here!"

They burst out of the cell only to find out that there were two exits. They turned to the right and ran for the daylight. But it wasn't any good – they were in a fenced-in stockade. The only way out was the way they had just come.

"Oh, no," Tim said, "this is the wrong way. We have to go back."

As soon as they turned to reverse their direction, they heard shouts coming from inside the hut. That way was no longer an option.

"Run!" yelled Tim.

"Where?" screamed Sabo. "Over behind that stone thing." They dove behind the rock platform that sat in the middle of the compound.

They huddled there long enough for them to catch their breath. Tim cautiously peeked over the top. He could see a man standing in the doorway of the hut. He aimed his pistol in his direction and pulled the trigger. The round splintered the doorframe and missed its target. The man ducked inside. Tim dropped down behind the platform. He crawled to the far end and looked around the corner. This vantage point gave him a clear view of the hut, yet minimized his exposure.

He took a moment to look down at his weapon. The guard's gun was a nine-millimeter Beretta, just like the one he had fired at Joe's battalion. It had a fifteen-round magazine. Just how many shots had he fired? He remembered shooting several times at the guard. If the magazine was full, he had ten, maybe eleven, rounds left. He regretted that he hadn't taken the time to check to see if the guard had another magazine. It was too late now.

A large black fly chose that moment to land on Tim's nose. He flicked it away with his hand. Then he became aware that there were lots of flies. He sniffed and thought he detected the nauseating odor of rotting meat. Black flies swarmed on the ground nearby. He looked closer to try to determine what was attracting them. He could see a dark stain on the ground. The same substance coated the rock platform.

He took a closer look. The stone structure was about three feet high, eight feet long and four feet wide. The cut stones were carefully fitted together to provide support for its flat top. Dark stains ran down its side.

On Tim's end, a second, shorter platform sat about two feet from the edge of the structure. It was about three feet square and only stood about eight inches above the ground. The dark stains covered most of the smaller platform with the exception of a one-foot square clean area in its center. It appeared to Tim that something might have been placed on the smaller platform that prevented it from being stained.

"What is this thing anyway?" Tim asked.

"It's a bad place," Sabo said. "I have heard stories of places like this. It is used to sacrifice people. Their heads are cut off. Evil *zoes* use a place like this to bring to life the powerful spirits from the underworld."

Tim pulled his hand back. Perhaps the dark stains were dried blood. Suddenly, it all began to come together.

"Is that why they're holding us here?"

"I believe so," said Sabo.

Automatic weapon fire rang out and bullets ricocheted off the stone altar. Tim pulled his head back and turned to Sabo.

"They're going to try to rush us. I won't fire until they get close. Maybe I will be able to get one or two. It doesn't look good. I only have ten bullets, and I have no idea how many of them there are."

Tim peered around the edge once again. He could see at least two guns aimed at them from the doorway. Another man came out of the door and made his way to the left. Tim aimed carefully, hoping to get off a lucky shot.

The burst of fire from an automatic rifle caused him to pause. He watched as the man was thrown against the wall. He slid down the wall, leaving a red stain on its surface.

"Tim, they are up there on the hill behind us."

Tim tried to see movement on the hill behind them. He saw nothing unusual. Just then another burst of fire rang out, and he saw a muzzle flash from the forest. He sighted the pistol in the direction of the fire. Another burst came from the hill. He almost pulled the trigger when it dawned on him that whoever was firing the weapons wasn't after them, but was shooting at the guards.

Hank, Joe and Charles had reached the valley before dawn and had found cover on the hillside above the stockade. Now Hank realized that it was the same place where he had witnessed Amahd's death so many years ago.

When it was almost daylight, they could see smoke rising from the cooking fires in the guards' hut across the valley. Later they watched as a lone guard walked down the hill and entered the hut.

Hank felt as chill run down his spine when he heard several muffled shots coming from inside the stockade. The other guards must have heard the shots. Four of them ran down the hill toward the ceremonial hut. Then he saw two people rush out of the hut door and stand in the middle of the compound.

It took him a moment to realize that he was looking at his son and a Liberian teenager. The two ran for the altar and dove behind it for cover. Tim had a pistol in his hand.

"Shoot anyone who tries to come out that door!" he yelled at Joe and Charles. "I'm going after the boys."

He ran through the underbrush to the trail. As he was approaching the wooden wall, he heard several bursts of automatic weapons fire. He ran along the wall until he saw a door that led into the hut. He moved carefully along the edge, until he came to the entrance. With his back against the wall, he reached into his fatigue jacket and pulled out one of the fragmentation grenades. He pulled the pin, stooped down and rolled the grenade onto the hut's floor.

He counted. He had reached "six" when the grenade exploded. Bits of shrapnel peppered the inside of the hut. He heard one piercing scream. He stepped inside, holding his M-16 and sighting down its barrel.

An explosion and two bursts of rifle fire were followed by silence. Both Tim and Sabo peeked over the top of the altar. They could see heavy, white smoke pouring out the door of the ceremonial hut. They could make out the form of a soldier in the doorway. The man was crouched in a combat stance and was holding an M-16. He moved stealthily around the side of the hut and disappeared. A few moments later, he reappeared and moved to the opposite side of the hut by the guard's body.

"Shoot him!" screamed Sabo.

Tim took careful aim. He was about ready to pull the trigger when he recognized the soldier.

"It's Dad!"

The soldier walked over and checked the guard's body. When he looked up, he waved at the boys.

Sabo shook his head. He was sure he must have been dreaming. This soldier was much taller than most Liberian men. His face had been blackened. He held the rifle just like he had done in the movie.

He recalled when he was back in school in Gbarnga. He and his classmates saved what little money they had so that they could watch videos at the Lebanese store. The enterprising merchant had acquired an old thirty-two-inch Sony television and a DVD player from an American who had left the country. Many times embassy staff or business people would sell their household goods. Liberians and third-country nationals would fight to pick up bargains.

The Gbarnga merchant had added an extra room to his store. He fashioned crude benches that provided seating for up to forty people. He charged his customers one dollar to watch a movie. Favorite movies included Kung Fu flicks and adventure movies. The action in these movies transcended the language barrier and any cultural differences.

Sabo had seen his favorite movie, *Predator*, four times. It starred Arnold Schwarzenegger, who played a mercenary soldier who battled an invisible alien being. The evil villain killed men and collected their skulls. Since the movie was set in the jungle, the Liberian boys loved it. Here was a man who battled a creature not unlike an *endosym*. Each time they saw it, they all cheered when the soldier prevailed. This soldier, wearing camouflage fatigues, was the meanest warrior they'd ever seen.

Now, here in this valley, Sabo saw the real Arnold, powerful, alive and walking in the sunlight. He even waved at them.

Tim nudged his friend. "Let's go. My dad has rescued us."

"That's your dad?" asked the astonished Sabo.

"Sure. Come on!"

Tim ran toward the man and threw his arms around him. Sabo only walked ahead, still puzzled.

"That's your dad?" he whispered. "Arnold Schwarzenegger is your dad?"

Hank's arm rested around Tim's shoulder. He hung his head briefly and took a deep breath. He thought he had lost his son. He had worse-cased Tim's gruesome death. The best he thought might happen was that he'd find him mutilated and in need of medical evacuation.

But Tim stood beside him now, laughing and acting more like a combat veteran than a teenager who'd been abducted, maimed, and held captive in a place as close to hell as anyone could find on earth.

"Joe!" Tim yelled, seeing his friend standing in the doorway of the hut. "Joe, you're here, too?"

"Sure," Joe answered, "we weren't going to let those guys keep you."

Another man stood behind Joe. He stepped up to shake hands with Tim.

"Tim, this is Charles Morray," Joe said. Tim shook hands and snapped fingers with Charles.

Hank stood back, taking it all in. Tim was dirty and his hair in disarray. He held his left hand close to his side. Hank could see that his finger was covered in gauze dressing spotted with dried blood. But Tim stood tall, making direct eye contact with the two men.

"Tempered steel. American made!" Hank whispered as he wiped a speck of dust from his eye. A boy had been abducted; a man had been rescued.

It was time to get moving. Hank broke into the animated conversation.

"Did you check the huts up on the hill?" Hank asked.

"Yes," Joe said. "We didn't find anyone. There are five dead guards. I guess that's all there were."

They turned, passed through the ceremonial hut, and headed up the trail and into the woods. Hank reached down and picked up the rucksack he had left earlier.

"I have to go back down there. You guys stay here. This is something I have to do alone."

"Not alone," said Charles. "I brought you to this place so many years ago. We'll go together."

"All right," Hank agreed, "but, Joe, if anything happens, you and the boys get out of here. Don't try to help us."

Hank reached under his t-shirt and pulled out the leopard tooth.

"Dad, you've got the leopard tooth!"

"Yes, Tim, your mother told me that it could protect us."

"It can," Tim said. "I saw it heal Joe when he had been shot."

"I sure hope you're right," Hank replied.

Hank and Charles returned to the hut. They stepped over the mutilated bodies of the guards who had been killed by the blast of the hand grenade. They saw that three small rooms had been built inside the hut. One had been made into a cell. The other two were larger and set on the opposite side of the hut. Ironwood doors fitted with padlocks secured the two rooms.

"Should we just shoot off the locks?" Charles offered.

"Just a minute," Hank said, approaching the body of a guard who had been shot three times in the chest. He rolled him on his back. He patted down the pockets until he found a key ring in the man's right pocket.

"Let's try these."

The second key that Hank tried worked, and the lock snapped open. He brought up his M-16, pointing it ahead as he pushed on the door.

He wondered if the M-16 would do him any good. Could it have stopped the thing he saw on the trail? Would it help him at all if he came face-to-face with the statue? The easiest thing to do was simply to turn and get the hell away from there, but Hank wanted answers. He knew if he didn't confront his nightmares, he wouldn't have a moment's peace for the rest of his life.

He kicked the door with his boot. Inside it was dark, yet some light filtered in from the hallway. He took one cautious step after another until he stood in the center of the room. He could begin to make out ceremonial clothing hanging from wooden pegs along the wall. A wooden table had been pushed against another wall. He unhooked a kerosene lantern that had been suspended from a metal rod in the ceiling. Using his lighter, he lit the lantern. The interior was filled with costumes and masks, like those used by the Poro secret society. The masks were hand-carved and highly polished. A collection of drums and woven baskets was piled in one corner.

His attention turned to a stone slab. On it was the ceremonial sword he'd seen so long ago. This one seemed larger than the one he remembered. A strong man would need both arms in order to wield it. It had the look of the old broadswords of England.

Hank's hand gripped its hilt. It felt cold, so cold that it almost stung his hands to touch it. He imagined blood spurting from headless corpses. He screamed and drove its tip into the dirt alongside the stone slab. He braced his boot against the steel, forcing the metal to bend against the stone. The veins in his neck protruded as he pitted his strength against that of the sword. He strained, emitted a low growl, and increased the pressure. The weapon snapped in two. Hank lost his balance and fell forward to his knees, gasping for breath.

Hank got slowly to his feet. Charles walked beside him as they made a thorough inspection of the room. They discovered two five-gallon cans of kerosene hidden beneath the wooden table. They set the cans in the hallway and moved to the second locked door.

The first key that Hank tried opened the lock. This room held at least another ten five-gallon cans, each heavy with the weight of the liquid contents. At least thirty lanterns were set along one wall. Besides that, the room was empty.

"Why so much kerosene? Why all the lanterns?" Hank asked.

"Why would anyone padlock a room full of nothing but kerosene and lanterns and keep it guarded twenty-four hours a day?" asked Charles.

"I was wondering the same thing," Hank said.

He scanned the room, searching for clues. Two rakes had been partially hidden behind the fuel cans. He detected fine lines of the tines in the loose dirt on the floor. He picked up one rake, inverted it, and began tapping the handle on the floor. A few minutes later, he heard a hollow thunk as the handle struck on the floor beside an outside wall.

"Bring that other rake over here," Hank said.

The two began raking the dirt back until they uncovered wooden planks. They kept at it until Hank's rake caught on a metal ring fastened to a trap door.

"Charles, light one of those lanterns and bring it over here," Hank said as he reached down to clasp the ring. He gave a strong tug, and the door came up. Charles held the lantern over the hole. They could see wooden steps leading down into the darkness.

Hank slung the M-16 on his shoulder and drew his pistol. He held the pistol in his right hand and the lantern in his left and began to make his descent. It took him about a dozen steps to come to a landing. He found himself at the entrance to a tunnel that seemed to lead to the center of the compound. Six-by-six timbers shored up the tunnel walls and ceiling. He could see a line of kerosene lanterns hung from the rafters, spaced at even intervals.

"There's a tunnel down here. It looks like it leads under the compound," he shouted back up at Charles. "Bring a lantern and come on down."

The tunnel had a downward slope. They followed it for nearly one hundred fifty feet until it opened up into a large room, perhaps one hundred feet across. It, just like the tunnel, was reinforced with heavy timbers. Hank estimated that the room's center was roughly under the aboveground altar. A ten-foot circular design had been etched into the middle of the floor. Its design seemed vaguely familiar. Hank lit several more lanterns that hung on posts around the room.

"Aren't you afraid they'll know we're here if we light the lanterns?" Charles asked.

"I don't care. If we need to get out of here in a hurry, I don't want to have to run with a lantern in my hand," answered Hank.

From what they could tell, the room was empty. Charles crouched down to get a better look at the center of the design. There appeared to be a stone disk, about three feet in diameter, at its center. Although it was made of stone, it looked similar to a manhole cover. Charles reached down to its indentations, figuring he could use them for handholds. He strained to lift the stone. It wouldn't budge.

"Give me a hand, Hank," he said.

Both men struggled, failed, and took a moment to rest. Then they gave it a second try. Finally, they tipped the slab on its side. Hank hung the lantern over the hole, revealing another set of stairs. These were carved from stone.

Hank felt a cool breeze coming from the opening. He settled himself on the edge and let himself down into another tunnel. Again, a series of lanterns hung from the walls at intervals of about fifty feet. This tunnel seemed much older, much more timeworn than the first. Although he saw occasional timbers, most of the tunnel was composed of just the native rock.

The tunnel sloped downward. Hank paused to light the lanterns as they went another fifteen hundred feet. They stopped at a heavy door, which was secured by a padlock. He pulled out the key ring and tried the only key he hadn't used before. It clicked in the lock. He reached for the handle.

"Hank!" Charles said as he touched Hank's shoulder. "Hank, look at the leopard's tooth."

"What the...?" Hank stuttered as he looked at the tooth hanging from the cord around his neck.

The tooth had taken on a green glow. Hank reached up and held it in his fingertips. It felt warm to his touch. In many ways, it looked like one of the chemical glow sticks he'd used in night operations.

He let go of the tooth, put both hands firmly on the door handle and gave it a tug. It opened into a natural limestone cavern. The room was too large for the meager lantern light to reveal its depths. Hank could see stalactites hanging like icicles from the ceiling. He heard echoes of dripping water.

He lit the lantern near the door. He could see yet another lantern farther along the worn trail. He moved along, lighting more lanterns and moving deeper into the earth. In many ways, it seemed like a typical limestone cavern. In some places it narrowed to a tunnel so small that the men had to crawl on their hands and knees. In other places, the openings were so large that the lantern light could not reach the top. Other tunnels branched off to the right or to the left, but they stayed to the more worn path and moved from lantern to lantern. They passed by several pools of crystal clear water.

To Hank, it all seemed too familiar. This was the long, dark tunnel of his dreams. This is where the bat-like creatures swirled overhead. Without thinking, he reached up for the leopard tooth. It continued to emit a green glow.

He paused to touch a coral-red outcropping when the toe of his boot came in contact with a circular object, about eight inches in diameter. He bent over and picked up a brass disk. It looked like an oversize doughnut, but had small, protruding bumps on its surface. It felt heavy. Hank guessed it might weigh as much as five pounds.

That's why the circle on the floor looked so familiar! It was a larger drawing of this same object. He'd seen similar objects in stores that sold African art in Monrovia.

"It's a Tien," Charles said, answering his unspoken question.

"A what?"

"Our people call them Tien or water spirits. They are found throughout Sierra Leone and here in Liberia. They are formed from bronze.

They're called lost-wax castings. Occasionally, they still wash up along riverbanks. They are very old. No one knows who made them. The people of West Africa never learned how to make them. They are far older than our people."

They continued deeper into the cavern, finding more and more of the brass objects along the trail. They varied in size, ranging from only a few ounces to nearly thirty pounds.

They reached another narrow spot, and they had to crawl several hundred feet until they came out into a large smooth-walled chamber with a ceiling more than twenty feet high. Hank reached out to light the wall lantern.

"Oh, my God!" Hank exclaimed.

They had reached a cache of stored objects including brass spears, wooden crates, large plates that appeared to be of gold, a wooden throne with inlaid precious gems and two large wooden statues. Hieroglyphics and multicolored drawings covered the walls. It seemed as if they had entered the treasure chamber of an Egyptian tomb.

Neither man was an archeologist, but this place appeared to be thousands of years old. Hank held his lantern up to a nearby wall.

"It looks like these pictures tell some kind of a story," Hank said. He moved to the far left where the drawings seemed to start.

The first scene depicted an open valley. Groves of trees spotted the green, rolling hills. Herds of animals were grazing. In the center of the scene, he thought he could make out a large stone statue.

"Isn't that the Great Sphinx from Egypt?" Hank asked.

"It looks like it. But this picture makes it look like it's in an area with trees and grass. I don't see any pyramids."

"When I was in college," Charles continued," I look a course on Egyptian antiquities. The professor claimed that some people believe that the Sphinx was built thousands of years prior to the pyramids. The erosion on the Sphinx seems to be from water, not just sand and wind. There had been no water in the Nile valley for ten thousand years."

The next pictures showed men bowing to two horned creatures. One was tall. The other was short and dwarf-like, perhaps only three feet tall. The creatures appeared to be arguing. The next picture showed the taller creature leading a group of men toward the Sphinx. The following picture seemed to indicate that the smaller creature led another group out of the valley. Other pictures showed human sacrifices.

One drawing appeared to be a map. Hank thought it looked roughly like the Mediterranean Sea and the western coast of Africa. Arrows indicated a route to West Africa by sea.

"Look," Charles said, pointing his finger. "That portion of the map looks like the Saint Paul River. They must have come from Egypt by boat up the river."

Other drawings showed men dressed in Egyptian costumes. They seemed to be greeting naked black men. Some black men were tied and bound together. Piles of the bronze water spirits sat nearby.

"They say that the Tien were used as money. Egyptians traded the bronze pieces for slaves," Charles explained.

In the next drawings, men were building a great city. Black slaves worked on temples. In all the pictures, the dwarf-like, horned creature appeared to be directing Egyptian priests.

Another map showed a road leading from the city into a valley. One seemed to show the inside of a cavern and the construction of another temple and amphitheater.

"Our people tell stories of an ancient city near the Saint Paul River fewer than ten miles from this valley," said Charles. "I'll bet that hidden in these jungles are the ruins of the city in these pictures. It must have vanished thousands of years ago."

In the next scene, a long line of demons, likely more than one hundred, marched out of the temple. The next drawing showed the demons and Egyptian warriors. Each pair had become one soldier-like being with the head of a demon.

"Those are *endosyms*," said Charles as he pointed at one of the soldiers with the demon head.

"Yeah, I remember when Joe Weah told us about *endosyms*," said Hank.

"Right, it's a bush demon and man living together in the man's body," Charles replied.

The final group of pictures was more crudely drawn than the others. Black men were attacking the Egyptians with spears. The city was in flames. Egyptians were placing stones across the entrance to the caverns.

At the end of the pictures was a young woman drawn life size on the cavern's wall. Lying at her feet were the bodies of two endosyms, their heads severed from their bodies. The woman was holding a sword over her head in her right hand. The sword appeared to be glowing green like the leopard tooth that hung around Hank's neck. Unlike the first crude drawings, this one was painted in vivid colors.

The woman appeared to be alive. She was tall, maybe six two with lean muscles. Around her waist was a leopard loincloth. Her small firm breasts jutted out from her lean body. She had fine features with a multiracial appearance. Her skin was light golden brown as was her long, straight hair that hung to her shoulders. Her eyes were almost golden in color. Hank stood still, mesmerized by her beauty.

"I'll be damned," said Charles. "The stories are true. Her name was Anaya. The legends of the tribes claim that she came from a far-away land and saved the Kapel people from a horrible evil."

"Do you realize that we have stumbled across a culture that existed here thousands of years ago?" Hank said. "Some of the pictures of the sacrifices look almost more Aztec than Egyptian. I wonder if there is an ancient link."

On the floor near the last picture, Hank found a bronze statue that he could hold in his hand. It was a replica of an *endosym*. Only ten inches tall, it was exquisitely carved and had been made using the lost-wax casting method. In one hand, it held an axe. In the other, it carried a spear. Its only garment was a small loincloth. Protruding from the backside, Hank could see a tail. Its ears were pointed. Its face looked almost Egyptian. Its chin sported the artificial beard as worn by the pharaohs. He tucked the statue in his rucksack.

"I'd sure like to know how old this is," he said.

They walked across the room until they came to a doorway carved in the rock wall. Two wooden *endosym* warrior statues, each almost ten feet tall, framed the doorway.

"This is a warning to go no further," whispered Charles.

"I know," said Hank. "I know, but I must go on."

"Then I'll go with you. I'm not staying here alone," Charles said. They passed through the doorway. They felt a sudden flow of air that extinguished both lanterns.

Hank tried to light one, but the breeze quickly blew it out again. Although it should have been completely dark, Hank realized that he could still see ahead. The light from the leopard's tooth was so bright that he couldn't look directly at it.

"Let's go," Hank said, stepping forward. He looked down in time to spot the trip wire. "Careful," he warned, pointing down. In the next hundred feet, they found two more trip wires, yet they stepped over each.

Ahead, they saw a light. As they went farther, it became even brighter. Finally, they stepped into a grand chamber, hundreds of feet in diameter. It had some of the features of a Roman amphitheater. Rows of benches faced a granite temple framed by marble columns.

"How could this have ever been built?" Charles said, marveling at the work it must have taken to complete it.

"I don't know. It would take hundreds of man-years to build. Nothing like this exists in the known world," Hank said.

The place was so large that it was difficult to see across. It was illuminated with a phosphorescent light.

"Where does that light come from?" Charles asked.

Hank reached out to touch the side of the rock cavern. When he pulled his hand away, his fingers glowed with the same light.

"I think it's some kind of algae that gives off light," Hank said.

They moved farther into the amphitheater. For the first time, they noticed something on the benches. Thousands of round objects had been placed side-by-side.

"What are those?" asked Charles.

"I don't know. Let's get closer," Hank answered. They moved down a rock pathway toward the center section. When they neared the first row, both men stopped. It had become apparent to both that the objects were severed human heads. Hank leaned down to get a closer look. Some still had dried flesh and thin strands of hair. The farther down they went, the more the heads looked like skulls.

"This has taken hundreds, maybe thousands, of years. This isn't just some renegade men trying to appease a bush spirit. What do you want to do?" asked Charles.

"Get the hell out of here," Hank said.

They moved out of the amphitheater. When they reached the room under the altar, Hank stopped and turned to Charles.

"I know this is bigger than just Carpai and his thugs, but we can do something to slow them down. Maybe we can stop them altogether."

He pulled off his rucksack and took out several blocks of C-4 plastic explosive. He examined the shoring and selected several timbers that appeared to offer the main ceiling support. He placed the explosives against the timbers then linked them together with detonation cord. He put a blasting cap into one of the blocks and cut the fuse, timing it to burn for thirty minutes. He inserted a fuse in the blasting cap and attached a fuse lighter. He lit the fuse. Finally, he punched the button on his stopwatch.

"We've got thirty minutes before this tunnel blows up," Hank said.

When they got to the last stairway leading up into the hut, he placed another explosive charge. Only fifteen minutes were left before the first charge was due to go off.

They climbed the ladder into the room above. He set another charge next to the drums of kerosene. He tied a white phosphorous grenade into the explosive with the detonation cord. When the C-4 exploded, the blast would rupture the kerosene drums. Simultaneously, the white phosphorous grenade would explode, saturating the blast area with burning chunks of phosphorous. The result would be a huge fireball. He took another look at his stopwatch. Only seven minutes remained.

"Let's make a run for it!" Hank said with a quick look at Charles.

When they reached the hillside where Joe, Tim and Sabo waited, Hank figured there were fewer than two minutes before the first charge would go off.

"Where have you two guys been?" Joe asked.

"Just watch," Hank replied. All five men lined up in a row looking toward the compound that shimmered in the morning light. There was no movement. There was no breeze. They could see the body of the guard that Joe had killed still leaning against the wall where he had fallen.

They heard a muffled rumble, then nothing.

"It must have been a dud," Tim said.

"Look!" Sabo said, pointing to a large crack that had opened in the earth only ten feet from the stone altar. Then the altar itself tilted and dropped about three feet. Another, much louder, explosion rocked the ground, and one side of the hut crumbled. The entire inner compound settled into the earth and the altar itself vanished. A ball of fire engulfed the hut and spewed smoke high into the air.

"Wow!" Tim said, staring up into the billowing cloud.

"I think you just put them out of business," Joe said.

"I hope so," Hank said. Then he reached down and lifted his rucksack to his shoulder. "Come on. We've got to find a place to hide out until tonight. Let's get out of here."

Moses Kayeh peeked around the tree at the smoldering ruins of the compound he had been sent to protect. How could the *endosym* have allowed such damage at this sacred place?

Before, he had thought himself fortunate to have been hired for such an easy job. No one dared enter this valley. His only duty had been to watch the prisoners. Since they were kept drugged, it was a simple task. Usually, the weeklong shift had been more like a vacation than a job. Now he was the only survivor.

He would have been gone, too, had he not suffered from severe stomach cramps the night before. They had gotten so bad that he had gone off into the forest to relieve himself. He had been squatting in the jungle, trying to ease the dysentery, when he first heard shots. He had pulled himself together and headed back toward the ceremonial hut when he saw the two soldiers go up the trail toward the sleeping huts.

Had he been a braver man, he could have easily killed the two men who searched the huts. Then again, he reasoned, he didn't know how many others there might be who might harm him. He had seen the three men walk alongside the boy prisoners and leave the grounds. Two of the men had come back and disappeared inside. One was a tall white man. The other looked like Charles Morray.

The two men stayed inside for maybe an hour. Then they burst out of the hut, ran up the trail, and vanished into the woods.

He had never before heard such an explosion. He stared in disbelief as the sacred site disappeared before his eyes in a giant fireball that rose high into the sky.

He kept hidden for another hour before daring to creep back to the sleeping huts. Inside he found the small wooden box, opened it, and took out the satellite cell phone. A phone was something alien to Moses. But Oscar Jalah had insisted that each of them learn how to push the red button and to wait for a beeping sound. Then he pushed the button that Jalah had painted white. Moses held the instrument near his ear, just as he had been told.

When he heard Jalah's voice coming out of the little holes, he began to tell the story.

# 28

***Lindsey had finally found comfort at the Myers' clinic. She was sleeping soundly. A voice had roused her to semi-consciousness.***

"TIME TO WAKE UP!"

"What?" Lindsey asked as she rubbed her eyes. "Is it already morning?"

Lindsey hadn't been able to get to sleep all night. She'd tossed and turned, worrying about the safety of her son and husband. She had finally given in to her deep sleep out of sheer exhaustion. Now a bright light came streaming through the shutters. Karen Myers, wearing a white smock, stood beside her bed.

"What time is it?" Lindsey asked.

"It's half past eleven. We'll be having lunch in a half hour."

"Lunch? You said I would have to get up early in order to help you in the clinic."

"Yes, I did," Karen said, "but you were sleeping so soundly. I felt that you needed your sleep. Besides, there's still plenty to do this afternoon. I took your clothes to be washed, so here is a smock to wear. Frank and I will meet you in the kitchen."

Lindsey hurried to get ready. When she got to the kitchen, she not only found Frank and Karen, but two young women. One was Julia Morray, Charles' wife whom Lindsey had met earlier. The other was a younger Kruman girl. Both wore white medical smocks.

"Lindsey, this is Julia's sister, Judie."

Judie flashed a smile, revealing her even white teeth.

"Pleased to meet you, Mrs. Martin."

"Call me Lindsey."

During lunch, Judie told how she had come to live with the Myers after government soldiers raided her father's plantation. It would be safer for her with the Myers, and she welcomed the opportunity to help out at the clinic.

Lindsey got her introduction to the clinic later that afternoon. More than twenty people had lined up to see the doctor. The patients, in many cases accompanied by several family members, sat on wooden benches in the shade outside the clinic.

Lindsey was stuck by the sweet-smelling odor of the native Kruman people. At first, it was almost overpowering. Karen had explained that the Liberians who lived in Nimba and Grand Gedah counties consumed large amounts of palm butter. They prepared the rich substance by crushing palm kernels. It forms a rich, red paste. It is cooked and eaten on boiled rice. Eating so much of it gave their sweat a distinct odor. Lindsey had laughingly told Hank that she could find their houseboy, Adam, even if she had been blindfolded. She insisted that he shower every day, but nothing could wash away the smell of ingested palm butter.

Throughout the afternoon, the stream of people in need of medical attention continued. Some had simple cuts, infections or stomach problems. Others suffered from the effects of the parasites that ran rampant in West Africa. One man, still in his twenties, had lost most of his toes and fingers from leprosy. Caused by the bacillus mycobacterium lepae, it formed nodules that became enlarged and spread all over the body. It resulted in loss of sensation and eventual paralysis, wasting of muscle tissue and physical deformity.

Lindsey was even more appalled by the condition of an old man who had been wheeled into the clinic. One leg and foot had become so enlarged that they were three times the size of his good leg and foot. His testicles had swollen to the size of bowling balls. Frank explained that worms cause the body to take on such a grotesque appearance. The worms invade the body and obstruct the lymphocytes.

The disease, called elephantiasis, was very painful and difficult to treat.

Although many of the cases she'd seen shocked Lindsey, none upset her more than that of a teenage mother who had brought her baby to Dr. Frank. She had patiently sat for hours, waiting her turn. She had swaddled the child in a bright, tie-dyed cloth. Lindsey had gone over to admire the baby. When the girl opened the cloth, Lindsey gasped. She turned and ran to find Karen.

The only starving children Lindsey had ever seen were on television. She'd seen the reports from places where famine had made death an everyday occurrence. But here in Liberia, the rain forests of West Africa provided abundant food. Yet this tiny baby looked like a miniature old man, his skin stretched so tightly that his eyes seemed to sink into his skull.

Karen rushed the girl and her baby to the front of the line. Lindsey stood nearby, watching as Frank examined the child. He pinched the flesh on the boy's arm and then released it. It remained puckered. Frank explained that one sign of severe malnutrition was the inability of the skin to return to normal. He estimated the child was about nine months old. He poked at the arm in an attempt to start an IV, but couldn't find a good vein.

"There's nothing I can do," he said, looking up at Lindsey and Karen. "He's too far gone. He won't make it through the night."

Lindsey looked down at the child. His large dark eyes seemed to look deeply into hers.

"What's wrong with him?" Lindsey asked.

"Nothing," Frank answered. "He's been starved to death through ignorance."

"I don't understand," Lindsey said.

"The mother's milk dried up. Since the Kruman nurse their babies for almost two years, she didn't know that she could have given him goat's milk or even solid foods. Instead she gave him nothing but the white water from the boiled rice. It had no nutrition," Frank said. "If only she had come to the clinic earlier. Even three days earlier, and I might have been able to save him. Some days it is so hard to deal with the things we cannot change. If only we could better educate them."

It was nearly six o'clock in the evening by the time the final patient had been seen. Frank and the women walked together back to the house. Frank planned to go back later to check on the six patients who'd been kept in the ward. Two of them were the girl and her dying baby.

Lindsey had been kept so busy during the afternoon that she barely thought about her husband and son. Now, totally fatigued, she slowly climbed up the steps to the house. Her anxiety returned. Tears came to her eyes, and she felt the familiar queasiness in her stomach.

"Oh, God, please bring them home safely!" she whispered.

# 29

***At the ambassador's residence, Vicki had gathered her team and the few dependents that remained in Liberia.***

"So, if you want my opinion, I think Steven Dowling has lost his mind. Julius Carpai's not that far behind. As a matter of fact, the whole government is teetering on the verge of complete stupidity. What on earth can they be thinking? Would you believe that they have locked up every single one of Joe Weah's officers for treason? Then they have the gall to crack down on Weah's old man and his village. They turned the most powerful Kapel paramount chief against the central government," said Dan Hamilton.

"Yes, but I heard that those officers confessed to treason. They also admitted to belonging to Morray's People's Party."

"Come on, Gordon, you don't believe their phony press releases? Hell, the stockade at Barclay Training Center is one step below Beliyela prison. They say that people are tortured there. Their wives and daughters are raped by Morris Kai's thugs."

"But, Dan, do you really believe all those rumors?"

"Damn right, I do. It's so bad that our President had directed Vicki to talk about it to Dowling tomorrow. Amnesty International has already lodged a formal complaint. Carpai has already fired the chief of staff, General Tarpeh. I guess Tarpeh was so shocked by what he saw at the stockade that he took his complaints straight to Dowling, bypassing Carpai. Sometimes I'm not even sure that Dowling is running the country. I don't know who is. Hell, maybe nobody is."

Vicki had stood silently next to the bar, listening to Dan Hamilton and Gordon Kennedy spilling their assessments of the country's deteriorating conditions. Dan was well on his way to getting flat-out drunk. Tonight, Vicki really didn't care. She considered getting a little drunk herself.

This was Lori Grant's last night in Liberia. The entire Peace Corps contingent had been withdrawn. Lori, in charge of the country's volunteers, had been reassigned to Washington, D.C. Even the Liberian staff that worked for the Americans had been dismissed. Vicki and the few wives who had stayed had served the dinner that had been prepared earlier in the day.

Vicki leaned her elbow on the bar and took a look around the room. People had gathered in small groups and were speaking quietly. This was so unlike the jovial farewell parties that had been so common prior to the horrible attack on the attaché staff. If they knew what she knew, they would be even more solemn. Only one other person in the room knew that Hank's son had been taken hostage.

Jim Parkinson stood by himself. His demeanor told her that they were on the same wavelength. He was the only one who shared her knowledge of Tim's capture. The more she worked with Jim, the more she valued his counsel.

"How are you doing?" Jim asked when he saw Vicki approach.

"OK," she answered.

"Any confirmation on Jerry Day's report from Sanniquellie?"

Earlier in the afternoon, a paid informant had relayed a story from a bar in Sanniquellie. He reported that two days earlier a white woman and a Kapel man were seen in a local bar. The man was identified as Lieutenant Colonel Joseph Weah. The woman was unidentified. She was described as a very tall woman, taller than any Liberian man. Her hair was blond. She had a noticeable scar on her cheek. It had to be Lindsey Martin.

"Vicki, we have no more information on the sighting. However, we can be sure something is going on. A number of helicopter flights have been reported flying out of Roberts Field."

"God! Jim, do you think they're after Hank?"

"I don't know. If they are, they don't know at the lower level. No one we talked to knew what was going on. Hopefully, it's just another show of force to intimidate the larger towns with government fly-overs."

"Jim, I don't know what's in store for us next. In the last six weeks, this country has deteriorated to the point where we have gone from Kruman against Kapel to Kapel against Kapel. If this continues, Monrovia could be on the brink of anarchy. Only the dusk-to-dawn curfew and the show of government soldiers in the streets are preventing the people from rioting. Now with this thing about General Tarpeh's being fired, we could be sitting on a powder keg."

# 30

***On a plot of high ground surrounded by triple canopy jungle, Hank and the men waited.***

HE PRESSED THE BUTTON ON HIS WATCH TO CHECK THE TIME. IT WAS ELEVEN o'clock. They needed to get moving soon. They had to link up with the truck at the Saint Paul River Bridge in two hours.

During the morning, they had stayed clear of the bush trail, working their way through the deep forest. They had crossed the river at a spot where it was fordable, but only in the dry season. Hank kept them on a compass course that would bring them within three miles of the main road. They settled in on a small clearing under the towering trees.

They broke out the MREs from their rucksacks. The two boys finished theirs quickly and looked around for something more to eat. It was only noon. They had a good ten hours to rest before they had to be on the move again.

Tim and Joe's cousin, Sabo, didn't appear to be adversely affected by their ordeal. In fact, they seemed to be enjoying themselves.

Hank thought back to his time as a second lieutenant in Ranger School. By the time they had reached the jungle phase in Florida, Hank had dropped a good twenty pounds. They had operated on less than three hours sleep within a seventy-two hour period. They were bruised and scratched. Their feet had been in water for days. Yet they could still laugh and joke. It hadn't been all that bad.

Hank moved close to Tim and sat down beside him.

"Son, I need to take a look at that hand."

"Dad, it's pretty bad. But right now it doesn't hurt much."

Hank wasn't put off by Tim's reluctance to let him examine the wound.

"Let's unwrap that gauze. I have some clean dressing and some Neosporin. Dr. Myers also gave me some pills for you to take. It's an antibiotic. I also have something for pain." Hank gently unwrapped the soiled bandage.

"I'll take the antibiotic," Tim said. "But I don't want any pain pills."

The finger had bled during the struggle and the gauze had stuck together. Tim grimaced as Hank pulled on it.

"Sorry," Hank said.

"It's OK, Dad. I can handle it."

When he finally had a chance to inspect the wound, he saw that the hand was swollen, but not severely. He opened the small first aid package and took out the sealed packets of alcohol-soaked gauze. He cleaned off the dried blood and looked at the stub of the severed finger. It had been neatly stitched and cleanly closed. He daubed the end with Neosporin. Frank had the foresight to include a rubber finger protector, like the type used to count money. Since it was thumb-sized, it was large enough to accommodate the fine strips of gauze Hank used to pad the wound. He taped plastic sticks on each side of the dressing so that wounded stub wouldn't be affected if Tim were to hit the end. Finally, Hank taped the protected stub to Tim's ring finger.

"How's that feel?"

"Great, Dad. Now I can use my left hand. How did you learn to do that?"

Hank laughed for the first time in many days.

"Dr. Myers, who you will meet tomorrow, told me what to do. Your mom is at the Myers' clinic waiting for us."

Tim suddenly changed the subject.

"Dad, do you think there is a devil?"

"Sure, son. I guess so. In the Bible there are stories of the devil tempting men."

"No, Dad, not that type of devil. I mean a devil that talks to you."

Hank paused, recalling what had happened on the trail.

"Son, sometimes people do see things that they can't explain. Why are you asking?"

Tim relayed his vision of the demon that bit off his finger. He told how the leopard had saved him.

When he finished, Hank didn't know what to say. Somehow he and his son had been tied together in this supernatural experience.

He hung his head for a second before looking at Tim. His son was no longer a child.

Hank spent the next two hours telling Tim what had happened since that day so many years ago when he first came into the sacred bush. He described what he and Charles had found hidden deep in the underground cavern. He told about the green glow from the leopard tooth. When he was done, both of them sat in silence.

Finally, Tim spoke.

"Our guard, Everyday Walker, who is really Chea Geebe, has the power to battle the *endosym*. He helped you destroy the ceremonial valley."

"Son, six months ago I would have told you that there is no such thing as an endosym, but right now, I'd have to agree."

Hank patted his son on the back and then stretched out, resting his head on his rucksack.

"And now we all have to get some sleep. Tonight we'll get out of here."

"One more thing, Dad."

"Yes, son?"

"Don't tell Mom about my finger. It would freak her out. You know how upset women get whenever a guy gets hurt."

"It's a deal. We'll keep it from your mom for now."

They both fell into a deep sleep.

When Hank woke up, it was half past ten at night.

"All right, everyone, it's time to move out. We'll work our way toward the main road, keeping close to its edge. There should be little or no traffic. If we hear something coming, we'll need to hide in the brush. Remember, don't move. If you keep still in the dark, you won't be seen."

Hank's knees were stiff, and his back ached. Sleeping on the ground was something he could learn to live without.

By midnight, they reached the main road. Charles took the lead. Hank, Tim and Sabo followed. Joe was at the rear. They encountered no vehicles or foot traffic. The moon wouldn't be out until one o'clock in the morning. Now, their only light was starlight. Moving along the road was a cinch compared to negotiating the jungle in the dark. The air was completely still. Even at midnight the humidity and temperature were oppressive.

In the night, sounds were exaggerated. A chorus of frogs near a small stream was deafening. The cicadas chirped in the brush. Occasionally, they'd disturb a larger animal, and it would crash through the undergrowth.

Charles held up his hand, and they came to a halt. Hank moved up close to him. Charles pointed ahead. Parked under a tall cottonwood tree was the mining company truck.

"Looks like they had no problem," Hank said.

"Should I signal the others to come forward?"

Charles hesitated. "I don't know. Something doesn't seem right."

Hank nodded. "I watched you on the way into the valley. You have a natural instinct found in few men. If you feel something is wrong, then we need to hold back until I can recon the area."

Hank directed the others to hide in the woods. He took off his rucksack and handed his M-16 to Tim. He screwed the silencer onto the barrel of his nine-millimeter pistol and tested the laser sight. He moved quietly through the brush along the edge of the road. Speed was not as important as stealth.

It took him almost fifteen minutes to cover the two hundred yards to a place where he could get a better look at the truck. He was only about one hundred feet from the truck. The moon was just beginning to rise. Gradually, the cab was basked in moonlight. He could see that two men were sitting in the truck. He watched, checking for movement. He saw none. Why would they be so still? He strained to get a better look. He sucked in his breath as he realized that bamboo sticks had been placed to prop up their heads. They were both dead, but had been positioned to make it look as if they were still alive.

Hank stepped backward and turned. A metallic click to the left sent him into a crouch. Any movement might betray his position. He watched as a soldier moved directly toward him. He prayed that the man would change his direction. He considered moving slowly out of the way, but the moonlight now streamed through the trees and lit up the areas on both sides.

The soldier stopped. He stared directly at Hank's hiding spot. He seemed to know that there was something ahead of him, but didn't seem to know what it was. He brought up his rifle and aimed. Hank felt the chill of defeat as he looked into the muzzle of the high-powered rifle fewer than forty feet away, yet he didn't fire, nor did he sound an alarm. The man began to advance, still sighting down the barrel.

Hank quietly raised his pistol and pointed it at the advancing soldier. He squeezed the trigger to activate the laser. A red dot appeared on the man's chest. A chest shot wouldn't work. Hank released the trigger. Even if the shot were fatal, the man would still have time to shout a warning. He raised the pistol again, this time aiming at the man's head. The red dot crossed the soldier's cap. As it settled on the man's forehead, Hank pulled the trigger all the way to the rear.

The nine-millimeter bullet left the silenced pistol with only a muffled spit. It struck its target above the right eye. When the bullet entered the skull, the round exploded, filling the brain cavity with mercury and shell fragments, turning the brain to mush. The soldier dropped in a heap. His legs crumpled under him. He fell to a sitting position, his head falling forward onto his chest.

Hank remained still for a full five minutes, waiting to see if the disturbance had alerted others who might be hiding in the bush. Then he rose and moved back into the brush.

"What did you find?" asked Charles when Hank returned.

"Not good. Your men are both dead. It's an ambush. I had to kill one of the soldiers. We have to get out of here before they find him."

"Where can we go?" Joe asked.

"They must have soldiers on the road. Therefore, we must stay off the road. Naama and Camp Jackson are ten miles to the south. We must cut cross country to the Camp Jackson Road."

Joe moved up close to Hank as they headed into the jungle.

"Do we have a plan?" he asked.

"Unfortunately, no," Hank answered. "As soon as they find the dead soldier at the truck, then shit will hit the fan. Since Naama is on a dead-end road and has an army camp, I'm betting that they will assume we would head back toward the main road. I think we will be better off hiding out in the jungle east of Camp Jackson. We can work our way around the town and camp. It may be necessary for us to lay low for several days until things cool down. As long as no one spots us, they will eventually assume we got away. Then, most likely, they'll pull the soldiers back. If not, we can cross into Guinea."

As if on cue, they saw headlights reflected on the trees ahead. They moved into the brush for cover. A military Hummer followed by six five-ton trucks loaded with troops sped past their hiding spot. The vehicles left a cloud of dust hanging in the still night air.

"Come on. While they're focused on the place where I killed the soldier, let's cut through the jungle to Camp Jackson."

Hank led the way through the bush, holding his M-16 at port arms. The others followed, walking behind him.

Major Edward Seah yawned. They had been there since late afternoon. It was now almost three in the morning.

"I have to take a shit. I'll be right back," he said to Captain Bobby Grebo.

He left the clearing where the helicopters were parked and entered the privacy of the forest. He pulled out his penlight, checked the area for snakes and lowered his pants.

He had just finished when he spotted shadows moving through the bush. He crouched down and moved cautiously forward. He counted five men silhouetted in the moonlit clearing. He pulled his pistol and moved forward.

It had taken three hours to reach the outskirts of Camp Jackson. Hank, Joe, Charles and the boys headed south around the post. Their plan seemed to be working. They hadn't seen anyone. As they approached a large clearing, Hank signaled them to a stop.

"What's the problem?" asked Joe.

"They're using this field as a staging area," Hank answered, pointing ahead to where four heavy-lift helicopters and two Hueys were parked.

"We'll go around the area. I can see ten to twenty men. Some are guards. The other must be the pilots and crew."

The five huddled together under a large tree to plan their next move.

A voice speaking in the Kapel language came out of the dark.

"I see you, Nah Weah of Zigda, son of Togba and Salmata."

Hank whirled and aimed his M-16 in the direction of the speaker. Joe reached out and held Hank's arm.

"No," he whispered. Then he spoke in Kapel. "I hear you, Tau Seah of Zigda, son of Jaleh and Famuah."

A Liberian Air Force major dressed in a Nomex flight suit stepped out of the darkness. He and Joe wrapped each other in a hearty embrace.

"Good to see you, brother!"

"Likewise," Joe answered. Joe brought the man over to the others.

"Let me introduce you to Major Ed Seah," he said to them. "This is Lieutenant Colonel Martin, the U.S. defense attaché, and his son, Tim. Do you remember Sabo?"

Seah smiled.

"You were just a little boy the last time I saw you. Now, here you are a brother. Your cousin Joe and I faced the great *Nangma* together many years ago. We ate the blood of our youth and felt the teeth of the *Nangma*," said Seah.

Then Seah noticed Charles Morray. He reached out his hand.

"I heard your speech to the House of Representatives five years ago. Your concerns are justified. You realize that the entire army is searching for you and Joe Weah?"

"Does that include you, Ed Seah?" Charles asked.

"If you had asked me that three months ago, it would have been true. As a major in the air force, it was my duty to follow orders. But in the last month, things have changed. Some of my friends have been arrested and falsely accused of treason. It had gotten so bad that General Tarpeh went to speak with President Dowling. He was fired for his efforts.

"Just yesterday, forces were alerted to support the garrison at Camp Jackson. We were told that the terrorists who killed the Americans were in the area. The officers were briefed to look for Charles Morray and a white mercenary. Many of us wondered why the terrorists would be working around Camp Jackson. I became even more suspicious when I discovered that Oscar Jalah headed up the operation. Now, I find you and this unusual group. Would you mind telling me what's going on?"

"Ed, it is a very long story. I will tell you everything, my brother. But I don't think we have time for that now. We need to hide out. Hopefully, you guys will give up and go back to Monrovia," Joe said.

Ed Seah stood in silence for a few moments, before making a decision.

"I may have a better solution. I think it may be time for a career change. Because I come from Zigda, it is just a matter of time until I will be fired or arrested. I don't like what I see happening. Do you think the People's Party can use an air force major?"

"We welcome every Liberian to our cause," Charles answered. "But I'm afraid we don't have our own air force," Charles said.

"Maybe not," Seah replied. "But I am prepared to offer you one helicopter."

"I'm afraid I don't understand," Charles said.

"I'll fly you out of here."

Seah walked back to the clearing. No one stood guard at his Huey. He walked to the door, slid it open and climbed into the pilot's seat. He turned the key and flipped the master switch. The instrument panel lit up. He watched the gauges, waiting the proper time. He engaged the starter and the rotor began to turn. With a puff of smoke, the turbine ignited. He brought up the RPMs. He looked out the window. No one seemed to register any concern. He raised the collective, adjusted the pitch of the blade and slowly lifted off the ground. He angled the Huey toward the edge of the clearing.

Grebo hadn't seen Seah return from his trip into the brush. He was surprised to see him crank up the bird. He watched as the chopper lifted off and headed toward the wood line.

"What the hell is Seah doing?" he called to the other pilots. One simply shrugged his shoulders. Seah settled in a hover. Grebo watched as five men emerged from the woods and ran to the aircraft. Even in the moonlight, he could tell that they weren't Liberian soldiers. He could see that they carried weapons.

"Stop him!" Grebo yelled.

He raced toward the hovering aircraft. Several soldiers joined him. Grebo pulled his pistol and opened fire at the helicopter. One of the figures stopped running toward the chopper and knelt. He saw a muzzle flash and heard the burst of the M-16 on full automatic. A soldier to his left screamed and went down. Grebo threw himself face down on the ground as he heard the rounds fly overhead. When he felt safe enough to raise his head, he saw the Huey clear the trees. He leaped to his feet, turned and ran to his own Huey. He ordered two nearby soldiers to get on board as he climbed in his seat and fired up his bird.

Hank made sure that Tim and Sabo were belted in. He crept forward and settled into the co-pilot's seat. He put on the earphones, turned on the intercom and spoke.

"Well done, major. It looks like we made it."

"Where are we going?" asked Seah.

"Sanniquellie," answered Hank.

"It should take us less than an hour and a half," Seah said.

"Do you have a frequency for this operation? I would like to listen in on what is happening."

"Sure thing, colonel," Seah replied.

Grebo ignored all the safety steps when he decided to lift off. The engine warning light had come on for a moment. At first he thought he had a turbine failure. Then the warning light went off. He had already climbed to seven thousand feet and was headed south, toward Nimba and Grand Gedah counties.

He decided to radio Jalah to keep him informed of the situation. He was about to report that he was in pursuit when he realized that the other helicopter would be monitoring the radio. He switched off the radio. His chances of finding the helicopter over the jungle in the dark of night were slim. He gambled that if the men were connected with the People's Party, they would be going to Nimba County. The best way to get there would be to follow the road.

But at seven thousand feet, it was difficult to make out the land features. He descended to four thousand feet. Ground elevation was two thousand. This put him at two thousand feet above the trees. If he went any lower, he would lose the ability to see any distance. The dim moonlight failed to provide enough visibility to spot the fleeing helicopter. He had about decided to return to Camp Jackson when he thought he saw something to his right. He made out the running lights of an aircraft. He banked to the right, slowed his forward speed and dropped behind the aircraft.

It still wasn't clear what type of aircraft he was following. When it crossed a road junction, he could see that it was the helicopter. Grebo laughed.

"Seah, you stupid son of a bitch, you forgot to turn off your running lights. I've got you now."

Military Hueys are designed to fly in complete blackout, yet in Liberia, the air force chose to use running lights at night to decrease chances of mid-air collisions. In Seah's haste to make his getaway, he had forgotten to turn off the running lights. It made him a sitting duck for the darkened Huey that followed him.

Grebo motioned to one of the two men behind him. The soldier cautiously moved forward and sat in the co-pilot's seat. The man had never sat up front before. He held tightly to the edge of the seat and looked from side to side. Grebo signaled for him to put on the earphones.

"What's your name, private?" Grebo said over the intercom.

"Wanabe, sir!"

"Wanabe, how would you like to be promoted to sergeant?"

"I'd like that very much, sir."

"Tonight you will become a hero to our country. Tomorrow Minister Carpai will make you a sergeant. But first I'll need your help."

"Yes, sir, captain."

"See that harness back there?" The man turned and looked behind him. "I want you to put on the harness. It will keep you from falling out. Then you'll open the door. Have your friend help you hook up the harness," Grebo said. "See that other helicopter ahead of us?"

"Yes, sir."

"Good. They are enemies of our country. They have stolen that helicopter. We are going to stop them. Are you a good shot with a rifle?"

"Oh, yes, sir. I'm a very good shot."

"Good! Good! Wanabe, once you get hooked up and the door is open, I will fly right up beside the helicopter. Then you will shoot at the front of the helicopter where the pilot is sitting. Do you understand?"

"Yes, sir."

"All right, go back and get hooked up."

Grebo felt the blast of warm air as the cargo door slid open. He dropped down until he was directly behind Seah's Huey. He moved to its left. This was too easy, he thought. The fools still had no idea they were being followed. Their first inkling that they were in trouble would be when Wanabe killed the pilot.

It would only be a few more feet, and he would be in the perfect position. He turned his head to check behind him. Wanabe was in position, ready to fire. He aimed the rifle directly at the pilot's seat.

Grebo steadied his helicopter and kept his eyes on the aircraft ahead. He failed to notice that at this exact moment, both helicopters were about to cross the deep gorge of the headwaters of the Saint Paul River. Even at night, the downdraft along the sheer walls of the gorge was significant. Grebo's helicopter took a sudden lurch to the left, tilting at almost forty-five degrees. Grebo corrected, grabbing the controls and slowing his speed as he fell in behind the other helicopter. Once he had steadied the craft, he glanced behind him.

"Holy shit!" he exclaimed.

The back of his aircraft was empty. Both men were gone. He looked down in time to see a hand gripping the bottom of the door. Gradually, the head and shoulders of Private Wanabe appeared. He pulled himself back into the helicopter. He'd lost his rifle. The other man, not attached to a harness, must have fallen out.

"Now what?" Grebo wondered. He'd lost the chance to shoot down Seah. He considered dropping down on top of its rotor with his skids. But that would result in both aircraft crashing in flames. He scratched that option. He fell back even further and climbed in elevation.

He decided the best course was to simply follow Seah and find out his destination. He focused on the running lights ahead of him, climbing to seven thousand feet.

No one on board Seah's Huey had any idea of how close to death they had come. They followed the road to Sanniquellie, flying two hundred feet above the trees at one hundred miles per hour.

"Sanniquellie is straight ahead," Seah said. "Where do you want to land?"

"Go north, over the small hill. You'll find a large clearing next to the clinic," Hank answered.

Seah throttled back the engine and began the descent.

Lindsey had dozed off while sitting on the couch in the living room. Frank had suggested that she go to bed. He reminded her that it could be several days until the men returned.

The "whop-whop-whop" of the Huey's rotors instantly woke her.

"There's a helicopter landing," Frank said as he came running from the bedroom. "This could be trouble."

"Why?" Lindsey asked.

"The only helicopters in Liberia are army helicopters."

"Oh, my God! What are we going to do?"

"Get outside and stay in the shadows. We can't let them find you here, Lindsey. Keep hidden in the clinic until I can find out what they want."

When they got to the porch, they could see the Huey sitting in the moonlight. Frank motioned for Lindsey to go around the side of the house. The pilot switched off the engine. For a few moments, the sound of the slowing rotor could still be heard as a distant echo. Then it was quiet.

The door slid open. Lindsey squealed and began running toward the helicopter.

"Lindsey, stop! Wait! Don't move!" yelled Frank.

But it was too late. She'd recognized the tall, thin form of her son in the distance. It was Tim. He was safe. He was alive. Never in her life had she been so relieved, so excited and so happy, all in the same moment.

"Tim, Tim... Oh, thank God! Tim, you're alive!" she said as she rushed toward him. No one saw the other helicopter turn and head back toward Camp Jackson.

# 31

***When Vicki arrived at the Liberian President's office, she didn't have to wait long.***

"PRESIDENT DOWLING WILL SEE YOU NOW, AMBASSADOR JOHNSON."

Dowling didn't bother to stand when she entered his office. She stifled a gasp as she looked at what used to be a vital man. Dark circles ringed his heavy-lidded eyes. Normally impeccably dressed, Dowling looked as if he had slept in his wrinkled suit. She caught a whiff of body odor, so out of the ordinary for him. She slid into a leather chair and looked across the disorderly desk at Dowling.

"Mr. President, the President of the United States has asked me to speak with you regarding our concerns about the treatment of prisoners in the stockade at Barclay Training Center. We have received reports of torture and beatings," she began.

"Madame Ambassador, these men are criminals and vicious murderers. They have killed your own citizens. They are traitors."

"But, sir, none of them has been tried for these crimes. Have any been proven guilty?"

"Of course not," Dowling scowled. "The trials will begin Monday. I assure you that these criminals will be found guilty. I am more concerned, Madame Ambassador, with your involvement with these traitors."

Vicki looked straight at him. She thought she must have misunderstood what he had just said.

"Sir, I'm afraid I don't understand."

"Understand!" Dowling shouted. "Woman, just what is it that you don't understand? A member of your embassy staff is working with Charles Morray to overthrow our government. Do you think for a minute that we don't know what Lieutenant Colonel Martin is up to?

"I plan to call your President tonight and demand your recall. I have no idea how he could have considered a woman for this important position. You are a disgrace to the diplomatic corps," he continued, pounding his fist on the desk for emphasis. "Colonel Martin has personally executed our citizens and our soldiers. I want that man jailed!"

Vicki sat speechless. Her hands began to tremble. She folded them tightly together to hide her anxiety. She struggled to gather her thoughts and to respond to Dowling's accusations. Yet she was handicapped – she had no idea what Hank had done. Even if she knew what he had intended to do, she wasn't sure that she could have stopped him. She waited, searching for the right response when the red phone on the desk rang.

"What is it?" snapped Dowling. Then his voice took on a softer tone. He stared at Vicki then began to speak in Kapel.

"She's sitting right here now, George. No she doesn't understand a word. We checked her out on her first visit," Dowling said. Then he was quiet for a while as he listened to the voice on the other end.

"So, he is in Sanniquellie. Morray and Weah are there, too?" He tapped his fingers on the heavy desk. "I told her I was going to have her recalled. It worked perfectly. You should see her. I'll bet she peed her pants. Don't worry, George. She's terrified. She'll do anything to prevent me from calling her President."

He hung up the phone. He suppressed a grin, staring down at his clasped hands. This was beginning to be most entertaining.

"Where was I?" he asked himself, savoring the memory of her discomfort.

"You were going to call my President," she said, barely audible.

"Goddamn it, woman, speak up!" he shouted. "I can't stand a sniveling, whining woman!"

Dowling leaned back in his padded swivel chair and readied himself to resume his tirade when Vicki suddenly stood.

"You want me to speak up?" With the same poise and confidence that had won her respect in the U.S. Senate, Ambassador Victoria Ryan Johnson looked him directly in the eye.

"You lying, sanctimonious, hypocritical son-of-a-bitch! How dare you sit there and call me a disgrace to the diplomatic corps. What exactly did you consider yourself and your six stooges as you stood naked while you beheaded Amahd Abram? How many other young boys have lost their lives in your evil ceremonies?

"As for Hank Martin, two weeks ago Lieutenant Colonel Martin was reassigned to Washington, D.C. He no longer works for me. I'm also somewhat confused about your statement that he has killed several soldiers. If my son had been kidnapped and mutilated, you can bet there would be more than a few Liberians killed. Mark my words, Dowling, you made a big mistake when you got involved with Colonel Martin's family. I know the man. He won't stop until he has you in his gun sights. Your days are numbered."

She moved to the office door. While her hand still rested on the polished brass handle, she turned back to him.

"If you are planning to have me recalled, allow me to thank you in advance. I took this job as a favor to the President. As ambassador, I am committed to my oath of office. Yet as a private citizen, I would be able to use millions of dollars of my personal resources. My husband is more than willing to support the charities that are working for Morray's overthrow of your worthless government."

Then in fluent Kapel, she added even more.

"I am afraid that I did not pee my pants while quivering in fear of the great Steven Dowling. That weakness is reserved for feeble old men like you – men whose manhood has shriveled to that of the size of a little boy. By the way, give my regards to George Sarday."

She swung open the heavy door and pulled it tightly closed behind her.

Dowling ran his thick fingers through his thinning hair. His knees trembled. Unable to stand, he simply stared out the wide office window and watched the passing clouds.

Dowling had been blindsided by Ambassador Johnson's reaction to his recall threat. How could she have known what was going on? Was she right about Colonel Martin actually helping Morray? Only this very morning, The Seven had met to discuss the disaster that had been reported the day before. Julius Carpai had told about the explosions in the valley. They had all been astonished that the powerful creature they all worshiped had allowed a mere mortal to wreak such destruction. One American soldier couldn't be so powerful. Each man had been shaken to the core. Even George Sarday, the *endosym*, had been rattled. Their meeting had collapsed into petty bickering.

He pounded the desk with his clenched fist and shook his head. Nothing was going according to plan.

"We're in big trouble," he whispered.

He planted his palms firmly on the edge of the desk, rolled back his chair and stood. He walked quickly to his executive restroom and locked the door behind him. He stared at his reflection in the mirror. His face revealed his inner turmoil. Dark folds of skin circled his bloodshot eyes. His skin lacked its previous luster. He scowled at his own image.

It all had seemed so easy. At first the sacrifices had turned his stomach, but the rewards had deadened his revulsion. For seventeen years, the group had committed their souls to the strange creature called the *endosym*. They had been nothing then, only minor government bureaucrats. Their shared secrets had brought each wealth and power.

Initially, he hadn't believed it possible. Together they had consumed the secret potions, mind-altering drugs that took them to the realm of the unreal. True, they may have distorted some secret Poro rituals, but their fantastic journey had taken them to the ceremonial valley.

Human sacrifice had been their ultimate ritual. His legs had weakened and the surge of vomit fouled his throat as he saw blood stream from the first severed head. He had to brace himself to keep from fainting. The creature had brought each man a heightened sense of power. Each of them was capable of determining life and death. He had seen himself step outside his physical being. He had risen to a new dimension, far above the pitiful essence of ordinary men.

The *endosym* had given them physical comforts and immense political power. In return, they presented human heads as tribute. It seemed to go on and on like the ticking of a clock. As each life was sacrificed, each of the celebrants saw his personal world evolve. More power. More wealth. More blood.

The facts were irrefutable. The creature had reigned for thousands of years in its sacred temple encased in the underground cavern. It had gained immortality.

Steven Dowling, President of Liberia, had every reason to believe that he, too, would live on forever in power and comfort. He imagined his own immortality.

But now things seemed to be falling apart. This American soldier had challenged the creature's power and had won. He had destroyed the sacred site. The ambassador knew too much. It may only be a matter of time until Colonel Martin would connect Dowling himself, not only to the sacrifices, but also to the murders on Embassy Row.

Carpai had been a fool to attack Martin's wife and son. Again Dowling felt himself soaked in his own sweat. He had no choice now but to break his bond with The Seven and renounce the *endosym* forever.

Once more Dowling leaned into the mirror. This time he placed one finger of each hand under its bottom edge. He slid his fingers outward until he felt two indentations. He pushed on them simultaneously. The mirror swung to the right to reveal a wall safe. He turned the dial until it clicked. He pulled out a thick manila folder. Inside was more than forty-two million dollars in negotiable stocks and bonds. He reached in the safe again and pulled out two stacks of one hundred dollar bills in U.S. currency. He thumbed through the bundles. It added up to at least two hundred forty thousand dollars. It would all easily fit into a single briefcase.

He had hoped to have a billion dollars. At least, that is what he had dreamed it would be. No matter, he reasoned, the money in this safe, added to his assets in Swiss banks, would still be sufficient to start a new life. He sorted through the certificates until he found what he had been looking for – a certificate valued at two million dollars in shares of stock from the company owned by the husband of the lady ambassador.

"Thanks, Madam Ambassador," he said.

Comforted by his secret stash, he carefully returned the envelopes and the cash to the safe. When he closed the safe and looked once again in the mirror, he thought he looked a little better. Wealth has its healing effects, he thought.

Back at his desk, he circled the date of the Saturday after next. He was scheduled to fly to Nigeria for the annual meeting of the Organization of African Unity. After the meeting, Dowling would not return to Liberia. He put a black X on the next Monday, the day of the treason trials. Another X went on the following Monday, the day of the executions. He closed his calendar, pressed the intercom, and told his secretary to cancel his afternoon appointments. He ordered his car and driver. He'd enjoy the afternoon at home with his wife. Things would all work out, he assured himself.

Cold cash could work wonders.

# 32

***Lindsey and Hank shared a bed in the Myers' guest bedroom.***

RUMPLED BED SHEETS TANGLED BETWEEN HER LEGS, LINDSEY STRETCHED AND yawned. She rubbed her eyes and squinted at the brightness streaming in through the shutters as she awakened from a deep sleep. It must have been a dream, a wonderful dream.

The gentle breathing of the man lying next to her assured her that it hadn't been a dream at all. She rolled to her side to take in the wonder of once again being with the man she loved. The wind-up alarm clock read seven o'clock. Myers' guest bedroom with its simple furnishings wasn't exactly a honeymoon suite, but for them, the night had been as magical as their first time.

They had been discreet. The Myers occupied the adjacent room. They had been slow and quiet. She shuddered, recalling their mutual pleasure.

She didn't get up. She just stayed beside him, watching the sleeping man and savoring each detail as if to etch the moment forever in her memory. She noticed the streaks of gray in his hair. Two weeks of beard growth also showed flecks of silver. In all the years she had known him, he'd always been clean-shaven. But he'd let his hair grow out and hadn't shaved. She knew he had deliberately altered his appearance.

She hadn't questioned him about what had happened on the rescue operation, yet she knew that both Hank and Tim had confronted their nightmare demons and had won. Neither had shared their experiences with her or the others. She guessed the silver in her husband's hair was not just the reflection of the morning sunlight, but also the physical remnant of what he'd seen and done.

Even Tim had changed, not so much physically as emotionally. He had passed up sleeping in the house and had joined Sabo in a hut north of the clinic. She couldn't decide how he'd changed, but she felt he had abandoned his awkward teen years and had emerged as an adult.

Tim had explained that he had crushed his little finger in the tailgate of an army truck when he had been taken prisoner. An army doctor had amputated the damaged portion and sewed up the wound. Frank had assured her that it was healing nicely.

Although the story seemed plausible, she still had lingering doubts. When she asked Hank about it, he had shrugged and asked why Tim would tell such a story if it wasn't true.

Little by little, they were beginning to get their lives in order. The savior helicopter had been concealed in a storage shed at the mining company. Arrangements had been made for a plane to land and take Lindsey and Tim on their way back to American soil. Hank had used the Myers' satellite phone to take care of the details of their departure. The church had provided the phone for emergency use only. Calls were far too expensive for casual use. Hank made a silent pledge that he would reimburse them for the cost of the calls when he got back home. He made one last quick call to his parents.

"Hello?" answered his mother.

"Mom, it's Hank."

"Oh, my God! Hank, where are you?"

"I'm in the village of Sanniquellie. Mom, Lindsey and Tim are alive and with me right now."

"Oh, Hank," she sobbed. "We've prayed every day. Wait a minute," she said and called out to someone. "Susan, it's Hank. Lindsey and Tim are OK!"

Lindsey's mother rushed to the extension phone.

"Lindsey?"

"Just a minute, Susan. I'll put her on," Hank said.

"Mom, Tim and I are just fine. Hank and some brave Liberian friends rescued him. Would you like to talk to Tim?" she asked as she handed the receiver to her son.

"Hi, Grandma Martin, Grandma Smyth." Both women questioned their grandson at the same time. "I'm just fine. Dad rescued me. I have this neat friend, Sabo."

Hank tapped his son's shoulder.

"Son, we'll tell them everything later. This call costs Dr. Myers a lot of money. Let me talk to your grandparents."

Tim handed the phone off to his dad.

"Mom, can I speak to Dad?"

"I'm sorry, but he and Virgil are driving to Florida."

Hank couldn't understand why his father and Lindsey's father had gone to Florida. "Florida? Why in the world are they going to Florida?"

"It was all Virgil's idea. The news media has been hounding us to interview you. We are telling them that you, Virgil and your dad are fishing in the Florida Keys. They're trying to help you get over your loss. They left yesterday and were supposed to stop in Miami to visit your aunt."

"Mom, if Dad calls, let him know we are all OK. I don't know when we'll get out of here. I'll try to call again," he said. "Oh, and one more thing, don't tell anyone that you talked to us or even that Lindsey and Tim are alive. We could be in big trouble if the wrong people found out."

"All right, son. We are all so happy. Come home soon."

Hank dialed a second number. The phone rang three times.

"What do you want?"

"Mai Lee, that's not the way to answer a phone," Hank laughed.

"Hank Martin, you back in Fayetteville?"

"No, Mai Lee, I'm still in Africa."

"Africa? You sound like you next door. I dreamed last night that you fight with demon and rescue Tim. That true, Hank?"

"Yes, Mai Lee. Lindsey and Tim are safe."

"I so happy for you. You want talk to Tiny?"

"Yes, Mai Lee. Is he home?"

"Tiny!" she screamed in the phone. Hank held the phone at arm's length.

"Colonel Martin! God, it's good to hear your voice. You found them?"

"Yes, Tiny. They're safe, but I need your help."

"Anything, sir."

"Can you come up with five or six retired special operations guys who'd be willing to come over here and train a military force?"

"Sure. That's easy. What else?"

"I need to get Lindsey and Tim out of this country. Their passports and visas are at the American embassy, and we're two hundred miles in the interior. Can your CIA connections fly into the air strip at the Liberian Mining Company?"

"No problem. I can probably fly in the trainers at the same time."

"Tiny, I also need some special equipment. I'll make arrangements to transfer one hundred thousand dollars from my mutual funds to your account to cover costs. Got a pencil, Tiny?"

Tiny nodded as they double-checked each item. When they finished, Tiny paused.

"Sir, someone wants to talk to you."

"Son, it sounds like you kicked butt!"

"Dad? What are you doing at Tiny's?"

"Drinking Tiny's beer and swapping war stories," laughed Bill Martin. "Virgil and I are having a ball. We helped close Tiny's bar last night. Those SF guys found out that an old engineer and an infantry grunt can drink any one of them under the table!"

"Dad, you'd better not let Mom find out."

"Don't worry, son. We're leaving tomorrow for Florida."

As they had arranged earlier, Hank called Tiny later that same day. An unmarked C-12 turboprop would land, bringing in the training team. When it left, it would fly Lindsey and Tim back to the United States. Hank had no idea how Tiny pulled the strings to get the CIA to fly the operation, but he would be forever indebted to him.

Lindsey eased herself out of bed, careful not to disturb Hank. She pulled on her clothes and slipped out of the room. Hank needed his sleep. She vowed to spend her remaining time in Liberia doing whatever she could to help out at the clinic.

Although she and Tim would soon be on their way home, she worried about Hank who had made plans to stay for at least another three weeks to set up the training for the military forces who would fight for the People's Party. It wouldn't be easy to leave Joe, Sabo, the Morrays, the Myers and all the others whose lives had become intertwined with theirs. The least she could do would be to work in the clinic, doing whatever she could to ease the suffering. She softly closed the bedroom door, taking a final look at her sleeping husband.

"Sleep tight, my love," she whispered.

When he rolled over, Hank's arm fell on the empty bed. His watch read half past eight. He hadn't slept so soundly in weeks. He stretched his arms out over his head, recalling the sense of relief and release he had felt at last while finally being alone with Lindsey. Now she had let him sleep, even though she herself had been through her own personal hell.

Safe at last, he pulled on running shorts and a pair of Frank's old sneakers. A morning run – at last a morning run.

He did some warm-up stretches and loosened his muscles. He used to just take off running, but now his stiff joints required some preparation. When he had satisfied himself that he wouldn't get a muscle cramp, he started his run.

Sanniquellie was about two miles down the road. Down and back would make it four miles, about right. Then he'd shower and head out to the camp where Joe Weah was training the People's Party militia.

Morray had designated Joe as commander. Hank was impressed by this significant appointment. Before, the leaders had all been Kruman. Now, Joe, a Kapel, and his tribal brother, Major Ed Seah, were to be key players. A steady flow of Kapel tribal members had been coming in daily to join up with the growing militia. Since Joe's father, a paramount chief, had denounced the Liberian government, Hank had gained even more confidence that the corrupt government could be overthrown.

Tim and Sabo came back to the hut on the clinic grounds each evening, but their days were devoted to helping with the training. Hank suspected Lindsey wouldn't approve. Tim had stood beside Joe as they taught the recruits how to fire the M-16. At least it wouldn't be for long, Hank rationalized. Tim would soon be on his way back to the U.S. But for now, deep in the jungles of West Africa, Tim had immersed himself in military training.

Hank clicked his stopwatch as he reached the edge of town. He'd made it in fifteen minutes. That translated to a seven-minute thirty-second mile. Not bad, considering he hadn't run in two months. He leaned forward to take a deep breath, bracing the palms of his hands on his knees. He turned and began to retrace his path. It wasn't long until he could once again see the clinic, but he stopped in his tracks when he heard a distinct sound. He scanned the horizon, but didn't see anything unusual. He looked again, this time to the west, when he saw them coming. The two dark, sinister shapes moved toward him. Even at a distance and at a high altitude, there was no mistaking what was coming.

"God, no!" he shouted as he raced toward the clinic.

Although Frank seldom took a break from his work, for some reason he had stepped out on the veranda to take in the beauty of the tranquil morning. He was startled to see a runner approach as if the devil itself were in pursuit.

Hank came to a stop at the steps, gasping for air. Streams of sweat ran down his face and dripped on his chest.

"Frank, evacuate the clinic. Now!" he blurted.

"Why would we want to do that?" Frank asked.

"Cobras!" Hank screamed.

"Snakes? Where?"

"No, no! Not snakes! Attack helicopters. Two. Up there!"

Hank pointed to the west. Frank pulled out his bifocals and squinted into the western sky. He had last seen that unmistakable shape in 1972.

In Vietnam, the Bell AH-1, called the Cobra, provided the fire support for airmobile and air assault operations. With its narrow body, seating a pilot and optional co-pilot tandem, the fast, sleek black helicopter looked as menacing as it was. Mounted on its nose was a multi-barreled, rotating 7.62-millimeter GAU-2 mini gun, capable of firing thousands of rounds per minute. It was an updated version of the old Gatling gun that used an electric motor. Each of its stubby wings was designed to carry rocket pods. Each rocket carries a high explosive warhead.

The Cobras served army aviation well in the seventies, but were eventually replaced with the more advanced AH-64 Apache attack helicopter in the 1980s. During the 1990s, the outdated Cobras were refurbished and sold through foreign military sales to third world countries. The U.S. had sold ten surplus Cobras to Liberia. Two of the beasts were now coming at them about three thousand feet above the treetops.

"They appear to be heading south," Frank said. "If they were in an attack mode, they would be flying at tree-top level, not way up there. Why should we evacuate?"

"Frank, just what do you think they're doing here? The government isn't going to waste the fuel and the wear and tear on the equipment just to fly around up there. When we rescued Tim and Sabo, we destroyed that whole damn valley. I would bet that Steven Dowling and his buddies are more than just a little pissed off!"

"Dr. Frank, Dr. Frank... the President is addressing the nation!"

The two looked up to see an orderly running toward them, carrying a large transistor radio.

"My fellow citizens, it is with great sadness that I must address you this morning. Monday, the military trials began against the thirty men accused of treason, treachery and murder. Wednesday the trials will conclude. Already sixteen have been found guilty of horrible crimes against our people. Several have already confessed to the killings of not only our people, but also men, women and children who were our guests. When the Americans were killed, I promised the President of the United States that I would find those who committed this evil act and administer swift justice. Holding true to my word, those found guilty will be hanged by the neck until dead in a public execution next Monday at noon.

"Yet, my fellow citizens, the crimes of these men pale in light of those evil leaders who gave the orders that these men carried out. I have been given their written confessions that point to the People's Party and their self-proclaimed leader, Charles Morray. Even more disturbing, we have evidence that Joe Weah, once considered a hero to the people of Liberia, has become like a rabid dog, a man bent on destroying his own great country. We know that he was personally responsible for the deaths of many of the Americans, pulling the trigger that killed several of the young children. This evil man has joined Charles Morray and his band of thugs.

"I can no longer sit and watch as the People's Party destroys our country. As your President, I have signed a proclamation denouncing the People's Party as a threat against all Liberians. Any person, town or village that harbors members of the People's Party will be considered an enemy of the state.

"At exactly nine o'clock this morning, all telephone connections to Nimba and Grand Gedah counties will be shut down. The rail line from the Liberian Mine will be closed, and no traffic will be allowed into or out of Nimba and Grand Gedah counties. This embargo will remain in effect until Charles Morray and the leaders of the People's Party are imprisoned in Beliyela Prison.

"If you have members of the People's Party in your village, rise up against them. If you feed, house or give help to the People's Party, you and your village will be considered an enemy of Liberia. I pray that you will drive out the traitors and join your country in destroying the People's Party."

A commentator came on the air. "The President's speech will now be translated into Kapel, then into Kruman," he said. No one spoke.

Moments later, the silence was interrupted by a woman's voice.

"Honey, we just lost power. Could you start the generator?" asked Karen from the clinic door.

"Sure. Right away," responded Frank.

Hank checked the time. It was exactly nine o'clock.

"The government just cut off power to Nimba and Grand Gedah counties," Frank said. There is one hydroelectric plant north of here. We might be able to change the transmission lines to provide some power."

Hank grabbed Frank's arm.

"Never mind that, and never mind the generator. We have to evacuate the clinic."

"My God, Hank! The helicopters are gone. Besides, the air force would never attack a medical clinic."

"Frank, listen to me. Didn't you hear what Dowling said? Any person, town or village that harbors members of the People's Party will be considered an enemy of the state. They know that Morray's headquarters are in Sanniquellie, and you can bet they know your relationship to Charles. Just humor me. Get everyone out of the clinic and into the woods."

The radio announcer droned on, translating Dowling's speech into Kruman and Kapel. Otherwise, it was a typical workday morning. A flatbed truck, a dented Volkswagen and a battered blue money bus made up the sum of the traffic on the laterite main street, each stirring up poufs of red dust. A scrawny black dog stopped to scratch its ribcage before settling in the shade. The cloudless sky, bereft of breeze, seemed especially blue.

Most people had been up since first light, working the rich farmland. School children had been at their desks for more than an hour. Sadly, only half the desks were filled. When the Peace Corps volunteers had been evacuated, many families had put their children to more useful pursuits in the fields.

The open market buzzed with the sounds of rural commerce. Brightly clad passengers got off the money bus in front of the Lebanese store. Old men hovered around a radio on the porch of a bar. Behind the huts, women ground rice or palm kernels while they watched toddlers playing in the morning sun. Young boys set up a primitive soccer game, using a grapefruit sized lump of latex as their ball. Someone pulled at the cord of the general store's generator, willing it to come to a sputtering start. No one seemed surprised at the power outage, a common occurrence in Liberia's interior.

The young soccer players were the first to notice the strange sight.

Sanniquellie's main road ran from southwest to northeast. To the southwest, it climbed a low hill. At the crest of the hill, barely above the treetops, flew two black Cobra attack helicopters. Like giant dragonflies, each carried two seven-round folding-fin aerial rocket pods. Each of the 2.75-inch rockets was armed with a high explosive head.

Although people living in developed countries might find it difficult to believe, an aircraft this far into the interior was a rare event. People put down what they were doing and came out into the open, curious to watch these strange machines that hovered, fixed in place, above the trees. Some pointed upward and talked quietly to each other, unsure of what they were seeing. Yet they were fascinated by it all. No one showed fear – after all, danger more often came from earthly creatures – never from clear, blue skies.

Oddly, just as the radio announcer finished his translation, the two black beasts glided effortlessly toward the village. Some people turned and ran into the buildings. Others rushed into the forest. Others clung tightly to those they loved. Many stood transfixed, startled and confused.

Like puffs of white cotton, tiny clouds of white smoke spit from the creatures' stubby wings as each aircraft launched six FFAR rockets. The metal tubes streaked forward at a speed of one thousand meters per second. One struck the produce truck, its high explosive warhead twisting metal and igniting fuel. Another four or five tore up the ramshackle building nearby. The mud-filled stick walls blew outward and the roof collapsed in a careless heap. Still others blasted craters two feet deep in the main road. Shrapnel, rocks and dirt flew though the morning air, pelting hapless creatures where they stood. Sharp steel fragments sliced through the air at thousands of feet per second.

The rockets maimed, mangled or murdered anything or anyone in their wanton path. One unfortunate soul tumbled to the ground, his head nearly severed from his twitching body. Blotches of spattered red appeared mysteriously on the backs of those who thought they could run away, the rocks and pebbles striking the soft flesh like a blast of shotgun pellets.

But that mayhem still didn't satisfy the two black merchants of death. They paused, taking a breather, before the mini-guns sent out thousands of rounds per minute, shattering the final vestiges of peace in the town of Sanniquellie.

The two Cobras pulled up, banked to the right and disappeared over the trees. After the brutal barrage, an eerie silence followed. Now only the crackle of flames and the pitiful moaning of survivors broke the stillness. Here and there, a bent and bloodied body pulled another damaged piece of humanity out into the street, away from the burning and broken buildings. Others limped from their shelter, huddling near the wounded to offer comfort.

They barely had time to apply makeshift compresses to gaping wounds or to press shut the eyelids of sightless and still victims, when, from over the treetops, the two Cobras reappeared.

At nearly sixty miles per hour the perverse pieces of machinery made their second strafing run. Their obedient rockets obliterated everything in their path.

Sanniquellie's peaceful morning had been transformed into a scene from the bowels of hell.

Dr. Myers urged his patients and their families to hurry forward and hide in the depths of the forest. Reluctant to leave the sanctuary of the clinic, they moved passively to a grove of rubber trees along the eastern side of the clearing. Staff members, including Frank and Karen, hoisted makeshift stretchers to carry out the bedridden. They went back to help the final six patients when a rumble of explosions erupted from the direction of the town. Seconds later, clouds of black smoke billowed from behind the hill.

Frank shook his head in disbelief. Martin had been right after all. Those black helicopters had let loose their venom on the town. He could only hope that the pilots possessed the compassion to spare the clinic. Mentally, he began to plan ways to help the villagers who must have suffered injuries in the brutal attack.

Frank and the others walked as swiftly as they could with the last six patients toward the shelter of the tree line when he heard the rotor blades.

"Run!" yelled Hank as he saw the dark shadow of the Cobra fall across the clearing.

Lindsey could see the deep forest hundreds of yards ahead. Although her legs felt leaden, she willed herself to lengthen her stride while clutching the tiny bundle in her arms. She had grabbed the fragile form of the malnourished child who had been brought in only four days earlier.

Frank had relinquished his initial hopeless opinion and had begun an aggressive and persistent treatment plan. He had finally been able to insert an IV in the baby's ankle. To everyone's surprise, the child not only continued to live, but also seemed to be making progress. Brain damage was still possible, but at least the child's body had begun to recover. By Lindsey's side, the child's young mother, wide-eyed and trembling, stumbled along in the race to safety.

The Cobra's pilot spotted the motley string of humanity dashing toward the deep undergrowth. He couldn't help but smile at his luck. He banked and lined up the fleeing figures with his helmet-mounted sight system. He pressed the red button at the end of the stick. Neither Cobra required a weapons operator. The pilot did it all.

A swath of fire erupted from the machine gun. He took aim at those near the head of the line. In seconds, he knew that pieces of torn flesh and puddles of warm blood would dot the clearing. Yet, even as he pressed the firing button, nothing happened. He swore and pushed it harder. A flashing light on the instrument panel indicated a weapons malfunction. He flew directly over the heads of the terrified runners. Their collective panic only served to reinvigorate him.

He banked over the trees and turned his attention to the clinic itself. His orders had been clear – destroy the cluster of tin-roofed buildings that housed the medical clinic. Four rounds sat ready in the rocket pods.

The last few weeks of Lindsey's life had been treacherous enough, but now when she felt the rush of air from the helicopter's rotors, she was certain that none of them would survive the imminent attack. She looked upward, only to catch a brief look at the Cobra's pilot. His sinister glare would be forever embedded in her memory.

Strangely, the aircraft passed over their heads without firing a shot. It was less than one hundred yards to the cover of the forest. She glanced quickly to her left, assuming that the baby's mother would match her pace. Yet the girl had reversed direction, her innate fear had pulled her back to the clinic's buildings. Lindsey handed off the bundle to an orderly and dashed after the frightened girl. Her chest heaved from fatigue, yet she kept running.

The clinic door stood wide open. She looked first to the left and then to her right. She panted, having difficulty catching her breath. She forced herself to scan the vacant room. Finally, she spotted a dark-skinned bare foot sticking out from beneath a heavy metal desk.

"Come on, dear," she pleaded. "We can't stay here. Come with me to the woods."

The girl's wide eyes peered upward, filled with abject fear. Lindsey continued her coaxing and reached down to clasp her hand. The girl reached up and held Lindsey's hand as she began to get to her feet.

Then the entire front of the building blew inward, its roof collapsing in smoke and flames.

# 33

*CNN World News, Monrovia, Liberia –*
*This is Richard Singleton reporting.*

As the situation in this small West African country continues to deteriorate, the Liberian government persists in denying charges from its opposition that more than three hundred innocent victims died in an attack on the People's Party headquarters in Sanniquellie.

President Steven Dowling said that the action taken by the nation's armed forces was no different than similar action taken against Middle Eastern terrorists in the past. According to Dowling, a strategic strike was ordered against the terrorist training camp of rebel leader Charles Morray. Members of Morray's People's Party who had been found guilty of the brutal murders of American Embassy personnel last month had identified the camp.

The Liberian government has issued a formal statement that his country will not tolerate the vicious acts of terrorism such as was witnessed here last month. Those who have been found guilty of such crimes are scheduled to be executed Monday. The camp where these men were trained has been destroyed. The government claims it will not rest until the People's Party is destroyed.

Yet despite such actions by the Liberian government, the People's Party appears to be not only growing in popularity, but also consolidating its hold on the Nimba and Grand Gedah counties. Following an attempt to shut off the territory from all outside support, rebel forces have captured the large hydroelectric plant on the Kruman River and have diverted its power to provide electricity to towns and villages within the territory. The Liberian Mining Company has also fallen under direct control of the People's Party, allowing the rebel forces direct access to the country's second largest airfield.

Arriving tomorrow on that airfield will be a Red Cross mercy flight carrying medical supplies and medical staff to address the injuries that occurred in the attack on the terrorist camp. This reporter will be on that flight. It is my goal to personally interview Charles Morray, the leader of the People's Party.

Stay tuned for further reports from Liberia.

Vicki clicked the remote, extinguishing the dismal news reports. Jim Parkinson and Jerry Day sat across the room, each on opposite ends of the couch.

"So, what happens now?" she asked.

"Richard Singleton is a tough investigative reporter. He was on the ground in Baghdad during Operation Iraqi Freedom. He has a knack at getting to the truth, and he isn't afraid to tell it as it is," said Jerry.

"What happens if he finds out that Hank Martin is out there supporting Charles Morray?"

"Then we're in big trouble," Jim answered. "So far, our sources in Sanniquellie only say that a missionary and his wife and son are in Morray's camp. They don't know who they are. But Singleton will ferret out the truth. When he does, we've got problems."

"Will he come to me before he goes public?"

"Vicki, I think we can arrange for him to meet with you first," Jim said. "I can't promise that it will do any good."

"All right," she answered. "I guess all we can do now is wait."

The three sat in silence. Vicki rattled the ice cubes in her heavy glass.

"Where does that leave us?" Vicki asked. "Our own country can't come in to help us. As long as Carpai and his pals have convinced the world that they're still in charge and that Morray is the real villain, we're just sitting ducks.

"If we don't hang on here, we can bet that our enemies will force their way in to establish a power base. Liberia's oil and mineral wealth is too tempting. We're teetering on the edge of a wider conflict."

Neither of her top-level advisors could argue with her reasoning. The Liberian government, no matter how corrupt, was in control of the nation's fate, and her staff was caught in the middle.

"All the men will be hanged Monday. I'm afraid that there is nothing that can be done to stop the executions. We know that the confessions were the result of trumped-up charges, and that these men were no part of any conspiracy. Yet our hands are tied. Nothing out of the ordinary has happened in Monrovia. The army continues to enforce martial law, but day-to-day activities are mostly normal. As the ambassador, I can't even issue a concern about the safety of the embassy staff in Monrovia."

"The capital may look normal on the surface," said Jerry, "but, if you ask me, this whole country is on the verge of coming apart. People out there on the street aren't as stupid as we might think they are. Anyone who's watched the trials on TV can tell that those men who are on trial are as much victims as the people who were killed. If Charles Morray marched into Monrovia tomorrow, half the soldiers would join him. If you want my opinion, I think this place is on the brink of complete collapse."

# 34

***Dr. Myers led the memorial service. The man not only healed bodies, but he also ministered to their inner spirits.***

"I LOOKED OVER JORDAN, AND WHAT DID I SEE? COMIN' FOR TO CARRY ME home. A band of angels comin' after me, comin' for to carry me home. Swing low, sweet chariot, comin' for to carry me home. Swing low, sweet chariot, comin' for to carry me home...."

The words of the American Negro melody sung by slaves one hundred sixty years before – perhaps sung by some who had stood on this very riverbank – echoed from the far shore of the slow-moving river. The sunlight filtered through the tall cottonwoods. Nearly fifteen hundred people gathered to say their goodbyes to loved ones, friends and strangers. So many lives had been lost in the attack. Many spoke no English, yet their lips mimicked the words, joining in an oddly surrealistic chant.

Frank Myers delivered his sermon in three languages – Kapel, Kruman and English. Although most of his listeners weren't Christians, they sensed the peace of this act of closure that gave them permission to move forward with their lives.

Lindsey twisted her stiff neck, painfully aware of how close she had come to death. Her arms and hands bore the scars of her injuries, yet she, unlike so many others, had lived. Gathered here in the morning, the survivors would bear deep, emotional wounds for the rest of their lives. The past three days had been an incomprehensible blur. No one could have imagined that their own government would have destroyed a town of innocents.

The young mother had been confused and frightened by the raid. Her panic had driven her back to the deserted clinic. Lindsey had followed her, only to find her huddled behind the doctor's desk. Lindsey could remember extending her hand, reaching down, and clasping the trembling fingers. The blast of exploding rockets erased her recollection of what happened next. It took rescuers more than an hour to lift the broken boards and crumpled metal from their tiny sanctuary.

If Hank hadn't insisted on the sudden evacuation, many in the clinic would have died or suffered serious injury. The only victims at the clinic were the two women. Each was scratched, bruised and covered with dust, yet neither the worse for the ordeal.

The staff and patients had stood before the broken building, exhausted, yet marveling at their own survival. Frank was the first to notice the tattered line of humanity making its way down the hill. More were sure to follow, if they could, he thought. He snapped into action, mobilizing the staff to probe the ruins to recover undamaged medical supplies. They loaded the clinic truck and headed for town.

Hank and Tim both begged Lindsey to stay in the Myers' house that had survived the attack with only a few broken windows. Lindsey shook her head, insisting on doing her part to help. Her only concession was to accept a ride on the truck, rather than to make the two-mile walk to Sanniquellie.

Nothing in her life could have prepared her for the horror on the town's main street. Lindsey found herself whispering the words of the Twenty-third Psalm.

"Yea, though I walk through the valley of the shadow of death."

Indeed, this peaceful village had become a valley of death. Except for the low moans of the injured and the burst of sobs from their loved ones, an eerie stillness filled the air. Lindsey covered her mouth and nose in an attempt to stifle her retching as she inhaled the smell of burned flesh and spilled body fluids. How could any human being unleash such ungodly horror? She hung her head and clutched her hands close to her as she prayed for strength.

Back home, she had watched the horror inflicted by terrorists as the World Trade Center and part of the Pentagon had been destroyed on that fateful September 11. She, like other Americans, sat glued to her television. Later she had seen the chilling photos in newspapers and magazines. But those were only images of death. Here, tangible human misery surrounded her.

For some reason, she thought about those soldiers who had suffered post-traumatic stress after being in combat. Some people thought it was only a sign of weakness. Now she knew what they were talking about. This nightmare would never leave her.

Hank barked out orders, organizing the survivors according to Frank's instructions. Sanniquellie's population had been near five thousand, counting the tiny hamlets on its outskirts. It had been one of the largest towns in Nimba County. Now it had been dealt a deathblow.

Many of the dead had been carried to a clearing north of the burning town. They were laid out side-by-side on the grass, never again to till the fertile soil or chatter in the country market. Teams of boys armed with slings and pebbles were stationed along the perimeter, ready to fend off curious vultures and hungry dogs.

Those who hung onto life were assembled in the market square. Lindsey helped with the triage, making life-and-death decisions as the medical conditions were assessed on the basis of urgency and chance of survival.

Frank quickly examined each victim. Some could survive their wounds with little care. Others required urgent medical attention. The third group had such serious injuries that they wouldn't survive. Even those who might have been helped if adequate equipment had been available were doomed to die a slow and painful death. Frank lacked even the basic painkillers that could ease their suffering. As their lives came to an end, teams of survivors wrapped the bodies in makeshift shrouds and carried them to the field of the dead.

For hours they made the heart-wrenching decisions. They moved like robots, doing all they could, but never doing enough.

Suddenly, their work came to a halt. The rumble of a large engine renewed their terror. To the south of the town, twin railway tracks had been used to haul raw ore to the Port of Buchanan. The government had shut down the rail lines. No one expected to hear the sound of a train engine. The train came to a stop on the tracks near the middle of the town. Frank couldn't believe what he was seeing.

Crews began unloading pallets of medical supplies, operating equipment and anesthetics. The mining company's doctor and nurse stepped down from the train and waved at Frank.

The two doctors directed the set-up of a small operating theater. Their work saved many who would have otherwise succumbed to their injuries. Yet the death toll continued to mount. In the seventy-two hours following the attack, more than four hundred bodies had been readied for burial in the mass graves. Another one hundred fifty were likely to die without major medical intervention. The exhausted workers received word that a Red Cross mercy flight was due to arrive within hours. But for so many, it would be too late.

Lindsey took a moment to sit on the ground, her elbows braced against her knees and her hands covered her eyes.

She couldn't help but wonder how Frank Myers' loving God would allow such suffering. Wars, so many wars. The living weep for their lost loved ones, their lives forever changed. How could something good come from all this horror?

She dropped her hands and looked up when she felt someone approach. It was her two men – Hank and Tim. They looked down at her. Each carried an M-16, casually slung over the shoulder. She saw the look of a soldier in their eyes. How was it that Tim got that look? Tim was just fifteen years old. Yet in so many places in so many wars, many fifteen-year-olds were soldiers. Now it was Tim's turn.

The arrangements had been made. In a matter of hours, Lindsey and Tim would board a flight back to the U.S. Hank would stay on. He planned to use his thirty days of leave to help train the ragged militia for its assault on the government of Liberia.

In September, Tim would blend in with the other American teenagers attending high school in Virginia. She shook her head in disbelief. How could Tim ever be the same again?

All around, the landscape had been transformed. Now the ridgeline was picketed with men. They were armed with hand-held surface-to-air missiles, designed to shoot down aircraft. Overnight, the sleepy village had become an armed camp.

After the support had arrived from the mining company, Hank and Tim had joined Charles and Joe at the militia training camp. In just two days, the People's Party had taken control of the Liberian mines and the hydroelectric plant. They had secured all the roads leading into Nimba and Grand Gedah counties. There wouldn't be another surprise attack. Yet Lindsey feared even more what lay ahead. When the militia made its move to overthrow the government, even more lives would be lost.

The frustration of the moment weighed heavily on Lindsey. When she looked up, she saw Sabo, Joe's young cousin and Tim's good friend. He, like Tim, had survived and escaped from Carpai's thugs. Sabo also carried an M-16, but what caught her eye was the young woman beside him. Charles Morray's sister-in-law, the beautiful young Judie Kerkula, was holding his hand. When the two looked at each other, it reminded her of the moment when the young Hank Martin had first stood at her apartment door on the night of their first date sixteen years earlier.

Then the realization hit her – they were in love.

It was a Kapel boy and a Kruman girl. The two tribes once waged war, but in these two young people, Lindsey saw a glimpse into the future. Perhaps Charles Morray and Joe Weah could bring the two tribes together to create a unified nation. It could prosper from the great wealth in oil reserves lying under the river delta.

Maybe God could make something good come out of the horror. She couldn't hold back her tears. She wept for the dead. She wept for the joy in what could lie in the future. She wept for herself and her family. In her tears, her deep burden found release.

"Are you going to be OK?" she heard Hank say as he stood behind her, resting his hand on her shoulder.

"Yes, I finally have come to a realization that things could actually get better. I have hope."

Hank reached down, placing his hands under her arms and bringing her up to his level. He held her in a comforting embrace.

"Come on. It's time to say goodbye. We'll be taking the train to the airstrip to meet your plane."

On the train, they sat side-by-side in silence. The only sounds were the rumble of the diesel locomotive pulling the passenger cars and the rhythmic click of metal wheels passing over the rail joints. Lindsey felt Hank's firmly muscled leg against her as they sat together on the polished wooden seat.

Opposite them, Tim stretched his legs across his own bench seat. The three kept their thoughts to themselves, aware that they had only hours left to be together before the family would once again be separated. The mining company had only six passenger cars. They must have been an afterthought compared to the numerous ore cars. Now the ore cars sat idle, and the passenger cars surged in importance. They ferried the militia between the mine and Sanniquellie. Across the aisle, Joe and Charles had joined them. There they would meet the retired Special Forces soldiers who would train the militia.

Lindsey turned her head to stare through the stained window at the passing jungle. Saying goodbye had been an accepted part of the life of a military wife as the family had moved from post to post. But having to leave the Myers had been a difficult goodbye. They still struggled daily. They worked as long as they could stand upright without giving in to their overwhelming fatigue. So many wounded. So many in pain. The Red Cross teams would be a godsend, yet so much remained undone. She knew Hank wanted her and Tim to be back safely in the U.S. He could work better at being a soldier if he knew his family was safe. She, too, felt compelled to assure their son's safety, but parting from Hank and leaving a job undone nagged at her sense of well being.

She watched Tim continue to stare straight ahead. If only she could read his thoughts. Usually, the three sat down and hashed out family decisions together. Tim, an only child, had always been included in adult-level conversations. Yet now the three sat in silence like total strangers.

"Dad?"

"Yes, son?"

"Dad, I don't want to leave Liberia."

"Tim, we've already discussed this. It's too dangerous for you and your mother to remain in country. Besides, you've got to get back in school."

"But, Dad, you need my help. You know that I can train the young Liberians better than anyone else. They feel that I am one of them. If I can fire a rifle, they know that they can do it, too."

Hank stretched his legs in front of him and ran a finger around the inside of his shirt collar. What Tim was saying made sense. It was time to change tactics.

"I'm worried about your mother. She has been injured. She has been attacked. I need you to take care of her. You're a man now. I have to stay here to coordinate the training. We can't leave her alone. She has to go back to the United States."

Hank glanced at his wife, sure of her support. Yet she didn't answer. Several minutes passed, and still no one spoke. Hank examined his fingernails, twisted his watchband and held his tongue.

"Mom is stronger than either of us," Tim said. "She got us to Zigda. You should have seen her when she nursed Joe back to health. She was so important that Joe's father, Togba, seated her as an equal among the men.

"Dad, we know what we are facing. Only you and I have fought the *endosym*. Chea Geebe told me that I would have to battle it. It will take both of us to win."

Tim stopped. His face was flushed. Hank felt his argument crumble. Now Lindsey would enter the discussion. She would come to his support.

"Hank, Tim, let me say something," Lindsey began. Hank breathed a sigh of relief. Now they would get somewhere.

"You're both right. My worst nightmare couldn't have been as bad as what has happened. I'm tired. I hurt, and I'm scared. Not just scared for myself, but for both of you. I want to go home. I want to sit on my porch in Virginia and listen to the birds sing. I want to drink my coffee and eat my breakfast.

"But there is no way I can walk away from the Myers and these poor people. Therefore, we will all leave together. Hank, when you have completed training the militia, your wife and son will fly out with you. Until then, we are in this together, as a family."

She folded her arms across her chest and looked at both men. All three sat motionless. Finally Tim broke the silence.

"Mom, you're cool."

That was probably the greatest compliment that a teenager could give to an adult.

"Shit," Hank sighed. "Lindsey, you realize that if you stay here, you could be killed, seriously injured, or even worse."

"William Henry Martin, those things can happen to us in the McDonald's parking lot in McLean, Virginia. It's settled. Tim and I are staying here with you."

Hank could only remember three times in their marriage that Lindsey had addressed him using his full name. Each time, he had lost the argument.

"All right," he conceded, "we leave together."

The dark cloud that had hung over them had now lifted. The atmosphere was completely transformed.

"Mom, Dad! Look at the pigmy hippopotamuses!" All three crowded at the window to watch the small creatures sun themselves on a sandbar. As the train rolled along toward the mine, the Martins had become a family once again.

Whatever the future held, they were prepared to face it together. It was early afternoon when the train came to a stop at the mine's station. The C-12 with six retired Special Forces non-commissioned officers would be arriving shortly. A van picked them up and headed for the airfield.

It stopped next to the control tower.

"Look, Dad!" Tim shouted. It's a C-130!"

"That's the Red Cross mercy flight that just brought in the medical supplies and staff for Sanniquellie. It should take about an hour to get it all loaded on the train," Charles said. The plane was parked at the north end of the field.

"We'll need to unload the C-12 on this side of the runway to be as far from that C-130 as possible," Hank said.

"Why?" Joe asked.

"My guess is that at least one reporter accompanied that flight. The last thing we need is for a reporter to find out that I'm involved in militia training to overthrow the government of Liberia. If that story breaks, you'll all have to visit me at Leavenworth Penitentiary.

"Place guards on the runway once the C-12 lands. Make sure no one leaves the area around that C-130 until we've unloaded all the passengers and equipment and the C-12 departs," Hank warned.

They had been sitting on a bench in the shade of a hangar. Their conversation stopped when they heard the engines from an approaching plane. To the west of the field, just above the tree line, they could see a C-12 turbo prop banking and leveling off to make its final approach.

The C-12 had served as a workhorse for the embassies since the early seventies. When equipped with special rough terrain tires, the plane could take up to eight passengers and their baggage into a thirty-five hundred-foot dirt landing strip. It could fly above twenty thousand feet. It was capable of all-weather flight and could cruise at more than two hundred sixty knots. Although not trans-oceanic, when fitted with wing tanks could hop to Europe via Greenland.

This one looked like the commercial version. It had been painted a dark green. As it got closer, Hank saw that it had been fitted with the wing tanks that would allow it to make long distance flights.

"Sure looks like it's coming in fast," Hank said.

It seemed as if the pilot had just come to the same conclusion. The pitch of the props shifted, causing the plane to make a sudden drop. Its wheels made hard contact with the gravel runway. It took a sharp upward bounce. One wing dipped to the right before the plane touched and bounced up again. It hit a third time, its right wing nearly scraping the ground. Finally, it settled on its three wheels and squealed to an abrupt stop.

A pickup truck pulled out onto the runway. The driver motioned to the pilot to follow. The pilot brought the plane to a wide area near the onlookers. Hank could make out the pilot's silhouette through the window as he leaned forward to cut off the engines.

A few minutes later, the door just behind the wing popped open. A bedraggled-looking man stepped out into the sunlight.

"Could it be?" Hank said out loud. "Who else?"

It was Roy, the crazy CIA pilot who had flown Hank into this same field only three weeks earlier.

"Well, Roy, it looks like you haven't learned to fly a plane any better."

"Do I know you?" he asked.

"You flew me from Upper Volta here a few weeks ago," Hank told him.

"You look different," Roy said.

"It's the beard."

"No, it's more than that. You look older."

Hank shrugged. "It's the job."

The first passenger stepped out. Lindsey wasn't sure what she had expected, but she was pretty sure it wasn't what she saw now. These weren't hard-charging Special Forces trainers. They were middle-aged men with gray hair, potbellies and bifocals. Each man greeted Hank as if he were a long-lost brother. Five of them gathered around Hank. He beckoned Charles and Joe to join them. Lindsey thought, by judging from the expressions on their faces, that perhaps the two knew several of the trainers. After a round of handshaking and animated chatter, Hank brought the group over to meet his family.

"Guys, let me introduce you to my wife and son," Hank said.

Here was retired Master Sergeant Jimmy Pullen, the medic who had patched up Hank during Desert Storm. Next were retired Sergeant Major Mike Kellogg and retired Sergeant Major Bill Catfield, both of whom had been members of the MTT to Liberia. They both knew Charles. Then Hank introduced retired Master Sergeant Charles Brothers and retired command Sergeant Major Gerald Murphy, both instructors from Fort Bragg. They had trained with Joe Weah.

"I thought Dick Savage was coming, too," Hank said.

"His doctor wouldn't let him come. He had a heart bypass four months ago," Murphy said.

"That's too bad," Hank said. "Dick was the second-best jungle tactics instructor in SF. We could have used him."

"Who was the best?" asked someone who was still inside the aircraft.

Everyone turned to see retired Command Sergeant Major Wilbur Sprague step down.

"You are, Tiny!" Hank yelled.

"Tiny!" screamed Lindsey. She ran up, threw her arms up around his neck and kissed him on the cheek. He held her at arms' length.

"You're as beautiful as ever!"

"You always had a way with the women, you sly old dog!" Lindsey laughed.

Now it was Tim's turn.

"Good to see you again, Sergeant Major Sprague."

Tiny reached out and shook Tim's hand. Tim's grip was firm, and he looked Tiny directly in the eye.

Tiny had to pause. He could see "the look" in Tim's eyes. It was the same look he had seen in so many men throughout his thirty-five years of military service. He saw it in Vietnam, Panama, Iraq and faraway places he would just as soon forget. It was the look of a man who had faced death and walked away to fight again.

How many years had it been since he had last seen Tim? Maybe six or seven? How Tim had grown! Tiny himself stood well over six feet six inches tall, and he was able to look down on most men. Tim was already almost six feet two inches tall. By the time Tim reached full height, he could be Tiny's equal, at least in height, if not girth.

"Tim Martin, if you don't give your uncle Tiny a hug, I'll whip your ass."

The boy couldn't help but smile. The steely glint vanished from the boy's blue eyes. He had Lindsey's smile. He threw his arms around Tiny, and they both laughed.

The boisterous chatter kept on. The old soldiers traded stories and shared memories. No one had taken notice of a passenger from the C-130 who now stood in the distance observing the reunion. He was a tall, thin man with a shock of unruly red hair. He moved slowly out from the shadow of the C-130's wing.

At fifty-four, he might have been recognized wearing his trademark safari jacket, faded blue jeans and sturdy walking boots. For thirty years, he had shown up in most any corner of the world where there was conflict. Because of him, the harsh facts of war came into living rooms throughout the world. His pockmarked face and ruddy complexion featured an over-large, hooked nose. No one would compare him to the handsome talking heads – he was far their superior and far better known. Anyone who watched CNN knew Richard Singleton.

Singleton had been the kid in high school who no one would remember. He had gained some minor fame as editor of the school newspaper, but he was never popular with the girls and was far too skinny for sports. He had battled a severe case of adolescent acne that didn't clear up until his mid-twenties.

He studied photojournalism in college. He landed a job as a CNN cameraman and volunteered to accompany one of the star reporters to the Middle East. When the reporter was wounded, Singleton took over the commentary. Even though bullets whizzed overhead, he maintained a cool detachment. CNN had been impressed, and Singleton, who'd never be pretty enough to be an anchor, became one of the stars of *World News Tonight*. So now he was in another part of the world, ready to take on yet another war. He'd hitched a ride on the Red Cross flight to help the victims of the attack on Sanniquellie. He'd done his homework. He intended to meet Charles Morray.

He climbed back into the hold of the C-130 and got into the driver's seat of a stowed surplus jeep. He slid the disk out of the digital camera and inserted it into the laptop computer. He and his cameraman, Brian Anderson, hadn't wasted any time when the plane had landed. They shot footage of the unloading of emergency supplies and looked around for other potential material. An armed militiaman had interrupted their work.

"No more pictures," he said. They were told that they were to be confined to the airfield for at least the next hour. Only twenty minutes earlier, they had watched the twin-engine turbo prop come in for a landing and taxi to the far side of the runway. They had seen two vehicles pull out to the middle of the runway. Armed soldiers appeared to be guarding the people who had gathered around the cargo doors of the C-130.

He had to be careful on this one. Any attempt to use the video camera might jeopardize his chances of getting an interview with leaders of the People's Party. Likely, it didn't matter anyway. The plane probably carried only more medical supplies. Yet his instincts kept him on the alert. There seemed to be too many white faces in the group. He moved out under the plane's wing and crouched in the shadows. He pulled out his small Olympus Zoom digital.

Slowly, Singleton lifted the camera to his eye. The guards seemed to be lounging in their vehicles several hundred feet away. Heat waves rose from the rocky runway, creating a visual distortion. If he moved slowly, no one was likely to notice his arm move. He clicked off thirty shots. Now, seated in the jeep, he checked out his work. Anderson peered over his shoulder as the first image came up on the laptop's screen. He could see the plane with its rear door wide open.

He zoomed in and brought the plane's tail number into focus. Anderson jotted down its number on his notepad. Singleton flicked through three more images before stopping on an image of a white couple. The tall, well-built man had a beard and wore military fatigues. Somehow, he looked vaguely familiar, but Singleton couldn't place him. The attractive blonde beside him was likely in her mid-thirties. She had an athletic build, a flat stomach and long legs. He focused on her face. Something didn't look right. He doubled the zoom, creating a fuzzy image, but one clear enough to make out a long, red scar that appeared to be a recent injury.

Moving ahead, he noted the image of a large man engaged in animated dialog with a young soldier.

"Hey, that's just a kid," commented Anderson.

Singleton guessed that he was maybe sixteen or seventeen. The white kid had an M-16 slung over his shoulder. Later images showed a black man that Singleton thought might be Charles Morray. The other black man also looked familiar.

"Brian, what do you think we have here?" he asked.

"I don't know, Richard, but this is more than a routine militia get-together."

Singleton pulled out his sat-phone and dialed the CNN research desk. He had a hunch, and, if it was true, he had quite a story to tell.

Stan Adams answered on the third ring.

"Stan, this is Richard Singleton."

"Richard! I thought you were somewhere in West Africa."

"I am."

"No shit? It sounds like you're in the next office."

"Yeah, this new sat-phone is unbelievable. Listen, Stan, can you do me a favor?"

"Sure. What do you need?"

"I understand that I can plug this phone into my laptop, and it will send e-mail. How do I do that?"

Stan took him through the steps, and he soon had it working. Singleton requested a photo of Lieutenant Colonel William Martin as well as photos of his wife and son. He figured the archives had their photos following last month's terrorist attack in Monrovia.

Fewer than ten minutes later, Singleton opened the e-mail attachments. He loaded the photos onto his computer, reduced each and copied them all as separate documents. On the same document, he copied a headshot from the digital camera. Now he could compare the photos with the individuals by the plane.

"What do you think?"

"Richard, there's no doubt. That's Lieutenant Colonel Martin, his wife and son. But I also remember where I saw that other black man with Morray. It was on a wanted poster in Monrovia," said Anderson.

"Brian, we've really stumbled on something here. Terrorists supposedly killed Martin's wife and son. The Liberian government claims that Joe Weah and Charles Morray were responsible for the killings. Now, we find the Martins, Morray, and what looks like Weah, meeting six guys on a plane. The general and his kid are dressed like People's Party militia. His wife looks like someone beat the crap out of her. On top of that, the whole group looks like they are all long-lost friends. We're not leaving until I find out what's going on."

"Are you going to notify the office?" Anderson asked.

"Not yet. Let's wait until we get to Sanniquellie and check things out."

# 35

*As the opposition to Steven Dowling's regime continued to grow, for those held in the stockade, all hope was gone.*

THOMAS SIO COULD TELL IT WAS LATE AFTERNOON BY THE WAY THE SUNLIGHT came in through the thin slit at the top of the thick concrete wall. He must have dozed, wasting the few, precious hours he had yet to live. He marveled at how slowly time seemed to pass, even though only three days remained until his death. He imagined the tick-tick of a heavy mantel clock. Each tick would be one last breath. Again, he thought of his fatal scene.

He imagined himself being led from the dark cell. His pace would match that of his keepers. They would march across the parade grounds. He'd see the observers surrounding the newly built platform that would be the stage of his final exit. Ten nooses would dangle from the heavy crossbeam. Ten trapdoors would open simultaneously. Ten men at a time would feel the snap of their fragile necks as they dropped, swayed, and lost all feeling.

Twenty men had been sentenced to death. He wondered if the second group would be forced to watch their comrades die.

Again he replayed the scene. He would march across the field. The grass would be a deep green and the sky a brilliant blue. The rough-hewn lumber of the thirteen steps would creak as he climbed to the platform. He would hold his head high, his shoulders square, and his back straight. He prayed that his bowels would not betray him, revealing his inner terror. Tom Sio would not crawl. He would not snivel. He would face death as a man. At least that was his hope.

Five men had endured their final days in this twelve-foot by twelve-foot concrete dungeon. A narrow trench ran parallel to the inside wall. At its left, an iron spigot protruded from the rough cement. He listened to the monotonous rhythm of its continual trickle. It served to clear the trench of body waste. The droplets from the faucet served as their drinking water. They had no beds or benches. The condemned men sat and slept on the cool concrete. Every other day, guards would force them out of the cell, walk them across the hall, cram them into a narrow space, and flush out the cell with streams of water.

Tom turned his attention to his cellmates. Curled in the fetal position in the corner was Captain Charles Edwawa. Badly beaten in his interrogation, the guards had to hoist his bruised body into a hard chair in order to question and torture him even more. Tom turned his head. He could only wish Edwawa a tranquil death. Perhaps he would die here in his sleep and cheat the Monday gallows.

Three others – Lieutenant Jim Bolley, Captain Kona Zorzor, and Lieutenant Sam Mawai – sat cross-legged near Tom. Tired old men now, their faces had become sallow, their shoulders bowed, and their eyes empty of hope. Each had shed weight. Each would periodically clutch his belly as spasms of dysentery doubled him over in agony.

A month earlier, they had been the pride of their families. Few Liberians could boast of such success. Tom had been one of the youngest majors in the Liberian army. He had it all – a beautiful wife, two healthy children and even a car, most unusual for a young officer.

He had worked hard to fulfill his duties. When the alert was issued, his battalion had been activated. His men had even located the missing woman and her son. He was the man who had assumed Joe Weah's duties when Joe told him he'd only be gone a short time while he ran an errand. He followed Joe's orders to stand down the battalion. Later, the men had either returned to the barracks or had gone home to their families.

The following day, Tom watched as six men stepped out of sleek, black official cars. All of them displayed their credentials as members of the elite corps from the office of the minister of defense. They moved into Weah's office as if they owned it. One after one, the battalion staff members were interviewed separately. Every move Weah had made that day had been carefully noted. In the late afternoon, government soldiers from the 1st Battalion showed up. Tom and his men were relieved of their weapons and confined to barracks. Officers were kept apart from the enlisted men. For the next two days, they underwent even more interrogations. The questions got more personal. Each man was asked about his political affiliation. On the third day, the officers were put under arrest and confined to the stockade. Not one of them was allowed to contact his family.

It was then that they had their first introduction to Major Morris Kai and his loyal staff. The stories people told of the conditions in the stockade failed to adequately convey the horror inside its chambers.

Stripped naked, the men were packed seven to a cell. No visitors. No counsel. No questions. Throughout the cool night, Tom and the others huddled in fear. Some men sobbed; others simply sat in silence, lost in their own inner terror. In the morning, one by one, the men were to be individually interrogated by Major Kai.

After the first man left, those who remained sat silently, listening for any clue as to what might be their fate. They didn't wait long. At first, they heard pleas for mercy, then shrieks of agony. Some were carried back, bloodied and beaten. Others were heaved through the cell door, unconscious. Two never returned. Tom watched as six went before him. He was the last to be taken.

Two guards, one on each side, pinched the flesh of Tom's upper arms as they pushed the shuffling prisoner down the long corridor. They passed cell after cell. Each chamber held those who had been Tom's fellow soldiers, his comrades, and his friends. The hallway intersected with another. They turned right at the corner and stood before a heavy, wooden door. One guard rapped three times. Within moments, it opened.

Tom's legs lost the ability to function. Only the pressure of the guards' grasp gave him any indication that a life force still flowed through his body. Banks of fluorescent lights hung from the ceiling.

There were no windows. There was no other exit. A single stainless steel chair sat bolted to the floor in the center of the room. Metal shackles attached to the armrests and chair legs momentarily gave Tom the impression that it could have been used as an electric chair in the days when criminals were routinely electrocuted. But Tom was no criminal.

Strong arms pushed him ahead. He felt bile rising in his throat. A foul smell made him nauseous. A pool of vomit, urine, excrement and blood filled the seat of the chair. It dripped to a larger puddle of waste on the floor beneath.

About six feet to the right, Tom saw a stainless steel table. A collection of objects was neatly arranged – a box of latex gloves, a metal instrument with exposed electrical wires, carpenter's tools and a hammer – all lined up almost as a surgeon would prepare his operating room.

Someone tugged on his wrists. The handcuffs came off. He was pushed into the chair. His naked buttocks slipped on the wetness. Someone else grabbed his arms, then his ankles and shackled them to the cool steel.

Then he was left alone. Tears welled up in his eyes, yet he forced himself to stay in control. He waited. He listened. It might have been as long as an hour. It might have been three hours. Finally, he heard noises outside. The door creaked open. Before him, stood the immaculate Major Kai.

Trim and fit, each aspect of the major's appearance indicated that this was a man who paid strict attention to detail. Although small in stature, Kai exuded superiority. His pant legs were sharply creased. His narrow mustache ran neatly parallel to his upper lip. Clipboard in hand, he wasted no time.

"Let's see," he smiled. "You are Major Thomas Sio, the executive officer of the Reconnaissance Battalion. Your wife is the former Fahn Kwekwe. Two children – Christina, age eleven, and Tommy, age seven. Your address – 1317 Montree Drive. Oh, and I see that you recently purchased a 1999 Nissan from Nowai Motors."

Kai paused to stare at his prisoner.

"Is this information correct?"

"Yes," Tom managed to answer.

"Good. Good. Now, let's finish this quickly. I have a dinner engagement in one hour. I am never late. Sign this confession, and you will be returned to your cell."

"Confession?"

"Yes," Kai said flatly. "You are a member of the People's Party. You and Weah led the terrorists who slaughtered the American families. You personally pulled the trigger and killed the young baby. You, Weah and your ruthless band of officers joined in a plot with Charles Morray to overthrow the government of Liberia and assassinate our President."

Kai's voice never wavered, yet Tom could sense his anger build.

"That's preposterous. There is no way I would confess to doing any of that. I've never even met Charles Morray. I am a loyal member of the armed forces of Liberia. I took an oath to defend my country. You can torture and beat me if you wish. I would rather die than to confess to such lies," Tom said with conviction.

Tom braced himself for the pain that was sure to follow. He willed himself to endure whatever happened. He turned his head and looked directly into Kai's eyes.

Kai frowned.

"I am sorry to hear that. You will not only sign this confession, but you will admit your evil deeds in court on Monday."

"And you can go to hell, you bastard!" Tom shouted.

"That won't be necessary. Hell is right here in this room, and you are already there," Kai sneered. He nodded his head in the direction of the door. It opened and six guards came in.

At first Tom was confused. How could this be happening?

"No... oh, no!" he sobbed. His beautiful wife, the innocent and loving Fahn, was their hostage. Naked, hands bound behind her, Fahn struggled; yet her slight build was no match for the burly men. Their eyes met – hers wide, her cheeks streaked with tears, and her mouth gagged with a red bandanna.

Kai leaned closer to his chair. Tom smelled his antiseptic breath.

"Thirty two guards stand ready," he said with a perverse smile. "Each one will service your wife. When they finish, I will personally slice her tender neck. You will see her bleed to death before your eyes," he paused to watch Tom's reaction.

"Then, your daughter. Her name? Oh, yes, Christina. Only eleven? Yet she'll do. Each man will be ready a second time. They'll use her. Then I will slit her throat, too."

Again Kai paused in order to watch the fear grow in Tom's eyes.

"Then the next. Your son. We'll do the same for your son," Kai said. Then his voice changed. His tone became deceptively gentle, almost conciliatory. "However, if you do as I have told you, this woman will be returned to her home. No harm will come to her or to your children. Following your trial and subsequent execution, your wife will receive a pension and the benefits due the widow of a Liberian officer."

Before Tom could answer, Kai turned to the guard.

"Begin!" he ordered. Two of the guards pushed Fahn toward the stainless steel table, bending her forward, and exposing her gaping buttocks. Tom heard the sound of a zipper as the first man dropped his trousers. His penis was already boldly erect. He placed his arms on either side of the fragile form and moved against her.

"Stop! Stop! I'll do anything you ask!" Tom screamed. "Just let her go!"

"Enough!" Kai yelled. The guard seemed as if he hadn't heard. He turned to look at his commander whose steely eyes told him what he didn't want to hear.

"Take Mrs. Sio home," Kai said. "No one touches her or any member of her family."

The guard, now flaccid, backed away. Two men lifted the trembling woman and carried her through the door. Kai snapped open the shackles on Tom's wrists.

"Sign here," he said, pushing a clipboard and a pen into his hands.

Tom watched his shaking hand confirm his own death sentence.

"Hey, Sio, you got a visitor."

"A visitor?" Tom mumbled.

"Yeah, get up. You're going to the visitors' room."

A second time, Tom was led down the long corridor. This time at the intersection, they turned left. Following the interrogations, they had been given their fatigue trousers. His loose pants had fit perfectly three weeks earlier. His boots, shirt and belt had never been returned. He grasped his pant loops, cinching the fabric to keep the pants from falling down. Although he had no way of knowing, he had shed more than thirty-five pounds since he'd been in the stockade. His skin had lost its tone, hanging in folds from his face, neck and ribcage. He must have looked sixty years old, not his actual thirty years.

They pushed him into the visitors' room.

"You have fifteen minutes. Just fifteen minutes," warned the guard.

"Fahn! Fahn, what are you doing here?" Tom asked.

"I had to see you, my husband."

Tom couldn't move. He couldn't think. He could only memorize the face and form of his wife. It had been twelve years. They had two children, yet he marveled at her beauty. Her breasts were high and firm, her stomach flat and her legs, long and well formed. Her skin, like velvet, was the color of palm kernel. Her wide, dark eyes looked deep into his heart.

"Have they touched you?" he whispered.

"No, the guards took me home. No one has bothered us," she said.

"You must leave," said Tom. "It is dangerous for you to be here."

"Oh, Tom! How will I live without you?" she cried. Tom reached out and caressed her cheek.

"I will be here on Monday to take your body back to our village," she whispered.

"No, no. Fahn, you must not come Monday!"

"But, my husband, your body must be buried in the sacred bush. Otherwise, your spirit will wander forever."

"Fahn, let my brother get my body. You must leave here today. Take the children and go back to our village tonight!"

"Tom, we can't just leave our home. Remember, President Dowling said that we will not be harmed."

"Fahn, oh, my Fahn, you can't believe what he says."

"I don't understand. He is the President. He said we would not be bothered."

"Fahn, those men tore your clothes and threatened you. That officer made me sign a false confession. They will hang me Monday. Every one of them works for the government of Liberia. As soon as I breathe my last breath, they will come and take everything from you. They will also do whatever they want with you, Christina and Tommy. Promise me that you will go home right now. Pack the car and leave for the village."

"But, Tom..."

"Promise me, Fahn. This is my last wish before I die. Please allow me to go to the gallows knowing my wife and children are safe."

"All right, Tom. I will do as you say."

"Time's up!" called the guard. Tom stood, bent over and gently kissed Fahn on her lips. He walked toward the door, stopped and turned to look one more time. The guard grabbed his arm and shoved him out the door.

Tom concentrated on one thing and one thing only – the softness of their last kiss. He vowed to hold onto that moment to his dying breath.

# 36

***While Tom Sio stared at the walls of his cell, five young officers sat at a picnic table on the north side of Barclay Training Center's parade field. It was one of three military posts in strategic locations throughout Liberia.***

Camp Jackson was located in the interior. Camp Schiefflin guarded Liberian interests near the rubber plantations. Finally, the Barclay Training Center provided protection for the country's major city, Monrovia.

Now Camp Jackson housed the 2nd Infantry Battalion. Camp Schiefflin, the major base, had six units, including the 1st Infantry Battalion, the recently deactivated Reconnaissance Battalion, the Artillery Battalion, the Engineering Battalion, the Support Battalion and the Air Corps. Monrovia's Barclay Training Center was smaller, billeting the MP Company, the Honor Guard and the Executive Mansion Guard.

Although the smallest, the Barclay Training Center, was the most impressive of the military sites. It took up more than sixty acres along the Atlantic Ocean in downtown Monrovia. Granite block walls fourteen feet high and two feet thick surrounded the facility. Guard towers were placed along top of its walls. The primary entrance was off of Tubman Boulevard. Its heavy gate was built of eight-inch thick teak planks. At the east end of the facility, another gate provided access to the motor pool. Finally, at the rear, a third gate opened to a grassy field that sloped to the banks of the Atlantic Ocean. The open field was framed by several groups of palms. Behind the trees, a high barbed-wire fence linked the compound to the river. It served to keep out the possible trespassers who occupied the nearby shantytowns. Standard troop barracks, reviewing stands, and a twenty-acre parade field was dwarfed by the center's most impressive structure, the stockade. Since 1900, the stockade had housed the nation's criminals. Serving as the jail, it covered one full acre. It was encircled by a ten-foot high concrete wall and topped with barbed wire.

As sturdy and impenetrable as it was, only those free to roam the facility knew of a shady area under the tall palms on the north side of the field where five young officers lounged at a wooden picnic table. On the bench sat a cardboard case of Liberian malt beer. It satisfied their thirst and relaxed their formal demeanor.

For five years, a handful of young officers had met almost every Friday afternoon. Sometimes the group swelled to nearly twenty, and the ritual camaraderie served to promote their unity. All graduates of the United States Army Special Forces-run officer candidate course, these men came to gatherings that were not unlike those happy hours enjoyed by military forces throughout the world. They celebrated the end of the workweek, let off steam, enjoyed their beer and reinforced the fellowship of those serving a similar mission.

Tonight the reunion had a different feel. Only five men had shown up. They included Captain Matthew Sayon and four lieutenants – James Sio, Henry Wreh, John Beahn and Sabutu Jauly.

Unlike the previous meetings, the men were unusually quiet, each pensive and absorbed in his private thoughts. Few words had been exchanged. All five sipped at their beers and stared down at the table, across the field or off into the horizon.

"So, there's no chance for a stay of execution?" Sabutu asked.

"I heard that some family members appealed to Dowling this morning. He heard their pleas and promised to consider their requests. But this afternoon, he ordered the stockade commander to proceed with the executions," said Matthew, who was a member of the Executive Mansion Guard.

"Dowling has stayed executions before. Why not now?" John asked.

James Sio, who sat with his back turned to the others, hadn't spoken. But now, the other four listened to his slow and measured words.

"We all know they aren't guilty. My brother Tom would never have killed those Americans," he said. "Hell, when we talked about the People's Party, Tom said he was against military officers joining any political movement."

"But they say he confessed," John said.

"Sure, he confessed. Wouldn't you confess if that son of a bitch, Kia, threatened to rape and kill your family?" snapped James.

"Why didn't Tom's wife report that to the judge?"

"Would your wife do that after seeing what Kia could do? You all have heard the stories of his interrogation chamber. Kia could make a rock admit its guilt."

Perhaps the ten percent alcohol in the Liberian brew had clouded their better judgment. Some would say they were simply honest men who, through circumstance, became heroes. Once again, they sat in silence. Matthew shook his head, stood, and placed one boot on the wooden bench.

"It might still be possible to convince Dowling to commute the sentence to life in prison," Matthew said. "He leaves tomorrow morning for Nigeria. Tonight he is supposed to be staying in the Executive Mansion. I'm sure Don Keah, the commander of the guard, will allow us to enter the mansion. We'll ask to speak to Dowling. We'll try to convince him to commute the sentences."

Each man, in turn, expressed his agreement, coming to terms with the details and timing of the plan. First they would go home, change into their dress uniforms and meet at the main gate at eight o'clock that same evening.

Jauly's wife, Mary, watched her husband eat his dinner in silence, consumed in his private thoughts. When he finished, he pushed himself back from the table and disappeared into the bedroom. Minutes later, he came back, wearing his dress uniform.

"Where are you going?" she asked. "You're going to be too hot in that long coat."

"We have a meeting with President Dowling," he answered, ignoring her penetrating gaze.

"You're meeting with the President?" she asked, surprised at his destination.

"Yes," he said, now looking directly at her. "We're going to ask him to commute the death sentences of Tom Sio and the others."

"But, Sabutu, it's night now. He will not see you."

"Oh, I guarantee he'll see us," he answered, fastening his cuffs.

Sabutu kissed his wife and walked out the door. He did not look back. Mary felt concerned and uncertain. The past month had been filled with such danger. First, there were the brutal murders. Then, there were the arrests of Sabutu's fellow officers. So many had been their friends. No one believed they were guilty. During the investigations, everyone feared a knock at their own door.

When the charismatic Charles Morray first formed the People's Party, both she and Sabutu had joined. Morray had vowed to rid the nation of the corrupt government. Since the killings, people had stopped talking about politics. No one commented on the trials. She shuddered. Sabutu shouldn't be meeting with Dowling. He would put their lives in jeopardy.

What Mary Jauly didn't know what that Sabutu had tucked his nine-millimeter pistol in his belt and covered it with his jacket.

If she had known, her fear would have been even greater.

# 37

***In the President's suite, Dowling and his wife drank a toast to their years together.***

"More wine, madam?"

"No, thank you, Morris."

The steward moved to the other end of the dining table and topped off the crystal glass in front of Steven Dowling.

The couple had elected to spend the night in the President's suite. At half past five in the morning, they would be driven to the airport. They would never return.

"Steven, Theresa said she would be here at ten o'clock. Will you be finished by then?"

"That should be no problem, dear. It is only eight o'clock. I have just a few changes to make."

Dowling stood, walked around the table and kissed Elizabeth on the cheek. "If you need me," he said, "I'll be down in the office."

"Hurry back. I want you here when we surprise Theresa with the tickets to London."

Elizabeth hadn't been filled in on all that her husband had planned. What she did know, she liked. They would spend the week in Lagos, Nigeria, attending the Organization of African Unity Leaders conference. Steven would deliver the opening remarks. After the conference, they'd join the family in London for a three-week getaway.

What a surprise this would be for Theresa and her family. They'd hand her the first-class tickets on British Air. It would only be one more week. Then they'd all be together again.

When she thought about it, she realized what a satisfying evening it had been. The smooth wine left her relaxed. She undressed and changed into her pale green silk pajamas. She curled up in on the ivory chaise lounge and clicked the remote. A satellite dish brought in stations from Europe and America. In fifteen minutes, her favorite show would begin.

Life was good – so very good, she thought. This trip promised to be the best vacation in years. Even her husband seemed unusually excited and anxious to get away. He needed the break. For weeks – probably even before the terrible murders and intense trials – Steven had seemed more distant, more preoccupied. She had been worried.

Often it seemed like he had no appetite and had been sick to his stomach. He tossed and turned, unable to sleep. Sometimes he would wake up screaming, bathed in sweat. She had gently asked him to share his concerns, but he had shrugged her off, claiming it was only the pressure of his job. Perhaps he was ill. Clearly, he had lost weight.

But this week, she had noticed a change. The curfew had been lifted Wednesday. The nation seemed to be returning to normal. When they talked about their vacation plans, he again became the man she remembered. Just last night, he had reached out for her for the first time in months. It had been good. Time hadn't diminished the depth of their love.

"And so, my fellow leaders, the future of Africa will be shaped by the Africans, those whose roots grow here."

"Done," he murmured, moving the cursor to the print command. He pictured the applause and the glowing words of praise. No one would realize it would be his final speech, his last comments as the President of Liberia. No one, not even Elizabeth, knew they would never return. He would safely steal away to Europe on the pretense of a family vacation. Theresa and her family would join them in London. Their other children were already comfortably settled in Europe or in the United States.

Once out of the country, he would convert several thousand stock shares to British currency. They'd buy an estate in England and claim immunity from deportation. He mentally measured his wealth. The bathroom safe held millions in stock shares and a half a million in U.S. dollars. Then there were millions in Swiss bank accounts. If they lived cautiously, he figured they'd manage.

He complimented himself on his foresight. His plans had been finalized after Carpai and Sarday had ordered the murders of the Americans. What had happened later only served to reaffirm his genius. True, they had all underestimated Colonel Martin. Not only had he rescued his wife and son, but also he had done the impossible – he had destroyed the sacred valley of the *endosym*. Dowling had already begun to question the creature's power. If its powers were truly so immense, how could a mere mortal have done so much damage?

Even the national deception hadn't really worked. He saw doubt in the eyes of his people. No one dared speak, but he knew they didn't believe that the men held in the stockade had really been to blame for the killings. In his Wednesday radio address, he had announced that the People's Party had been eradicated. But he had lied.

Indeed, the opposite was true. The Kruman had seized that mine and its hydroelectric plant. After Joe Weah sided with Charles Morray, even more Kapel had pledged to work for the rebels. To add to the threat, Martin continued to be a player. He had heard rumors that white men were training the rebel militia. The tide had turned. It wouldn't be long until the government would crumble.

Yet he, Steven Dowling, and his family would be living in luxurious exile in England. He glanced at the antique clock on the wall. In ten hours, they would be on their way to freedom.

The dark blue carryall pulled up to the front gate of the executive mansion on Friday at eight-thirty p.m. The guard peered in the driver's side window. Recognizing Captain Sayon, he saluted.

"Good evening, sir. You're working late."

"Yes. We have a meeting with the President."

The guard leaned in the window and made a cursory check of the passengers. Four others, all officers in dress uniform, sat in silence. The guard snapped to attention, saluted and waved them on.

The carryall pulled through the gate, turned right and followed the road to the rear entrance. It pulled into a parking stall marked "Military Vehicles Only." The five men got out and walked to the rear door. Sayon pulled out a plastic security card from his wallet. He swiped the card through the slot next to the door handle and listened for the metallic click. He pulled the handle down and pushed. The door swung inward.

The five officers entered a long, fortified hallway. Overhead fluorescent lights cast an eerie glow on their faces. No one spoke. The only sound was the tap-tap of their polished dress shoes on the concrete floor. Their steady footsteps echoed off the thick walls.

The hallway led to a staircase. One flight up, they stopped at a landing in front of yet another secure door. Again, Sayon used his security card and the door clicked open. Inside, they entered a dimly lit office. Wide wooden desks stacked with piles of folders and loose papers ran in rows across the room. Sayon flipped the switch on the light panel. The men threaded their way through the office furniture to yet another door on the far wall. Before swiping his card, he turned to his fellow officers.

"Wait here. I'll be right back."

Sayon walked down the hallway to the office at the end. He knocked on the door. Moments later, a Liberian officer opened the door. Sayon recognized his friend Captain Don Keah.

It took ten years and a flawless record for a man to make captain. The two career soldiers had served together on many operations. Even their families had become close. At first, Keah was startled to see Sayon. Friday night visits to the mansion were rare. Keah searched his friend's face. He suspected that Captain Matthew Sayon had more serious motives than just a social visit.

"Captain Keah, we need to speak with the President. Do you think he would listen to a plea for leniency for our brother soldiers who have been sentenced to death?" asked Sayon.

He didn't wait for a response.

"Is the President here? Can we speak with him?" Sayon demanded.

Keah paused before answering. His duty was to provide security at the mansion, but here before him stood a fine man, one of his Liberian brothers. He, too, had been shocked and saddened by the imprisonment of his friends.

"The President and Mrs. Dowling are staying in the suite tonight," said Keah.

"Do you think he'll hear our request?" Sayon asked.

"I don't know. I will take you up to the suite, but you will be on your own. He might refuse to see you. If he does, you must leave. Follow me."

The officers followed him. The group passed through the doorway, down another hallway and into the rotunda. At eight-forty p.m., only a handful of people occupied the building. Some twenty guards, plus the custodial staff, were the only ones on duty. Two men pushed vacuum cleaners over the plush red carpet.

Walking purposefully, the men moved across the rotunda until they reached the wide staircase that led to the President's office and his private quarters. Reaching the foot of the stairs, they stopped abruptly at the sound of a commanding voice.

"Just where in the hell do you think you're going?"

"Oh, shit," whispered Keah. "It's Colonel Zaza."

Following the assassination of Hans Kruger, Colonel Augustine Zaza, formerly his deputy, had been promoted to chief of security. Dressed in a tailored gray suit, the frowning Zaza approached them.

Keah stepped forward.

"Good evening, sir."

"Keah, who are these officers, and what are they doing here?"

"Sir, you remember Captain Sayon. He is also a member of the mansion guard."

"Look, Keah, this place isn't a tourist attraction. The executive mansion is closed and off limits. I don't know what is going on, but whatever it is, you can do it somewhere else."

James spoke up.

"Sir, I am Lieutenant Sio. Major Tom Sio is my brother. I have come here to ask President Dowling to spare his life."

"Well, you just wasted your time," Zaza growled. There is no way that I will allow you to see the President. As for you brother, he and the rest of the Reconnaissance Battalion scum will hang on Monday. If you want my opinion, hanging is too good for them. If I had my way, I would truss them up by the legs, cut their bellies open, and let the flies drink their blood as they slowly die in the hot sun."

James raised his fist and swung at Zaza.

"You son of a bitch! Tom is innocent!"

His fist never reached its target. Zaza easily blocked the punch with his left arm. His right arm shot forward, his fist striking James with sufficient force to send him flying backwards. He sprawled helplessly on the floor. Zaza reached into his jacket and withdrew a nine-millimeter pistol. He pointed it directly at James.

"You're under arrest. Get up."

James stared up the barrel of the pistol. In a split second, shots rang out. James' vision was still blurred from the force of Zaza's punch. At the first crack of the shot, he had closed his eyes, bracing for the pain of the bullets that would pierce his flesh. Eyes still shut, he heard nothing and felt nothing.

Cautiously, he opened his eyes to see the faces of his friends huddled above him. To his right, he made out an out-of-focus lump on the floor beside him. When he blinked, his vision cleared. The lifeless body of Colonel Augustine Zaza lay only inches from him.

Sabutu Jauly, in his impeccable dress uniform, still held his pistol in his hand, pointing at the corpse. Keah reached down to take James' hand and pull him to his feet.

"What happened?" stammered James.

"Zaza decked you. Then Sabutu shot him," Keah answered.

"Jesus," James said, shaking his head in disbelief. "Is he dead?"

"Looks like it," Thomas said.

Several members of the Mansion Guard stood nearby. Every now and then, one would glance at the body. Strangely, they took no action. Like elsewhere in West Africa, soldiers were trained to take orders from their immediate commander. Captain Keah was their superior. He only stood there. He showed no reaction to Zaza's death.

"What now?" James asked.

"We find Dowling," said Sabutu. He turned and started up the stairway to the second floor. Little did he know that two special security service agents who were assigned to guard the President had heard the shots and had run from the second floor hallway to the top of the stairway.

The mansion had been designed as the showplace of the nation. Its ballroom could hold three hundred guests. The large rotunda featured a main entrance with double doors six feet wide and ten feet high. The west wing of the building housed the executive office. Nearly two hundred government employees worked there during the week. The second floor consisted of the President's office, his immediate staff and the House of Representatives. Temporary yet lavish living quarters were adjacent to the offices. An express elevator and the circular stairway provided access from the rotunda to the second floor. The stairway itself was twenty feet wide and totally suspended from above. Its sixty-five steps were covered in the same plush red carpet as the floor of the rotunda.

Sabutu Jauly bolted up the stairway. Near the top, the two secret service agents opened fire. Sabutu dropped to the carpet as bullets whizzed over his head. He returned fire at the unseen assailants. He knew he'd found his target when he heard a man scream after taking a shot to the chest. In the silence that followed, he got back on his feet and continued up the stairs.

Sabutu assumed there had been one man waiting above. He didn't know that the second agent had taken cover to the right of the stairs. When Sabutu neared the top steps, agent Walter Saigbe figured he could take out the intruder in one easy shot. Had he succeeded, the momentum of the overthrow of Liberia's government might have come to an abrupt end.

Saigbe fired six times. He missed all six times. Even with both hands firmly grasping his pistol, he saw his own arms shake so uncontrollably that he couldn't line up the sights of the pistol with the man who was charging up the stairs toward him. He squeezed the trigger again, only to discover he had spent his last bullet. He fumbled for a second clip. When he looked up, he saw the muzzle of Sabutu's nine-millimeter pistol only inches from his eyes. He knew he was about to die.

Sabutu reached out and took the pistol from Saibge's quivering hand.

"My juju is more powerful than yours," he said firmly. "Go now, and you will not be harmed."

Saigbe got to his feet, stepped over his dead partner, and walked toward the elevator that took him directly to the basement exit.

In the years that followed, the details of the night's events would be told and told again. Saibge's account of Sabutu Jauly, the hero of the revolution, grew in its glory and magnitude. This Great Man had been shot six times. Each bullet tore through the fine uniform and pierced Sabutu's beating heart, yet the courageous patriot never faltered. The spirits of Sabutu's ancestors had healed his wounds. Finally, Sabutu's infinite compassion allowed Saigbe to walk away a free man.

Sabutu stared at the top of the staircase and watched as the elevator's doors closed. Pistols ready, the others had joined him at the top of the stairs. The group had grown from the original six to fifteen men.

"Which way is Dowling's suite?" Sabutu asked.

"This way," said Keah, as he led the men down the corridor to a heavy, carved door. He tried the knob, but the door was securely locked.

"Do we break it down?" James asked.

"No," answered Keah. "We knock."

He hammered on the door with his fist.

"Who is it? Who's there?" a woman asked meekly.

"It's Captain Keah. We must speak to President Dowling immediately. Unlock the door."

"He's not here. Go away!" she pleaded.

"You must open the door now, madam!"

"Please, please ... just go away!" she cried.

"We must speak to Dowling now," Keah demanded. "Open the door, or we will break it down!"

"He's not here! Go away!" she insisted.

"Where is he?"

"In his office," she sobbed.

Sabutu glanced at Keah, and then sized up the door.

"Shall we break it down?"

"No. Let's try the office first," Keah said.

They reversed direction and headed down the wide hallway to the double doors that led to the visitor reception area. The doors were wide open, and the men walked into the large room. Behind the receptionist's desk, they saw another door. A brass plaque identified it as the office of the President. Sabutu tried its brass handle, but the door wouldn't budge.

"Use your pass card," Sabutu said.

"I can't," Keah answered. "This door has a higher clearance level."

"Then we break it down," Sabutu said, leveling his shoulder firmly against its unhinged edge.

"Won't work," Keah said. "It's blast proof. The doors and walls were designed to withstand a blast or bullets."

James, who had come in behind them, had another idea.

"Would the SSS man in the hall have a security card that would work?"

"It's possible. Someone check out that dead SSS man. You need to find a card that looks like this," Keah said, pulling out his plastic card.

Two men nearest Keah nodded, ran down the hallway. They returned minutes later. One man handed Keah the blood-smeared card. Keah wiped the plastic on his pant leg and inserted it into the slot near the handle. No one spoke, listening intently for the click as the electromagnet freed the bolt. Each man smiled at the sound of the click.

Sabutu went in first. He pushed open the door. Pistol ready, he walked into the room. The others followed. None had ever before been inside the President's office. None had ever before seen such opulence. The massive mahogany desk was centered on the deep carpet. On the wall behind the leather swivel chair hung two elephant tusks. Tusks of that size hadn't existed on the African continent for more than a hundred years. Photographs along the wall showed the smiling Dowling with international heads of state, including the President of the United States.

The mere men who had invaded this inner sanctum felt like awkward trespassers in another world.

"No one's here," James said, scanning the room.

But then he focused on a side door.

"Where does that door go?"

Not waiting for a response, he approached the door and tried the knob. It didn't give. It was only a simple wood door, very plain compared to the elaborate double door entry. There was no keyhole or card slot.

Sabutu stepped forward, pushing James aside. He aimed his pistol to the left of the knob and fired. His hand jerked back with the recoil as the bullet splintered the soft wood. He tried the knob again, but it still wouldn't move. He fired again. This time he grasped the knob and pulled. It swung outward. Sabutu stumbled back into James.

Inside, the room was dark. Sabutu ran his hand along the wall until his fingers found the light switch. He flipped it up and the lights came on, revealing a large, well-appointed executive restroom. Sabutu, James and two others stood in the center. To their right, they saw a large walk-in closet. Several dozen dark suits and formal dress shirts hung above a row of highly polished shoes.

"Sabutu," Keah said, "take a look at this."

Keah stood near the sink. He pointed at a large, black leather briefcase. He snapped open the latch.

"Jesus!" he said as he saw what was inside. Bundles of hundred-dollar bills in U.S. currency were packed tightly in the briefcase. Careful printing in a neat, black pen identified each bundle as twenty-five thousand dollars. A manila folder held a sheaf of papers. Keah thumbed through them.

"These are stock shares," he whistled. "Must be worth millions."

Behind him, he heard a commotion as the others searched the room.

"We found him!" one man shouted. "He was cowering in the shower."

Two soldiers grasped the trembling Steven Dowling by his elbows.

"Take him out into the office," Sabutu said. The two men pushed the disgruntled President into an upholstered chair near the window.

The others stood in a semi-circle surrounding him.

"What do you want? What are you doing here?" Dowling demanded.

He got no response. Each man simply stared at Sabutu, awaiting his move. Since his brave charge up the stairway, Sabutu had become the de facto leader of the band of men.

"Sir," stammered Sabutu, "we are here to ask you to commute the death sentences of our fellow officers to life in prison."

Dowling, for all his faults, was no fool. A politician all his life, he had perfected the art of intimidation and manipulation. When he had first heard shots, he had secured the office door. Heavily reinforced, he was sure no one could break through it. His best move was to sit tight until the situation resolved itself. For reassurance, he had gone into the bathroom, opened the safe behind the mirror and unlocked the briefcase. Loud voices in his office had interrupted his work. Initially, he assumed the sounds came from members of his staff who had the situation under control. He turned toward the bathroom door just in time to hear a bullet strike the door. Splinters of wood pelted the floor. He turned, running into the tiled shower and huddled in the far corner.

When the two soldiers pointed their pistols at his head, he felt certain that his life was over. But now, he knew he had been issued a reprieve. He could see the uncertainty in this man's eyes. Addressing the group with all the authority he could muster, he looked directly at Sabutu Jauly.

"You all have committed a most serious offense," he said, pausing for effect. "You realize you could all die for what you have done. Your families could be imprisoned for the rest of their lives."

Dowling knew his performance had worked. Each man stood silently, measuring the weight of his words. They seemed to have forgotten that they held guns in their hands.

Dowling seized their moment of indecision. He placed his palms on the armrests of the chair and lifted himself to a standing position. Each soldier took a step backward, in awe of this illustrious man. Yet Dowling showed his compassion, smiling broadly, his former threats now lost in his concern for his fellow Liberians.

"Of course, I realize you worry about your friends. As President, I care deeply for all my people. The lives of these men will be spared," he said, his eyes brimming with false concern. "But first, you must go back to the shelter of your homes. You have my promise that you will not be punished for what transpired tonight."

Sabutu spoke. "We must talk," he said to the others. He turned to a young private who held a pistol. "Watch him," he ordered.

The men moved toward the double doors, leaving Dowling standing near his desk. The private, a man named Harrison Dugbe, stood by his side, his pistol pointed directly at the President's head.

"What do you think?" Sabutu asked.

"There is no way he's going to let us just walk out of here," said Sayon.

James shook his head. "But we only wanted to talk with him. When Zaza attacked me, Sabutu shot him to protect me. It wasn't planned. It wasn't our fault."

"Sure, but what about the secret service agent that Sabutu killed? Do you really believe that he will let us just go home?" Don Keah asked. The young officers immersed themselves in their mutual despair. Dowling couldn't help but smile at their foolishness and congratulate himself on his cunning. He would be jubilant when each of the traitors dangled at the end of a rope. No one could be so stupid, so dense, and so unaware as to assume that he would allow them to walk away after breaking into his inner sanctum and daring to lay hands on him. He turned his wrist to check the time on his Rolex.

He'd had enough bullshit. He was ready to make his move.

The private continued to point his pistol unsteadily, glancing from time to time at his superiors who appeared deep in discussion.

"Give me that gun, you stupid idiot!" Dowling ordered.

He wasn't sure what to expect from the immobile guard, but he hadn't anticipated what he saw next. Something was wrong with the man. Dowling caught the wild look in the youth's dark eyes. For only a split second, Dowling felt a chill run through his limbs and dizziness in his head as he heard a click when the soldier pull back the hammer of his pistol.

"I say that we take the money and stock papers. We hold President Dowling as our hostage. We go to the airport and make them fly us to Sierra Leone," Wreh suggested.

"Doug, how will we get to...?"

Before Sabutu could finish his sentence, the blast of the bullet from the handgun echoed through the closed room. The men turned, pointing their own weapons in the direction of the shot.

Blood pooled beneath the body of the nation's highest official. Flat on his back, Dowling's right eye stared vacantly at the ornate ceiling. A neat, round hole filled the space where his left eye had been only seconds before.

"What have you done? Why did you shoot him?" screamed Jauly, while grabbing Dugbe by the loose fabric of his shirtfront.

"What in the hell did you think you were doing?"

Dugbe stammered, his eyes filled with tears. "I ... I wanted to see the bullet pass through him."

"Through him? What do you mean? How could the bullet pass through him?" demanded Sabutu Jauly, whose strong wrists held tightly to the young man's fatigues.

"People say that the President is a powerful *zo*. Bullets pass through him. He cannot be harmed," the private sobbed.

"Look! Look at him!" Sabutu demanded, releasing his hold and pointing at Dowling's body. "Does he look alive?"

"No, sir," the private admitted, sinking to his knees and leaning his back against the desk.

At a quarter past nine in the evening, Steven Dowling, President of Liberia, lay dead on the plush carpet of the executive office in the nation's capital. The men, all proud members of Kapel and Kruman tribes, stood passively, staring at the corpse.

Following the tradition of his ancestors, each man instinctively knew what had to be done. Henry Wreh pulled out his buck knife and handed it to Sabutu Jauly. A powerful chief, lost in battle, must be disemboweled to be truly dead. Sabutu knelt next to the body, carefully cutting through the belt, the shirt and the trousers. The sharp point pressed into the soft flesh above the pelvic bone and cut upward to the bottom of the ribcage. The abdominal cavity exposed, Sabutu's hand reached inside and extracted a fistful of intestine.

Sabutu rose to his feet, holding the bloody knife in his hand. His right forearm and shirtsleeve were slick with blood and flecked with the contents of the dead man's belly. Sabutu raised both arms above his head and screamed in the ancient tongue of his people.

"The chief is dead!"

One by one, the men joined in the chant, repeating Jauly's words. Their echoes began to mesh in a pulsating rhythm, rising in volume and intensity.

Then they went wild. Pistols fired into the brocade wall coverings, into the plaster ceiling, and into the textured fabric of the cushioned furniture. One man pulled on an elephant tusk, loosening it from its brackets. He heaved it through the tempered glass window. It fell onto the circular drive one floor below.

Just as quickly as their rampage had begun, it ground to a stop. The men surveyed the shambles of the corrupt Liberian regime.

Sabutu Jauly raised his arms again. His booming voice announced their next move.

"To the stockade," he bellowed. "Release our comrades!"

Down the stairs and through the rotunda, the small group grew to a crowd and then to an unruly mob. Cars were overturned and set aflame. No storefront along the wide Tubman Boulevard was left undamaged as looters joined in the growing riot.

# 38

***In the dark cell, day or night made little difference. Tom Sio knew that now time was irrelevant. He had been deep in a dreamless sleep. When he awoke, he had forgotten where he was. The concrete beneath his aching back brought him back to reality.***

Charles Degoto crawled to Tom's side and tapped him on the arm.

"What is it?" Tom asked.

"Something's going on."

Tom sat upright, massaging his lower back. The two helped each other stand. The others were already crowded against the barred window. They couldn't see much more than the stockade's interior wall.

"Listen!" another prisoner said.

No one moved. All they could hear was each other's breathing. Then they all heard the distant gunfire followed by a burst from an assault rifle on full automatic. Judging the distance was another matter. The shots were close, perhaps coming from inside the training center itself.

The men huddled together and speculated on what could be happening. Tom drew back and moved to the cell door. Before, they had always been able to see the armed guard at the table in the hall. Tonight, no one was there.

"Hey! What's going on?" Tom shouted. He tried again, but still no one answered. He turned to the others. "The guards are gone."

Twenty minutes later, the shooting had diminished to sporadic bursts. A deafening crash rattled the cell walls, startling the men. Then they heard renewed shooting that seemed to be coming from the end of the hallway.

"Tom! Tom! Where are you?" someone shouted. Tom froze in disbelief then hung on the cell door.

"Jimmy? Jimmy! Over here!" he screamed. He heard people running down the hallway. Leading the handful of men was Lieutenant James Sio, Tom's brother. When he got to the cell door, Jimmy forced the heavy metal key into the lock. The bolt released, and the door opened.

"Jimmy!" Tom said as he pressed his brother close to him. "What happened?"

"You're all free!" he shouted, wrapping his arms around Tom's thin form. They stumbled out into the hallway, walked past the bodies of the two guards and emerged into the floodlighted courtyard. A five-ton cargo truck sat steaming near the gate, dripping liquids from its bashed-in radiator. The stockade gate had been no match for its bulk. Near it, a guard cradled his right arm as his blood seeped through his fingers. Another guard lay motionless, his legs crumpled under the tread of the oversized tires.

None of them stopped to look. The free men and their saviors marched right by the truck and passed through the broken gate. Hundreds of soldiers milled about on the parade field. Some saw the gaunt men.

"They're free! The men are free!" shouted someone.

Tom and his brother, arms locked together, faced the crowd. Cheers broke out, and men jubilantly waved their arms as they celebrated the bold release. Perhaps he was still dreaming. How could it be that Tom could stand here on the lighted parade field? Where were the bars, the guards, and the concrete walls? He felt his legs give way beneath him. Only his brother's strength kept him upright.

It was no dream.

A small group of men wove their way through the crowd and emerged before the gate. They pushed Major Morris Kai to the front. Clad only in boxer shorts, Kai's spindly body evoked peals of derisive hoots from the crowd. Yet, even in his nakedness, Kai's presence brought fear back to Tom's consciousness.

"You stupid fools," Kai snarled. "I will enjoy torturing each of you until you beg for the mercy of death."

When he saw Tom before him, he became even more irate.

"As for you, Sio, I let your woman go the last time we met. Never again. Tomorrow, I'll bring her to your cell. I'll skin her alive while you watch!"

Tom didn't flinch. He gathered up the fabric of his loose trousers in his left hand. He reached out with his right hand to the soldiers nearby.

"Give me a gun," he said deliberately.

A nine-millimeter pistol was thrust into his palm. Kai saw the movement, but only laughed.

"Sio, a worthless bastard like you doesn't have the guts to use a gun!"

Tom lifted the weapon and aimed its barrel directly at Kai's face. He pulled the trigger three times. Kai crumpled to the ground. Tom emptied the remaining rounds into Kai's back. Tom felt a nudge on his arm. Degoto stepped forward, holding an M-16. Degoto fired all twenty rounds, transforming what had once been Kai's body into a mass of bloody tissue. One by one, each of the former prisoners followed suit, emptying their weapons into the tattered remnants of flesh and bone.

"What do we do now?" Jimmy asked.

"Now?" Tom asked. "What do you mean?"

"We didn't plan for this to happen. All we wanted to do was to ask the President to convert your sentences to life in prison. Somehow, it all got out of hand. Tom, you're the senior man here. You have to lead us."

It took Tom a moment to grasp what his brother was saying. He lifted his head, his eyes sharp and his thinking clear.

"We need to place men at all the gates and on top of the walls. I want the officers and NCOs to come to the administration conference room."

Tom turned and walked unassisted across the parade field. He felt the cool, wet grass under his bare feet. He never knew anything could feel so good.

Halfway across the field, they heard the first shot then another. Tom didn't turn to look, nor did he flinch. His fellow prisoners were dealing out justice to the guards who had abused and humiliated them.

Jimmy and Sabutu fell in step alongside Tom.

"Jim, find me a belt to hold my pants up. I'll need a shirt and some boots, too."

Near the edge of the field, Tom caught sight of the gallows.

"Sabutu, I want those gallows burned."

"Yes, sir," Sabutu answered.

For the first time in a long while, Tom smiled.

# 39

*In the briefing room at the American Embassy, Vicki looked around the table at the haggard faces of her staff. Most of the men hadn't showered or shaved in days. A dozen M-16 rifles leaned up against the wall near the door. She had picked up her notes and was just about to start the meeting when the lights flickered and went out. No one spoke. In a matter seconds, they blinked again and stayed on.*

"MUST'VE JUST SWITCHED TO GENERATORS," SOMEONE SAID.

"Might as well start at the top," Vicki said. "Gordon, fill us in on the status of our supplies."

"We have enough diesel fuel to run the generators for fifteen days. We could extend that to thirty days by shutting off non-essential equipment and providing power only to the operations center. Water tanks are seventy-five percent full. With all the third-country nationals and Americans on the grounds, it will be gone in twelve days unless we can figure out how to get more. Water should be used only for drinking.

"If we issue MREs to each person on the compound, we have about ten days' supply of food. We managed to pick up some rice and vegetables this morning. We had to get it on the black market. They want cash only – just U.S. dollars. Liberian dollars aren't worth the paper they're printed on.

"The arsenal consists of thirty M-16 rifles, six M-60 machine guns, twelve nine-millimeter pistols, several cases of grenades

– both fragmentation and smoke – and about fifty thousand rounds of ammunition."

Gordon Kennedy stopped and looked at each person.

"Any questions?"

"How many embassy vehicles do we have?" Doug Baxter asked.

"Five sedans, eight carryalls and four armor-plated Ford Excursions. We also have three flatbed trucks and a dozen personally-owned vehicles."

"Do we have any communication with the established government of Liberia?" Vicki asked, looking at Dan Hamilton.

"Not one word. As near as we can tell, there is no government. Of course, after we lost power two days ago, the phones don't work. Attempts to reach any government officials by satellite phone have been fruitless."

"Where is everybody? Are they all dead?"

"It's possible. From the information we've received from the Liberians on our embassy staff, Steven Dowling is definitely dead. Other government officials are either dead, or they have gotten the hell out of town."

"Jerry, give me your take on what you think is going to happen," Vicki asked.

"Things are sketchy. As near as we can tell, Dowling's assassination wasn't planned. After the President was murdered, the men who killed him freed those prisoners who were supposed to hang on Monday. It seems a group, consisting primarily of former members of Joe Weah's battalion, has consolidated forces in and around the Barclay Training Center. Why the army didn't go in at the time, I have no idea. Whatever the case, Major Sio appears to be in command. Sio was Weah's executive officer. Rumor has it that he and Weah have already been in contact. Sio has indicated that his troops are willing to throw in with Charles Morray.

"Perhaps the man with the greatest claim to power in the government is Julius Carpai. He has massed close to six thousand soldiers at the Roberts International Airport. They are not letting anyone into or out of the country. He has not answered any requests for help for the besieged embassies. It seems that he has basically written off Monrovia.

"Our greatest danger, however, comes not from Morray or Carpai, but from the rogue gangs that are fighting for a piece of the city. They're made up of street gangs from the ghettoes, soldiers who have walked away from their units, and the tribal groups. Somehow these gangs have picked up a supply of weapons from the government arsenal on Monkey Island. They live by the law of the gun and will kill without hesitation. Right now, outside these walls, this place is in absolute anarchy."

Vicki pursed her lips and tapped her pen against her left hand.

She wondered if it could possibly get even worse. She covered up her anguish by sticking to business.

"Jim, what's your assessment?"

"I think that Carpai is building up sufficient forces to take on Morray's militia. He could care less about Monrovia. It could burn to the ground for all he cares. Right now, Sio and his men are boxed in at the Barclay Training Center. The gangs are out there keeping themselves occupied by fighting against each other. Carpai's more concerned about Morray. He knows he has to get him. After he accomplishes that, he will worry about Monrovia. Frankly, I don't think we have any other choice but to get the hell out of here."

# 40

***On the way to the militia training camp, the old mining company truck creaked and groaned as it wound its way up the narrow road. Overgrown branches slapped against the windshield and scraped against the sides.***

THE THREE WOMEN RODE IN THE CAB. LINDSEY DROVE; JULIE AND JUDIE HAD come along. Lindsey's hands gripped tightly to the steering wheel as she moved it right to left and left to right, negotiating the deep ruts. She wondered how long the vehicle's frame and springs could hold up to such torture.

The truck's bed held more than twelve hundred bags of rice. Two other trucks moved along with them in a convoy. The women had volunteered to make the delivery. It would give them a chance to see their men.

Lindsey jerked the wheel to the left to avoid a deep hole. When she swerved, a thick branch whipped against the driver's side mirror. When she reached the top of a hill, two men carrying M-16s stood in their way. After they squeaked to a halt, another six armed men emerged from the thick brush. She turned around to look out the back window. She had felt the truck bounce as one of the men jumped onto the load.

She slipped the transmission into neutral, opened her door and stepped onto the ground. A young man, likely not much more than twenty years old, came around the side. By his distinct features, Lindsey guessed that he was Kruman. Shirtless, Moses Yarboy's chest was marked with the ritualistic scars that proclaimed him a warrior. Barefoot, his only garment was a pair of torn jeans. Were it not for the casual way he carried his M-16, a pistol belt and two ammo pouches, he didn't seem much different than any young Liberian who might have been working the fields or out hunting for food.

His wide grin eased her initial concern. Lindsey had become quite well known as the wife of Colonel Martin and the mother of Tim. Yet her fame didn't end there. The story of the tall, white woman had spread from Zigda to the Kapel villages and across the border. The people of Sanniquellie knew how she had saved Joe Weah's life. They had learned how the great chief, Togba Weah, treated her with high regard, not simply as a woman. After all, this woman didn't act superior to the Liberians. She had tirelessly nursed the sick and injured.

Lindsey was regarded even more highly than the Myers who were loved by the people of Sanniquellie. Lindsey had the protection of the great leopard spirit. The most powerful *zo* in Zigda had bestowed this woman with the power of the leopard. Even in battle with the dark spirits of the bush, she would be endowed with all the magic of the great Chea Geebe.

Lindsey reached out to shake the young man's hand. He spoke softly to her as befitting her reputation. He opened the truck's door and helped her climb back in. She placed her hand gently on his arm, settled in her seat, shifted into gear and pulled away.

Behind her, Moses caressed the spot on his arm where this white woman had laid her hand. He was certain that her touch would protect him once the battle began.

"Did you get some good shots?"

"Sure, no problem."

"OK, then let's get out of here."

The two men moved back over the crest of the hill. They continued to wind their way through the brush. It was easier going than it might have been because the entire area had been clear-cut fifteen years earlier and the underbrush burned. The new growth provided cover from the road below and it allowed easy movement. After about an hour, the lead man signaled them to a halt. They knelt in the shade of a palm tree.

"Let's take a look at what we've got on that video camera," said Singleton.

Anderson flipped open the viewing screen and pressed, "play." They watched images of a white woman passing easily through the roadblock. When they zoomed in, they could see the faces of both the woman and the young guard. Even on the tiny screen, it was clear that this was Lindsey Martin.

"The people act as if she is some kind of white goddess," Anderson said.

"I don't know about that, but I'll tell you what she isn't. She sure isn't little Miss Missionary."

When Singleton had spotted the Martins with Charles Morray five days earlier, he knew that he had stumbled onto one big story. He and Anderson had flown in with the Red Cross medical team to Sanniquellie. In the last four days, they had gotten great shots of the team assisting with the injured. The Liberian government had done one hell of a job on their own people. As tragic as it was, Singleton had been in enough third-world countries to know that similar atrocities happened almost daily in many parts of the world.

In Sanniquellie, they had met the Myers, the missionary couple who ran a medical clinic just outside of town. He had also been introduced to a Lindsey Smyth, just another of those committed missionaries from the United States. Dr. Myers said that she was a housewife from Virginia, sent by her church on a three-month tour. The good doctor had requested that none of the missionaries be photographed. He explained that if the government knew they had been helping the wounded, they would be forced out of the country.

They had honored Myers' request. Singleton had to give her credit. Although he knew that that woman wasn't what she said she was, she sure played the part well. She was right there in the thick of it, working like a combat nurse. He watched her every day, working with the sick and wounded. He stood behind her as she held the hand of a dying child, talking softly to the girl until the child's eyes glazed over. Then this "housewife from Virginia" gently closed the girl's eyelids. Her compassion gained the respect of everyone she met. Singleton had picked up bits and pieces of stories of this woman's incredible feats. Even if they were only partly true, this was a most unique individual.

The irony was that although she and the Myers stayed closed-mouthed about her identity, the Liberians readily told everything they knew. Singleton had heard many stories about the woman's son and about Joe Weah.

But finding out the whereabouts of Lieutenant Colonel Martin and their son was more difficult. The two of them – and almost every other able-bodied man – had disappeared. Singleton was determined to find out what was going on.

Yet as the days passed, Singleton, a man who never let his heart interfere with a story, was somewhat reluctant to follow up on anything that might harm this woman. Although he wouldn't admit it, he felt drawn to Lindsey Martin. He found himself staring at her as he watched her work. Usually, his experiences with women were mostly shallow. His romances never lasted. But several times he found himself daydreaming about a relationship with this remarkable woman.

He got to the point where he was almost ready to forget the whole thing. They could just finish up the story on the medical team and get out of the country. But the story wouldn't quit. Civil war had broken out in Monrovia. The President had been assassinated. Some claimed that Charles Morray was planning to march on the city. Others said forces loyal to Joe Weah already held part of the capital and were expected to join Morray's militia.

In the two days following Dowling's alleged assassination, hundreds of young men had made their way through Sanniquellie to get to Morray's training camp. Just the day before, they had seen government soldiers, weapons in hand, move through the town. They had joined the exodus from the capital and were going to throw in their lot with Morray. It didn't take a journalistic genius to suspect that a huge story was about to break. Whatever happened, Richard Singleton would have his byline.

Earlier in the day, Singleton and Anderson had slipped away from the clinic and fell in line with the men marching to join up with Morray. The Liberians seemed indifferent to the presence of the two men from CNN.

But Singleton remained cautious. Getting inside the camp wouldn't be easy. They hung to the back of the line of the thirty or so young men until they approached a roadblock. The two cut off from the group and went into the forest. They made their way through the secondary growth and climbed a low hill. From there, they could monitor the roadblock. That's where they spotted the heavily laden truck and its white female driver.

Singleton nodded to his companion.

"Let's move in closer and try to get some shots of the training camp itself. It can't be much farther up the road."

Two miles down the road, the women reached a wooden gate flanked by sandbagged bunkers. M-60 machine guns pointed outward. At least twenty armed guards stood watch. A radio alert from the men at the first checkpoint authorized the guards to push the gate wide open. The three trucks rolled into Morray's camp without stopping.

Although they had some knowledge of the camp's activity, all three women were astonished at what they saw.

Back in 1987, a private logging company had cut a deal with the Liberian government to harvest the hardwood in the several-thousand-acre forests south of Sanniquellie. Nearly twenty thousand acres of trees had been clear-cut. Not long after, the company had gone bankrupt. Buildings and equipment had been abandoned. A feeble attempt had been made to convert the land to farming, but the poor soil couldn't support agriculture without the addition of tons of fertilizer. Moreover, it was too far from the labor force. Twelve miles from Sanniquellie, it took workers too long to get there.

Yet now the cleared land had found a purpose. So large that it could be seen from outer space, the area now served as the training site for the army of the People's Party. It bustled with activity. Groups of anywhere from thirty to one hundred men were practicing for war. Small arms fire from the several ranges echoed across the barren hills.

Lindsey spotted what appeared to be the principal building. She threaded her way through the crowds and pulled up to its wide veranda.

"You've got to be the best looking truck driver I've seen today," someone said.

"Oh really? And just how many good looking truck drivers did you see yesterday?" she asked, turning around to see her husband behind her.

"All right," Hank said. "You're the best looking truck driver, period."

He reached out his arms and held his wife close.

"That's better," she grinned, resting her head against his shoulder. "Oh, by the way, I brought some good-looking assistants."

Julia and Judie came around the other side of the truck.

"OK, is anyone going to tell me what's going on here?" Hank asked.

"We decided that you needed a break from all this training, so we volunteered to deliver the rice and brought along a lunch. That is, of course, if you can spare some time from training and spend it with us."

"I guess we can take a few minutes from our busy schedules to eat lunch," Hank admitted with a laugh.

Charles Moray, Tim and Sabo joined them. Hank led them to a palm grove a hundred yards from the lumber company offices. Sabo and Judie moved off to a secluded spot a short distance away.

Lunch included fried chicken, hard-boiled eggs and fruit. After they ate, they stretched out and kept their conversation simple. These precious moments wouldn't be wasted talking about the threat of war that would soon consume the small West African nation.

"Getting all this?" Singleton asked.

"Sure, boss. The zoom on this video camera brings them up so close. It's like I'm right there with them eating lunch. I can almost taste that fried chicken," Anderson said.

They had found an excellent vantage point to watch the activity in the camp. They lay low, stretching flat on their stomachs. Thousands of men were in training. This militia could be a force to be reckoned with.

Anderson kept the video rolling while Singleton scanned the area with a 10x20-millimeter pair of binoculars. He had settled on three white men who seemed to be directing groups of Liberians. But none of that was as interesting as the cozy little picnic that featured the Martins and the Morrays.

"Martin and Morray are as thick as thieves. How do you suppose that relationship came about?" Anderson said.

"I have no idea," Singleton answered, "but it would be great to find out."

Singleton focused on Lindsey Martin. He liked her smile. He watched the interaction between husband and wife. They seemed so at ease together. Obviously, the two had something special, something that he had never known in his inconsequential liaisons.

Martin was clean-shaven and his hair closely cropped. The Martin kid also sported a butch haircut. He shifted to Morray and then to the black kid sitting next to the pretty girl. They and the other trainers had unusually short hair. If this was any clue, the bunch looked like they were on their way to becoming real soldiers. He set the binos aside for a moment. Martin just might be able to make a difference in this rag-tag group of simple natives fresh out of the bush.

"Ouch! What the hell are you doing, Brian?" Singleton complained. He had felt a sharp jab in the small of his back. He rolled over.

"Oh, shit!" he whispered. Two militiamen towered over them, their M-16s inches from their faces. His bowels churned. His breaths came in short gasps. One man gestured for them to stand. He heard the brush move behind them.

Another Liberian, most likely an officer, glared at the two.

"And so, we have some spies here," said Jeffery Gbam, Morray's deputy.

"No, sir, we aren't spies," Singleton managed to say. "I'm Richard Singleton from CNN. This is my cameraman, Brian Anderson. We're here to do a story on the People's Party."

He pointed to his press card that hung from a clip on his shirt pocket.

"You're spies! You came into our camp without permission!" yelled Gbam.

He yanked the press card from Singleton's pocket. It fell to the ground near Gbam's boot. In one quick side step, he crushed it into the ground.

"Do you know who this man is?" Anderson asked.

Gbam nodded at the soldier who stood next to Anderson. He snapped his fingers. The soldier reversed his rifle and jammed the butt end into Anderson's mid-section. Anderson hunched forward, grabbing his stomach, and gasping for air as he crumpled to the ground.

"You fucking son of a bitch!" Singleton snarled as he swung his fist at Gbam.

But it never connected. A second soldier was quicker. His rifle butt struck a glancing blow to Singleton's temple. Singleton collapsed on to his back.

Gbam placed his left boot on Singleton's neck and pointed his pistol right between Singleton's eyes.

"All spies die. Today you die!" he grinned.

Singleton had been in many dangerous situations in his career, but none frightened him as much as this one. He stared into the dark, narrow tunnel at the point of the pistol. Never in his life had he been this close to the barrel of a weapon. Never had one been pointed directly at him.

Gbam's finger twitched slightly, tightening on the trigger. Singleton heard his own heartbeat pound in his head. He thought he might faint. He closed his eyes. He had only seconds to live.

Lunch over; it was now time for both Hank and Lindsey to get back to business.

"It's going to happen soon, isn't it?" she asked as they walked back to the truck.

"We will attack in less than seventy-two hours," Hank said.

"My God, Hank, I thought you were just going to train the militia then we'd be leaving."

"This situation has changed. It's complete anarchy in Monrovia. Tom Sio has only about five hundred soldiers holding the Barclay Training

Center. Gangs of rogue soldiers and street orphans have divided up the rest of the city. No one is safe there."

They walked several more yards in silence.

"I talked to Jim Parkinson on the radio this morning," Hank said.

"Jim?" asked Lindsey. "Is everyone safe at the embassy?"

"So far, they are. Apparently they have been paying one of the street gangs for protection. Jim said if we want to go to lunch, we should meet soon."

"Lunch?" asked Lindsey, puzzled by the reference.

"It's a code we use," Hank said with a grin. "Jim is telling us that the situation is so bad that they're on the verge of closing the embassy. If we want out, we better get back to the embassy soon."

"Are you going to attack Monrovia?"

"No, we plan to attack Camp Schiefflin. Julius Carpai has declared himself President. He has about five thousand soldiers. Apparently, he made a deal with both Sierra Leone and Guinea. Both countries agreed to send troops. We believe that if we don't move quickly, Carpai will launch an attack on us. Joe Weah is bringing five thousand weapons and twenty-five tons of ammunition across the border tonight. We have already begun to move our forces toward Monrovia."

Hank stopped talking and turned toward the hill behind him.

"That's funny," he said.

"What's funny?" Lindsey asked.

"That's the third shot I've heard from that hill above those palm trees."

"Maybe they're just training," suggested Lindsey.

"No, we allow no shooting except on the ranges. I need to find out who fired that weapon."

"I guess that means it's time for us to go back to the clinic," said Lindsey.

"Lindsey?"

"Yes, Hank?"

"When we move toward Monrovia, you'll go with us."

"Oh, Hank, I can't believe this is happening."

"I know what you mean. Every time we were called on alert back at Fort Lewis, no one knew if it was a drill or the real thing until we were in the air. When we opened the ammunition boxes, if they were blanks, it was a drill. If they were full of live ammunition, we were going to war."

Hank turned Lindsey's shoulders so that she faced him. He kissed her softly on the lips. Both knew there was no need for further talk.

Lindsey settled herself into the driver's seat and took one last look back at Hank. He waved, then turned and walked toward the hill.

# 41

***In front of the embassy offices, Jim Parkinson stayed partially hidden behind the wide fronds of a date palm. He watched the conversation unfold outside the embassy gates. Gordon Kennedy's broad gestures helped him to communicate with the three young Liberians near the front gate.***

THE MEN HAD COME IN TWO PICKUP TRUCKS. BOTH VEHICLES IDLED NEXT TO the fence. M-60 machine guns had been fastened to gun mounts in each truck bed. The gun crew consisted of six armed men who perched on the rails of the trucks.

The three at the gate appeared to be the negotiators. Two of the men wore the uniform of the Liberian army, which indicated that they were junior enlisted men. The third wore a green sports coat, white shirt and tan pants – likely the spoils from a looted clothing store in the business district. He looked to be about seventeen or eighteen years old. Parkinson had him pegged as the leader.

He called himself Amos. Just weeks earlier, his only claim to fame was that he headed up a small group of orphans. Now his influence had spread. His powerful, armed gang controlled a large part of the city, including most of the embassies.

It pissed Jim off, knowing that this rag-tag bunch could hold the American Embassy hostage, but he could do no more than watch as Gordon handed Amos a packet. This was the almost-daily payoff, a bribe to buy assurance that the embassy would have the gang's protection.

It wouldn't work for much longer. The cash was almost gone. This bunch would soon tire of the protection racket and storm the compound. Three embassies had already fallen. Their fleeing staffs had sought refuge with the Americans.

Once the transaction was complete, Jim walked back toward the building. Vicki waited at the door.

"Can you believe that the embassy of the greatest nation in the world is being held hostage by a group of young thugs fresh out of the jungles?" she asked.

"It's hard to believe that the whole city has collapsed in less than a week," answered Jim.

"Are you sure about tonight?"

"Before you request that we totally evacuate the embassy and bring down the flag, we have to give the State Department a true assessment of what it is like on the streets."

"If it's so dangerous on the streets, how will you be able to check out the city safely?" Vicki asked.

"Three of us will use one of the armored Excursions. We'll be armed and blend in with the mobs."

"How in the world can you blend in with those horrible people?"

Jim laughed. He had a plan.

"My three-man team consists of myself, Lance Corporal Russell Ward and Private First Class Mark Tate."

"You're all black!"

"That's right. In this situation, equal opportunity means that you're just one of the crowd. We'll be wearing tattered blue jeans. Over our Kevlar vests, we'll have on old tie-dyed t-shirts. Since everyone else in town seems to be carrying a gun, our M-16s will be right in style."

"But, Jim, won't the embassy Excursion stand out like a sore thumb?"

"Oh, I don't think so," Jim smiled. "Why don't you come on down to the motor pool and see what Mark and Russ have done with your new Excursion?"

"Sure, let's go," Vicki said.

When they got to the motor pool, they found the two Marine guards who had been recruited to take on the assignment. Both men saluted when Jim and Vicki walked into the building.

"Men, Ambassador Johnson said she'd like to see what you've done to the Excursion."

Corporal Ward hesitated.

"Sir, beg your pardon, but are you sure you want her to see it?"

"Sure," said Jim.

"All right. We have it parked in bay one."

Russ lifted the bay door. There sat the embassy's ninety thousand dollar custom black Ford Excursion.

The latest model, it had only about fifteen hundred miles on its odometer. Customized for government use, it had it all – armor plated sides, bulletproof glass, protected radiator and custom tires with steel mesh webbing. The tires were so specialized that they allowed the vehicle to be driven at speeds in excess of eighty miles per hour, even if they had no air in them. Its unique carbon-filtered air system allowed the all-wheel drive vehicle to operate in an environment filled with smoke or poison gas.

"Oh, my God!" Vicki said. "What have you done?"

It had once been a sleek and classy vehicle. Now the hood and doors were scratched and dented. The front bumper hung at a lopsided angle. The thick plastic covers of the parking lights had been crushed. The finish was splotched with white, yellow and red paint that had been mixed with dirt and even chicken feathers.

"Will it run?" Vicki asked.

"Perfectly," Jim answered. "We kept the headlights in excellent condition, but there are no tail or brake lights. The smoked windows keep anyone from seeing inside. To your average guy, this just looks like another one of the wrecks driven by the gang members.

"Our plan is to recon the city at three o'clock in the morning. Most people will be asleep. We'll go out for no more than two hours. In that time, we should be able to make a pretty good assessment of the actual conditions here in Monrovia."

"All right," Vicki said. "Go ahead and recon, but don't do anything dangerous. Be ready to get back here in a hurry."

It was half past two in the early morning when Jim opened the door to the motor pool. The power was out again, and the generators had been shut off to conserve fuel. They might as well be in some remote mountain village as in the country's major city, thought Jim.

The Excursion had been driven forward. He could make out the shape of its dark hulk. He saw two figures standing near the car's hood. At first, Jim assumed it was Russ and Mark. When he got closer, he was surprised to see Jerry Day and Vicki leaning against a dented fender.

"Good morning! You're up early! What a nice day for a tour of Monrovia," Jim said with a grin.

Russ Ward and Mark Tate, the two Marine guards, were dressed like Jim. All three wore torn and faded blue jeans and tie-dyed shirts. The two were young. Russ was just twenty-two, and Mark was only nineteen. Despite their age, Jim had complete confidence in their ability to handle the situation. The Marine Corps selected only its best to serve as embassy guards. These were two of the finest.

"Gentlemen, we're on the verge of requesting an emergency evacuation of the embassy. Since the collapse of the Liberian government, we have been virtual prisoners on the compound. You'll be providing us with an eyewitness evaluation of conditions here in the city. Please be very careful. Since it's so early in the morning, activity is rather limited. You have your best chance of getting a good assessment," Vicki said.

She shook hands with the young men and stood before Jim. She grasped his outstretched hand and looked him in the eye.

"You be careful, Jim."

"Don't worry, Vicki. We don't plan to stop or get out of the vehicle."

Jim turned to his men.

"Russ, you drive. I'll ride shotgun. Mark, you take the back seat."

The three men climbed into the battered vehicle. The big V-8 rumbled to life as soon as Russ turned the key in the ignition. When the gears engaged, the doors locked automatically. It pulled forward to the embassy's reinforced outer gate. Three armed Marines checked the area immediately outside the gate. When they signaled that it was all right to proceed, the Ford Excursion rolled down the street and toward the city. The gates closed and locked tightly behind them.

Russ didn't turn on the vehicle's headlights until they were a good half-mile from the embassy. Then he switched on the halogen lights that lit up the road ahead.

"Where to, sir?"

"Let's take a pass through the downtown area. Most of the gangs aren't too well organized, but try to avoid any roadblocks and any place where we might be trapped."

Monrovia, with its blend of colonial and modern architecture, had once been considered one of Africa's most beautiful cities. The city center's wide boulevards were punctuated with islands of palms and tropical flowers. Even the side streets were landscaped. The city had no arrogant skyscrapers. Only two and three-story buildings stretched lazily along the avenues. Some people said that the city's beauty was reminiscent of pre-Castro Cuba.

Days of rioting and looting had taken their toll. They could hear broken glass crunch under the vehicle's tires. Through the darkness, they could see smoldering coals. The hot spots were lingering reminders of the fires that had flared out of control. Burned and abandoned cars littered the streets. Rotting and bloated corpses lay along the sidewalks. Body parts could be seen partially poking out from gutters. Without the special ventilation system in the Excursion, the men would have been overwhelmed by the stench of death.

Every so often, they saw the gleam from the eyes of an animal – rat or mongrel dog – in the glare of the headlights. Many didn't bother to run. Emboldened by their easy harvest, they didn't flinch, but briefly looked up before continuing their meal. Invisible in daylight, the predators ruled the night. Bones, stripped of flesh, were piled haphazardly, like little shrines to the horrors of hell.

"Let's drive out by Mamba Bluff and see how that part of town fared," said Russ, who averted his eyes when he caught a glimpse of a dead child.

He turned sharply onto a side street.

"Whoops!" he said. "Not a good move."

A makeshift roadblock loomed before them. Two men jumped out and opened fire. Russ switched off the headlights and made a tight U-turn. They heard bullets ricochet off the armor plating.

"Don't seem real friendly," Mark said.

The move worked. Russ accelerated down Tubman Boulevard. There were more abandoned vehicles, but fewer bodies. Turning into Mamba Bluff, they noted a burned-out Mercedes that partially blocked the roadway. The driver's charred remains slumped over the steering wheel.

Even the prestigious homes of Mamba Bluff hadn't been spared. Many were burned to the ground. Others stood like skeletons, their doors and windows wide open and their broad lawns strewn with what remained of their contents.

"Wait! Pull over here," Jim said.

Russ pulled up on the sidewalk.

"Cover me," Jim said, stepping out onto the lawn. Flashlight in hand, he ran up to the porch. The front door hung partially open. He ripped it from its hinges. He took out his pistol. With the gun in his right hand and the flashlight in his left, he cautiously stepped inside.

The stench of feces made him want to retch. The beam of the flashlight reflected on the interior. Holes had been smashed in the walls, pictures slashed, and furniture overturned and torn. Anything that hadn't been stolen had been destroyed.

He nearly tripped on a small, hard object as he turned to leave. He pointed the flashlight at the tip of his boot. A porcelain figurine, a little Spanish Lladro duck, had survived. He reached down, scooped it up and slid it into his pocket.

Back at the car, he snapped open the glove box and put the brightly painted duck inside.

"What's that?" Mark asked.

"That? Just all that's left of our life in Liberia," Jim said.

Jim took a quick look at his watch.

"I've seen enough. Let's head back to the embassy."

The Excursion began its return trip; no one seemed to know what to say. A few minutes later, they turned a corner and the headlights fell on a group of people huddled around a smoldering fire in front of what was left of one of the larger homes. The lights lit up the scene for only a moment.

"Sir, there was a white woman in that group we just passed."

"What did you say?" Jim asked.

"Sir, I'm almost certain that I saw a white woman back there sitting next to the fire."

"Let's check it out. Mark, you come with me. Russ, stay here. Keep the engine running. We might have to get out of here in a hurry."

They pulled off the street about a block away from the group. The two worked their way through a neighboring yard until they reached a point where they could get a better look. There were six men, all armed with rifles. At least three wore Liberian army uniforms. Jim saw a light-skinned person on one side. Another smaller figure sat cross-legged on the ground. One of the men threw dried palm boughs on the fire.

The light of the flames made it easy to see the faces of a white woman and a child. When the woman turned her head, Jim recognized Jessica Richardson. Her daughter, Elizabeth, had been in his son's class at school. Her husband Darrel had worked as an accountant at the Ford dealership. He had been the son of a missionary couple and had lived his entire life in Liberia.

"We've got to rescue them," he whispered. "Go back and get Russ."

When the two joined him, Jim had developed a plan.

"All right, I want both of you to set up good firing positions right here. If things come apart, shoot to kill."

"What are you going to do, sir?" Mark asked.

"I plan to talk to the gentlemen. But I have no idea how successful I'll be."

He passed his M-16 to Russ, unbuckled his pistol belt and let it fall to the ground. He tucked the pistol in his hip pocket.

"Here goes nothing," Jim said. He sauntered toward the group until he could be heard. "Hey, my man! What's happening?"

The three men who had been standing turned and pointed their weapons directly at him. If they opened fire, he would be dead before he hit the ground.

"What do you want?" asked the man in the middle.

The three who had been sitting got to their feet.

It couldn't have been a better move as far as Jim and his men were concerned. Now all six stood close together. If it came to shooting, they'd be easy targets.

"Just like ducks in a row," he thought. "Hey, all I want to do is talk," he said casually.

"Talk about what?"

"About the white woman and the girl."

"What about them?" said the one who appeared to be in charge.

"You want to sell them?"

"No way, man. They belong to Amos's gang."

The name was familiar. This was the bunch that was supposed to be protecting the embassy.

"I got good money. U.S. dollars. I pay good for woman and girl."

"You want to use woman or girl, give us your money. We'll watch. But they not for sale."

"If they not for sale, I be going," Jim said while he backed away.

He watched them talk in low voices. Clearly, they couldn't agree.

"Stop where you are, man!" said the leader. "You be going nowhere."

"Shoot them!" Jim yelled, throwing himself face down on the road. He reached around, pulled the pistol from his pocket and emptied all fifteen rounds at his six targets.

Russ and Mark opened up with the M-16s. None of them had ever fired at another human being, yet all three had undergone extensive training. All had qualified on rifle and pistol ranges. Realistic training with live ammunition was an annual requirement. Their deadly, accurate fire cut down all six men. The Liberians failed to return a single shot.

Jim pulled himself up onto his feet, and his two men came up alongside him. Mark checked each of the bodies to be sure the men were dead. Russ handed Jim his pistol belt. Jim inserted another clip in his pistol, wrapped the belt around his waist and stepped around the bodies to where the woman and the girl sat.

Despite the violence only a few feet away from them, neither had moved during the firefight. The woman continued to stare blankly into the coals. As he neared them, Jim saw that the woman was naked from the waist up. Barefoot, her only clothing was a pair of dirty white shorts. Her skin was bruised and scratched. Her hair was matted and filthy. Spots of dried blood dotted her cheeks. The barefoot child in a torn dress had pulled her knees into her chest and sucked on her thumb.

"Put this on," Jim said, stripping off his t-shirt. The woman accepted the shirt and pulled it over her head while still sitting. Her gaze never left the dying fire. She did not acknowledge them at all. It seemed that she didn't know who they were. Probably they were only three more thugs who would continue the abuse.

"Jessica? Jessica, I'm Jim Parkinson. You know, Jimmy's dad. Jimmy is in your daughter's class at school. Maggie is my wife."

"Jim? Jim, what are you doing here?" she asked, finally looking at him.

"I've come to take you to the embassy where it is safe. Are you able to walk?"

"I think so," she said meekly.

"What about Elizabeth?"

"I don't know."

"Sir, I hate to interrupt, but we have a problem."

"What is it, Russ?"

"There are two pickups coming in this direction."

"Oh, shit!" Jim exclaimed. "Russ, pick up the girl. Jessica, come on. We have to get out of here right now!"

Jim grabbed her hand and pulled her to her feet.

"Back to the van! Fast!" he shouted.

They melted into the darkness, away from the firelight. When they got to the thick bushes, Jim paused to look back. The two trucks had stopped by the bodies. One man wore a green sports coat.

"Run!" Jim screamed.

As they neared the vehicle, Russ pushed the button on the Excursion's key chain. The doors automatically unlocked.

Before they could get in the car, all hell broke loose. M-60 machine gun bursts echoed through the neighborhood. Tracer rounds lit up the night sky. Two trucks forced their way through the thick hedge.

Mark dropped to one knee and fired his M-16 at the first truck. It veered to the right and struck a tall palm. The other truck kept coming.

They ran toward the Excursion. The two Marines climbed in the front; Jim, Jessica and the girl crouched down low in the back seat.

Russ jammed the key into the ignition, cranked the starter and floor boarded the accelerator. He forced the gearshift into drive. All four wheels spun on the loose gravel as he roared into the street. The pickup followed, only a few hundred feet behind them. The Excursion's rear window fragmented in a web-like pattern as rounds from the truck-mounted M-60 hit the bulletproof glass.

"Lose them!" Jim yelled.

"I'm trying to, sir. This beast is so heavy. The truck is faster. I think they're gaining. Those M-60 rounds will break through the armor plate if they get close enough."

Jim looked back. He was right. They were getting too close.

"Wait a minute," Jim said. "Isn't this an all-wheel drive vehicle?"

"Yes, sir," Russ said.

"Then get us the hell off the road!"

"Better buckle up!" Russ yelled.

Jim pulled the seatbelts around the woman and the girl before fastening his own.

"Go for it, Russ!"

The Excursion cut to the left and aimed for the four-foot chain link fence that separated Tubman Boulevard from a field along the ocean. All four wheels left the ground as it crashed through the fence, tearing up the brush and knocking down some small trees. It moved deeper into the wide field. They wove in and out around the larger trees, yet the truck kept up with them. Jim figured that the truck was also an all-wheel drive vehicle. At least it wasn't getting any closer. He feared that if they got bogged down, they would meet face to face.

"Guys, we're going to have to fight," Jim said. "Russ, pull the Excursion sideways. We'll exit on the opposite side of the oncoming truck. When it comes at us, open fire at its radiator and windshield."

Russ waited until they started up a low hill then he jerked the Excursion to the left.

"Everyone out the right side!" Jim yelled.

He yanked Jessica and the girl from the vehicle and ordered them to lie flat on the ground.

Still very dark, they couldn't see much farther than two hundred feet. He had gambled that the men would have left their headlights on.

When the pickup spotted the Excursion sitting askew, it pulled to a stop. Just as Jim had figured, the lights were on. He sighted his M-16 on its headlights.

"Leave your selector switches on semi-automatic. Fire directly at the headlights. If they go out, keep firing at the same spot. Fire until your guns are empty," Jim said.

Just as the men began firing, the truck's M-60 opened up on them. Bullets struck the Excursion. Jim's finger never left his trigger until his entire magazine was empty. Just as quickly as the whole thing had begun, it now ended.

"Do we go back to check if we got them all?" asked Russ.

"No," Jim answered. "Everyone, back in the Excursion. Let's get the hell out of here!"

They kept driving through the field for another mile until they veered back toward the road.

There were no more signs of pursuit. Jim glanced over at Jessica Richardson who hadn't spoken a word nor shown any emotion. He concluded that the woman and her daughter must have been brutalized. Since her attackers were all black men, she was likely afraid of him, too.

"Jim?"

Jim almost jumped when he heard her speak.

"Yes?"

"Did Maggie and the boys make it safely out of Liberia?"

"They're back home in Baltimore with Maggie's parents," he answered.

"Oh, thank God. Jim, I've got to tell you what happened."

"Jessica, you don't have to do that."

"Jim, I have to. If I don't, I'll lose my mind."

As they headed back to the embassy, Jessica told their story. When the embassy had been evacuated, all nonessential personnel were asked to leave. That included any Americans who lived and worked in Liberia. Her husband, Darrel, had scoffed at the suggestion, claiming that the officials were overreacting.

Not long afterward, rumors of the President's assassination began circulating. Jessica had been even more concerned, but Darrel insisted that he knew more than she did about the country. After all, he had grown up there; she had been raised in New Jersey. He assured her that they were in no danger.

Their home had escaped the looting that had occurred at Mamba Point. Fluent in Kapel, Darrel had established a kind of rapport with the wandering groups. But later, the character of the groups changed. A new group emerged from the ghetto. None of them spoke Kapel. Darrel tried to reason with them, but they didn't want to listen. A single shot through the chest killed him instantly.

Jessica and her daughter had been taken. Each had been sexually assaulted numerous times by one after another of the belligerent men. When they tired of them, they traded them to another band of thugs. They had been with the six men for several days when Jim and the two Marines had rescued them. She hung her head when she explained that she had made up her mind to kill her own child to spare her from further torture. The rescue had been nothing more than a miracle.

The battered Excursion pulled up to the embassy gate just as the first light of dawn began to appear over the eastern hills. Jim spoke briefly with the Marine guard. Both looked up and down the wide street to check for anything unusual. Satisfied by the quiet early morning, the guard signaled and the gate opened.

The gate fastened securely behind the battered Excursion. The guard resumed his post.

A lone figure stepped back from his position behind a palm across the street. Mabuta had fulfilled his duty. Amos had asked him to watch the embassy and to report any suspicious activity. He figured Amos would like to know about the car that just pulled into the gates, as well as its late night exit.

Jessica and her daughter were moved to the embassy clinic for immediate attention. Jim went directly to the ambassador's office to confer with Vicki and Jerry Day.

"You agree that we have no choice but to close the embassy," Vicki said.

"Yes," said Jim.

"Yes," said Jerry.

"Very well," Vicki said, reaching for a paper on her desk. "This is the message I am prepared to send to the secretary of state."

TOP SECRET:

Sensitive Information

To: Secretary of State

From: Ambassador to Liberia

Situation has deteriorated. Population of embassy has reached fourteen hundred twenty. Government of Liberia is non-existent. Hostile forces surround embassy. Fall of embassy deemed imminent. Immediate evacuation requested.

Victoria Ryan Johnson, Ambassador

# 42

*While the embassy personnel prepared for evacuation, plans for the assault on Sarday's forces were in the final stages in the large conference room at the timber company.*

TALL-SCREENED WINDOWS LET IN LIGHT FROM EACH SIDE. IN THE FRONT, blackboards lined the wall behind the raised platform. A large map of Liberia had been fastened to one blackboard. Another board listed types and number of available weapons. A third had a tally of number and location of personnel. Backless benches were nailed to the floor in parallel rows.

Compared to a tactical operations center in a typical infantry brigade, the whole set-up was a joke. This so-called military force was planning an assault on the national forces of Liberia. Yet, somehow, Hank Martin and his retired military friends had patched together an organization that did have the semblance of an armed force. It still remained to be seen if this militia could perform in combat.

The militia's leaders briefed the senior officers. The forces would begin moving toward the city to confront the troops commanded by Julius Carpai, who had proclaimed himself in charge.

"So far, our forces have met little resistance," said the first speaker, Alfred Jlayou. "We found the garrison at Camp Jackson manned by fewer than fifty soldiers. It appears that most of the army units have been moved to Camp Schiefflin."

The next speaker was Henry Wlue, who briefed them on another troop movement. Some fifteen hundred men had been moved to the outskirts of the town of Yorba in the southwestern section of the country.

Joe Weah then addressed the group.

"Monrovia has fallen into the hands of street gangs and renegade soldiers. Major Thomas Sio and five hundred former members of the Reconnaissance Battalion hold the Barclay Training Center. Carpai has about seventy-five hundred troops at Camp Schiefflin. He has put together a deal with both Sierra Leone and Guinea, who are sending in military forces to back him up. Then he'll name himself President. We've got to attack Camp Schiefflin before the reinforcements get there. Now, I'll turn this over to Lieutenant Colonel Martin who will outline our battle plan."

Hank stood before the map with a thin wood stick in his hand.

"Can you believe they're going to do it?" asked the CNN cameraman.

"If anyone can, Martin can," replied the reporter.

Singleton watched as Hank began. He had seen military briefings during Desert Storm and Operation Iraqi Freedom. He'd seen others in Bosnia. The presenters there had used state-of-the-art software and computer-enhanced graphics.

What he was seeing here was only one step ahead of what George Washington must have used at Valley Forge. Even two days earlier he wouldn't have given this operation a chance in a million. But now, he hung on every word.

He wasn't the only one. All around the room he saw militia officers intently focused on Lieutenant Colonel Martin. Only one – Jeffery Gbam – stared with pure hatred. Even looking at Gbam caused a chill to run down Singleton's spine. He had never really feared anyone before, but he was terrified of Gbam.

Gbam and his four militiamen had discovered the two journalists hiding out on a bluff overlooking the camp. Gbam had knocked Singleton to the ground. He drew his pistol and aimed it between Singleton's eyes. Gbam left no doubt as to his intentions – he was going to kill both of them.

Singleton had heard the gun go off. He had felt the burning of the powder. He had heard two more blasts, yet he didn't move. He kept his eyes tightly closed, sure that he would die. But he hadn't. When he opened one eye, he saw the sneering Gbam only inches from his face.

"You foolish white man. Spies are not given the privilege of a quick death," Gbam said.

One of the soldiers jammed his knee into Singleton's chest. Another pinned his arms to the ground.

Singleton wondered what they were planning to do. Then he saw the machete Gbam held in his right hand.

"So that you know your fate, white man, I am going to cut off both of your hands. Then you will be free to go."

Singleton could feel his heart beat in his throat. He had witnessed such atrocities before. In 1999, he had filmed the horrific mutilation of men, women and children during the war in Sierra Leone and Liberia. It was routine to amputate the hands or feet of opposition forces. Many victims bled to death. Others survived, only to spend the rest of their lives as beggars, living off the charity of others. The memory of those terrible times continued to torment Singleton in his nightmares.

But this was no longer just a nightmare. Now it was going to happen to him.

"You can't do this!" Singleton gasped.

"What can you do to stop me?" Gbam said.

Singleton struggled to free himself, but couldn't. He saw Gbam lift the machete above his head with both of his hands. Singleton couldn't take his eyes off the sharp blade. He imagined himself wandering through the jungle. He would have two bloody stumps where his hands had once been. He would stare back at his severed hands. He would remember the searing pain as the machete split the bones in his wrist. He saw Gbam lower the machete with all the force he could muster. Singleton shrieked in terror. His imagination transcended reality. From out of nowhere, he saw someone coming up behind Gbam.

A hand grabbed Gbam's wrist, arresting the force of his swing in mid-air.

"What the fuck do you think you're doing?" yelled Hank.

"This is none of your business, Martin!" Gbam said firmly.

"Well, Jeffery, I'm making it my business."

Gbam seethed with anger.

"Take Colonel Martin back to camp!" he snapped to the two men who were watching.

When the first soldier moved toward him, Hank pivoted on his left foot, striking the man nearest to him with his right boot. The kick forced the man backward and knocked his partner off balance. Both fell helplessly to the ground.

Gbam let out a yelp and came at Hank with the machete. Hank thrust his fist in Gbam's solar plexus and knocked him breathless. He crumpled to his knees.

"Get back to camp," Hank told the four militiamen. Without hesitating, all four turned and scrambled down the hill.

Hank picked Gbam up by his collar and set him on his feet.

"Jeffery, you come at me again, and you're a dead man," he said while tightening his hold on Gbam's collar. "Now you and I are going to escort these two gentlemen back to camp. By the way, Jeffery, you and I will walk down there like we're good friends. Do you understand what I'm saying?"

Gbam coughed and nodded.

When they arrived in the camp, the two journalists got their chance to meet Charles Morray, yet the rebel leader stipulated that no reports could be released until the attack on Monrovia was under way.

Now the two sat in the back of the briefing room and watched Lieutenant Colonel Martin conclude his remarks. The two journalists from CNN were safe – at least for the time being. They would be billeted with Martin and the Special Forces NCOs.

Singleton knew one thing for certain – he vowed that he would stay as far away as possible from Jeffery Gbam.

# 43

***Aboard a McDonnell Douglas C-17, everyone was more than ready to jump. U.S. forces were on their way to rescue embassy personnel in Monrovia.***

HE HAD ALREADY BEEN IN THE JUMP SEAT FOR MORE THAN TEN HOURS. NOW with all the gear on, he was even more uncomfortable. When he shifted his weight, the straps of the chute dug into his shoulders. The cross straps on his chest made it hard to breathe deeply. The leg straps dug into his groin, causing sharp pains that radiated up to his guts. A ninety-pound cargo pack balanced between his legs. It was attached to quick-release clips on the front of the harness.

When he jumped, the cargo pack, tethered to a fifteen-foot nylon rope, would dangle below him. It was designed so that the pack would hit the ground first. If he hit the ground with the heavy pack between his legs, it would either kill him or make him wish he were dead. The pack held an assault rifle, extra ammo, Claymore mines, plastic explosives and MREs. It had everything a man would need to survive and accomplish his mission.

The chute was made of zero-porosity mixed fabric so it would retain its shape and buoyancy through sudden changes in air currents. The canopy was slightly elliptical with a tapered wing. It could be steered much like a hang glider. The jumper could accurately "fly" to a target ten feet in diameter.

Lieutenant Commander Glen Jordan took a quick look around the cargo hold. He wore a black Nomex high altitude jumpsuit and Gortex gloves that would protect his hands from subzero temperatures. His hip holster carried a silenced nine-millimeter "Hushpuppy" automatic pistol. His Kevlar bulletproof vest had side pockets for flashlights, flares, hand grenades, additional pistol magazines and maps. Before jumping into the subzero environment, he would don his respirator mask. It had a large, shatterproof and tinted eyepiece, which allowed wide visibility. Just ninety minutes before, he had chuted up. In fewer than twenty minutes, he'd step off the tailgate into freezing darkness.

The tactical transport aircraft was cruising at five hundred eighteen miles per hour, some twenty-four thousand feet above the Liberian jungles. The sound of the four Pratt and Whitney F-117-PW-100 turbofans generating thirty-seven thousand pounds of thrust could barely be heard from the ground. But in the cargo hold, the steady rush of air was deafening. It was nearly impossible to hear when someone tried to speak.

The men stared ahead, each lost in his thoughts. Some seemed to be praying. Others went over each step of the mission, just to be sure.

The mission order read:

The influx of refugees to the American Embassy in Monrovia, Liberia has left its staff short of food and water. Rebel gangs may attack. If they do, the embassy will fall.

The task force can't launch the Marines on the helicopters for another twenty-four hours. If there is an assault on the embassy, the task force will launch F-14 Tomcats. They could be on target within one hour.

The President has ordered the task force to avoid mass citizen casualties at all costs. For this reason, SEAL Team Six will reinforce the Marine guards and attaché staff until rescue forces arrive.

The thirty-man SEAL team will conduct a high altitude, low opening (HALO) parachute jump from twenty-four thousand feet. Embassy staff has been alerted to light the drop zone near the tennis courts using vehicle headlights. Since the city is blacked out due to lack of electrical power, the team should have no problem finding the DZ.

The jump will take place in less than one hour.

Each man had that mingling of fear and exhilaration that comes to those who dare to step out into the unknown.

To Jordan's right sat Chief Petty Officer Gerald Mason. He leaned close to Jordan's ear.

"Sir, hope there's not a crowd standing around at the embassy when we land," he shouted. "I've got to pee so bad that my teeth are floating."

"I know what you mean," Jordan nodded. "Every time I get suited up and then have to sit for two hours, my bladder fills up."

Mason was Jordan's senior non-commissioned officer. They had served together for almost three years. Even though they were senior and subordinate, the two were good friends. Navy SEALs became more than co-workers; they were a close-knit family.

The lights in the cargo bay flashed three times in succession. The jumpmaster, Chief Petty Officer John Pittman, stood next to the ramp at the rear of the aircraft. He held both his hands palms up. Then he held his right hand up once.

"Fifteen minutes!" he shouted.

The aircraft began to slow down. It had to reduce its speed to one hundred-fifty miles per hour before the men jumped.

He gestured to the men to put on their respirator masks. All thirty jumpers, each member of the flight crew and the jumpmaster himself adjusted their masks. Once satisfied with the fit, each man pointed his right thumb upward. The cargo bay began to depressurize. Only four minutes later, the interior pressure was equal to the air pressure at twenty-four thousand feet. Each man leaned to his right, to check the man next to him for signs of oxygen deprivation.

"Five minutes," the jumpmaster indicated, signaling the men to stand.

The SEALs pulled themselves to their feet and waddled toward the cargo ramp. Heavily laden with their gear, they looked more like Ninja Turtles than fearsome Navy commandos. The Air Force crew chief pressed a button that activated the electric motors on the hydraulic ramp. It began to open. The drone of the aircraft's engines became a deafening roar.

The inside temperature dropped to twenty-four degrees below zero. The men worked their way back to the edge of the ramp.

"One minute," the jumpmaster signaled.

The first man on each side of the ramp stared at a red light on the side of the hold. It flashed green. One after another, the thirty men stepped off the ramp and into the cold darkness.

Petty Officer Frank Springer had quit counting the number of times he had jumped. The total likely surpassed fifteen hundred jumps, most of them free-fall. While others complained of the freezing cold, Springer relished the exhilaration of flying through open space. He exited the aircraft with his arms pressed tight to his sides. He plummeted downward at nearly ten thousand feet per minute. He quickly stabilized while slicing through the thin atmosphere.

Beneath him, the surface of the earth was almost completely dark. Only pinpoints of orange glow from burning buildings dotted the landscape enough to indicate the existence of a city. Springer angled his body and aimed himself in the direction of the fires. At five thousand feet, he would activate the chute.

This was Lieutenant Junior Grade Josh Iverson's first combat mission. He failed to share Springer's enthusiasm for leaping out of an aircraft. He had completed his rugged SEAL training only six months earlier. He'd been with SEAL Team six for only the last three months. Even his graduation from Annapolis hadn't given him more of a sense of accomplishment than had having earned the coveted SEAL badge. He loved nearly every aspect of this life as a SEAL.

Only one thing – parachute jumping – filled him with fear, so he forced himself to overcome this weakness. He volunteered for more than the minimum number of jumps that were required to maintain proficiency and earn jump pay. Yet each time, he was terrified. He could feel his anxiety peak as he stood waiting for the light to turn green. He imagined his chute failing to open, his body plummeting to the earth. These high altitude, low opening jumps were the worst. Often the nightmare of free-fall would disrupt his sleep.

When it was Iverson's turn to jump from the ramp, he gritted his teeth and stepped into the darkness. His body twisted and turned. The heavy cargo pack strapped to the harness made stabilization nearly impossible. He fought for control for what seemed like an eternity. He knew he must stabilize before reaching five thousand feet. If he didn't and tried to deploy the chute, he might become entangled in the nylon lines.

At last, he managed a semblance of stability. He looked around him for the other members of the platoon. In a night HALO jump, each man activates a chemical nightstick. Its green glow is too dim to be detected from the ground, but allows the free-fall team to locate their teammates. He turned his head and squinted. He saw one, then another, and yet another. They were together. It was just in time. At five thousand feet, the barometric release opened his chute.

Nearer to the ground, he could see the fires burning out of control. No law and order. No fire department. No water. No one really cared. Sometimes he could see a single building on fire; other times it appeared an entire city block was engulfed in flames.

One lighted area was different. He could make out the landing zone. Fifteen vehicles had been parked in a circle, their headlights illuminating a one-hundred-fifty-foot area in a field adjacent to the tennis courts. Landing there would be no problem for an experienced jumper with a steerable chute. His chute had deployed, and he was able to maneuver. His stomach was no longer caught in his throat.

He steered toward the drop zone. He picked out what appeared to be the building that housed the offices of the embassy. Across the street he could see a burning building. Part of their preparation had been to study maps and aerial photos of Monrovia. They had reviewed the latest situation report. He knew that the British Embassy had been evacuated. It looked like their ambassador's residence had been set on fire, sending spikes of red-orange high into the air. Even from twenty-five hundred feet, the light from the fire illuminated the road and the surrounding buildings.

For the first time since he had left the plane, Iverson felt a sense of assurance that this portion of the mission would be a success.

Jimmie Gato stifled another yawn. He had no idea why Amos had wanted them to patrol the road in front of the American Embassy. After all, where could these people go? They were basically hostages. The patrol wasn't his idea of fun. Besides that, he was annoyed that they hadn't even been permitted to loot the British Embassy. Now that would have been fun.

He sat in the pick-up next to Henry. He drove the truck on yet another pass up and down the street. Massa and Steven hung on to the railings on the side of the bed, ready to man the machine gun if necessary. Jimmie couldn't help it. He closed his eyes and began to drift off to sleep.

"Jimmie!" someone shouted as the truck braked to a stop. "Jimmie, something not right's happening here. Come look!"

Jimmie stepped out of the truck and stood alongside Henry.

"What?" he asked.

"Look up in the sky!"

"I don't see nothing. What are you talking about?"

"Over there," Henry insisted, pointing up into the night sky. "Over there, above the American Embassy!" Jimmie stared in the direction of Henry's finger. This time, he could make out dark shapes illuminated by the light of the flames from the British Embassy. At first, he wasn't sure what he was seeing. They seemed like large, dark birds, circling in the sky. He realized that they were coming closer and that they weren't birds at all – but objects dangling from parachutes. He rested his arm on the truck's fender to steady himself. Lots more of the man-like objects neared the ground. He ran around to the back of the truck, settled in behind the machine gun, swiveled the weapon and pointed its muzzle upward.

He depressed the trigger and the M-60 obediently began to spit out thousands of rounds of 7.62mm ball ammunition directly at SEAL Team Six.

Every fifth round was a tracer, and he could see the red streaks lash out at their targets. "Shit!" he swore.

The firing didn't seem to be doing any good. He swung the machine gun back and forth, spattering more shots through the field of falling chutes. A blinding explosion lit up the sky. All four men screamed excitedly as they watched the flurry of invaders, their chutes ripped to shreds, tumble out of control while crashing to the ground.

Petty Officer Second Class John Pittman floated in the midst of ten jumpers. The first man had just touched down when he saw the tracers streak through the cloud of descending parachutists.

For more than sixty years, the concept of moving troops into battle by having them parachute from aircraft had been a vital tool in a military campaign. "Death from above" was the motto of these brave men who could strike fear into the hearts of their enemies. The truth was that the mission was only successful if the troops landed behind enemy lines under the cover of darkness. The greatest danger was when they came under fire while still descending. The drifting chute was an easy target for enemy firepower. Even a duck in hunting season had a better chance of survival than the figure of a man suspended from an open chute.

Pittman whispered a prayer. His only hope was that whoever was doing the shooting would be a lousy shot or that the darkness would keep him safe. Yet as he drifted down, he felt the bullets rising to meet him. He heard a man to his left scream in agony as he was hit. Pittman tried to will the chute to safety, but he dropped directly into the line of fire. He heard the whiz of bullets nearby and, simultaneously, felt a bolt of pain shoot up his leg. He looked down to see a rip in the toe of his right boot. He was relieved – a foot wound wasn't fatal.

The next round struck his flak jacket, hitting a fragmentation grenade in his right pocket. It had sufficient force to detonate the grenade. It, in turn, detonated the other four grenades he carried. The force of that explosion set off the four Claymore antipersonnel mines in his cargo pack.

Pittman's body, blown to bits, scattered throughout the sky. Everyone within two hundred feet of the blast was peppered with shrapnel, fragments of gear, and tiny pieces of human flesh.

On the ground, Marine Gunny Sergeant Erick Wilson and Lance Corporal Brent Jones gazed skyward, watching the SEALs careen through the air.

Then they heard the M-60 open up.

"Open the gate!" yelled Wilson. Both men ran toward the pedestrian gate. Jones lifted the heavy bar and swung open the door. Wilson ran past him, ordering him to close and lock the gate behind him. The street was deceptively quiet. He was looking from side to side when he heard a burst of machine gunfire. It was coming from a pick-up truck parked mid-road in front of the burning British Embassy. The flaming backdrop revealed the silhouettes of four men. One hunched behind the machine gun; he was pointing and gesturing with outstretched arms.

Palm trees along the side of the road masked Wilson's movement toward the truck. He crouched behind a wide tree trunk about one hundred feet from the truck when an explosion lit up the sky. Torn parachutes spiraled to the ground. Two screaming and battered SEALs crashed to the pavement only yards in front of him. All around him, he heard the thunk-thunk of other debris striking the ground.

Wilson stepped out from his cover and planted his boots firmly on the sidewalk. He pulled a fragmentation grenade from his vest and hurled it at the truck. The men in the truck couldn't hear it hit because of the noise from their weapon. Wilson watched as the grenade rolled under the vehicle. He hurled a second grenade. It landed in the bed of the truck. One of the Liberians glanced down at the grenade, totally ignorant of its deathly purpose. Neither the man in the truck nor Wilson moved.

One after another, the grenades exploded, engulfing the truck in a burst of flames. Three of the men died instantly. The fourth was thrown backwards onto the pavement. He struggled to his knees and tried to rub the blood from his eyes. When his vision cleared, he saw an American Marine pointing an M-16 directly in his face.

Wilson pulled the trigger. Three rounds penetrated the man's skull.

Wilson turned on his heel to examine the broken and lifeless body of Third Class Petty Officer Michael Hitachi. He ran his arms under Hitachi's legs and shoulders and gently lifted the man's body. He carried it to the embassy grounds. He then made a return trip to retrieve the body of Chief Petty Officer Gerald Mason. After he laid Mason's body inside the embassy gate, he fell to his knees and wept at the senseless loss of such fine men.

Iverson had been one hundred fifty feet above Pittman when the explosion tore Pittman apart. Shrapnel peppered Iverson's legs and hips. Although the particles caused only superficial wounds, they hurt like hell. His wounds were the least of his worries.

He was drifting away from the landing site and falling far too rapidly. His chute had been damaged by the blast, and now he had no directional control. He panicked. Instead of cutting away the main chute and activating the reserve, he jettisoned his cargo pack. That served to slow his descent, but only slightly. He still was falling too fast. The dark shadows of the buildings loomed larger and larger.

He was still struggling with his chute when he struck the ground at close to thirty-five miles per hour. It was as if he had jumped from a moving vehicle onto hard asphalt. He managed to roll over. He heard himself moaning then forced himself to be quiet. He lay still for moment, getting his bearings. He pulled at the tangled lines in an attempt to disengage himself from the tatter of the parachute. A few minutes later, he freed himself and crawled away from the knot of silk and lines.

He looked up to find four Liberians standing over him. Each held a rifle in his hands. Iverson imagined his mutilated body being dragged through the streets of the city.

"Oh, shit!" he murmured, lowering his head to his bloodied forearm.

**FLASH MESSAGE** TOP SECRET

TO: TASK FORCE COMMANDER

INSERTION FLAWED

7 KIA, 6 MIA

EMBASSY SECURED

SEND MARINES ASAP

# 44

*The former ore train was headed west to Buchanan, forty miles southwest of Monrovia.*

SINGLETON MUST HAVE DOZED OFF FOR ABOUT A HALF HOUR, BUT NOW HE woke up. It was so dark inside the railway car that he couldn't see his own hands in front of him. Yet he remembered that his photographer, Brian Anderson, sat next to him on the wooden bench.

"You awake?" Singleton whispered.

"Yeah. What time it is?"

Singleton pushed the button on his watch.

"It's half past one. We should reach the coast in about two hours."

"Good. It couldn't be soon enough. This hard seat is killing me."

"Don't complain. We're lucky. We could be one of those soldiers stuffed into the ore cars."

The Buchanan facility served as the terminus for the ore trains that carried the iron ore pellets that were loaded onto ocean-going freighters. Now, with weapons and ammunition provided by the Ivory Coast, the train carried the arms, equipment and men to face Carpai's forces. Both journalists knew their lives could be in jeopardy. They also knew that they were perched on the edge of what might be one of the year's biggest stories.

Six hours earlier Morray's men had breached the government road-block on the rail line. More than three thousand troops had been crammed into the ore cars. Only one passenger car had been added to the long, slow-moving train. Other cars carried extra ammunition, surface-to-air missiles, anti-armor weapons. The passenger car held several key staff members, including Lieutenant Colonel Martin and two American advisors. The two journalists squeezed in one of the rear seats.

When Singleton thought back on the plan of attack, he couldn't help but think it was all too simple. He had been surprised that Martin endorsed such a basic approach.

One of the militia's largest forces, composed of about five thousand men, had been fighting along the main highway. Their mission was to drive the government forces back toward the capital. The three thousand soldiers on board the train would occupy the ore-receiving plant. Later they would march toward Camp Schiefflin and attack Carpai's forces on their left flank.

All together, the four-thousand-man militia would face a force that could be as large as twelve thousand – many of them the reinforcement troops from Guinea and Sierra Leone. Clearly, the odds were in Carpai's favor.

Yet Martin, backed up by Weah, insisted that a flank attack coming from the ore plant could overwhelm the government troops garrisoned at Camp Schiefflin. Whether it was going to work or not was no longer a question. The plan was in motion.

"I'm going to try to get a little more sleep," Singleton said with a yawn. He hunched down on the seat and forced himself to concentrate on the rhythmic rumble of the train.

# 45

***Back in Monrovia, the ambassador's staff once again gathered around the conference table.***

RATIONAL THINKING WAS IN ABOUT AS SHORT SUPPLY AS WAS FOOD AND WATER. Everyone was on edge, yet Vicki's staff forced themselves to come to grips with their status. Needless to say, it was even more difficult to think straight at half past two in the morning.

Commander Jordan had just completed his cold assessment of their readiness. Of the thirty SEALs who had dropped onto the embassy grounds, seven bodies were lined up side by side in the maintenance warehouse. Another six were missing. No one would even venture a guess as to whether they were dead or alive. Another two were seriously wounded. One had a broken leg. At least a half dozen more had been treated for minor wounds and injuries. More than half of the SEALs were out of action before the sun had even come up.

Despite the terrible losses, Jordan spoke as if it were nothing more than a routine operation.

Inside the embassy compound, things hadn't been going well. Tension had taken its toll. Vicki had heard of hostility within the ranks of the refugees. Food and water was rationed. They had given top priority to the children. Shouting matches had erupted among some of the adults. Just the day before, two Marines had to restrain two diplomats who were on the verge of punching each other. If this so-called King Amos decided to attack, she wasn't sure how long they could hold out. She turned to her strongest staffer for his advice.

"Jim, do we still expect the Marines to come in this evening?"

"Based on our last message from the task force commander, the first choppers should land around eight o'clock tonight. The Marines will secure the perimeter. Then the choppers will begin the evacuation," Jim reported.

"The order of evacuation will be women and children, foreign embassy staff and third- country nationals, and non-essential staff. The last group will be the country team and myself," Vicki said. "Until tonight, we'll just have to hold the fort. Continue to give me hourly status reports. That will be all."

The staff rose and filed out of the room, leaving the ambassador to her private thoughts. She had only one: Could it possibly get any worse?

# 46

***Still far from its destination, the ore train suddenly jackknifed, and the passengers were sent reeling to the left.***

SINGLETON HAD JUST GIVEN IN TO AN EXHAUSTED SLEEP WHEN HE SUDDENLY found himself buried in a tangle of arms and legs on the floor. He heard screams and curses of the others who were thrown unceremoniously on the wood floor. The forward motion stopped. Unhurt, Singleton staggered to his feet.

"Everyone out of the car and into the woods! Move! Now!" ordered Hank.

Singleton had no choice. Those behind him prodded him with their knees and elbows as they pushed their way toward the exit. He made his way down the metal stairway until his feet crunched on the gravel roadbed. He stared upward. It was still so dark that he could barely see the outline of the tops of the trees in the faint starlight. He blindly fell in step with the others who were making their way into the brush that paralleled the tracks. The four or five ore cars ahead of his car had been toppled to their sides. Militiamen spilled out into the open and joined the frantic rush into the forest.

A bright flash was followed by a loud blast. Then they heard the "pop-pop" of gunfire. The mob's escape escalated into a mad dash for cover.

"Jesus Christ!" Singleton yelled. "Those were gunshots!"

Now aware that they had been ambushed, Singleton seethed with anger. He dove into the bush, cursing the fools who had jeopardized their lives.

"Stupid idiots!" he screamed. "You fucking, stupid idiots! You got us right into the middle of an ambush!"

"Singleton? Anderson? Where are you?" someone called.

"Over here!" Singleton shouted, hoping to be heard over the roar of battle. Lieutenant Colonel Martin crawled alongside him. Behind the colonel, he could see Anderson, his eyes wide with fear.

"Come on!" Hank said. "We're getting out of here!"

"And going where?" Singleton demanded.

"Back in the direction we just came. Keep up with me. I don't have time to carry you."

Hank didn't wait for their response. He turned and led them off through the brush along the edge of the tracks.

About a half hour later, the battle sounds had either stopped or faded away. Hank moved out to a more open area along the tree line and picked up the pace.

"Where are we going?" Singleton shouted.

"I don't have time to talk," Hank said without turning around. "Save your breath and keep moving."

Singleton felt another surge of anger. Lieutenant Colonel Martin was nothing more than a goddamned coward who'd abandoned the pitiful militiamen who were sure to be killed. Yet he'd been careful to save his own ass. He had run from the battle like a whipped dog. Singleton pledged to himself that if they got out of this alive, he'd do everything possible to see that Hank Martin was publicly denounced for the coward that he was.

"Faster! Keep moving!" ordered Hank.

# 47

***Once they got on the paved road at Kakata, the seven military Hummers raced along at nearly fifty miles per hour.***

THE TRUE LIBERIAN GOVERNMENT WAS PREPARED TO FACE THE REBELS AND their evil American friends. Their leaders told them they must do what was necessary to save their homeland.

Two vehicles drove side-by-side in front. Behind them, another two drove parallel to one in the middle, which flew the colors of the chief of staff. Two more followed directly behind.

Each guard vehicle sported an M-60 machine gun mounted on a turret between its front and rear seats. In addition to the driver, each Hummer carried five members of the elite cadre assigned to protect the chief of staff. This early in the morning, the road was free of local traffic. In less than an hour, the group of vehicles would reach Camp Schiefflin.

General Oscar Jalah was more confident than ever. So far, the campaign had been successful beyond his wildest expectations. The People's Party had been thwarted, literally stopped dead in its tracks. The ambush of the train had been a fatal blow. Morray's forces had scattered in panic. It was only a matter of time until the new government's troops would move in and assume control.

Only a month earlier, Jalah had been a mere major. Today he wore the uniform of a four-star general. He had a direct link to Julius Carpai, who had entrusted him with the entire military operation.

He could hardly believe his good fortune.

It had all turned his way the night President Dowling had been assassinated. His brother, Peter Jalah, had been in command of the nation's SWAT team. His orders were to secure the stockade at Barclay Training Center. When Peter and his thirty-man team arrived, the front gates stood wide open. Inside, there was nothing but darkness.

Bodies of bullet-ridden guards were strewn haphazardly near the entrance. They had arrived too late. The prisoners had already fled the stockade. Making their way deeper inside, Peter himself had nearly slipped on the bloody pulp of what had once been the government's chief interrogator, Morris Kai.

They made their way across the parade grounds when bright lights suddenly blinded them as the powerful floodlights lit up the area. They whirled around to assume a defensive position, only to find themselves surrounded by nearly two hundred armed rebels who held them in their gun sights.

"Drop your weapons!" ordered the voice of Major Tom Sio over the loudspeaker. "Drop your weapons, or you will join Major Kai in death!"

There had been no choice. Outnumbered and outgunned, Peter and his men had been forced to give up their weapons, equipment and even their clothing.

Although Peter had anticipated their swift execution, he and his men had been led to the gate and released. Peter had made his way to Oscar's house. He had worn only his boxer shorts. Oscar had found him a shirt, pants and a pair of shoes. Together the Jalah brothers had driven to Carpai's residence to report what had happened.

They had taken Carpai's Cadillac and rushed to Camp Schiefflin. Carpai had ordered an alert. The battalion at Camp Jackson was relocated to Camp Schiefflin. Troops then secured the nearby international airport.

Carpai had decided to amass all available troops at Camp Schiefflin. Rejecting any formal ceremony, he had also proclaimed himself as head of state. The nation's mission – now more than ever – was to destroy the rebel Charles Morray and all who followed him. Once Morray and the rebel People's Party were killed or contained, Carpai's troops would reoccupy Monrovia and put down the lawless gangs.

Yet not every commander had supported Carpai. Some had even dared to question his authority to appoint himself as President. However, Carpai, anxious to demonstrate his benevolence, had told them they would be free to leave if they wished. Two dozen officers had taken him up on the offer. Carpai had promised an escort back to the city. They would be driven in two five-ton cargo trucks. Carpai had even assigned Major Oscar Jalah as their official escort.

If any of these men had doubted Carpai's sincerity, they had failed to heed their inner misgivings. Most likely, they had no inkling that their destination wasn't the streets of the capital, but a remote beach along the Atlantic Ocean. When they had arrived, they had been ordered to get out of the trucks.

Oscar Jalah himself had handpicked the death squad that waited in the shade of the tall trees. One after another, the officers had been shot in the back of the head and their warm corpses loaded onto the truck beds for the trip back to Camp Schiefflin.

The following morning, Carpai had ordered a formation. All five thousand officers and men who had been garrisoned at Camp Schiefflin had assembled on the parade grounds to hear an address by the nation's new leader.

Dressed in formal attire, a brilliant gold sash ran diagonally across Julius Carpai's chest. He had stood confidently in the morning sunlight and looked out over his assembled troops.

"The new order of Liberia...," he began, his gestures, bold and dramatic.

He had gone on to tell them that each man had been blessed to have been chosen to be a part of this fateful day. Liberia would rise to claim its destiny as the jewel of West Africa. Its vast oil reserves would bring untold wealth to each loyal subject.

Yet, he had warned, some would dare to try to thwart the glory they deserved. Already, some evil ones had plotted against his life. But good would prevail, he had vowed. He had raised his right arm and nodded to his left.

Two five-ton trucks had pulled in front of the reviewing stand. One by one, the corpses of the slain officers had been ceremoniously laid in tidy rows before the assembled troops.

Carpai had nodded once again. This time, Oscar Jalah had come to attention beside him as Carpai pinned on Oscar's new rank as his top general. The message had been clear: Anyone who attempted to desert would be shot.

Carpai and his right-hand man, Oscar Jalah, were firmly in charge of the new Liberia.

Even before the seven Hummers reached the entrance, the gates at Camp Schiefflin swung open to admit the chief of staff and his escort. Bright floodlights had been installed to illuminate the heavily fortified entrance.

Only fifty miles away, the capital still struggled in darkness, lacking both power and water.

But here, the massive turbine generators, running on JP-4 jet fuel, provided plenty of electricity to run the lights at the fort and airport. No riots or mob rule here, the military was in complete command.

The Hummers pulled up in front of the headquarters building. A soldier rushed to open the general's door. Out stepped Oscar Jalah, Liberia's top military man. The guards snapped to attention and saluted sharply.

"Good morning, General Jalah. Minister Carpai is in the briefing room," said a major who had been manning a desk in the hallway.

"Thank you, major," said Jalah's escort. A guard posted at the door saluted and opened the door. The headquarters building was constructed of solid brick. It had been built in the early fifties by a British construction company. The plans for the headquarters building were patterned on similar buildings in the old British Empire. Inside, it boasted rich hardwood floors and inlaid teak walls.

The conference table in the briefing room was made of highly polished wood. A stage ran along the far wall. Other walls were lined with topographic maps. Six men nodded as General Oscar Jalah entered.

"Oscar, welcome back," said Carpai, who stood and offered his outstretched hand. "We've been reviewing the reports. Everything has gone far beyond our expectations."

The other men also had stood when Jalah entered the room. Each of them came forward to congratulate him on the successful engagement with Morray's forces.

Carpai grinned as he brought the meeting to order.

"Let's go over the final plans for the total destruction of the People's Party," he said. "General Grebo, how many Cobra attack helicopters are now operational?"

Captain Bobby Grebo had been promoted to brigadier general and commander of the air force.

"Six, sir."

"Good," said Carpai. "What about the heavy lift helicopters?"

"We have ten. We are capable of transporting three hundred assault troops in one lift."

"Thank you, general," said Carpai, satisfied with the answer. "Now let me introduce the commander of the special action force from Guinea, James Ogalla," Carpai continued. "One hundred Guinean soldiers will be brought in along with two hundred of our loyal Liberian soldiers. In charge will be Jeffery."

Jeffery Gbam beamed at his introduction. He would teach Charles Morray and that arrogant Hank Martin that no one could humiliate him. Morray had sided with Martin on the incident with the two newsmen. He would get back at both of them.

Gbam had struck a deal with Carpai. Privy to the briefings at Sanniquellie, Gbam had provided details of the planned rebel attack on Camp Schiefflin. Carpai had arranged to pick him up by helicopter and fly him to Camp Schiefflin as Morray's forces moved out of Sanniquellie. It was a direct result of Gbam's information that ten thousand soldiers had been sent to thwart the attack.

Ambushing the train had been the crowning achievement. Later, monitored radio contact between Sanniquellie and the fleeing men had verified that the militia was in complete disorder. Joe Weah and Lieutenant Colonel Martin were reported missing and presumed dead. Rebel commanders had been ordered to withdraw their remaining forces and retreat to Sanniquellie.

When the rebel forces made it back to their base camp at Sanniquellie, they would find nothing left. Although most of the Liberian forces would continue to pursue the scattered militia, some three hundred soldiers, supported by six attack helicopters, would destroy Morray's headquarters. Gbam would personally lead the attack in order to assure himself that Morray and his family, the Martins, and even the Myers, would all die. Gbam had already been assured that his work would earn him the governorship of Nimba and Grand Gedah counties.

"I want the forces to lift off by seven-thirty a.m. By noon, the People's Party will no longer exist," announced Carpai.

He pushed himself back from the table, turned to the bar and brought back a tray holding a bottle of Seagram's Crown Royal and seven glasses. He filled each glass to the brim.

"To the new order of Liberia!"

"To the new order of Liberia!" they repeated, downing the drinks in a single swallow. Carpai set his glass down heavily on the table and turned his wrist to check the time.

"It's now five o'clock. The forces will be in the air in a little more than two hours."

# 48

***In the isolated American Embassy, things looked mighty bleak.***

FEW WERE ABLE TO SLEEP MORE THAN AN HOUR OR TWO AT A TIME. ONE OF the wounded SEALs had died from his injuries. Vicki's team had gathered around a long, folding table in the recreation room. She crossed her arms and rested her head on her forearms. Jim Parkinson stood nearby, staring at the tips of his scuffed boots.

"My eyes feel as if someone has poured acid in them," Vicki said.

"I know what you mean," Jim said. "It seems like everything just gets worse."

They listened to the hiss of the Coleman lanterns that provided the only light. Generator power had been limited to the main building.

"It looks as though Carpai's forces have beaten back Morray," Jim said.

"Oh, Jim, do you think Hank, Lindsey and Tim could have escaped all that?"

"Vicki, I have no idea. We can only hope that they're not with the forces that came south."

"Do you think that this Amos character will attack us here?"

"It wouldn't surprise me. Although he appears to be a certified nut, he sure seems to have a lot of followers."

"You have to admit that demanding that 'his property' be returned was something right out of the Dark Ages."

"How true, especially when that property was an American citizen and her eleven-year-old daughter, both of whom who had been raped by his thugs. The fact that we took out one of his trucks might also make him unhappy."

Jim paused to look at his watch. It was half past five in the morning.

"In thirteen hours, the Marines will arrive. We can hold out until then."

"Let's pray that we will," sighed Vicki.

# 49

*Carpai's forces at Camp Schiefflin's airfield would soon be celebrating victory.*

ALONG THE EASTERN HORIZON, THE SKY HAD BEGUN TO LIGHTEN, SIGNALING the dawning of a new day. The Liberian general walked the flight line, personally overseeing the final fueling of the heavy-lift helicopters. Six Cobras were armed and ready for take-off. Clear skies and the prospect of an easy victory made it a perfect day for flight operations.

General Grebo stopped to chat with the excited aviators who busied themselves making their last-minute checks. It was now quarter to seven in the morning, Grebo noted. Flight command had scheduled the arrival of combat troops for seven o'clock.

Grebo paused at the door of the operations building, suddenly aware of the distinct whop, whop of a Huey. At first he suspected that someone had defied orders and, in his excitement, had lifted off early. He vowed to discipline whoever failed to follow the plan. He squinted into the eastern sky. The noise was getting louder. It seemed to come from the direction of the rubber plantation. He watched as the red-gold semicircle began its ritual ascent above the tree line. He shaded his eyes with his outstretched hand in an informal salute to the sunrise.

He still couldn't see the Huey, but he had no doubt of its presence. The engine noise and the cut of the rotors were unmistakable. Again, he looked. This time he saw it, hovering one hundred fifty feet above the misty rubber trees. It hung in mid-air and came toward the airfield. Grebo wheeled around and stepped through the doorway. As soon as he was inside, he hesitated then turned around to take another look. Something wasn't right. He shielded his eyes to look again.

The Huey headed straight at him before banking to the right. Its doors had been removed. An M-60 machine gun had been mounted on board. Clearly, this was one of his birds, but none of his had gun mounts.

"Oh, shit!" he shouted as he bolted toward the flight line. He recognized the Huey. It was the one that Major Edward Seah had stolen when he defected to join up with the People's Party. This one was in Morray's hands. Its presence meant trouble.

Airmen along the flight line looked up. They were startled when they saw Grebo running toward them. He was shouting and waving his arms like a madman. Confused by his odd behavior, they just stood and watched, unaware of the imminent danger.

The Huey came in faster than Grebo could run. It dropped down to only fifty feet above ground. It came so close that Grebo could see the faces of the men riding inside. The Huey had two M-60s, one on each side of the opening. All he could do was watch as they swung the barrels of the weapons, sighting in on their targets.

A burst of machine gunfire stopped Grebo's charge. A spatter of rounds hit the tarmac. Another burst chipped at the parked Cobras. Grebo felt the ground around him shake as the ordnance detonated. In an instant, all six Cobras vanished. They were transformed into a scorching, red-orange inferno. A rush of hot wind knocked Grebo off his feet. Tiny fragments of metal – shrapnel from exploding rockets and ammo – tore into fuel tanks, parked vehicles and human flesh. Grebo looked up and saw the lethal Huey move in closer to target the heavy-lift helicopters. He struggled to get himself to a standing position. Bloodied and bruised, he could only stare at the hellish sight. In a matter of minutes, the Liberian Air Force had been obliterated.

Julius Carpai sipped at his strong, dark coffee while jotting notes on a yellow legal pad. He tapped his pen on the surface of the wide desk, pausing from time to time to collect his thoughts. Near the airfield, Carpai had taken over the office of the former commandant. He wanted to be prepared for victory. He searched for just the right phrasing for the speech he would deliver once he knew for certain that Morray was dead.

The blast from the exploding Cobras shattered the office windows, blowing shards of glass across the room. His back to the window, Carpai hadn't been hurt. He scrambled for cover in the kneehole of the desk.

"What the hell is going on?" he shouted.

He reached up to muffle his ears from the deafening blasts and sporadic bursts of gunfire. He felt a warm trickle from behind his left ear. He pulled his hand away and saw his own blood coating his fingertips. He crawled back to the shelter of the solid wall and stood. Hand over hand, he made his way to the door and finally out into the hallway.

"We're under attack!" he screamed. Major Droba huddled on the floor beside a filing cabinet.

"Droba! Get the garrison commander and have him place men on the perimeter!"

Back in the hallway, Carpai ran to the radio room. The radio operator stood, hands in pockets, staring out his unbroken window at the flames rising from the airfield.

"Get General Jalah on the radio!" he yelled. "Now! Quickly! Move!"

His trance broken, the man turned to his desk and placed the earphones on his head.

General Oscar Jalah's head bobbed from side to side as the Hummer sped up the road to Kakata. His intent was to accompany Liberian forces that would drive the militia back up the road. After the successful air operation, a helicopter would pick him up and transport his base of operations to Sanniquellie. Lost in an exhausted sleep, he felt a nudge on his shoulder.

"What.... What is it?" he mumbled.

"Sir," the driver said, "Minister Carpai is on the radio."

Jalah reached for the mike and pressed, "Talk."

"General Jalah here, sir."

"Oscar, Camp Schiefflin has been attacked."

"Attacked? Who attacked?"

"We don't know. It might be one of the gangs from Monrovia. There have been several big explosions over by the airfield. Also, some small arms fire. I'm trying to get a status report."

"What can I do, sir?"

"To be on the safe side, I want you to send one thousand soldiers."

"Sir, I won't be able to get reinforcements to Camp Schiefflin before this afternoon."

"Do what you can, Oscar. We have the three hundred strike troops and about two hundred garrison soldiers. We should be able to hold off until you arrive. If it is the gangs, they aren't well trained. But I still want those reinforcements here by dark."

"Yes, sir. I will organize the reinforcements and personally bring them to Camp Schiefflin," promised Jalah.

"Shit!" he said quietly. Everything had gone so well up to now. What in the hell could be going on at Camp Schiefflin?

Four officers stood with their backs to the hallway wall as Carpai paced before them. "You're telling me that every helicopter has been destroyed? How could that happen?"

"It was Major Seah. That was the helicopter Seah stole when he defected. Nothing else has happened since," said Colonel August Mustafa, trying to offer some reassurance. "This might be Morray's last-ditch effort. This just delays the fall of his headquarters...."

Mustafa was cut short when three more explosions rocked the building.

"Now what?" demanded Carpai.

A captain burst through the front door.

"The fence to the motor pool and the south wall of the parade field has been blown up!"

"Get men to those sites!" shouted Carpai. "They're trying to breach our security."

The officer saluted and turned on his heels. Out the door and at the top of the steps, his body was knocked backward by the force of a 7.62-millimeter rifle bullet that pierced his chest.

From a low knoll to the west of the airfield, Singleton watched the black smoke pour from the burning helicopters. Even the breeze was co-operating, blowing toward the military compound, obscuring the enemy's vision and fouling the air.

After the train ambush, Singleton had been convinced that Martin had run from the battle in abject terror. Now he knew he was wrong. Martin had pressed him and his cameraman to keep up. The three had traveled for nearly an hour. Martin turned on a narrow dirt road that crossed the tracks. He stopped when the road made a sharp bend. He took out a small penlight from his vest pocket. It had been equipped with a red lens cover. He flashed the light three times. Singleton looked ahead along the wood line. Another small red light flashed three times in response.

Singleton flinched when he heard the brush rustle behind him. He turned to see about a dozen men dressed in camouflage step out.

"Everything ready?" Martin asked.

"We're in position and ready to go," answered Joe Weah.

"Come on," he gestured. "The chopper is in the clearing."

The group moved up the road until they came to a cleared field. In the darkness, Singleton could see only a few feet ahead, but in the clearing, he made out the unmistakable shape of a helicopter. Martin's wife and son were already on the chopper.

They all crowded on board and flew to a staging area six miles east of Camp Schiefflin. The Huey made six trips to ferry the force to the staging area. From there, they marched to the rubber plantation.

No one filled him in on the details, but Singleton could make the connections. It appeared that the militia along the road and rail line was only a part of the operation. True, the ambush had been a surprise, but it hadn't been the deathblow the enemy had envisioned.

Aware of the potential for information to reach the opposition, the rebels had specially trained a seventy-five-man team. As the militia's large military force headed toward Monrovia, Carpai would find it necessary to deploy the bulk of his forces to meet them. Then the militia would withdraw, sending the impression that they were beaten and in retreat.

Carpai's men would be preoccupied in the interior while the seventy-five men attacked the poorly manned garrison at Camp Schiefflin.

Even though they were outnumbered, the team would have the advantage of surprise. Besides that, Martin and his Special Forces men had a few tricks. A Huey had been outfitted with M-60 machine guns, rigged like they had been in Vietnam. The best sharpshooters would act as snipers, using a dozen M-14 rifles with eight-power scopes that had been brought in on the C-12 aircraft.

During the night, two twenty-man teams had crawled up to the chain link fence that surrounded Camp Schiefflin. Another team had infiltrated the airfield complex on its commercial side. Its mission was to secure the control tower and place six snipers in the tower.

All seventy-five men wore Liberian army uniforms. If spotted, each would be dismissed as yet another soldier. To keep them from shooting each other and to avoid being shot by their own snipers, red bands of half-inch fabric ringed their sleeves above the elbow. All soldiers without a red band were the enemy.

At first light, the Huey attacked the airfield and took out the attack and support aircraft. The destruction was even greater than expected because the Cobras, loaded with ammunition and rockets, exploded. In the chaos following the attack, the six-sniper team took over the control tower. The other six secured the knoll about four hundred meters from Camp Schiefflin's outer fence.

From his vantage point, Singleton could see Martin's son, Tim, stretch out flat out on the ground; he had his weapon before him while he scanned the airfield. The boy's mother was hidden in the rubber trees two hundred yards to the rear.

It seemed strange that this high school kid would be making life-and-death decisions. Singleton noted that it would take a sharp eye and a steady hand to make a kill. The thin, red armband was the only protection for friendly soldiers. A tough call from so far away, Singleton thought.

A moment later, Singleton saw the militia breach the fence. The two teams were moving in. Within the hour, the course of the battle would likely be determined. If the People's Party were to succeed, it would have to do it now.

General Oscar Jalah stood beside his Hummer and conferred with Brigadier General Edward Sacker, the commander of the 1st Infantry Brigade. Efforts to obtain the reinforcements for Camp Schiefflin had been unsuccessful.

When he had first arrived in Kakata, he found that militia soldiers, instead of retreating, had moved back into positions outside the city. The brigade was totally engaged, and Sackor was reluctant to release troops from the battle.

Jalah had just received word that the force pursuing the retreating militia along the railroad tracks had also encountered stiff resistance from entrenched militia soldiers. Repeatedly, Jalah had tried to reach Minister Carpai to apprise him of the situation, but he hadn't been able to get through to Camp Schiefflin by radio. Without guidance, Jalah took it upon himself to order Sackor to begin pulling back all forces and to return to Camp Schiefflin.

Somehow the attack on Camp Schiefflin had something to do with the sudden reversal of the retreating militia. He radioed the commander of the force that had been engaged along the railroad tracks and ordered him to withdraw his troops.

Carpai didn't like what he saw happening at Camp Schiefflin. For the first time, Carpai worried about the outcome. The three hundred soldiers he planned to load on the helicopters had been deployed to the breaches in the fence. It should have been a quick fix, but the reappearance of the deadly helicopter changed the situation. It had opened fire on the deploying soldiers, killing or wounding more than one hundred and scattering the others. Surface-to-air missiles had been rushed into place, but the chopper's pilot seemed to know what was up, and he disappeared over the distant hills.

Sniper fire from a high spot on the rubber plantation and from the airfield's control tower killed or maimed Carpai's forces. Other militia streamed through the broken perimeter fence and engaged in hand-to-hand combat. Liberian soldiers sometimes attacked their own men in the confusion. Most combatants wore the national uniform. Who could tell who was friend or foe?

Less than an hour after the helicopter attack, Camp Schiefflin had fallen to the militia. Only one building – the sturdy, brick headquarters – hadn't yet been taken. Inside, twenty-five men including Carpai himself – had barricaded the windows and doors. Surely, it wouldn't be much longer before Jalah and the reinforcements would arrive.

Yet those troops would never come. Jalah had pulled back, and the militia had broken though his lines. Thousands of Morray's forces pushed ahead, bypassing the Liberian forces while storming down the main highway to Camp Schiefflin and then on to Monrovia itself.

More than two hundred Liberian and Guinean survivors sat in rows on the parade field. Those who were unhurt did what they could to ease the suffering of their wounded comrades. A pile of confiscated weapons and gear was stacked near the flagpole. Twenty militiamen held them in place, their guns ready to stem any attempt at escape. Only twelve militiamen had been lost in the attack. Now Morray's forces controlled the international airport and Camp Schiefflin itself.

Only Carpai and a couple dozen troops, holed up in the headquarters building, refused to surrender.

# 50

***The ornate Ducar Hotel on First Street had become the royal mansion for King Amos. Its marble-floored lobby now served as his throne room. His powerful gangs had now spread his influence to nearly every corner of the capital city. Anyone who dared to dispute his sovereignty would die.***

AMOS PACED BACK AND FORTH. HIS AIDES COWERED, FEARING HIS WRATH. He sneered at the five corpses lying near the entrance. Five white men, each dressed in black, had dared to invade his realm. They had attempted to land within the confines of the American Embassy. They failed. Now their bullet-ridden bodies stunk up his quarters. He looked down at the piles of their gear stacked beside them. The very presence of these fools and their equipment served to sharpen his rage. He clenched his fists and swore his revenge.

He had only tried to help the Americans. He had provided them protection from his rival factions. Then they had kidnapped the white woman and her daughter. In the process, they had killed one of his officers and several of his men. They refused to honor his request that the females be returned.

"The Americans must pay for what they have done," he vowed.

"But, Amos, what can we do?" asked Alford, his number two man.

"We will kill them," Amos replied. "We will kill them and burn the embassy to the ground."

"The Americans have guns and know how to use them," Alford said.

"That may be true, but we have many followers. We can attack in force. I want you to begin firing at the embassy this afternoon. Make them use up their bullets. As soon as it gets dark, we will mass our forces and make our attack. Tell your people that there is much wealth hidden on the grounds. As soon as they take the embassy, they can have whatever they find."

Alford was reassured by Amos's words. The king had spoken. In a matter of hours, the cornered Americans would wish they had obeyed the orders of Amos, King of Monrovia.

# 51

***In the motor pool building at Camp Schiefflin, three men stood in the doorway. Two stood calmly with their hands in their pockets while listening to the third, larger man make broad gestures while he attempted to explain his plan to take over the headquarters.***

HANK'S FORMER SERGEANT LAID OUT THE DETAILS OF HIS PROPOSAL.

Wilber "Tiny" Sprague had come up with his idea after he had heard Hank talk about the advantages of taking Carpai alive. Hank figured they could use Carpai to get the Liberians to lay down their weapons. Hank reasoned that his surrender would reduce the number of casualties on both sides.

Tiny pointed to two light armored vehicles (LAVs). Swiss-designed and Canadian built, U.S. Marines had used the 6x6. Later, they had been exported to several third-world countries.

"These babies resist the impact of small arms fire," he explained. "Each one holds a dozen men."

Joe Weah interrupted Tiny's non-stop talk.

"So, what are we going to do, pull up and offload and walk in the front door?"

"No, sir. I plan to drive this little baby right up the front steps and through the front doors," Tiny said. "Do you think it has the power to go up the steps?"

"Sure, sir. The British loved to build big buildings. The stairs are concrete and more than twenty feet wide. The main entrance has double doors, a good eight feet wide. The hallways have ten-foot high ceilings and are twenty feet across. We can take these two armored cars right up the steps and directly into the building. Most important, I personally, will drive the lead vehicle right up those steps!"

Hank had enough of the talk. He glanced at his watch.

"It's already two o'clock. We have to do something," he said. "Let's do it. Joe, we need our best men for this operation. I'll be in the lead vehicle with Tiny. Joe, I want you in the second vehicle. We'll move out in twenty minutes."

Headquarters, Camp Schiefflin

Two officers cautiously approached Julius Carpai who had holed up in the G-2 intelligence office on the second floor. The interior room had no windows and therefore was safe from small arms fire.

"Why don't we just surrender?" suggested one of the men.

Carpai glared at him.

"There is no way I will surrender to Lieutenant Colonel Martin. That man wants nothing more than to have me surrender."

"Sir, excuse me, but what other options do we have?"

"Oscar Jalah will bring help. He has never failed me."

Carpai hesitated. He was about to offer more self-reassurance when gunfire erupted from the floor beneath them.

"They must be trying to approach the building!" the other officer said. He turned to face the doorway. More gunfire broke out, followed by the sound of breaking timber and shattering glass.

They heard the roar of a heavy engine. The floor beneath their feet began to shake.

"Jesus Christ! They're going to blow up the building!"

The screaming officer yanked open the door. The two men ran down the wide hallway, leaving Liberia's new President standing alone in the dimly lit room.

From across the quadrangle, two armored vehicles had roared toward the headquarters building. The first had hit the lower steps at nearly twenty miles per hour. Its six all-terrain tires grabbed at the concrete steps as it bounced roughly up the stairs. As it crashed through the wide, reinforced doors, the upper beam had given way. Debris from the unsupported second floor rained down on the vehicle.

It never paused as it rolled down the hallway. It finally had come to a halt just short of the operations room. Directly behind, a second armored vehicle stopped as soon as it crossed the entrance. The back doors opened and two dozen armed warriors jumped out and took up positions at intervals down the hallway.

A few of the holdouts had offered sporadic resistance. Yet their efforts were short-lived. The shock action had not only surprised, but also demoralized, the holdouts. It only took minutes and the building had fallen. Hank looked around, but his prey – Carpai himself – was nowhere in sight.

"This man says Carpai was upstairs in the G-2 room just a few minutes ago!" yelled Joe, who held a pistol to the ribs of a trembling officer.

Hank ran for the stairway. Tiny was at his heels. The other militia had already swept the second floor, bringing down staff members who rested their hands atop their heads in surrender.

"Is there anyone still upstairs?" Hank asked one of the men he passed on the stairway. "No, colonel. These were the only people we found."

The two men paused, standing motionless in the second floor hallway.

"It's too damn quiet up here," Tiny said.

"I know he's still here," Hank said. "I can feel it."

"Well, sir," Tiny smiled, "there is only one way to find out. Let's search the place."

They pushed open the door to the G-2 office. The dim light from the hallway offered limited visibility. The room appeared to be vacant.

Without speaking, Hank moved to the right as Tiny went left. Both held their nine-millimeter pistols in the classic combat stance. They looked under desks and behind partitions, being careful to check anywhere a man could hide. There was no sign of Carpai. Back out in the hallway, they searched the other second floor offices. Still, they found no one.

"I can't understand this," Hank whispered. "I still have an uneasy feeling that Carpai is up here somewhere."

The two men began to descend the stairs, when Tiny suddenly stopped.

"Well, I'll be a son of a bitch!" he said. "I know where he is!"

He turned to Hank to explain.

"We had a mobile training team mission to India. The old headquarters building there had the same floor plan. That room on the second floor that they use for G-2 has a hidden room. Come on, I'll show you!"

The two bolted back to the darkened room. Holding his finger to his lips, Tiny signaled silence. He moved to the wall that was lined with maps and let out a roar like a wild bull. He raised his right foot and drove his size sixteen boot into the wall. He put all of his three hundred pounds of body weight into the blow. The entire section of wall gave way, opening a hole in the plasterboard.

He pushed his way through the opening. Tiny returned, just seconds later. In one hand, he held up Carpai by the collar of his fatigues.

Tiny's grin stretched from ear to ear.

"They stored maps behind the boards," Tiny laughed. "This bastard figured no one would know about that empty space behind the map boards."

Here was the man who had haunted Hank Martin's dreams for years. Here was the man who had ordered the attack on Lindsey and Tim. Here was the man responsible for the mutilation of his son's hand.

Every single day since he had returned to Liberia, Hank had plotted how he would kill Carpai. His death had come in so many ways. Carpai had been strangled, stabbed and shot. He had died quickly; he had suffered slowly. Hank had experienced the exhilaration of victory. He knew Carpai would be more valuable while still alive, but he was tempted to carry out his fantasy execution. All he had to do was to nod, and Tiny would hand him over.

Hank could only stare at the dangling scarecrow at the end of Tiny's thick arm. Carpai was a small man. Next to Tiny, Carpai looked like a grade school kid.

Carpai didn't even struggle. He only stared blankly across the room. White streaks of dust from the plaster of the collapsed wall clung to the coils of his thinning gray hair and filled the narrow wrinkles of his face and jowls. Hank tried to calculate his age. Back in 1992, he had likely been in his forties. Hank figured Carpai must be near seventy by now. He was an evil, old man – but mostly, a pathetic, old man. Hank's desire to kill Carpai had vanished. It was replaced by simple revulsion.

"Bring him downstairs. I'm sure that Joe Weah will be happy to take care of Minister Carpai," Hank said. He turned and walked toward the door. He had no desire to ever look at Carpai again.

In a house along the ocean less than five miles from Camp Schiefflin, George Sarday sat on the wide porch staring at the waves lapping against the beach. He could hear the explosions and gunfire coming from the camp. He knew that all of his plans were unraveling. He closed his eyes and bowed his head. He could still create havoc.

"Come on, little man, you have a date with justice," Tiny said, still holding Carpai by the collar. Tiny tightened his big fingers on Carpai's arm and shoved him forward.

In the half-light, neither Hank nor Tiny had noticed that Carpai was undergoing subtle changes. Had they been watching more closely, they would have noticed his pupils fade until his eyes had become two blank, white orbs. His face, once devoid of emotion, began to show a flicker of slight amusement. He ceased moving as Tiny tried to pull him along. Tiny shoved, but it was like trying to move a concrete post.

"What the fuck?" Tiny said. He pushed again, but Carpai didn't budge. He dug his fingers into the man's upper arm. Instead of the soft flesh of an old man's arm, Tiny felt rock-hard muscle.

In an instant, Carpai turned and pulled himself free of Tiny's grip. Now face to face with Tiny, Carpai's hands tightened on Tiny's thick arms, constricting the blood flow with the force of a steel vise. Tiny felt a shiver run up his arms and down his spine as he looked into a face that was far from human.

As a non-commissioned officer, Tiny had never addressed Hank Martin by his first name. It had always been "captain," "colonel" or a simple "sir." Now he could only manage one faint word.

"Hank..." he called softly.

Hank had only gone a few steps down the hallway when he heard his old friend's cry. He swiveled in place, only to be confronted by the impossible.

Carpai stood in the middle of the room, his back to the door, his upraised arms holding Tiny over his head as if he were an inflated balloon in the shape of a man. Hank hesitated, unable to comprehend what he was seeing.

With an easy toss, Carpai threw the three-hundred-pound man across the room. Tiny's body slammed into the wall, knocking plaster, maps and ceiling tiles to the floor. Hank's faithful friend lay in a crumpled heap, still and silent.

Hank willed himself to regain his self-control. He screamed and rushed at Carpai. But the man stood his ground, stuck out his hand palm up, and landed a blow to Hank's chest.

Hank's forward momentum was reversed. He flew back over the surface of a cluttered desk and landed on the floor. His fingertips located a sore spot on his chest. He thought that his sternum had been broken. His breathing became labored. At the very least, he had cracked several ribs.

It was clear that bare hands would not stop his attacker. He fumbled at his side, reaching for his pistol, but only found an empty holster. He blinked, trying to bring his surroundings into focus. He spotted the black metal object a few feet from the threshold. He struggled to stand, but doubled over in pain. He began to crawl on his elbows toward the pistol.

"You're wasting your time, foolish mortal," a voice said. It was followed by a high-pitched laugh. "You actually believe you have the power to stop me!"

Hank shook his head in an attempt to clear his senses. The voice was familiar. It was the same mocking voice of the dwarf-like creature he had encountered in the bush. He turned toward its source, expecting to see the creature. Instead, he looked down the barrel of the nine-millimeter pistol that Carpai pointed between his eyes.

Again the voice spoke. It came from Carpai's lips, but it was far from the voice of an old man. It was the haunting sound of the creature. Its eyes – white and lacking pupils – were those of something other than a human being.

"So now, mortal, your soul joins all the others who serve me," it said. "Your death will come from the weapon I hold in my hand. It is so much better than the stones and spears of the mortals who first served me."

Hank saw the finger tighten on the trigger.

It stood fewer than ten feet from him. It couldn't miss. Hank braced himself for certain death.

The pistol fired once and then once again. In the confines of the room, the sound of the weapon's blast intensified. Each time the walls shook, Hank felt his ears nearly burst with the impact. Surely, he had been shot, yet he felt no pain. Two more rounds were fired. Still he felt no pain. Hank looked straight ahead at Carpai who shaded his eyes with his left hand. Another shot. Again, there was no pain. Perhaps Carpai couldn't see in the darkness.

Hank became aware of a green glow that began to fill the room. He ran his fingers over his fatigue jacket that had torn when he had been thrown over the desk. He fumbled until he found the leopard tooth amulet suspended from the leather cord around his neck. He looked down to see an emerald glow emanating from the tooth itself.

Another shot rang out. This one passed so near Hank's head that he felt the rush of air as the bullet streaked by him. Even though this creature couldn't aim, death might come from a single, lucky shot.

Hank turned to dive for his pistol. It was right there on the floor, only a few feet away. He reached and his fingers closed around the butt of the pistol. As he rolled to his right, another shot embedded itself in the wall only inches above his head. He pulled himself to a sitting position and fired three shots in rapid succession. Each blast struck Carpai in the chest.

"You can't hurt me, mortal!" he sneered, but as Carpai spoke, Hank could see the dark stains spreading across the man's chest.

Perhaps even though the creature had endowed Carpai with superhuman strength, maybe immortality wasn't included in his being.

Hank fired two more times. Each bullet found its mark. Hank watched as the white orbs in the eye sockets changed to the terrified and tortured eyes of a pitiful old man. Hank leveled the pistol and fired three times directly into Carpai's face. The body fell backward and collapsed onto the floor. A mist rose from Carpai's body as the demon evaporated.

Hank pulled himself up to a standing position. He approached the bullet-ridden corpse. He kicked at it once with the tip of his boot. Assured that Carpai would never again be a threat, he took one long step over the body toward Tiny who lay motionless on the floor nearby. He reached down and caressed Tiny's weathered cheek.

"It's over, old friend," he said softly. "Carpai's down."

# 52

*From the rooftop of the American Embassy, five men looked through the night-vision glasses at the street below. The entire street had taken on the look of a photographic negative done in green. Commander Jordan could make out a number of young punks sporting assault rifles. They stood in groups or casually leaned against the palms across from the embassy's main gate.*

JORDAN AND FOUR SEALs HAD POSITIONED THEMSELVES ATOP THE EMBASSY roof. They trained the scopes of their sniper rifles on the mob. Lacking the firepower to take out large numbers of armed attackers, they scanned the crowd for the big mouths and agitators. By shooting them, they could create indecision in many of the others. They hoped to leave the mob in disarray.

"I'm going downstairs to talk with the ambassador. If something happens, call me on the radio," Jordan said.

The ambassador, Major Parkinson and Jerry Day sat at the table in the main conference room. The table was littered with discarded packaging from the MREs brought in by the Marines.

"Would you care for an MRE, Commander Jordan?" asked Vicki, offering him an unopened meal packet.

"No, thank you, Ambassador Johnson. I have to check the men. I just wanted to let you know that the last two helicopters should be returning in less than forty-five minutes. Everyone will go out on those two birds."

He hesitated, as if he wanted to say something more.

"Is there something else, commander?"

"Just that we better be sure that the staff members are armed. The crowds are still milling about the area. When they see that we're about to withdraw, they might rush the embassy. If they do, things could get a little sticky."

He saluted and left. For a few moments, no one spoke.

"I can't believe it is going to end like this," Vicki said to no one in particular. In the middle of the table, someone had placed a neatly folded United States flag.

Gunny Sergeant Wilson had taken it down only fifteen minutes earlier. In terms of protocol, the United States Embassy in Liberia no longer existed. Vicki ran her finger under her eye, stemming the all-too-obvious tear. So many lost. Hank, Lindsey, Tim – were all senseless casualties – the slaughtered families, attaché members and then the Navy SEALs. And it wasn't over yet. She stood, turned her back to the others and took a moment for herself in order to regain her composure. What could she have done differently? She had no answer.

"Come on, gentlemen," she said with conviction. "We're going to lock up the embassy offices. Those thugs out there will break in five minutes after we leave, but, by God, it will be secure when we leave."

Chief Petty Officer Brian Scott knew better than to relax his watch. He used his night vision scope to scan the road in front of the embassy. He picked out several men who sat on a curb. He had heard some sporadic gunfire, but nothing serious. Suddenly the sound of automatic weaponfire broke out at the end of the street. It erupted into what sounded like a serious firefight. Strangely, it didn't seem to be directed at the embassy. The men on the curb had run in the direction of the gunfire. Now he heard a barrage of weapons. He swung the scope in the direction of the sound.

"Oh, shit!" he whispered. He picked up the radio. "We've got a problem here."

"I'm on my way," answered Jordan.

In less than fifteen seconds, Jordan was at Scott's side on the roof.

"What's up?"

"Look up there toward the end of the street."

Jordan twisted the focus until the image became clear.

"You're right. We have a problem."

They could see eight armored cars moving slowly down the street toward the embassy.

"I thought we were dealing with poorly equipped street gangs," Scott said.

"Well, I would assume that the Liberian army had armored cars. Maybe they were abandoned during the collapse of the government. Whatever the case, those cars could easily break through the barricades at the front gate."

Jordan pressed the talk button on the radio, which linked them to the task force.

"Eagle," he said. "This is Falcon."

"Go ahead Falcon."

"Request immediate air support against enemy armor."

Jordan didn't take the time to check, but he figured his pulse rate was at least one hundred twenty beats per minute. The eight armored cars were now right outside the front gate. The generators still cranked out enough juice to keep the floodlights on. They provided sufficient light to reveal what was transpiring on the street. The cars had spread out in a semi-circle, all facing outward. Their exit ramps backed up to the embassy gate.

"Gee, sir, when they exit those armored cars, they'll walk right into our gun sights."

"Well, Scotty, no one said this group was smart. I'm surprised they even know how to operate an armored car, let alone deploy one."

They heard the creak of the ramps as they began to open.

"This is it," Jordan said. He had lost thirteen of his men to these dickheads. He had been given the authority to make the decision. This enemy hadn't fired a single shot, but he was not about to wait around to lose another man. He picked up the mike and pressed the talk button.

"Black Stallion, this is Falcon."

"Go ahead, Falcon."

"Black Stallion, the attack has begun. You may remove the targets."

"Roger, Falcon. We are sixty seconds out and closing. Keep your heads down."

Marine Corps Captain Ron Clements piloted the lead Harrier. He pulled the aircraft into a dive and began his run. At last, after all these years of playing at war, he would finally take out a live enemy target.

The heat generated by the engines of the armored cars lit up his view screen. The semi-circular arrangement of the vehicles stood out clearly. The laser-guided bomb (LGB) would easily locate the target. He couldn't wait to get back to the ship and talk about the kills.

Clements' hand closed around the joystick. Funny, the firing mechanism on the Harrier was just like the sticks used on video games. The only difference here was that the targets were real.

Flesh and blood would fly when the LGBs struck the target. No one would survive.

Jordan and Scott peeked over the edge of the wall on the embassy's roof. Each armored car had lowered its ramp, depositing more than one hundred twenty men to exit and spread out between the vehicles.

"This is payback time for the men who were killed by these assholes," Jordan whispered. But Scott hesitated, placing his hand on Jordan's arm.

"Oh, my God! It's Lieutenant Iverson!" Scott shouted.

"What?" Jordan asked.

"Sir, look! See what's coming out of that armored car. I see a bunch of white people. One of them is Josh Iverson."

Jordan dove for the radio and grabbed the mike.

"Black Stallion, abort! Black Stallion, this is Falcon. Abort! I say again, abort your mission. We have friendlies in the target area."

Jordan squeezed the mike so hard that his knuckles turned white. Was he too late? Had they already launched?

He didn't have to wonder for long. The building shook with a deafening roar. Jordan rose shakily to his feet, expecting to see the total annihilation of the armored cars and the troops around them. Yet everything was completely intact. Looking up into the night sky, he could see the glow of the Harriers' afterburners as they pulled up from the aborted attack.

"Falcon, this is Black Stallion," said a voice on the radio. "We're back in standby. Let us know if you want us to make another run."

"Black Stallion?" answered Jordan.

"This is Falcon. Negative. We can handle the situation from here. Thanks, guys. You saved some lives. Falcon out."

Jordan lowered his head to say a silent prayer. Those hours of practice between the SEALs and the flight crews had paid off. He vowed to buy those four pilots a beer when they got back to Norfolk.

"I'm going down there to check out what's going on," Jordan said.

In a few minutes, he stood at the pedestrian entrance. He signaled for the Marine guard to open the door. Less than thirty feet from him stood Lieutenant Iverson, leaning against the armored vehicle.

"Are you OK, Josh?"

"Yes, sir. I have a little shrapnel in my legs and a lot of bruises, but no broken bones," said Josh.

"What's going on here anyway?" Jordan asked.

"Major Sio of the People's Party militia found me when I landed. These guys are the good guys," he said, pointing at the group near the vehicle. Another man came out from behind the car. It was a tall, white man who was dressed in Liberian Army fatigues. He limped toward Jordan. He seemed to favor one leg over the other. One side of his face was bruised and dirty. Jordan figured that maybe this was a mercenary who had joined up with the guys in the armored cars.

"I'm Commander Jordan. And who are you?"

"Lieutenant Colonel William Martin, U.S. Army."

"I didn't realize that we had U.S. troops on the ground."

"We don't," grinned Hank. "We sort of got caught up in the fall of the country."

"Sir, may I ask who these other people are?"

By now, others had moved in closer.

"This is my wife, Lindsey," Hank said.

"How are you, commander?" Lindsey said, offering her hand.

"Just fine, ma'am."

Martin's wife wore soiled blue jeans. Her blouse was wrinkled and dirty. An ugly red scar ran down one cheek.

"This young man holding up my sergeant major is my son, Tim," Hank continued.

Jordan did a quick appraisal of the twosome standing next to Martin's wife. The kid seemed not much more than sixteen. He was also dressed in Liberian fatigues. A mountain of a man leaned against him, clearly in need of support. His right arm was in a makeshift sling, his face bruised, and one eye was swollen shut. He stared ahead at Jordan with his good eye.

"I know you, commander," said the man, "I taught you jungle tactics at MacDill Air Force Base in 2000."

Jordan smiled. He remembered the big man.

"You're Command Sergeant Major Sprague," Jordan said. "You were one tough instructor."

"Still am. Maybe a little shaky tonight, but I can still march thirty miles," Tiny beamed.

"I remember that jungle training," said a Liberian officer who came up beside Colonel Martin. "It was a tough course."

"This is General Joe Weah, commander of the People's Party militia. Joe commands these and about fifteen thousand more troops. He graduated from the Special Forces Qualification Course at Fort Bragg," Hank said.

"We were fighting to gain control of the capital when Iverson told us that the embassy was being evacuated tonight," Joe said. "I decided to escort these people here. It looks like we made it before the last choppers lifted off."

"Yes, sir. The last two choppers will be landing in a few minutes."

"Good," said Hank. "General Weah will keep the site secure until we lift off."

Jordan decided that this wasn't the best time to tell them that only a few minutes earlier, the entire group was within ten seconds of being blown off the face of the Earth. On further thought, he decided that he'd never mention it.

The crowd parted to allow two other white men to come forward. The taller one wore a hunting vest. A CNN press ID dangled from a cord around his neck. Another CNN man stood behind him.

"Colonel Martin, Brian and I will be staying with General Weah and the militia," said Singleton. "I just want to take a moment to thank you for saving our lives."

Singleton reached into his pocket and retrieved a digital disk wrapped in a plastic bag.

"What's this?" Hank asked.

"A small souvenir for you, your wife and your son," Singleton said. "They're the digital photos from the airfield. Oh, by the way, for your information, Brian and I have never met or seen you, your wife, your son or any retired non-commissioned officers during the entire time we spent with the People's Party militia."

"Folks, I hate to break this up, but we need to get back on embassy grounds. I can hear the helicopters," Jordan said.

Lindsey turned to Joe. She embraced him and kissed him on the cheek.

"You be careful, Joe."

"Don't worry, Lindsey. I'll keep my head down."

# 53

***On the embassy tennis courts, two CH-53E Sea Stallion helicopters gently set down. Crews had removed the fencing. The net posts had been cut off flush with the ground. The concrete court made a perfect landing pad for the huge helicopters. Each could carry fifty-five fully equipped soldiers.***

VICKI SAT ON A CONCRETE BENCH NEAR THE POOL AND WATCHED THEM COME in. She figured they only needed one helicopter. After all, not more than forty people were left at the embassy. Maybe they had the other one for back up, she thought.

It would only be a matter of minutes until the generators were shut down and the entire compound would be plunged into darkness. They'd load the helicopters and lift off. This West African plot of ground would no longer be held by the United States.

Although she didn't see or hear anyone, Vicki sensed someone standing beside her. It could only be Jim Parkinson, but it wasn't.

"Hank!" she said as she threw her arms around his neck and kissed him.

"Careful, Vicki! I think I have some cracked ribs."

"Sorry, Hank. I am so glad to see you!"

She paused, her voice tempered with concern.

"What about Lindsey and Tim?"

"Standing right over there by Jim," Hank said.

"My God, I can't believe it. You're all OK. Where have you been?"

"It's a long story," Hank said.

"Vicki?"

"Yes, Hank?"

"Julius Carpai is dead."

"Did you kill him?" she asked.

"Yes."

Seventeen years earlier in Vicki's hut in West Africa, she had argued with a much younger Hank Martin that killing another human being could never be justified. But now her opinion had changed.

"I'm glad you did," she said.

Suddenly it was completely dark. With the generators down, only the operating lights of the helicopter lit the way to the makeshift-landing pad. Passengers made their way to the choppers and settled in their seats. The flight crew checked the seatbelts. Both choppers would carry the passengers, splitting the group in two. Hank, Lindsey and Tim watched from the second bird as the first one lifted off.

The seventy-five-foot rotor blades began to turn, kicked to life by the two four thousand three hundred eighty-three-shaft horsepower GE engines. Then the Sea Stallion began its gentle ascent, climbing at a rate of twenty-five feet per minute. Then it was their turn.

As the CH-53 banked to the left, Hank caught a glimpse of a raging fire burning by the docks along the river. Flames leaped hundreds of feet into the air. Hank leaned forward to take a second look. Through the early morning darkness, he imagined the image of the horned statue rising in the flames.

Imagined? He wasn't sure. He opened his fatigue jacket and held the leopard tooth between his fingertips. It felt cool to the touch. He lifted it out to take a look. There was no green glow. He turned again to look at the fire. The image had vanished.

The helicopter cleared five thousand feet. Low intensity interior lights were switched on. Hank leaned over to Lindsey and reached for her hand.

As a family, the Martins had faced an evil that had permeated the government of Liberia to the very doors of the Liberian President's office. They had fought against something that had hidden in the jungles of Liberia for centuries. It was something that had wanted their very souls, but had failed in its attempt to get them.

"I love you," he whispered.

She smiled.

"I love you, too."

He turned to Tim and held out the leopard tooth necklace. Neither spoke. Tim lifted it over his head and pulled it into place around his neck. He looked at his father, raised his right hand to his brow and saluted. Hank grinned in response. Then he looked at his son and returned the salute, the time-honored gesture of respect.

# EPILOGUE

*Two years later*

THE BLACK STRETCH LIMO PULLED UP IN FRONT OF GARFIELD HIGH IN Alexandria, Virginia. Three men in three-piece, dark suits got out. One reached to open the back door. Two more well-dressed men stepped out. All five climbed the wide steps of the school's main entrance.

From his office window, the principal, Dr. Howard Simpson, watched the men come up the walkway. With only three weeks left until summer break, he had been enjoying the unusually calm day. In a school with twenty-five hundred teenagers, quiet days were the exception. Perhaps that was about to change.

"Dr. Simpson?" said his secretary as she opened the office door.

"Yes?"

"Some gentlemen would like to see you," she said, handing him a business card.

It introduced Malcolm MacDonald, United States Secret Service. Not your usual high school visitor, Simpson thought.

"Show them in, Marilyn," he said.

Moments later, all five sat in his office.

"Dr. Simpson," one said. "I'm Special Agent MacDonald. This is Special Agent Stevens and Engles. We're here to accompany two very good friends of our country. Allow me to introduce the President of Liberia, Charles Morray and his minister of defense, Joe Weah."

Simpson shook hands and exchanged greetings with the men. Their precise English surprised him. He was even more astonished to learn that

Morray had graduated from the University of California, the same school where he had done his graduate studies.

"Tell me, Mr. President, what can we do for you?"

"Dr. Simpson, we are on our way to the airport following a meeting with your President. We only have a few minutes. We would like to speak to one of your students."

"One of our students? Who?"

"Tim Martin. I believe he is a senior. We spoke to his mother, and she gave us permission."

"I'm sure that we can have him come down. School will be out shortly," Simpson said as he pushed a button on his desk.

"Marilyn? Could you have Tim Martin report to my office."

Weah asked the principal if he knew Tim well.

"Gentlemen, in a school this size, you get to know the top and bottom five percent. Tim is in the top five percent. He's vice president of the senior class, captain of the soccer team, president of the karate club, and we just found out that he's been given a four-year R.O.T.C. scholarship to the University of Virginia," Simpson said.

"And just how did the soccer team do this year?" asked Weah.

They continued to visit for another five minutes. Then the office door opened.

"Tim's here," announced the secretary.

"Have him come in."

Tim had grown since the last time he'd seen his two old friends. Now six feet four inches tall and weighing in at two hundred pounds, he filled the doorway.

"Yes, Dr. Simpson, you wanted to see me?"

"Not me, Tim, these gentlemen asked for you."

"Joe! Charles! It's great to see you guys. I saw you on TV with the President."

Joe embraced Tim with both arms.

"This can't be the young warrior who fought beside me as we defeated our enemies! Look at you!" he said, holding Tim at arm's length. "Why every virgin in the village would want you when they danced for the winners of the games!"

Tim blushed.

"Come on, Joe, you're still the greatest warrior in Zigda. Now, tell me about Sabo, is he well?"

"You mean Lieutenant Sabo Weah?"

"Lieutenant? You mean to tell me that Sabo is a lieutenant?"

"Yes, and I have good news for you. Sabo and Julia will be coming to America in two years to attend college. You know, they are already married."

"Joe, I'll be going to the University of Virginia. Wouldn't it be great if we could go together?"

"Anything is possible," said Charles.

Joe had a question for his young friend.

"Tim, do you still walk with the great leopard spirit?" Joe asked.

Tim reached in his shirt pocket and pulled out a gold chain. He held it at arm's length. An animal tooth dangled from the necklace. It swayed gently before the men.

Joe looked at Tim, a slight smile forming on his lips. He nodded at the brave young man whose life had been transformed in Africa.

"The leopard tooth," said Joe.

"Yes," Tim answered. "Yes, Joe, I still walk with the leopard's spirit. I hope I always will."

New York City – the same day

As he often did, Dr. George Nah Sarday, former chancellor of the University of Liberia and now assistant professor of African studies at New York University, sipped his latte at a table in the corner of the coffee shop. It was a good spot to relax after his afternoon class. He laid out his New York Times and began to take in the day's news. One story caught his attention. He saw a picture of five flag-draped coffins.

"The remains of five servicemen killed two years ago in the evacuation of the American Embassy in Liberia were personally returned by the President of Liberia, Charles Morray. Morray said that the people of Liberia considered these five men heroes of the revolution.

"According to Assistant Secretary of State Victoria Ryan-Johnson, who served as ambassador to Liberia during the overthrow of its government, Morray had brought a new prosperity to Liberia."

His hands trembled as he read the article. He had hidden among these foolish creatures for ten thousand years. They thought they were worshiping some ancient spirit. The statue and all the chanting was just a ruse to make them believers. He and the demon were one being, an *endosym*. He gave them their power, and he could take it away. Next time, he would not be thwarted.

"Hi, George. May I join you?"

He had no choice but to respond.

"Hello, Fred. Yes, please have a seat," he said to his friend and fellow professor, Fred Rice.

Fred looked at the headline.

"Will you be going back to Liberia?"

Sarday's face seemed to change. He took on an almost inhuman look. Even his eyes seemed different. It unnerved Fred. He felt a chill to the depths of his very soul. Then it passed. Fred gasped as Sarday responded.

"No, Fred, I won't be going back. What I want is here in America."

The adventure continues
Read book two available at amazon.com

THE DOORWAY TO THE OTHER WORLD WILL OPEN

# ENDOSYM

# THE PLANTATION

RELIGIONS DEPICT DEMONS AS EVIL BEINGS. A MAN POSSESSED BY A DEMON becomes an Endosym: Two entities living in one humanoid body whose goal is to become the "Apex Predator" of the Planet.

WHEN DOCTOR GEORGE NAH SARDAY, THE LEADER OF THE NEW AGE cult *Dacari Mucomba*, purchased the old Johnson Plantation in Johnsonville, Virginia as the site for the School for West African Spiritual Studies, Chief of Police Brian Bishop had little reason to be concerned.

LITTLE DID HE REALIZE THAT IT WAS FAR MORE THAN JUST ANOTHER FAKE religion bilking money from its followers; the School was hiding the creature whose existence would threaten not only the City of Johnsonville but also the very existence of the human race. With time running out and marked for death, Chief Bishop finds an unlikely ally in Tim Martin, a senior at the University of Virginia who knows to well what they must face when they meet the *endosym*.

ARE *ENDOSYMS* REAL? WOULD YOU LIKE TO MEET THE AUTHOR? READ A preview of the next book in the series? Join in the *endosym* Blog?

VISIT WWW.ENDOSYM.COM.

Made in the USA
San Bernardino, CA
29 November 2014